⟐

"Do not play with me, Saxon."

"I like playing with you, Viking."

"Stop now, or—"

"Or what?"

She had no idea what . . . because the impertinent, arrogant, born-to-be-a-libertine was lowering his mouth toward hers. And she was frozen in place. Maybe it was because she had a pigeon in one hand and a ladle in the other, but more likely it was because her lips had somehow parted of their own volition. She wanted his kiss. She wanted it badly.

"Tyra," he whispered against her mouth just before his lips claimed hers. The man was proving to be a master at a number of things. Medicine, for a certainty. And now kissing.

She did not allow herself to ponder what other areas of expertise he had.

The VIKING'S CAPTIVE

SANDRA HILL

(Originally published as *My Fair Viking*)

AVON
An Imprint of HarperCollinsPublishers

Originally published under the title *My Fair Viking* by Dorchester Publishing in April 2002.

AVON BOOKS
An Imprint of HarperCollins*Publishers*
10 East 53rd Street
New York, New York 10022-5299

Copyright © 2002, 2011 by Sandra Hill
ISBN 978-0-06-201908-0
www.avonromance.com

First Avon Books paperback printing: January 2011

Avon Trademark Reg. U.S. Pat. Off. and in Other Countries, Marca Registrada, Hecho en U.S.A.
HarperCollins® is a registered trademark of HarperCollins Publishers.

Printed in the U.S.A.

10 9 8 7 6 5 4 3 2 1

This book is dedicated with much fondness and respect to Alicia Condon, who had been my editor for seventeen novels and two anthologies.

We have both moved on, but the fact remains: Alicia is an editor extraordinaire. Better yet, she shared my sense of humor. The only idea she ever nixed was my wanting to make one of the Three Wise Men a romance novel hero. I'm still hoping to slip that one by some editor someday.

Alicia made my books better. What else could any author want?

Seafarer, may the sweet
Songs of the god of verse
Drench your mind, and may your
Men's lips be stilled by art.
For in the far and rich
Fields of Norway the seeds
My song sows will ripen,
so men may taste its fruit.

EGILS SAGA
Circa tenth century

Reader, may the sweet words of my muse
Drench your mind, and may you stand in awe
Of my books. For in the far and rich fields
Of my imaginations, the seeds of ever more
stories do ripen, so that all of you may
taste of its fruit.

SANDRA HILL, 2002
A shameless play on Egils's words

The
VIKING'S CAPTIVE

PROLOGUE

❧

The way they were . . .
It was alms day in the market town, and hundreds of people, many of them children, crowded the minster steps, screaming and pushing for the loaves of dark bread to be handed out by the clerics.

Among the poor who lined up for their weekly pittance of food were seven-year-old Adam and his four-year-old sister, Adela.

"Don't be afeared, Adela," Adam said. "No one can hurt ye . . . leastways, not whilst I'm here to protect ye."

Adela stared up at him adoringly, her thumb planted firmly in her mouth, as it always was. Despite her being covered with filth from bare feet to lice-infested head, as he was, too, Adam thought she was more comely than a harem princess . . . not that he'd ever seen a harem princess, but he'd heard sailors speak of such as they strolled the city. Adela was the only family he had since their mother had died a year past and left the two of them to roam the wharfside streets on their own. Adela meant more to him than anything. He promised himself in that instant that someday he would replace her threadbare garments with jewel-studded silks. And she would take a bath sometimes, too. Most of all, he would always, always be there to protect her.

"Now, ye mus' stand right here, Adela, whilst I try to get us some bread. Do ye promise not to move?"

"Yea, Adam." She nodded her head up and down, eyes wide with fright as she watched him make his way craftily to the front of the mob, pinching a buttock here, darting between legs there, finally pulling a small loaf out of the priest's fingers just as he was about to hand it to an old woman in rags.

"Come back, ye bloody toad," the woman screeched, to no avail. Many in the crowd turned to watch his progress, some trying to snatch his precious booty. But there was no way he would give up his hard-won food. He shoved it down the front of his dirty tunic and ran for his life toward his sister.

Reaching Adela, Adam quickly broke the loaf in half, and the two of them gobbled the moldy bread ravenously. It was the first they'd eaten in a day or more, but more important, the food was safer in their stomachs than in their little hands where those larger than they would think nothing of killing them for the crumbs.

While his mind had wandered, a lady had hunkered down on her haunches in front of Adela. She was a tall lady, but not so big as the man who stood behind her . . . the size of a warhorse, he was, and mean, would be Adam's guess, by the scowl on his face. Both of them had pale blond hair, which probably meant they were Vikings . . . not surprising, since this was the Norse capital of Britain. The place was flooded with the bloody sea pirates.

"What's your name, little girl?" The woman reached out to brush some lank strands of hair off Adela's face as she spoke.

Although the woman looked harmless enough, there

were evil folks lurking about the city, and Adela recoiled. "Adam," she whimpered, reaching for him with one hand, while the thumb of the other shot immediately into her mouth.

"Why do ye want to know?" Adam demanded, narrowing his eyes and putting his hands belligerently on his hips.

"You two shouldn't be out on the streets like this. Where are your parents?"

"Got none."

"Did they . . . die?"

"Yea, our mother died. What matters it to you?"

The lady inhaled sharply. "When was that?"

"Last winter."

"A year! And who do you live with now? Your father?"

"Huh?"

"Rain, we have lingered here overlong," the blond man interrupted, taking her arm.

Rain, he had called her. What an odd name.

"Just a moment, Selik," the lady insisted.

"Remember the woman in childbirth," Selik reminded her.

"Oh, I forgot," she said, shooting a look of apology at another man standing beside the Norseman. It was Uhtred, a resident of Jorvik that Adam had seen about on occasion. His wife was big—*very big*—with child these days. She was nowhere around now. No doubt she was off somewhere in a pile of straw, popping out her latest bratling.

The lady Rain was addressing Adam again. "Who did you say was taking care of you?"

He raised his head defiantly and snarled, "I take care of me sister and meself."

"I just want to help—"

"Hah! Just like Aslam—"

"The slave trader?" Selik asked with surprise.

"Yea, the slave trader. Keeps tryin' to ketch us, he does. But I be too fast fer the fat old codsucker. Says he knows of a sultan in a faraway land that wants ter have us fer his very own children, to give us a home and good food, but I know what he wants. Yea, I know."

"What?" Rain exclaimed, even as Selik said a foul word behind her.

"He wants to bugger us both, he does, to stick his cock up our arses," he declared with a streetwise explicitness that he hoped would shock the lady into going away. He spat at her feet, grabbed Adela's hand, and disappeared into the crowd.

"I only wanted to help you," she called after them.

Those words rang in Adam's ears, false as they must be, and he slowed his pace. For some reason he could not explain, he decided to follow the blond giants hurrying to keep pace with Uhtred, whose wife was apparently unable to pop out their latest babe with her usual ease.

At one point, when he drew close to them in the crowded sector of Coppergate where all the tradesmen had their stalls, he overheard Rain complain to Selik, "We should have stayed and helped them."

"You're out of your bloody mind. I want no children of my own, and for certain I will not care for anyone else's bothersome brood. Get that through your thick head."

"But, Selik, did you see that little girl's eyes when she looked back at us over her shoulder? They were pleading for help."

"You see and hear only what you want, wench. Did you hear the coarse-mouthed, filthy pup? He wants no help, and I daresay the tough little whelp could survive on a battlefield, let alone the streets of a market city."

It took Adam a few moments to realize that the "coarse-mouthed, filthy pup" Selik referred to was him. He growled and would have pounced forward and taken a bite out of the man's leg, but Adela held him back. She did, indeed, have a pleading look in her blue eyes.

"Please, please," Uhtred was begging, pulling on Rain's sleeve. "My wife is dying, and you stand here prattling about worthless street children."

Rain turned on Uhtred with anger. "And what makes you think your unborn child is worth more than those two precious children?"

Precious? Who? Us? In that instant, Adam's heart felt as if it were growing and growing. He could love this woman, he decided . . . like a mother. Then he shook his head fiercely to rid his brain of the witless notion.

A dream was born . . .

Hours later, Adam stood peering through a wide crack in Uhtred's miserable hut. Adela was asleep in the lap of Selik, who sat under a nearby tree, his long legs stretched forward and crossed at the ankles. How that had come about, Adam wasn't quite sure, but he did know that there was no way he was leaving Uhtred's home, despite Selik's harsh reprimands that birthing was no sight for a little boyling. If Selik called him a "little boyling" one more time, Adam vowed he would give him a famous Anglo-Saxon gesture. But he'd best be ready to run when he did, with Adela in hand and not cuddled in the Viking's lap.

The thing that enthralled Adam was what Rain was doing inside the hut. She was a healer, apparently. Not just a midwife, as some old crones were, but an actual trained physician. Amazed, he watched as she turned the babe inside the woman's womb with her hands shoved inside, made a small cut in the place between her woman-folds, then helped to ease the babe out when it was ready.

Adam was only seven years old. He was not given to religious turns, having given up already on the God his mother had prayed to . . . or was it God who had given up on him and Adela? But somehow, Adam came to an insight way beyond his years. It was his destiny to protect Adela, of course, but he had another destiny, too. He was going to become a doctor. Yes, he was.

He swaggered over to Selik with as much confidence as he could display and announced, "Guess me and Adela will be going home with you tonight." It wasn't as if anyone had invited them, but sometimes Adam had found it was best to take the first step.

Selik looked as if he'd swallowed a frog. Actually, his scowling face turned a shade of green.

But he didn't say no, which Adam took for a good sign.

It appeared he and Adela would have a home of sorts . . . for a while.

NORTHUMBRIA, A.D. 960 (TWENTY-THREE YEARS LATER)

And then his dreams crashed to an end . . .

Adela was dead.

Adam the Healer dropped to his knees and beat his breast. Muttering to himself rather than to anyone who might hear in the crowded hospitium at Rainstead, he berated himself, "Two life missions I have had—only two; to protect Adela and to be a healer. I have failed at both."

For the first time in Adam's thirty years, he cried. In fact, he wailed his grief to the high heavens and pulled at his hair. "I should join my beloved sister in death. The pain is more than I can bear."

"Nay, master, do not speak such sacrilege. Only Allah, or your Christian God, should make such destiny-decisions," his assistant Rashid cautioned softly, putting a comforting hand on Adam's shoulder.

But there was no comfort to be had this day.

Adam leaned forward over the pallet and pressed a soft kiss on his sister's already cool cheek. Death wasted no time once the last breath was stilled. Soon the body stiffening would take place, and the skin color would change. He was a physician; he knew these things too well. "Good-bye, sweet Adela," he whispered. "Forgive me for coming too late."

A monk from the minster in Jorvik knelt on her other side and started to speak the last rites over her. It was a routine the priest must have played out over and over. Did his faith ever falter? Did he ever wonder why his God would take so many innocent people?

With a sigh, Adam rose to his feet and let Rashid lead him down the rows of pallets where dozens of people lay sick and dying of the wasting disease that had hit Jorvik with such devastation these past months. The toll in lives thus far was horrible to contemplate.

"Healer, help me," one dying man called out to Adam.

"Master Adam, Master Adam . . ." another entreated.

"I hurt," a child's weak voice whimpered.

Over and over, the sufferers called for Adam and his healing skills, but he had nothing left to give. If he had not been able to save his sister, how could he help them?

Adam followed Rashid outdoors where the fresh air was at first a balm to his raw lungs. It was a momentary ease, however, for as his eyes scanned Rainstead for the first time in five years, he did not see the manor house, the orphanstead, the weaving sheds, stables and out-buildings, the hospitium . . . all that Rain and Selik had built over the years to aid the homeless of Jorvik. What he saw was the grave mound being dug for his sister.

Grieving mightily were Selik, who had adopted him and Adela all those years ago . . . and his wife, Rain, who had been more than adoptive mother to him. Rain, a far-famed healer, had taught him all she knew of medicine and encouraged him to study further in the Eastlands, where the Arab physicians were at the forefront of research amongst all those in the world. Rain and Selik had passed many winters together, having seen more than fifty good years. Today they looked every one of those years, while Adela had been a relatively young woman . . . only twenty-seven.

If only he had not stayed away so long!

He'd received the missive a month ago from Rain, informing him of the epidemic and how it was hitting so many in Jorvik and at her orphanage. "Come home, Adam. You are needed here."

Adela had not been afflicted then, but he had made all possible haste at the summons. Immediately after receiving the letter, he'd left the caliph's palace in Baghdad, where he'd been conferring with physicians who'd gathered from all sectors of the Eastlands to share their knowledge, but his longship had had to be prepared for the journey and then they had been delayed by sea storms for a sennight and more. He'd arrived two days past to find Adela near death.

"You came," Adela had whispered on first seeing him, raising a hand weakly to caress his face. Already, the death rattle had been in her voice.

Then, "Thank you, dear brother, for caring for me all those years."

And finally, "I love you, Adam. Be happy."

He'd tried frantically to save her . . . everything Rain had taught him, everything the world's best physicians had taught him . . . but nothing had worked. She'd died in his arms an hour ago.

"What will we . . . what will *you* do now?" Rashid asked.

Adam shook his head with indecision. "I must stay for the burial. Viking funerals are elaborate, drawn-out affairs. After that, I do not know. Mayhap I will go to Hawkshire . . . that small estate Selik and Rain gifted me in Northumbria years ago. Mayhap I will return with you to the Eastlands."

A long silence settled over them as they walked aimlessly about the grounds.

Finally Adam said, "One thing is certain. No longer will I answer to the name of healer. I am forswearing medicine."

CHAPTER ONE

☖

The Viking warrior was a warrioress . . .

"With all due respect, Master Adam, you need a harem."

"No harems, Rashid."

"Just one."

"Not even one."

"Dancing girls?"

"Nay!"

"A Nubian concubine?"

"Nay!"

"Triplets from Cordoba who could give a man thrice the pleasure?"

"Nay, nay, nay!"

"Hmph! Man was not intended to live this way. Truly, I do not understand how you can be content to live as a . . . a . . . hermit. 'Tis unnatural."

"No harems," Adam repeated.

Rashid muttered one of his usual proverbs, in this case, "Even paradise is no fun without people." With a grunt of disgust, he gave up, for the moment, and returned to his work.

Adam, on the other hand, stared off into space, realizing with some amazement that he actually *was* a con-

tented man, just as his faithful assistant had inferred.
That realization came to him with such suddenness that
Adam, rather stunned, set his quill down and smiled to
himself. Despite all the misery and grief—and, yes,
self-pity—peace had somehow crept up on him. Mayhap his inner wounds were finally healing.

But wasn't that an irony in itself . . . that a man who
had been renowned for his adventuresome spirit, wicked
sense of humor, and wanton ways now took great comfort in *contentment?* It was a graybeard's word. Next he
would be calling for a hot posset and a cane.

Before he had a chance to catch himself, Adam sighed
aloud.

"There are harems, and then there are *harems*," offered Rashid, misinterpreting Adam's sigh. "I'm especially fond of women who can dance the Ritual of the
Veils. Or those who are double-jointed. Or those with an
ample set of buttocks. Or those with breasts like pome-
granates. Or those—"

"Pfff!" was Adam's only response.

Rashid's biggest complaint about the Saxon lands
was its dearth of women . . . especially *talented* women.
He was of the firm conviction that the answer to any
male difficulty could be found between the thighs of a
comely woman, with or without talents, and he did not
mind sharing that conviction with one and all. 'Twas
best to ignore him betimes.

Adam picked his quill up, dipped it in the ink pot's
treacly *encaustum*, and resumed scratching on the parchment pages of his herb journal. In some ways, this two-
year respite from medical practice had helped Adam
become a better doctor. He was assimilating all his
thoughts and research from the past ten years or more
and putting them on parchment.

Some physicians studied the human body, head to

toe. Others believed in the theory of humors . . . that everything that happened to the body was related to bile, blood, phlegm, or water. Adam had come to believe that there was much more he did *not* know about the body than what he did know, so he limited his studies to herbs and their medicinal uses. Even then, it was complicated. The same plants grown in different geographical areas displayed different properties. The time of year an herb was picked could be important. And, of course, the roots, seeds, leaves, spores, pollen, and flowers all served different purposes . . . not to mention how they were preserved or prepared.

Rashid continued to fill small pottery containers with *propolis*, the reddish resin produced by honeybees. Adam's stepaunt by marriage, Eadyth, one of England's most famous beekeepers, had sent him a goodly supply last sennight. He used the base substance as a balm in treating wounds, while scenting the rest with lavender, rose, and sandalwood for gifting on occasion to his women friends. It was an excellent unguent for softening hands and other body parts. Not that he had all that many women friends of late. Adam also used honey as a dressing for wounds or, mixed with salt, as a cleansing agent.

He and Rashid worked in companionable silence in the round tower room overlooking the courtyard. Its eighteen arrow slit windows gave more light for his studies than any other chamber in this dreary keep. While many men measured their wealth in gold and land, Adam prized the rare books that filled a shelf on the far wall. An amazing six in all. Few kings had as many. They were worth a fortune. *Bald's Leechbook*; Pliny the Elder's *Natural History*; Hippocrates's medical observations; the works of Galen, surgeon to the Roman gladiators; the notebooks of the revered Arab doctor, Rhazes; and, of course, his stepmother Rain's journal.

The books had been translated from their original languages into English, most often by monks, but ofttimes by Adam himself, who was fluent in five tongues. Of course, he hadn't translated Rain's journal—the one he consulted most—because it had been in English to begin with.

There was valuable information in all the books, but much to be scoffed at as well, such as Pliny's advice to eat a mouse a day to prevent tooth decay.

"If this lowly servant could be so bold," Rashid said, breaking the silence, "a harem could be just the spark you need to fire up your life again."

By the rood! Is Rashid still on that selfsame subject? "A harem? A harem in Saxon lands? I'd like to see that. Better yet, my dour-faced neighbors, far distant as they are, would love to see it."

"You could start a trend. Lucky for you, I know just where to gather a harem."

"I'd wager a camel's hump you do, you conniving scoundrel."

"In Baghdad."

"Aaaahhh! So that's where this conversation is headed . . . as always. Home to the desert."

"Truly, it is past time that we return to the warmer climes, oh, wise one."

Rashid always threw in "oh, wise one" when he wanted something. His machinations were as transparent as Lady Eadyth's wispy beekeeping garments.

"It is so cold and damp in this land that I swear I found mold betwixt my toes this morn. And there was frost on my nose, yea, there was, and it is only September. Mayhap you could accept the sultan's offer of a small palace in Cairo in return for becoming his personal physician.

And, of course, there would be a harem." Rashid smiled widely, as if he'd just said something brilliant.

Adam glanced up from his work to see if Rashid was serious.

He was.

"I do not need a woman. I sure as bloody hell do not need a harem. And how many times do I have to tell you, I am not your master, Rashid?"

"As you say, master."

"And we are not going back to the Eastlands anytime soon."

Rashid scowled at being thwarted, but then tried a different approach. "A thousand pardons, master. Perchance you would not be so ill-tempered if your body humors were leveled out. Everyone knows that a man must empty his sacred vessel on occasion lest the biles rise in his body."

Adam shook his head at Rashid's persistence. He had a fair idea of what "sacred vessel" Rashid referred to, but, being a physician, he had to ask, "Which biles would those be?"

Rashid brightened, no doubt thinking that he was making some progress. He wasn't. "The biles that create dark moods."

"Rashid," Adam said with a weary sigh, "I am not in a dark mood . . . especially not a dark mood caused by sexual deprivation."

"Hah! You are always in a dark mood. The grooves betwixt your eyebrows have become a permanent fixture. You have set aside your fine apparel. The coins you earned on one battlefield or another have been stored away, along with the treasures given for your great medical achievements. And this home given to you by your adoptive father Selik is certainly dark and gloomy," he said, waving a hand at their surroundings. "There is no gaiety in your life. What you need is gaiety."

Adam's lips twitched with suppressed mirth. "And that gaiety would come from . . . let me guess . . . a harem?"

"I knew you would agree with me." Rashid puffed his chest out with self-satisfaction.

"I do not agree with you. Stop being unreasonable."

Rashid unpuffed his chest. "You could start small, with one or two females. That would be reasonable. You wouldn't need to have a full harem right away. You've heard of that famous Arab proverb regarding harems, haven't you?"

"The one which says, 'If there is no nubile female about, a camel will suffice'?"

"For shame!" Rashid exclaimed, but his lips were fighting a grin, too. "Nay, I refer to the one which says, 'A man's staff needs constant polishing.' "

Adam shook his head with amusement.

Rashid's dark-skinned face turned somber. He put a hand on Adam's shoulder. "In all seriousness, my lord, I worry about you. You have become a recluse here in your own land. You do not mix in society. You make no attempt to refurbish your keep so that others may visit. Most worrisome of all, you continue to refuse to treat the ill and dying who come seeking your healing skills."

Adam should have been affronted. Rashid went too far, for a servant. But then, he was not really a servant. He was a friend. And Adam had given him good cause to worry.

Adam squeezed Rashid's hand on his shoulder and motioned for him to move to the other side of the table where work awaited him. "I'm getting better, Rashid. Really, I am. I know I have been morbid overlong, but—"

Rashid made a snorting sound of commentary on just how morbid he had been of late.

"—but I have been thinking of establishing a small hospitium in that old weaving shed near the moat. What think you of that?"

Rashid gave him a look that said, without words, that he would have been much more impressed if he'd said he was thinking of establishing a harem . . . even in the old weaving shed.

"I knew you could not walk away from medicine permanently," Rashid said. "Why else would you maintain your studies? Why else would you continue to gather herbs? Why else would you correspond with healers of other lands? You may call yourself knight or land owner, traveler or hermit, but at heart you will always be a physician. Till the day you die. For the love of Allah, 'tis time you stopped fighting your fate."

Rashid's wise words did not require comment, but Adam did ponder all he had said. A long period of silence followed.

Adam worked with great concentration, writing in his journal. Rashid, giving up on his harem exhortations for the moment, sat on the bench across the table from him, looking for more work to do now that he was finished with the beeswax balm. After years of noisy towns and battlefields, after the turmoil of personal tragedies, after so much death . . . well, the familiar, peaceful sounds of his quill scratching on parchment and Rashid's pestle now moving rhythmically against fragrant herbs in a stone bowl were oddly soothing.

Alas, their solitude was broken of a sudden.

Clang! Clang! Clang! they heard, accompanied by huffing-and-puffing noises and a few muttered expletives. There were also the neighing of horses and the rhythmic clatter of shod hooves on wood, probably the drawbridge planks.

Adam and Rashid turned as one with surprise toward the windows that looked out over the bailey, then toward the open doorway that led down to the great hall. The sounds seemed to emanate from somebody, or somebodies, stomping through the courtyard and up the steps to his keep.

"Did you forget to pull up the drawbridge?" Adam asked sardonically.

"Ha, ha, ha! May Allah be laughing at your marvelous wit," Rashid replied. Adam, Rashid, the cook, a chambermaid, and a stable boy were the only people living in this cavernous wood castle. There was nothing worth stealing. And the drawbridge was rusted into a down position, as they both well knew. "No one ever comes to this desolate place. You live like a hermit."

"You already said that."

"Some things bear repeating."

"Not that."

"Mayhap it is your stepuncle, Lord Eirik, returning with yet another invitation to spend the coming harvest season at Ravenshire."

Adam peered out through one of the arrow slit windows. "Nay, these men appear to be Viking soldiers and a *hersir*, by their attire and weapons." Although Eirik was half Viking, he had long ago adopted Saxon ways, including his manner of dress.

"Your other stepuncle, Tykir, then? He is a full-blooded Viking, is he not?"

Adam shook his head. "Tykir is Norseman to the bone, but he would not venture past the bounds of Dragonstead in Norway . . . not at this time of year . . . not with his lady, Alinor, breeding yet again at the advanced age of five and thirty, no less."

Adam shrugged with unconcern. They had naught to fear; there was nothing worth stealing. Even so, they both grabbed short swords lying nearby and made for the doorway.

Clang! Clang! Clang! Huff, puff, huff, puff. "Bloody damn hell!" The noises made by the intruders were getting louder as they climbed the steps. Adam heard a female screech of dismay . . . probably Emma, the cook. No, there were two female screeches, combined. It must be Emma *and* Bridget, the chambermaid. By the timbre of their screams, you'd think a dragon had entered his keep.

The huffing-and-puffing, the clanging, and the expletives, he understood immediately. After all, there were thirty-seven steep stone steps leading up from the bailey to the double doors of the great hall. He knew because he'd counted them on innumerable occasions and cursed fluently in several languages, especially when he was suffering from mead-head.

Adam and Rashid were making their way down the interior stairway when Adam stopped abruptly at the bottom, incredulous at the sight he beheld. Rashid slammed into his back.

"Oh . . . my . . . God!" Adam muttered.

"For . . . the . . . love . . . of . . . Allah!" Rashid muttered.

They were standing next to each other by now, gaping at the other side of the great hall, where a small entourage of Viking warriors stood, broadswords drawn and battle-axes at the ready. They were a fearsome group of fighting men, massive in height and breadth, clad in furs and armor, wielding weapons that could cleave a grown man from head to groin with a flick of the wrist. That was what had caused Emma and Bridget to scream, no doubt; both women stood leaning against a nearby wall, fanning themselves with their aprons.

"May God help us!" Adam exhorted.

"Hah! I prefer the proverbial wisdom, 'Call on your God, but avoid men with sharp blades.'"

In truth, these Norsemen did not frighten Adam, his words prompted more by surprise than fear. Even though he was Saxon by birth, he and his sister Adela had grown up in a Norse household. It was not the sight of armed Vikings that had caused Adam and Rashid to go slack-jawed with amazement. It was the leader of the Norse troop that drew their attention. Tossing aside a full-length, midnight blue, wool cloak lined in gray sable, the Norse chieftain stood before them, arrogant and proud.

It was a woman.

A woman warrior.

A sudden thought occurred to Adam, and he turned on his assistant. "Rashid! You didn't! Surely this is a coarse jest, even for you."

"Me? What have I done?" Rashid slapped a palm over his heart, as if suffering some great insult.

"The harem nonsense," Adam reminded him. "A short time ago, you urged me to start a harem, and now *this*," he said, indicating the Amazon who had resumed her bold approach toward him, followed closely by a dozen soldiers. The woman even walked like a man, in an exaggerated, swaggering sort of way.

"Are you mad? That . . . that man-woman is not what I would consider for a harem." Rashid practically sputtered with indignation.

"What then? A Valkyrie?" He'd heard the tales of the legendary female gods who led brave warriors to the afterworld.

"That is no Valkyrie," Rashid asserted. "That man-woman is live and human ... I would swear it on Muhammad's grave."

As the group drew closer, Adam got his first good look at the woman through the light provided by the open doors and meager arrow slit windows. And he had to agree with Rashid's assessment. This was no goddess, come from the other world. She was flesh and blood ... and definitely woman.

The oddest thing happened then. Fine hairs stood out all over Adam's body. His heart stopped beating for a second, then raced wildly. Most remarkable, a surge of energy slammed into his loins, pumping hot blood into the region, and settling there, thick and pulsing. Like the drawbridge, he'd thought his manpart was rusted down. He was wrong.

She was tall, for a female. In fact, Adam was very tall himself and he had only a half head on her. Despite being slender, she was well muscled, as any soldier would be. The short-sleeved tunic she wore, belted at a narrow waist, left bare her arms, which bore etched silver armlets over well-defined muscles. Even her forearms displayed the raised tendons and ropy muscles of a swordsman. Exceedingly long legs were encased in skin-tight, soft hide leggings which also showed the delineation of musculature ... no doubt from long hours atop a warhorse.

That image—female legs spread wide, the rhythmic up-and-down canter of the horse pressing against her womanplace—caused the throb in his manhood to intensify. *Bloody hell! It feels as if I have a heartbeat there.*

She must have been wearing flexible chain mail, because he could see its hem beneath the thigh-high tunic, and because it molded her body in such a way that her breasts were upthrust against the fabric of her tunic.

From a distance, she might have resembled a man-woman, as Rashid had referred to her, but up close she was all woman, in Adam's opinion.

To his utter shock, the woman did the most outlandish thing. She scratched at her groin . . . as men were wont to do. He could swear she did it deliberately, to reinforce the notion that she was a manly woman, or mayhap just to startle them. Repulsed as he was by the crude gesture, his manpart knew no better . . . it still throbbed.

Two years without a woman, and the first one that arouses me is wearing chain mail and scratching at her groin. Some celestial being must have a twisted sense of humor.

Who is she?

The richness of the jewel-brooched garments and gold-studded belt she wore, along with the silver-scabbarded weapons, bespoke a personage of high rank. He thought he knew all the families of Viking nobility, but this woman did not strike a memory chord.

Even as he stared at her rudely, the woman pulled the fitted leather helmet off her head, causing thick, pale blond braids to fall out, then cascade loose from their leather ties into what could only be described as skeins of golden silk.

He gasped.

And throbbed some more. Good thing he wore the loose Arab robe he favored when in his own home, or he would embarrass himself.

Under his breath, Rashid murmured in Arabic, "On the other hand . . ."

Adam arched an eyebrow in question.

"On the other hand, yon man-woman might make a magnificent harem houri. Dost think she would consent to wearing pierced bells on her breasts?"

"Shhhhh," Adam cautioned, then added, also in

Arabic, "It would be more likely she would pierce your balls with bells, my friend. This is no tame desert damsel, eager to please her master."

Eyes of cerulean blue pierced them both, almost as if she understood their words. Her men snickered under their collective breaths.

"Which of you is the healer?" she asked, speaking for the first time.

Her voice was deep and husky, but not at all manlike. Nay, Adam could imagine that voice whispering wicked things to a man when they were both stoked to passion. He could imagine it suggesting ways to cure the pleasure-pain that continued to envelop his loins. He could imagine—

"Well?" she interrupted his reverie. "Enough time have I wasted, traipsing across this wretched land. Which of you is the healer I have been searching for?"

He and Rashid exchanged a long look, not sure if either of them wanted to be the subject of her search. Finally, Adam admitted, "I was . . . am . . . Adam the Healer."

Rashid piped in, "And I am Ibn Rashid al Mustafa. Your humble servant." He performed a peculiar obsequious bow native to his country, involving the rapid touching of his forehead, nose, mouth, and heart.

"I have been trained as a physician," Adam continued, "but I no longer treat patients. Perchance I could recommend another doctor for you . . . there are several monk healers in St. Peter's ministerium at Jorvik. What exactly is your problem?"

"It's not *my* problem that causes me to seek you out," she explained, the whole while motioning with hand gestures to Emma and Bridget that they should provide drink for her men who were sitting down at the long trestle tables. Adam should have been embarrassed at not offering the hospitality himself, but he was too confused by this woman and her mission. "'Tis my father, King Thorvald of Stoneheim, who needs your help. He is gravely ill of an unknown malady. Dost know of him?"

Adam shook his head slowly.

"He is called Thorvald the Wolf."

"Aaaah. Now I recall. His kingdom is in far northern Norway . . . Halogaland." Adam's stepuncle Tykir lived in Dragonstead, at the end of beyond in Norway. Men had body parts frozen off there if they were careless enough to venture outdoors overlong during the winter months. Stoneheim was even farther north, in the most primitive, mountainous area . . . a land nigh uninhabitable.

She nodded. "How long will it take you to pack your medicinal supplies?"

"I beg your pardon, m'lady . . . I mean . . ." He paused meaningfully, not knowing her name. *If this woman, magnificent as she is, thinks I am going anywhere near the frigid mountains of that godforsaken section of Norway, she is sadly mistaken.*

"Tyra. Tyra Sigrundottir. Tyra, Cub of the Wolf. Tyra First Child. Tyra the Blonde. Tyra Brave One." She shrugged as if to say she would answer to any of those appellations.

"Or Tyra Warrior Princess," he offered, half in jest.

To his surprise, she agreed. "That, too." And she didn't even smile as she said it. Of a certainty, the woman was full of herself, and lacking in humor.

But her ego was of no consequence. He, and an important part of his body, thought she was glorious. Especially since she had not scratched herself again . . . thanks be to God! If she belched or did something else of a distasteful masculine nature, he might just cry with disappointment.

"In any case, *Tyra*, I regret to inform you that I cannot

help your father. I have not practiced the healing arts these past few years. When, or if, I resume treating patients again, it will be here in Britain. My traveling days are over. Under no circumstances would I be willing to go so far."

She made a scoffing noise. "I do not recall *asking* you to come. You will come, of that there is no question."

He raised himself to his full height, which was more than considerable, and fixed her with a glower. "I will not."

Tyra rolled her eyes as if to say, *Here we go again!*

Some of her men sniggered and began to talk amongst themselves. He understood the Norse tongue perfectly. These sea pirates were placing bets . . . *against* him in this battle of wills.

"Uh-oh," Rashid said and danced quickly away from his side.

Adam's glance wavered briefly. In that instant when he looked to Rashid to see what the problem was, then glanced back, he saw that the demented woman had her broadsword raised high above her head and was lowering it. *Toward him*, of all things. He had no time to duck aside. The flat side of her sword hit him on the crown, causing him to see stars and his knees to buckle.

The warrior princess bent over him in the rushes, admonishing, "See what you made me do, you dumb dolt!"

He *was* a dumb dolt, because all he could think about was the magnificent set of breasts jutting out above his face.

Just before the blackness overtook him, the most amazing thing of all happened. She picked him up— *she actually picked him up*—and tossed him over her shoulder.

It appeared he was going to Norway, after all.

CHAPTER TWO

✣

Never trust a blue-eyed rogue . . .
    The man was beautiful.

Tyra normally did not notice such things, surrounded
by men as she was day and night. For the most part,
men were smelly, flea-ridden creatures with overblown
egos and a ridiculous tendency to think with their male
parts. In fact, they had a tendency to scratch intimate
body parts . . . a habit she was trying to mimic, to her
own disgust, to fit in better with them. Belching at will
was harder . . . a dubious talent she'd not yet mastered.
Truly, men were good for one thing only. Fighting wars.
But this man . . . for the love of Frey . . . this man was a
god in human form.

She'd laid him out on one of the trestle tables where
he still "slept" from the tap she'd administered to his
head with her trusty sword, "Good Friend." His assistant, the Arab chatterbird Rashid, was off packing
leather bags and wooden chests with clothing and medicinal supplies, under careful guard of the leader of her
troop, Rafn the Ruthless. The rest of her retinue sat
about the great hall, which seemed to have been unused
for some time, eating a cold repast of mead, flat bread,
and sliced mutton.

The physician's unconscious state gave her an opportunity to study him more closely. He was tall—even

taller than she was—and perfectly proportioned. He lacked the bulk of an active soldier, but he was not un-muscled. His shoulders were wide and his waist narrow, if she could judge by the full, belted gown. She wondered idly—or perchance not so idly—what he wore under the garment . . . if anything. Her face heated at her vivid imaginings.

It was his face that drew her most. Thick, thick black lashes fanned his eyelids and matched the overlong hair, which hung down to his shoulders in a silky swath. She recalled that his eyes, now closed, were clear blue like the waters of the North Sea on a summer day . . . as she'd been told hers were. His nose was straight. His lips were full. His cheekbones high . . . almost ascetically so.

Tyra had seen many a handsome man in her day. In truth, Viking men were reputed to be more splendid in appearance than the average man of other countries. But something about this man touched her in a way she had never experienced before . . . something she did not want. She had seen twenty and five winters. There was no place in her life for a man. Not anymore. Not that he would be willing. Not that he would even look at the likes of her.

But he *had* looked at her. Tyra had seen that. And a part of her thrilled at the glow of arousal she'd seen in his blue eyes . . . a glow that would have prompted a sharp punch in the stomach if given by any man in her company. The look of appreciation he'd given her was the kind normally reserved for one of her four sisters . . . never for her. She was too big, too crude, too unfeminine, too . . .

Enough! I have no interest in this man, or any other. Not that way.

And, really, the rogue would not be lifeless for long,

she reminded herself. In fact, she would wager that the man, once he awakened, would be madder than a castrated bull at being bested by a woman. She had better restrain him now while she had the opportunity.

She had just finished tying his wrists and ankles when she noticed those sinfully thick eyelashes fluttering open. Although he did not rise immediately from his supine position atop the wide table, she saw awareness in his blue eyes.

"My lady warrior, you are in big, big trouble," he said, low and ominous.

Barely had the words left his mouth than the man—a man she had clearly underestimated—performed a move that would do the bravest Norse *hersir* proud. The loop of his arms went over her head, drawing her forward to land atop him. At the same time, he flipped them both over so she was the one flat on her back and he was the one leaning over her, belly to belly, thigh to thigh.

Her guardsmen rushed forward to her aid, swords and daggers aready, but she warned them off with a sharp command, "Stay!" A good soldier knew when to pick his battle, when to proceed and when to yield. She'd chosen the latter course because the physician's bound wrists were resting at her neck, both thumbs pressed against her windpipe. Before a blade could enter the knave's back, he could choke her, or break her neck. Besides, she needed him alive if her father was to live.

But it was humiliating to have been caught thus by the lout. He was not even an active warrior, as she was.

He leaned forward, so close his lips almost touched hers. "Order your men to go out to the courtyard and await you there. Tell them to sheathe their weapons, carefully. We are just having a little . . . discussion."

"Stop choking me, you Saxon maggot," she said. But

what she thought was, *Holy Thor, his breath is sweet and warm and inviting. I wish . . . I wish . . . nay, I do not wish . . . I do not wish . . .*

"I'm not choking you, wench. If I were, you would know it."

"I am not a wench."

"I am not a maggot."

"Hah! So you say!"

"Do as I say," he demanded and pressed his thumbs tighter.

There would be bruising on the soft flesh of her neck by nightfall, and the brute well knew it. He was delighting in putting his mark on her.

"Go out to the courtyard, all of you! Put your weapons aside," she yelled out to her guardsmen in a voice they would know brooked no argument. "I am safe. The Saxon pig just wants to . . . talk."

"A pig, hmmm? Do you say I am malodorous? Or my facial stubble prickles you? In any case, your tongue outruns your good sense, *wench*." He shifted his body atop her, letting her know that the bulge between his legs was there . . . for her. And that more than talk would be in store for her if he had his way.

Despite his pincer grip on her throat, she tried to wiggle her body upward to escape the press of his masculinity.

He just followed her—a sensuous, body-to-body scraping—and grinned wolfishly. What she'd accomplished, instead of escape, was the raising of her tunic hem. The only thing between them now was the fabric of her *braies* and his robe, and heat . . . the most agonizing, delicious heat.

"Are any of these men your husband?" he asked.

The question surprised her. She shook her head hesitantly.

"Good," he said and grinned some more.

Good? What does that mean? Hell and Valhalla, this man is much more clever with words than I am. "Why would you care, one way or another?"

"I have no idea," he admitted. "But I do."

Oooh! Tantalizing words to a woman who had only garnered attention for her skill with sword and lance.

"Tyra!" Rafn, her chief bodyguard, exclaimed.

"Master!" the Arab servant exclaimed at the same time.

The two of them must have just returned to the great hall from the tower stairwell.

Tyra was suddenly alarmed. She did not want Rafn to overreact, putting her life in peril. "I am safe, Rafn. Do not proceed farther. Go about the business of packing. I am just . . . uh, talking . . . with the Saxon physician."

"Talking!" Rafn declared with a snort of disbelief. "Methought you were about to couple."

"Couple? Couple?" the Arab inquired with great interest. "Two years my master has remained chaste. 'Tis past time for a bit of coupling, if you ask me. By the by, Master Rafn, do you have harems in the Norselands?"

A dozen or more voices shouted from the courtyard steps through the open doorway, "Two years!" All eyes turned on the healer, who still lay atop her.

Adam groaned and pressed his forehead against the witch's.

Damn, damn, damn! Rashid of the Running Tongue just had to expose all my secrets. I am going to cut off his tongue the instant I get off this woman. He raised his head and gazed down upon the woman, who gazed right back at him, chin raised high with pride, not the least bit frightened. He realized then that the last thing he wanted was to get off this woman.

"Two years?" she asked. "Are you a monk healer?" The questions were simple, but the tone was taunting.

"Yea, two years. And, nay, I am no monk," he grumbled. "How long has it been for you?"

Despite all her efforts to appear masculine, she ducked her head, but not before he saw the less-than-masculine blush that bloomed there. "A virgin!" he guessed. "A thirty-year-old virgin!"

"I am not thirty years old. I am only twenty-five," she asserted too quickly, before she realized what she had revealed. It wasn't her virginity she had denied, just her age.

He smiled.

She snarled.

"What are those stains upon your tunic?" he inquired, suddenly noticing the blotches that marred the fine wool fabric.

"Blood."

"Yech!" He started to raise his chest off her chest, but then changed his mind, deciding he'd rather feel her breasts pressed up against him, despite the blood. Still, he asked, "Whose?"

"Some bloody Saxon who had the temerity to be in my way when I stepped off my longship in Jorvik."

This woman was certainly unlike any he had ever met. "You killed a man because he was in your way?"

"And because he laughed at me."

"Remind me never to laugh at you," he said, and did just that . . . laughed at her.

She stiffened, which caused her body to rub slightly against his. He felt the whisper of a caress from her metal-webbed breasts to the soft mound of her sex. "I can scarce wait till we make love," he whispered against her ear.

"You go too far, Saxon," she hissed back in his ear.

Little did she know how erotic her breath felt there. He wished she would dip the tip of her tongue in, as well.

She made a snorting sound, as if she sensed his thoughts.

That felt good, too.

"Enough of this nonsense!" he said finally.

"I agree. Let me go."

He nodded. He wanted her free so that her hands could roam his body, just as he intended his to do to her. "First, let us come to an understanding. I will not be leaving my keep, but you are welcome to stay as long as you want. No repercussions." That was rather magnanimous of him, he concluded. But then, he wanted her in his bed furs that night. "Well?" His tied hands still gripped her neck. He would not let go till she gave her word.

She seemed to be gritting her teeth. He thought she murmured, "Toad."

"What did you say?"

"Load . . . I said you are a heavy load on me."

He smiled, sensing that his "load" was not all that burdensome to her.

"You make me breathless," he informed her. Women liked to know that their charms heated the male blood.

"You suffocate me," she said.

The woman really was lacking in charm, he decided, though she had other assets to make up for that deficit. And, really, he could teach her how to be charming. It was an art form he'd developed at an early age. And no doubt she was acting foul-tempered to hide the fact that she was as aroused as he, even if she was a virgin, which he could hardly credit at her advanced age.

"Give your word and you are free," he told her.

Her only response was to arch her hips and rock from side to side.

His toes curled and blood rushed to all the important parts of his body. His pleasure at the brush of her sex against his was so intense that he felt like roaring and whimpering at the same time. "Your word, m'lady," he nigh begged.

She indicated with a jerk of her head that he should come closer. Then, into his ear she whispered, "There is a game you Saxons play in your high courts. 'Tis called chess, I believe. Are you familiar with it?"

He nodded, even as he frowned with puzzlement. His mind felt dull with arousal. "Yea, I know the game, but what has chess to do with us?"

"If you know the game, then you will understand this," she announced with a hoot of glee. "Check and mate!"

Too late he realized that a sharp blade in her hand was pressed into his neck and was already drawing blood from the point imbedded in his skin just above the pumping vein. "Do not make a wrong move, Saxon, or you are dead."

It appeared he was going to Norway, after all.

Two days later, somewhere on the North Seas

How about a little bondage, baby? . . .

On second thought, Adam decided, the wench wasn't all that attractive.

In fact, after two and a half days of being tied to the mast pole of a rolling longship . . . up one wave, down one wave, up one wave, down one wave . . . well, to say that his stomach turned at the thought of Tyra was a vast understatement. To make matters worse, each evening just before dusk the warrior-woman hoisted him over her shoulder and carried him ashore for overnight camping. With his head going ka-thump, ka-thump against her backside, he was definitely un-enthralled with the outrageous wench . . . even if she did have a decidedly delicious backside.

Despite his best intentions—and his being unenthralled—he had to admire her expertise and that of her warriors, who appeared equally at ease at sea or on land. He was on one longship and Rashid was on another, each ship manned by sixty-five vikings. There were no rowing benches. Instead, thirty-two men sat on their sea chests working the thirty-two long oars. The other thirty-two spelled them when their arms grew tired, while a helmsman guided the rudder. The Vikings hung their decorated shields along the sides of the dragonships, both for display and to stop arrows in case of a sea battle. Square sails of red and white stripes fluttered high atop both ships from single masts and yardarms. A group of horses were corralled with ropes in the center of each boat, including Adam's and Rashid's.

In all, this Viking warrior-princess led her soldiers, even on the seas, with remarkable skill. As Rashid was fond of saying, "An army of sheep led by a lion would defeat an army of lions led by a sheep." It was clear that Tyra was a lion . . . but then, her hard-muscled warriors hardly counted as sheep.

That fact had been demonstrated to Adam only this morn when a Viking pirate ship attacked them. Out of the mist, the grotesque dragon prow of the marauding ship had appeared, like a giant sea monster. Reinforcing that image had been the battle shrieks of the pirates, like howling creatures from Niflheim, the Norse afterworld. Tyra's other ship had been too far ahead to be of assistance. Tossing grappling hooks attached to strong ropes onto Tyra's ship, the pirates—three dozen in all—had managed to pull the two ships close enough to each other to jump aboard.

Tyra had led her men in the counter attack, slicing one man in the neck and heaving his lifeless body overboard, grabbing another smallish Viking pirate from behind around his neck and squeezing till he fell dead to the deck. Grunts and shouts and screams and muffled cries had filled the air, but mostly there had been just the metallic sounds of swords and axes hitting one another. The skirmish had lasted barely a half hour before the pirates disembarked Tyra's ship, cut the grappling rope, and rowed off, leaving behind ten dead pirates and much blood. But it had been long enough for Adam to see that Tyra was indeed a Viking warrior, woman or not.

And much to his dismay, he'd heard Tyra ask Bjorn, a berserker who also happened to be a blacksmith, if he wanted her to drain the still-warm blood from one of the pirates into a bucket to take home. The blood of an enemy was used betimes to "quench," or harden, white-hot swords during the pattern-welding process . . . though more times than not, water would suffice.

He had been fairly certain at the time that she had been serious, but mayhap she had been trying to shock him.

The bloodthirsty wench was about to walk by him now—and wasn't that an amazing sight? Whenever she remembered to do so, the woman swaggered—shoulders back, stride aggressive. Adam had lots of time to study this phenomenon and he'd come to the conclusion that Tyra deliberately tried to take on male characteristics. Perchance she thought they would give her greater authority. She even scratched her groin on occasion, as men did, and she spit over the side of the ship.

Now she was about to swagger right by him, as if he were invisible, on her usual manly stroll from stem to stern to supervise the work of her sailors. He gritted his teeth with chagrin at her easy disregard of him, or his comforts. Luckily, his teeth were no longer chattering. Before taking him forcibly away from his home two days ago, the woman had given him an opportunity to change from his robe into *braies*, a wool tunic and heavy cloak, but, being exposed to the open air aboard ship, those garments had soon became soaked with sea water . . . until today when they'd seen their first warm sunlight. Now they were covered with residual sea salt. His situation was no different from that of every other person on the longboat. The Viking vessels rode low in the water, sloshing water in as a matter of course, and everyone was sodden most of the day. Baling water was a never-ending job.

"My lady Viking," he called out, unable to control the sarcasm in his voice.

Tyra paused and arched one eyebrow in question. "What? More complaints? Too cold? Too wet? Too hungry? Too tired? Too sore? *Too, too, too . . .*"

He barely restrained himself from snarling. Quickly he banked his temper.

"Now that you've kidnapped me, why won't you untie me?" he asked, not for the first time. "I concede I'm a prisoner, but prisoners have rights, too, you know."

"I wouldn't precisely call it kidnapping," she contended.

"Really? What would you call it?"

"A forceful invitation to visit my homeland."

"Word games!"

"And as to why I won't release you, look what you did back at your keep when my mind wandered for a moment. Flat on my back I was with your clawlike fingers at my throat."

Flat on her back. Yea, that is where women should be . . . rather, that is where this particular bothersome woman should be. And she will be, eventually, if I have my way.

God, what is it about this woman? One moment I wish my hands were free so I could wring her neck. The next moment I wish my hands were free so I . . . so I could do other things.

"My fingers are not clawlike. In fact, I have been told by many that my hands are quite attractive . . . and clever."

"Clever hands? No doubt 'twas a besotted maid who spoke those words."

"Does that make my hands less clever?"

"This is a pointless conversation. The reason I won't release you is that you might try to escape."

He looked all around him. Water, water, everywhere. "As talented as I am in many ways, I do not think I could survive a two-hour swim to shore."

She shrugged. "You have a slick tongue, Saxon. You might try to convince my men to turn against me."

"Mutiny? Pirates do that, don't they? Not civilized folks."

"You consider us civilized?" She fair beamed at the presumed compliment.

"I was speaking of myself."

"Aaarrgh!" she said and walked away.

He watched closely as she reprimanded one of her sailors for some misdeed, then moved on to a young boy, Alrek, who couldn't have seen more than ten winters. He was an apprentice who was trying desperately to impress his leader by maneuvering an oar bigger than himself. Adam had observed that the boy had great spirit and determination, but mostly he failed miserably at every task he tried, from scooping out bilge water in the early morning hours to archery practice during the evening exercises.

Tyra instructed Alrek with gentle firmness now, showing him how to handle the oar so it put less pressure on his shoulders and back. When he still failed to understand, she took his place on the sea chest and began to row, expertly. My God! The woman had muscles in places women were never intended to have muscles. And, by damn, they looked good on her.

Soon she was back in front of Adam again. "Would you like me to bring a bucket so you can relieve yourself, or turn you so that you can aim overboard? It has been a long time since our morning ablutions, and Rafn is too busy right now to handle the chore."

He stared at her, bulge-eyed with horror. "Nay, I do not wish to piss in a bucket, or overboard . . . whilst you watch."

"Well, then, would you like a serving of *gammelost* to break your noonday fast?"

"If I never taste another bite of that stinksome cheese, it will be too soon."

"I am so sorry I have no sweetmeats to tempt your palate."

"Sarcasm ill suits you, m'lady. Do you not have some enemy to go bedevil, lop off a head or two, or something equally unfeminine, and leave innocents like me free of your word barbs?"

"Innocent? You? Methinks you were not innocent even when you came squalling from your mother's womb." She sniffed the air around him then and remarked bluntly, "You need a bath, my healer friend. I cannot fathom why you will not bathe along the shore in the evenings with my men."

"I am not going into any body of water with my arms and legs tied."

"Perchance you would like me to remove your garments now so Rafn can hang you over the side with a rope till the currents wash you clean . . . let us say for an hour or so. What say you to that?"

She was probably teasing.

But then again, she might be serious. He remembered vividly the morning's events and the ill-fated pirate she'd chopped in the neck with her broadsword.

"I am not a bloodthirsty man," he said evenly, "but it becomes increasingly clear to me that I am going to have to kill you."

She laughed . . . she actually threw her head back and laughed at him, exposing white teeth and a mouth that was big enough to . . . well, suffice it to say, it was big enough. In deference to today's heat, she had forgone her cloak and tunic. Instead, she wore only a short-sleeved mail *shert* over tight leggings tucked into leather half-boots. But Adam was too angry now to admire the jut of her breasts or the taper of her waist.

He sniffed in an exaggerated fashion, mimicking her. "Come to think on it, you are a mite rank yourself. That no doubt is why you scratch so much. Wouldst consider letting me remove *your* garments? We could both hang over the side together. I know, I know . . ." he said, as if suddenly inspired. "I will wash your back"—*and other places*—"if you will wash mine."

"For a healer, you are not all that bright, are you?" Her eyes swept over him meaningfully from wind-blown, salt-lank hair to booted toes. "You are hardly in a position to harm even a flea, rope-bound as you are." It appeared she was going to ignore his naked-hanging-over-the-side-washing-backs business. But her pinkened cheeks indicated that his comment had had its desired effect.

"I will not always be bound."

"Ah, so you are saying that the moment you are released, you will attempt to kill me? See, I was right when I said it would be unwise to untie you. But, truly, dost think it wise to give me fair warning?"

He shook his head. "Nay, I will not kill you immediately." He let his eyes sweep over her body now, just as hers had done to him. "I have other plans for you first. And the longer I stand here tied to this bloody pole, the more detailed my fantasies become."

"Oh?" Clearly interested, she put her hands on her hips, her legs widespread to balance herself on the moving ship.

Oh, yea, really detailed. Keep standing like that and give me more ideas. "First, I intend to tup you till your toenails curl."

She gasped. His remark had caught her off guard.

It had caught him off guard, too. Who knew he was going to say such a thing?

"Then I will tup you again till your eyes roll up into your head." *My tongue seems to have developed a mind of its own.*

She regained her composure and glared at him, almost as if to make sure her eyes weren't rolling. "Has the sea air turned you barmy?"

"And then I will make love to you again and again till you beg for more. That should take, oh, a sennight or two . . . or five. I cannot wait. How about you?" *Mayhap Rashid's flapping tongue has rubbed off on me.*

"Pffff! You overstep yourself, Saxon, to speak thus to me. The only thing bigger than your nerve is your ego."

"Or something else." He glanced significantly downward.

She did not answer. In truth, she could not answer, for her mouth was hanging open. With shock or interest, he could not say, but either possibility marked success to his mind.

"Then . . . and only then . . . will I kill you," he concluded, and grinned mirthlessly at her.

She stared at him, pondering all he had said. After a
while, her hand moved through the air in a gesture of
unconcern. "You'd have to catch me first."

"Oh, m'lady, you should see me run."

Tapping her foot with exasperation, she bared her
teeth and nigh growled at him. "Dost think you are man
enough?"

He wasn't sure if she referred to the tupping or the
running. Either way, he knew the answer. "I know I am."

She swiveled on her heel and stomped away from
him, muttering something about coarse, dirty-minded
oafs. But he could tell that he had disconcerted her,
which had been his goal. He'd been trained as a soldier
as well as a physician. After all, he'd been raised in a
Viking household. She was not the only one well versed
in the strategies of battle.

He'd just declared war on his captor.

She tried to persuade him . . .

On her return trip across the decks, she remarked, as
if their conversation had not been interrupted, "Your
crudity knows no bounds, but what could I expect from
a bloody Saxon?"

"My Saxon heritage didn't seem to concern you when
you were on a physician hunt. By the by, I meant to ask
you afore, how did you hear of me?"

"Tykir of Dragonstead recommended you. I asked for
his advice when he came to visit my father. He said you
are the best healer in all of Britain, but he said naught
about your refusal to practice the healing arts."

"Tykir? My stepuncle betrayed me? I can hardly
credit that."

"He did not betray you. All he said was, 'If you want

the best healer for your father, go get Adam.' He did laugh in a most peculiar manner afterward when I told him that I would do just that."

"I am not surprised. Tykir always did have a warped sense of humor."

"Don't you want to know about my father's illness . . . so that you may be prepared to cure him when we arrive at Stoneheim?"

"Why should I inquire about his symptoms when I do not intend to treat him?"

Her face was turning red with frustration. He could tell that she would love nothing more than to punch him in the stomach, but she feared alienating him more than she already had.

"Why won't you treat him? Why have you given up medicine? Why do you disdain the talents your One-God gave you? 'Tis selfish, if you ask me."

"That is my business, and mine only. 'Tis not for you to know."

"Hmph! Well, I will tell you anyhow . . . so you can ponder your method of treatment, despite what you say. He was struck down in a minor battle about three sennights ago . . . a blow to the head from a spiked mace ball. He has been drifting in and out of sleep ever since."

"Did you hit him over the head?"

"Nay, I did not."

"Do not be giving me a look of such affront, as if you'd never struck a man over the head with a deadly weapon. I know better than most that you have, as evidenced by the goose egg on my crown."

The woman did not even have the good sense to look guilty. Instead, she raised her stubborn chin arrogantly.

Suddenly another thought occurred to him. "Your father has been unconscious for three sennights and you expect me to cure him! What happens if I fail? I'm wagering on a head-lopping for such a serious offense. It's an impossible task you ask of me, my lady. *Impossible!*" He made a grunting sound of incredulity. "Are you demented, woman? I am a healer, not a magician."

"Nay, I am not demented. Just desperate," she said.

Adam could tell that the admission cost her much in pride. He knew too well how it hurt to lose a loved one. In a softer voice, he commented, "You must love your father very much."

To his surprise, she shrugged. "The old sly-boots is even more selfish than you are. Of course, I want him to live, but mostly because once he is well, I can convince him to . . ." Her words trailed off, and her face turned an even brighter shade of red.

Now this was interesting. "Convince him to what?" he asked when she looked everywhere but at him.

"Never mind," she said and stomped off.

He considered her methods of persuasion laughable . . .

On her next pass by him, she continued the conversation. "If you must know, I have four sisters," she informed him.

"Huh?" He didn't recall asking her.

"Four sisters! And all of them nagging and pulling at me for just one thing."

"And that would be?"

"A husband."

Uh-oh!

"You see, my father's family has a tradition . . . an ironclad one, passed down through many generations. The daughters in the family can only be married in the order of their birth. The first daughter must wed afore the second. The second must wed afore the third. And so on."

Tyra looked so doleful he almost felt sorry for her.

Almost. Humor outweighed pity, however. "Let me guess. You are the eldest."

She nodded.

"Why not just get married?" he asked when he was able to bank his mirth.

"Look at me," she said, sweeping a hand from her blond head to her big-booted toes.

I'm looking. I'm looking. I'm looking way too much. "What is your point?"

"My point is that I do not have the usual feminine attributes that attract a man."

I beg to differ, my lady. "If you say so."

"Besides, by the time I had seen ten winters, my father realized that his seed was only going to bear girl-fruit. He decided that if he wanted his kingdom to pass to his blood kin, it would have to be me. So he trained me to be a soldier . . . a *good* soldier. That's why it's urgent that you heal my father. If he should die, I must continue to lead his men."

"I'm confused. If your father dies, you will lead his men. So, if you want your father to live, it must be so you will be able to find a willing husband."

She glared at him. "Nay, you dunderhead. Do you deliberately misunderstand? I do not want a husband, but I *do* want my sisters to be able to wed. And I want my father well again. Then he can take back his chieftain duties. Then I can announce the severing of our kinship . . . a divorce, if you will. If I am no longer his daughter, there is no need for me to take on a loathsome oppressor . . . in other words, a husband . . . for my sisters' sake."

"If this severing is such an easy task, why have you not done so before?"

She blushed. "'Tis a recent idea of mine."

"This is the most far-fetched bit of feminine ill-logic

I have ever heard," he said. "What in the name of God would you do if this . . . this . . . divorce took place?"

" 'Tis simple. I will join the Varangian Guard."

"In Byzantium?" His jaw hung open for a moment before he noticed and clicked his teeth in place. "I have never seen or heard of a female in that prestigious group of Viking warriors."

"I have already spoken with the emperor's captain. He thinks a female addition to the Guard would not only be permissible, but highly desirable." She raised her chin another notch, daring him to disagree.

All he could say was, "Oh, my God!" Adam started to laugh then. And laugh. And laugh.

When he told the story to Rashid that evening, he was still laughing.

Rashid, of course, homed in on the most irrelevant part of the story. "Four sisters! Five in all! Dost think that is a Norse version of a harem? Allah be thanked, that it might be so!"

"Five sisters do not count as a harem. Definitely not! And do not dare bring up the subject!" He couldn't stop laughing, though.

However, his assistant saw things in a different light. "If her father dies, mayhap her tribe, including the sisters-harem, will look for you to be the warrior princess's husband."

Adam stopped laughing.

CHAPTER THREE

❧

You could say he was Alrek the Klutz . . .

"I will *never* become a fierce Viking warrior," Alrek complained dolefully. Tears pooled in his green eyes which he quickly wiped away on the sleeve of his tunic.

Adam was still tied to the mast pole, but he'd sunk down to the deck. The boy, whose hair was bleached almost white by the sun, had plopped down beside Adam and was now munching on a piece of *gammelost* wrapped within a slice of manchet bread. Every time he took a bite, he pinched his nose to avoid smelling what he was eating.

"Why do you eat the overripe cheese if it tastes so bad?" Adam had asked him more than once.

Alrek had replied, " 'Cause I need to eat so I kin grow big and strong."

Both sets of legs were extended outward. Alrek's were half as long as Adam's . . . and so skinny, it was pitiful. Even more pitiful were the bleeding blisters that marred the palms of his hands—testament to his dogged determination to become a sailor and a fighting man.

Alrek had a habit of hanging around Adam when he wasn't busy elsewhere. He liked to spout off endlessly about all his failings. In truth, he liked to spout off on any subject. It didn't matter if Adam contributed to the conversation at all; Alrek just wanted someone on whom he could unload his problems.

Adam's eyes kept coming back to the open blisters on the boy's hands. Finally he advised, "You should dip your hands in salt water every chance you get. It will burn like Hades, but the salt helps to keep the wounds from festering, and the blisters will heal faster."

Alrek nodded. "Eyvind, my rowing partner, says horse piss will serve as well."

"Eyvind is teasing you."

"Really? Ah, well, good thing I could not get Rafn's stallion to stand still whilst I held a bucket under him. That's how I got this knock on my knees." He motioned with his bread toward a knobby knee that was bluish-black and turning yellow on the edge. "Kicked me good, the bloody horse did. Tyra, our chieftain, said it would have served me good fer being such a lackwit. She is a fine leader . . . I will give her that . . . but, whew, she can be hard fer a woman. What do you think of her?"

Adam didn't know what to think. The way Alrek's mind moved from one subject to another, he could scarce keep up.

"Huh? Huh? What do you think of her?"

"I try not to think of her," Adam said, choosing his words carefully.

"Some say she is still a verge-on, which is no doubt true, her being so big and tall and fiercesome. Puts the men off, you know."

"Alrek, do you even know what a virgin is?"

"'Course I do," he said with affront. "'Tis a woman what has had no man's longship up her fjord, so to speak."

"Well, that is one way of describing it." Adam should have warned the boy of the inadvisability of speaking so intimately of one's superiors, but all he could do was grin.

"And a man is a verge-on when his longship has never set sail, so to speak."

Longship? That certainly is a new name for a man's best friend. Adam started to cough and couldn't stop.

"I'm a verge-on," Alrek admitted in an undertone, as if disclosing some big secret.

Adam coughed some more, then choked out, "Of course you are. Ten years old! I would hope so."

"How old were you when yer longship first went . . . uhm, a-Viking?"

If this little whelp thought Adam was going to discuss his sex life, he could think again. 'Twas long past time to change the subject. "Why is it so important that you become a Viking warrior?" The boy was going to kill himself trying, if what Adam had observed the past two days was any indication.

"A *fierce* Viking warrior," Alrek corrected him. "'Cause it be a noble profession. 'Cause 'tis the only way fer a homeless boy like me to gain lands and riches. 'Cause I would rather drink goat piss than stay behind at Stoneheim with King Thorvald's daughters. Tyra is not so bad, but wait till you meet her four sisters! Many a man in King Thorvald's court has gone a-Viking just to escape their doings." He rolled his eyes dramatically.

"You're too little to go a-Viking. You should be home playing youthling games."

"I'm ten years old. I am not little," he asserted, puffing out his little chest. "Besides, I have no home. This ship is me home. When I am back at Stoneheim, I sleep on the floor of the great hall."

"Where are your parents?"

"Me father left when I was five. Some say he is a fighting man in the Rus lands; some say he is dead." He shrugged with indifference. "Me mother died last year of the childbed fever. She were a kitchen helper. Two sisters and a brother I have back at Stoneheim. I am the oldest, so I mus' support them with the silver coin King Thorvald pays me each year."

"That is very interesting. Well, it has been nice talking with you. Farewell." *How is that for a not-so-subtle hint? The boy always overstays his welcome, not that he is ever really welcome. I would rather be alone. 'Tis best to keep my distance from each and every one of these vicious Vikings.* He turned to look at Alrek and almost laughed aloud, then immediately made a correction in his mind. *Each and every one of these vicious Vikings, including the want-to-be vicious Vikings.*

"I heard you were an orphan one time, too."

Adam groaned. *I knew there was a reason why I wanted him to go away.* "Who told you that?"

"Rashid."

"Rashid talks too much."

"He does? It took me ever so long to get any useful information from him."

"Are you a spy sent by your leader to pry secrets from us?"

Adam had been jesting, but Alrek's eyes went wide with amazement that anyone would credit him with such responsibility.

"Nay, I am not a spy, but I will mention yer idea to Tyra. Dost think yer recommendation will have influence with her?"

"About as much as your talking has on me."

Alrek beamed as if Adam had paid him a high compliment.

"As to what I was sayin' afore . . . do not be so hard on Rashid. Mostly, he sez nothin' of import. Jist things like 'Allah save me from pestsome gnats,' or 'You chatter more than a harem houri.' What is a whore-he? Is that a whore what is a man?"

Adam would have put his face in his hands if his hands were free. "Don't you have to go back and row some more?"

"Nay! I am done with that job fer the day. I am going to mend nets this afternoon."

Jesus, Mary and Joseph! "With a needle?" *He is going to turn those blistered palms into a war field.*

Alrek nodded and stood.

Bless the saints! He is going to leave me alone.

"There is something I wanted to ask you."

I should have known. The boy is not leaving after all. Now he gets to the reason for his visit . . . what he has been leading up to all along. On the other hand, mayhap this is some form of Norse torture I have never heard of in all my living amongst Viking families. Torture-by-boy-with-blathering-tongue.

"How long were you an orphan? Rashid said you and yer sister were adopted by a Viking man and his wife. Do children ever get adopted when they are no longer . . . um, ah, children exactly?" The whole time Alrek sputtered and stammered to get his question out, he stood as tall as his spindly frame would stretch, with chin held high and face flaming with color . . . all this to demonstrate that *he* was not a child exactly.

After he killed Tyra, he was going to kill Rashid for getting him into this predicament.

"Alrek, do not waste your time dreaming impossible dreams. We were fortunate, Adela and I," he said, then had to pause after speaking his sister's name. Had he ever spoken her name aloud these past two years? When he was more calm, he continued, "It was just a chance circumstance that brought Selik and Rain to that place in Jorvik at the same time my sister and I were there.

Most often, orphans are left to fend for themselves, as you do. And, really, 'tis not—"

"A miracle? It was like the miracles yer One-God promises in his Bible." Alrek was staring at him as if he'd just spoken some magic words. "So what I need is a miracle?"

"Nay, nay, nay! It was not a miracle."

"The only gods I know of are Odin and Thor and Frey and Loki. Perchance you could pray to yer One-God that he would send us a father and a mother . . . a family . . . you know, a miracle."

"Alrek! I am not praying. I do not believe in miracles. And I think I see Gorr the Netmaker motioning for you."

Alrek turned to look at Gorr, who was indeed scowling his way, no doubt because he would be saddled with the bratling next. Alrek waved a hand at the netmaker, indicating he would be there shortly. But before he left, he smiled widely at Adam. "Thank you very much, Lord Adam."

Adam didn't even want to know what he was being thanked for. And what was this *lord* business? First he had to contend with Rashid referring to him as master, and now Alrek called him a bloody lord. Next he would be proclaimed king . . . when what he felt like at the moment was the lowest of animals for having inadvertently offered hope to the boy when the chances of his ever having a family were hopeless.

Adam didn't think his life could get any worse.

He was wrong.

Alrek offered him these departing words: "Methinks yer One-God sent *you* to me as a miracle."

The loathsome lout a miracle? . . .

Miracle of miracles, Alrek finally seemed to have mastered the rudiments of archery.

Oh, Tyra wasn't deluding herself. The boy could scarce lift the heavy bow, and everyone ducked when he did, but at least he'd hit the target. Off center, of course, but after two dozen tries, having hit it at all was a real accomplishment.

"Good job, Alrek," she complimented him with a pat on the shoulder.

The boy's face fair glowed with pride. You'd think she'd just laid a treasure chest at his feet . . . or granted his most fervent wish . . . a family, of all things . . . something he told everyone who chanced to cross his path.

She and her men were camped for the evening along the North Sea shore; tomorrow they would head north up through the fjords to her father's holdings. While their evening meal was being prepared—a freshly killed red deer roasting on an open spit—they were exercising in a clearing with sword and lance and bow, as was their daily practice.

"Betcha yer thinkin' it was a miracle . . . that I hit the target," Alrek said. He and Tyra were picking up arrows that lay about in the grass.

"I wouldn't exactly call it a miracle," she replied with a laugh. "Hard work always pays off in the end. Haven't I told you that afore, Alrek? You always want results immediately, but you must learn patience. Someday you are sure to be a good Viking warrior. Give it time."

Alrek tilted his head and considered her words. "Nay," he concluded. "It was a miracle. Jest like Lord Adam is a miracle fer me, too."

"*Lord* Adam? Your personal miracle? Did he tell you that?"

"Not precisely," he admitted, "but I jest know his prayers will shoot up in the sky to his One-God who is gonna find me and me brother and sisters a family. A miracle, to my mind."

Alrek's logic boggled the mind and did not bear questioning, lest he translate her inquiries into license to fantasize even more. Tyra started to walk away toward the target, where she hoped to find at least some of the arrows that had gone astray.

"By the by, are you gonna be in Lord Adam's harem?"

Tyra halted in her tracks and peered back over her shoulder. "Are you referring to Adam the Healer? He has a harem?"

"Well, he does not have one yet, but he is putting one together. Leastways, that is what Rashid said. Rashid thinks you would make a glorious first addition."

"Alrek! Do not dare repeat that tale anywhere! Dost hear me?"

He nodded reluctantly.

"I am not now, nor will I ever be, interested in being a member of any man's harem. Is that clear?"

He nodded again. "I did not mean offense."

"I know you didn't, but you can be sure I will give *Lord* Adam an earful on this topic. A harem! Indeed!"

A short time later, she was bent over picking up the remainder of the arrows when she heard a whistling whirr—a sound she recognized too well. It was too late to move away. Almost at the same moment as she heard the sound, she felt a sharp pain in her right buttock.

She stood quickly and spun on her heel. Peering over her shoulder, she saw her worst fears realized. There was an arrow protruding from her behind. Then she raised her narrowed eyes to pierce the culprit on the other side of the field.

Alrek at least had the grace to turn gray and mutter, "Uh-oh!"

As she began stomping toward the inept rascal, she shouted, "Now would be the time to pray for a miracle,

Alrek. Pray that I fall over dead afore I get my hands around your scrawny neck."

Alrek, smart boy that he was at heart, ran for his life.

Some things always come back to bite you in the arse . . .

"I thought you would have come up with an escape plan by now," Rashid complained to Adam.

They were sitting next to each other, tied to adjoining tent poles. Their legs were free, but their hands were bound behind their backs. There were several burly Vikings sitting before the nearby campfire, tending a deer that was being roasted for dinner. Every couple of minutes the guardsmen looked their way, just to make sure they hadn't mysteriously disappeared.

"What? You think I'm a magician, too?"

"Nay, master, but I see the way the warrior princess looks at you. Methought you would have charmed her into releasing us by now."

"The only way I see her looking at me is with disgust. In fact, she said I stink."

"You do. I mean, you did," Rashid commented bluntly, "until we bathed this evening."

"And I have no idea where you got the notion that I have the ability to charm anything, let alone a thick-headed Viking woman who can't decide whether she wants to be a man or a woman."

"I got the notion from watching you take one woman after another into your bed over the years. Isobel. Sari. Katlyn. The Princess Neferi. Ester. Magdalene. I could go on and on. That was afore we came to Britain, though. Now your male parts must have dried up from lack of use."

"My male parts are just fine, thank you very much."

"Then why have you not seduced the warrior woman?

Alrek says she has shown more interest in you than any man before."

"That's because she wants me to heal her father so she can be disowned and go off somewhere and be free to lop off heads and other gruesome things, without the burden of a husband. No doubt my head will be the first one to be lopped once my healing talents are no longer needed."

"Huh?" Rashid said to this long-winded discourse.

"Never mind. Speaking of Alrek, look over there."

Alrek was running through the clearing where the tents were pitched, dodging tent poles and campfires, his skinny legs pumping madly as he panted like a war-horse. Adam looked at Rashid, and Rashid looked at him; then they both shrugged, indicating their confusion over why Alrek was on the run.

Soon they discovered the answer. His pursuer was about to pass them, stomping doggedly in Alrek's path. She didn't bother to swagger now, so angry did she appear to be. But that wasn't the most amazing thing.

"Oh, Mistress Viking!" Adam called out.

Reluctantly, Tyra stopped and glared at him. "What?" she snapped.

"Did you know you have an arrow sticking out of your backside?"

Her hands fisted, her face went rigid, and a sound came from her throat that sounded very much like a growl. "Yea, you lunkhead, I know there is an arrow in my backside. Why did you think I was chasing after Alrek? And wipe that grin off your face, man, or I will do it for you."

"Would you like me to remove it?" he asked sweetly.

"What? The grin?"

"The arrow."

"Nay, I do not want you touching any part of my

body, and certainly not that part. Besides, I thought you had given up medicine."

"For this, I would be willing to make an exception." He was still grinning, but he meant it. For a view of her naked backside, he would do just about anything.

Tyra told him to do something that he was fairly certain was physically impossible and continued on her pursuit of Alrek.

God, he was beginning to develop a taste for sharp-tongued women. That surprised him mightily. He'd always preferred gentle, soft-spoken women in the past.

"Well, so much for your seduction skills," Rashid opined dolefully.

A short silence ensued before Adam turned to stare at his friend. "Why are your eyes closed? Why are your lips moving without making a sound?"

"I decided the best course is to join Alrek in praying for a miracle."

Some deals are sweeter than others . . .

"We have to talk."

Oooh, lady, talk is not what I have in mind. My arms and legs ache from being in the same position so long. My buttocks feel like they have no flesh on them from sitting on this hard ground. Come closer, you irksome, infuriating daughter of the Devil, and see what kind of talk I have for you.

It was dusk, more light than dark yet, and Adam had been resting. He opened his eyes now . . . just a crack to look at Tyra, who was easing herself down to the ground beside him. He noticed that she lowered herself to her knees, not her backside, and that she winced at one point from stretching the skin surrounding the wound, which had apparently been stitched up an hour ago by the sometimes blacksmith, sometimes berserker, Bjorn.

"Lackbrain lad!" she murmured as she rubbed one nether cheek. Obviously, she was referring to Alrek, and not Bjorn. He wondered if Alrek was suffering a sore backside as well . . . sore from the whip of a birch branch which he'd seen Tyra brandishing a short time ago. Once settled on her knees, she groaned softly.

Good! I hope your arse pains you mightily, wench, because you have been more than a pain in the arse to me. He decided not to share those opinions with her now, but he surely would later.

Instead, he said, "I'm not talking to you till you release these bonds. You need a lesson in diplomacy, my lady," *amongst other things.* "One should not maltreat the person from whom one seeks favors. And, believe you me, asking a physician to treat a man unconscious for sennights is a big favor, especially when he will no doubt be surrounded by a horde of bloodthirsty Vikings who would as soon lop off the physician's head at the first sign of death pallor in the patient." He pressed his lips together in an exaggerated fashion, indicating that his talking time was over.

From inside the tent where Rashid had already gone for the night, following a meal of venison and venison . . . and more venison—but at least not *gammelost*—he heard his busybody Arab friend add to the conversation, uninvited, "The wise man treads softly amongst tigers."

"What does that mean?" Tyra asked him.

He refused to respond, but what he thought was, *Who says Rashid's proverbs have to mean anything?*

"The whisper of a pretty girl can be heard farther than the roar of the tiger," Rashid added.

He sent Rashid a mental message; *Shut your teeth.*

"Listen. I will admit that I was perhaps less than tactful in convincing you to come with us. If I had had more time, my men and I could have partaken of your hospitality, and . . ."

Hah! No hospitality was offered by me. He felt a twinge of guilt at that reminder . . . a *tiny* twinge. Could it be that the warrior-wench would have acted differently if he'd acted hospitably? *Nay, nay, nay! I will not allow her to turn the tables on me here. She is the guilty party. She will be the one to pay. Not me!*

". . . and mayhap I would not have acted so . . . um, rashly."

Rashly? Rashly? I would hardly call whacking a man over the head with the flat side of a broadsword merely rash. More like brash. Yea, a brash act, not a rash act. He smiled inwardly at his own wit.

"So, what I wanted to say was . . . hmmm . . . well . . . you see . . . I didn't come to your keep *intending* to harm you in any way. Nor did I *plan* to take you by . . . uh, force." Her face bloomed pink as she stuttered to get the words out . . . hard words for a prideful woman.

Is this your sorry excuse for an apology? Hah! You will have to do much better than that. Much!

"When you think on it, I am certain you will realize that you have not been treated so badly." She waved a hand dismissively as if anticipating his disagreement. "I know you resent the ropes, but other than that, you are a guest. Really."

Adam bit his tongue to keep from speaking his grievances aloud, but he couldn't keep his eyes from widening with indignation. *Guest? Guest? Do you tie your guests like a harvest-fat hog? Do you toss your guests over your shoulder like a sack of barley?* He scowled his fiercest scowl and made sure that his tongue was firmly in place, so tempted was he to reply.

"All right, I can see that the guest appellation does not go down smoothly . . . that it sticks in your craw . . ."

How about indigestible?

". . . but what can I do to make things better? I mean, how can we start over?"

Is the woman lackwitted? Or deliberately obtuse? She knows exactly what she must do. Adam craned his neck to look pointedly over his shoulder at his hands tied behind his back and around the tent pole.

She got the message.

Her shoulders sagged. Then she seemed to come to a decision and braced both palms on her thighs and leaned forward to address him . . . which was a big mistake. *A huge mistake!*

For the first time, he noticed her attire. She must have bathed sometime after the evening meal because her hair, in long braids, was still damp. Her face was shiny clean, and clear as new cream, except for the dotting of a few freckles on her nose. Instead of chain mail, she now wore a hip-length, faded blue linen *shert* over her usual tight wool *braies* and half-boots. The *shert* was belted at the waist.

She was a big woman, Adam observed, not for the first time. Her height was immense for a woman, due to her exceedingly long legs. Her hips were ample, as were her breasts, though both were offset by a comparatively narrow waist.

Oddly, her bigness was not unattractive. On the contrary. Overall, she was well proportioned so that all her bigness just contributed to a picture of woman in all her glory. She was almost more than a man could take in.

He forced his eyes to move higher, and the picture was the same. Her lips were full. Her teeth were big. Her eyes were wide, thick-lashed, and crystal clear as blue lagoons. Even her blond hair would be big when loose, he would imagine.

And he was imagining.

But that wasn't what had caused his chin to drop to his chest. It was her posture, leaning forward on muscled thighs, which resulted in her *shert* gaping open at the laced vee-neckline, giving him an enticing view of an ocean of skin and the top swells of two very curvaceous breasts.

Adam had a weakness for curvaceous breasts. Well, actually, he had a fondness for all kinds of breasts— small, big, round, pointed, flat, whatever. Leastways, he had in the old days when he'd jumped from one lady's bedchamber to another like a randy rabbit.

"So, what do you think?" Tyra said.

Huh? He hadn't realized that she'd been talking all this time.

He arched a brow in question. He hoped he appeared more mature than he felt. *Thinking about breasts! By the rood! I'm behaving worse than an untried youthling.*

"Did you hear one word I said? Stop looking at me like that."

He shrugged to indicate confusion, but he knew exactly how he'd been looking at her. The shrug just covered all grounds. To his mind, shrugging was a man's best tool.

"Some men feel they must pretend to flatter me, just because I am a woman. Well, forget about that. I am a soldier first and foremost, and I know better than most how unattractive I am to men. Frankly speaking, I am stronger and larger in size than many men . . . not Norsemen, who are better endowed than normal men, but other males. Like Saxons. So save your ogling eyes and drooling lips for mush-headed maids who would appreciate the effort."

Is the woman daft? Unattractive? If I were any more attracted, my male parts would set themselves afire.

And I am very well endowed, thank you very much, even if I am only Viking by adoption, not birth. Furthermore, I most certainly did not drool. He licked his lips all around, just to make sure.

"Back to what I was saying afore—what would you say to a truce?"

He might be interested. Truth to tell, he was bored to death with sitting about, rope-bound, all the time. He tilted his head to indicate she should continue.

"I would set you free . . . under guard, of course . . . or two guards." She added that last after giving his body a quick head-to-toe scrutiny.

Aha! She is probably noticing my . . . endowments.

"I have no fear of your doing harm to me, or my men . . ."

Mayhap not.

". . . but you might find a way to escape, and I am honor bound to deliver you to my father's bedside."

Honor, hmmm? He could understand that—the need to fulfill a pledge. But there was something missing from this truce offering. She had told him of what she would give. What did she expect in return? The answer was forthcoming.

"Your uncle Tykir claims you to be a trustworthy man . . . one whose word, once given, is solid as ice on a winter fjord. If you would give your vow not to attempt escape till you have examined my father and done whatever you can to help him, then I will cut your ropes myself right now."

He considered her offer for a long time. The occasional snort of Rashid's snoring was the only thing breaking the silence between them. Their eyes held the entire time as each weighed the other and wondered if trust could be given.

Finally he nodded.

She smiled widely—a big spontaneous expression of joy—and a hard core of something he could not name began to melt inside him. "I hoped you would agree," she said, standing with a groan and pulling a long knife out of a scabbard at her belt. She was about to cut his ropes.

"Wait!"

Surprise flared on her face, and her smile faded. Odd how that latter affected him adversely! Her short-lived trust was replaced with suspicion.

"A truce goes both ways. You set *your* conditions, to which I agreed. Now I set mine."

She still stared at him suspiciously, the knife poised in her hands. "I'm listening."

Since she was standing tall over him, he had to crane his neck to look up at her. Shifting slightly, she adopted a legs-spread stance.

He hated that arrogant posture. Unfortunately, a familiar part of his body . . . one that had not been in use for an aeon or so . . . liked that arrogant legs-spread stance very much.

"If I am unable to help your father . . . if I try my best and 'tis not enough"—he paused to quell memories of a time when his best had most definitely not been enough—"if he dies under my care, I want your promise that you will shield me with your own life. Rashid, too."

She nodded. "'Tis a fair request you make. I agree." She started to relax.

"There's more."

She went stiff again, but kept her legs spread. Blessed Lord, if she only knew what her pose did to him!

"I want one night in your bed furs. Dusk to dawn. You, naked. Me, naked. Oh, do not be enraged without hearing the rest. You would not have to touch me, and I would not touch you . . . unless you asked."

He saw anger in her fiery eyes, and hurt as well, as if his proposition offended her deeply. "Why?"

"Because I want to."

"Nay!" she declared emphatically and stomped away, muttering something about "lying lackwit Saxons who think with their male organs."

"Wisdom has two parts: one, having a great deal to say; and, two, not saying it," Rashid proclaimed from inside the tent. Apparently, the snoring had been a ruse to cover his eavesdropping. And, apparently, he believed that Adam had said too much . . . too soon.

"She will be back," Adam predicted, ever the optimist . . . or was that ever the egotist?

"Every ass loves to hear himself bray."

"Rashid! Are you calling me an ass?"

"Nay, it is just that you bray overmuch. Comes from having an overlarge ego, I would say."

I guess that answers my question about optimist or egotist. Adam laughed, but only for a moment.

Tyra was returning. There was a glow of determination in her eyes, but her cheeks bespoke great embarrassment.

"I agree."

"You agree?" That part of Adam's body that had come to life miraculously of late now stood at attention. Talk about miracles! This one was better than any of Alrek's, in Adam's opinion.

"Under my conditions," she added.

"Oh?" Adam tried not to sound as interested as he was.

"One night, and one night only. No touching."

"Unless you ask me to . . . or unless you insist on touching me," he quickly reminded her.

She glared at him as if to say *that* would never happen, but in truth she looked adorable when she glared at him. Mayhap he would tell her that . . . later. "And do not forget the naked part," he threw in for good measure.

"How could I? There is one other thing. I agree to this suggestion, scandalous as it is, only if my father lives. If he dies, the pact is canceled."

Adam wanted to argue, but, really, he had been only half serious to begin with . . . although the half that was serious was very serious. Besides, who wanted to sleep with a grieving woman?

He nodded his head.

Soon his ropes were cut and Tyra motioned to two of her biggest guardsmen, ordering them to stand outside his tent. Before he knew it, she was gone in a huff.

"I told you she would be back," Adam gloated to his friend as he crawled into the bed furs inside the tent, after untying the Arab's ropes.

"Feather by feather, the goose will be plucked," Rashid declared with a laugh, rolling over and away from him.

"Precisely," Adam said.

"I was referring to you as the rooster, not her," Rashid said with dry humor.

"I know."

CHAPTER FOUR

er in a harem? Hah! . . .
Tyra couldn't stop looking at the man.

He'd caught her in mid-ogle once or twice. On one occasion, the rogue had actually winked at her; the other time, he'd just grinned. In any case, his smirking, as if he thought she was remembering her promise to him— *which she was not . . . definitely not . . . well, hardly*— cured her of her infernal staring . . . for a few moments, leastways.

It had been a busy day, starting with their early morning turn from the North Sea up the headwaters of Ilsafjord—one of the thousands of rivers interlacing the Northlands. Not all of them were connected, unfortunately. In fact, twice today they'd had to portage the two longships. Portage was a long, arduous enterprise that involved removing all the men and animals from the crafts, then carrying the boats overland to the next waterway . . . or pushing the boats over hastily made wooden rollers, if the distance was far and the pathway open.

All that time, Adam, to his credit, had contributed his fair share of muscle to the hard labor. And, yes, Tyra was beginning to notice, to her chagrin, that, for a healer, he had a fair share of muscle . . . not like her Viking warriors, whose very livelihood depended on their being in perfect physical condition. But he held his own, and that was remarkable in itself. She supposed it came from being raised in a Norse household, even though he was Saxon by birth.

Tyra suspected that one of the reasons Adam worked so hard was to escape Alrek, who had developed an attachment for the healer, despite Adam's best efforts to avoid the boy and his never-ending questions. He seemed especially uncomfortable with Alrek's view that he was a miracle sent to change his life. Why he could not just laugh off the outrageous notion was beyond Tyra's understanding.

Oh, well. In the next day or so they would enter the edges of her father's vast land holdings. Then she would be faced with a whole other set of problems.

A wicked man's wink would mean nothing to her then.

Well, almost nothing.

She hoped.

"What troubles you, my lady?" Rashid asked, jarring her from her reverie. Rashid and Adam traveled on the same longship, now that their bonds had been released. Rashid had just given up his spot on a sea chest to Adam, who was teaching Alrek how to row without hitting himself in the face on the backswing of the heavy oar. The boy had gotten two bloody noses yesterday. No doubt, Adam's reasoning was that an exhausted Alrek would be a silent Alrek.

Tyra glanced up from the rudder she was steering . . . easy work now that they'd entered the wide river, Drisafjord. There was no wind to carry the sails, but the current ran smooth.

"What troubles me?" She gave her full attention to the Arab—a handsome, dark-skinned man with a full mustache but a hairless chin, which he plucked meticulously every evening, to the wincing fascination of her men. Tall and slim, he was an attractive man who was probably much favored by women. Alrek, who had latched on to the Arab as well as his new best friend, Adam, claimed that Rashid was the son of some desert sheik. She would have to ask Rashid later why a prince of the desert would have left his homeland. "Everything troubles me. My warriors and I should be off protecting our southern boundaries. Pirates and outlaws abound. My sisters are up to Odin-knows-what mischief. My father hovers at the doors to Valhalla. I have wasted much time searching for your physician friend to help my father. What should have been an easy task has proved bothersome in the extreme. 'Twould be a shame to have accomplished one goal . . . saving my father . . . only to lose his holdings for lack of diligence."

"Diligence! You toil beside your men. You work your fingers to the bone. With all due respect, my lady, you do your bloody well best."

"With all due respect," she repeated back at him, "hard work matters not if there is no success. And do not dare quote me a proverb about that."

"Why go looking for trouble?" Rashid persisted on the same subject. "Did a messenger from Stoneheim not arrive this morn, informing you that your father still lives?"

"Yea, but that could change at any moment."

"Like I said, do not borrow misery. Believe me, trouble finds you, as certain as the thirsty hump-backed beast seeking a desert oasis. Allah willing, of course."

What was it about her that brought out the religious fervor in these two men? Rashid was always quoting his God, or the prophet Muhammad. And every time Adam came into her company, he invariably said, "My God!" Usually it was after staring unabashedly at her breasts, or her buttocks, of all things.

"You are thinking about my master again, are you not?"

"I . . . was . . . not," she lied, then felt guilty for being dishonest, even about such a trivial thing. "Well, mayhap a little. How could you tell?"

"Your face betrays you. One of two expressions do you show whenever he is about, both of them accompanied by flushed cheeks. The first is anger, and then your eyes turn fiery blue, nigh flashing with sparks. The other is arousal, and then your eyes fade to a smoky blue . . . dreamy."

"Oh . . . oh . . . oh . . ." Tyra sputtered. "I have never been aroused!" was the only retort she could come up with, so roiled was she with consternation.

"You haven't?" Rashid was clearly surprised, and amused.

"Not by that . . . that infuriating man! And my eyes have never gone dreamy either, for him or any other man. Really, what kind of leader would I be for my troops if I went *dreamy* every time a handsome man walked by?"

"Aaaah! So you think my master is handsome?" he commented, homing in on the most irrelevant part of what she'd said.

"Yea, the man is handsome, as if that matters a whit when—"

"Oh, it matters, m'lady. When it comes to seducing a maid, being comely in appearance can be a decided advantage for a man. By the by, my master tells me that you wish to be disinherited by your father if he lives . . . though I can hardly credit the logic of that. But I was wondering . . . I do not suppose . . . well, would you be interested in joining a harem? It is quite a coincidence, but I know of one that is being formed."

She made a tsk-ing sound of disapproval. "I have heard this harem nonsense that you blather to my men. It is not good to plant such ideas in their heads. Bad enough that some Norsemen practice the *more danico* and that they often have several wives and mistresses, if they can afford them. But a harem!"

"Was that a yea or a nay?"

"It was a nay, you fool."

Rashid's shoulders slumped with disappointment. "That is unfortunate. You would make a good houri, I believe."

"I would not!"

"You would," he disagreed. "Any woman who moves the way you do, in battle-sport or sailing-sport, would move very well in bed-sport, too."

It was hopeless trying to talk to the thickheaded Arab. "I cannot believe that Adam, presumably a noted healer . . . in a Christian country, no less . . . would countenance a harem. It is so . . . so . . . uncivilized."

"I beg to differ, m'lady. It is a most civilized custom." Rashid ducked his head then and confessed, "Actually, my master has not precisely given his permission for me to put together a harem for him."

She narrowed her eyes at Rashid. "*Precisely* what has he given permission for you to do?"

Rashid looked everywhere but at her. Finally he told her, a hint of dismay in his voice, "His precise words were 'No harem. Not now. Not ever.' But I think he will change his mind once he sees what I have to offer. He would definitely change his mind if you were the first houri to join the troop, so to speak."

She laughed at the wily Arab's persistence . . . and at the image of her lounging about in some man's *troop* of pleasure trifles.

"You would look good in sheer silk scarves and bells on your toes," Rashid said, taking her laugh as a melting of her resolve.

"Mistresses are supposed to be tiny, giggly, fragrant, pretty creatures, not sometimes-malodorous, giant Amazons with big bones, big feet, and a tendency to guffaw on occasion."

"See! You would be the first. No doubt you would set a new fashion. Every sheik and sultan from Baghdad to Samarkand would be searching for Amazon houris once they heard of my master's prize possession."

Possession? That aspect would rule me out. Never will I be any man's possession. "Rashid," she said with as much firmness as she could. "No harem. Not now. Not ever."

Beware of a rascal's wink . . .

Adam was standing at railside next to Tyra late the next morning, watching the dragon prow of the ship dip and rise proudly through the waves, like a sea monster.

"Do you have to stand so close?" she snapped.

He smiled at her, knowingly.

Holy Valhalla, she hated it when he smiled like that.

"Do I make you nervous?" he asked innocently.

Hah! The man did not have an innocent bone in his body. She hoped he was much more serious about his medicine.

"Nay, you do not make me nervous. But I do not like you touching me all the time."

He held his hands aloft as if to demonstrate that he had not been touching her.

"You do not have to use hands to touch, as you well know."

"You are correct, of course, my lady Viking. There is touching . . . and then there is *touching*." The hot look he gave her both confused and angered her. Was he referring to their pact wherein he had promised *not* to touch her naked body?

"You promised not to touch me," she seethed in an undertone. "I knew I could not trust you."

Rashid leaned around his friend and advised Tyra, "There is a famous Arab proverb: 'Trust in Allah, but tie down the tent.' "

"You and your proverbs, Rashid! Do you have one for every occasion? Actually, the Norse sagas have a similar one. 'Pray to Odin, but sharpen your sword.' "

"I said I would not touch you in the bed furs *unless you ask me.* I never said I wouldn't touch you *ever*," Adam said, as if affronted that she'd questioned his integrity. "Bloody hell! I'm not a complete lackwit." He conveniently ignored Rashid's and her proverbs.

She was beginning to think that her promise had been a mistake. She was about to suggest a modification of the rules but had no opportunity because just then her longship made the last bend in the wide river amidst wild, mountainous terrain. The ancient forests here in the Northwest were dark and menacing, and an ominous mist arose to the snow-capped peaks. Against this backdrop, her father's strong and imposing keep, Stoneheim, came into view.

Adam gasped, as did Rashid on his other side. It was the usual reaction of people getting their first eyeful of the most outlandish Viking stead this side of the Other World . . . and its equally outlandish inhabitants.

Her men groaned on first seeing their homestead. That, too, was the usual response. Not that they weren't happy to be home, reunited with wives and lady loves. 'Twas just that Stoneheim did not resemble the usual stark Viking fortress . . . especially in the far North. Here, the winters were long and bitter, often with only one or two hours of daylight; survival took precedence over all else . . . or it should have.

Stoneheim's keep was a wood fortress, like most others throughout Norway. But that was the only way in which it was similar.

Stoneheim was built back a considerable distance from the river frontage, with the harsh mountain as a backdrop. Many additions had been built on to the original royal longhouse, many of them set into flat ledges or carved out of the mountain itself, some of them two and three floors in height. And that did not include the outbuildings, or the village homes that lay in an ever widening half circle below the keep. The homestead was an immense hodgepodge of styles, its door lintels and eaves highly carved with Nordic symbols, even the frames of the windows . . . many of which contained skins oiled and rubbed until they were nigh as transparent as glass.

All this building was the work of Tyra's sister Breanne, who had told her father over and over that if he was not going to find her a husband, then she was going to while away her time doing construction work. That was Breanne there atop the pigsty, looking beautiful as ever, even wearing men's *braies* and tunic, her red curls tucked under a stable boy's cap; she was helping her workers put new sod on the roof. Breanne was the daughter of an Irish thrall, Fiona, who had died of childbed fever just after wedding with Thorvald, her father, thus giving the newborn babe legitimacy. In fact, all of Tyra's sisters were legitimate. Her father had a tendency to marry his women, even more than one at a time. All the mothers were dead now. Although Breanne was wearing men's breeches, and did so whenever engaged in hard labor, she donned women's apparel on all other occasions, unlike Tyra.

At least the pigsty had not been decorated during Tyra's absence.

"I have never seen anything quite like this in all my life," Adam remarked, his mouth agape.

"Well, yes, you have," Rashid disagreed. "Remember all the colorful gardens in the harems of Baghdad?"

There the rascal went, bringing up harems again. Adam was referring to all the flowers and vividly hued bushes and autumn-leafed trees that adorned almost every available space outside the royal keep.

"Yea, you are correct," Adam said, "but I have traveled throughout Norway and the other Northlands and never have I seen flowers growing in such profusion. You would think the cold would kill them off in the bud."

"That is the work of my sister Drifa. Her mother Tahirah came from your lands, Rashid . . . a concubine of my father's, and later his wife. She missed the warmer climes of her homeland so much that Father allowed her to plant a flower or two to halt her constant weeping. Little did he know that it would lead to this . . . this extravagance of floral madness. She even brought a tree indoors one time. Tahirah died five years past . . . some say of the yearning for her homeland that never left her . . . but her daughter Drifa has carried on in her stead."

She pointed to a nearby terraced garden where a petite woman—petite by Norse standards—was kneeling amidst a profusion of autumn flowers, her dainty hands covered with dirt. Her raven hair and slightly slanted eyes were the only signs of her half-Arab heritage. Otherwise, she looked like a dark-haired Viking woman.

"It certainly is . . . pretty," Adam commented, his mouth still agape.

"Pretty!" a nearby soldier said with a snort of disgust. "What kind of keep is this for fierce fighting men?

We should have dirt-stomped exercise fields, but, nay, Drifa had to plant grass there and shrieks every time we trample it with our heavy boots. And the great hall! That is where the other sister, Vana, reigns. Thor's balls, a man should be able to put his feet up in the hall, belch if the meal is particularly tasty, bring his dogs inside, spit in the rushes if he wants . . . not that there are rushes in this great hall. Nay, Vana says the dirty rushes breed maggots. We cannot even take a piss in the courtyard if the need comes on quicklike from an overabundance of mead. And we men must wipe our feet afore entering the great hall. Can you imagine that?" That last was spoken with such horror that you would have thought the men were required to cut off a limb . . . or a manpart . . . before dining.

Adam and Rashid looked to Tyra for an explanation. The soldier had stomped off with a curse to help Alrek toss ropes to the lad on the wharf so the longboat could be tied and pulled in close for landing. Twice so far, Alrek had missed his target.

"That would be my sister Vana he refers to . . . Vana the White she is called because of her white-blond hair. Her mother came to us, via my father's bed furs, from Iceland. What can I say? She likes cleanliness."

Rafn passed by and muttered under his breath, "Pfff! *Like* would be too weak a word. More like she worships at the altar of the god of cleanliness. The woman is a tyrant, I tell you, a tyrant. What she needs is a husband to beat her on occasion. Yea, she does." You'd never know it by his words, but Rafn was in love with Vana. When asked by his comrades on many occasions how he would be able to abide living with such a zealot, Rafn always grinned and said, "I will give her more to occupy her time than brooms and lice."

"Does the Norse religion have a god of cleanliness?" Rashid wanted to know.

She and Adam looked at each other and smiled . . . and wasn't it amazing how her heart turned over at the small gesture of shared amusement? How pathetic she was! And how interesting that she had never noticed all these years how needful she was of a man's attentions.

Or was it just Adam's attentions that touched her so?

Now, that was an alarming prospect. Best to think of other things. What was it Rashid had asked? Oh, about a god of cleanliness. That was all Odin and Thor would need—a Vana-style goddess insisting that the great hall of Asgard be spotlessly clean! Asgard was reputed to be big enough to let 800 armed men stomp in with their dirty boots through 540 doors . . . doors with brass hinges that would need polishing.

"Alrek says there are two dozen spotlessly clean garderobes at Stoneheim," Rashid commented, "and as many outside privies."

"Alrek was jesting," she said. "There are only ten . . . each."

"Nice to know, though, that the bed furs will be clean and fragrant at Stoneheim," Adam said. "I do so like to have clean bed furs when I am"—he paused long enough for her to look at him and blush—"sleeping." He winked again, then leaned down to pick up his leather medical bags.

"I would pick you up and toss you overboard if I did not need your skills so much," she snarled.

"Lucky me!" Adam murmured, a somber expression on his face now that the time to revive his medical talents was at hand.

"Skills? Skills?" Rashid hooted, obviously inferring that she'd meant a different kind of skill altogether.

"His *medical* skills," Tyra emphasized. Then she did

to Rashid what she would have liked to do to his master. She picked him up and tossed him over the side into the icy water.

She glanced around then to see everyone staring at her. The men were laughing. Her sisters were frowning with disgust.

And Adam—the bloody rogue—safe ashore . . . he winked at her.

A hole in his WHAT? . . .

A short time later, they were in her father's bed-chamber.

With an authority and expertise he hadn't displayed before, Adam ordered everyone from the sickroom except his assistant and the king's resident healer, Father Efrid, a monk from a monastery in Ireland. Thorvald practiced the Norse religion, but was Christian, too, when it was convenient. And everyone knew the monk healers were the best physicians . . . next to Arabs, that is.

Adam had also ordered Tyra to depart, but she'd dug in her heels, and he'd finally relented, saying firmly, "Stay, but keep your distance and shut your teeth, or I will remove you bodily myself." She stood at the back of the room, watching with silent fascination as he did his work.

Adam laid his various vials of ointments, linen packets of herbs, and instruments such as lancets and cautery rods on a small side table before turning to examine her father. With gentle efficiency, he removed the king's garments, exposing a big body which was still wide-shouldered and barrel-chested and bulky, though his muscles had no doubt lost their firmness from lying abed so long.

He pushed back the king's eyelids and examined the whites of his eyes. He pressed his ear against her father's chest and seemed to be listening to his heartbeats. He examined her father's fingernails and toenails, even his genitals. The wound itself at the back of his head garnered the most attention.

Quietly he asked questions of Father Efrid, whom Tyra knew from experience to be a good man and a good practitioner of the healing arts when less serious injuries were involved. In truth, she knew of no physician who had a high rate of success when mortal wounds were involved. Mostly, it was luck, or in the hands of the gods. Still, she had heard of Adam the Healer's reputation and knew she had to let him try his particular talents on her father, even if it turned out to be a futile effort.

"How long has he been thus? Does his condition never change?" Adam asked.

"Do you manage to get food and liquid into his body?"

"Does he pass water regularly? What is the color of his waste?"

"Any fever?"

"Does he appear to be in pain? No screams, or excessive groaning?"

"When did the bleeding stop?"

On and on his questions went. During the course of the examination, her father's eyelids fluttered occasionally, and once or twice he even muttered aloud. Father Efrid reported that the king had regained consciousness a few times while Tyra was gone. They'd been able to feed him thin gruel and liquids, and he did swallow with ease. All these things Adam seemed to take for good signs.

When they left the room, after an hour-long examination, Tyra walked with Adam back to the great hall. "Can you help him?" she asked.

He shrugged. "I just don't know. There are some good signs, but the length of his unconsciousness troubles me deeply. There is something I could try, but . . . nay, I will not do it."

"What?"

"You have put me in an untenable situation, and I resent it mightily."

She tilted her head in question.

"I could try drilling a hole in his skull to reduce the swelling. Trepanation the procedure is called. It has been done afore, and even successfully in some of those cases. But . . ."

"But?" she prodded when he did not immediately explain.

"But it is extremely dangerous. And once again, I find another person's life in my hands, and I do not want that responsibility. I do not!"

"What is the alternative?"

"There is always the possibility that someday your father would awaken on his own, but, frankly, that would be practically a miracle. 'Tis more likely that his brain would continue to swell within the confines of his skull, and his body will begin to wither away, and he will die a slow death."

"Nay!" she asserted, much too harshly. Realizing she was directing her outrage to the wrong person, she lowered her voice and told the physician, "My father would abhor that kind of death. He would rather die on the battlefield, but if not that, then under your knife."

"Do you have the authority to make that decision on his behalf?"

"I do."

"I just don't know. I did not think it would be this bad. I was hoping . . . well, I was hoping for something else."

"Please," she said, putting a hand on his forearm. "Try this trepanation."

He looked at her hand, big and callused; then he looked into her eyes.

"Please," she repeated . . . a hard word for her to say and one she could not recall using for years and years.

His face was rigid and unyielding. She could see that a myriad of emotions warred beneath the surface.

"So be it," he said finally. "God help me, but . . . so be it."

CHAPTER FIVE

❧

Would they have to learn to belly dance? . . .

"I'm thinking about joining a harem."

Tyra's sisters giggled at their sister Drifa's remark, but Tyra reacted quite differently. The remark was so unexpected and outrageous and out-of-character for her timid sister that Tyra just about fell out of the tub as she was rising from her bath.

The big brass tub that she and her sisters shared had been set up in the kitchen so that all of them could grill her with questions without pulling their sister Ingrith away from her cooking. Actually, there were a cook and several kitchen maids to perform such menial duties, but Ingrith's special interest was cooking and she made sure all her directions were followed to the letter. In truth, all the meals at Stoneheim were feasts, thanks to Ingrith's talents, unlike the unpalatable fare the men had eaten aboard ship. Some of Ingrith's dishes were basic recipes that appealed to all, but some of the frothy, sauce-covered concoctions had the big Norsemen blinking down at their plates with confusion . . . and a fear of ruining their fine physiques with excessive fat.

In most Norse households, the cooking was done on a large central hearth in the great hall, the site of most communal activities. Because of the large size of the resident population at Stoneheim—more than three hundred fighting men alone—most of the cooking was done in this separate kitchen with its immense hearth and stone ovens. Meanwhile, the five open hearths down the center of the great hall were there to provide heat during the cold winter.

But a harem? Drifa is thinking of joining a harem. "Drifa!" Tyra exclaimed.

Drifa might be half Arab, but that was as close to an Eastern harem as she'd ever been, having resided in Norway all her life. Tyra couldn't imagine her performing the wanton things a pampered concubine would do.

Drifa continued to arrange large bunches of autumn flowers in a pottery jug filled with water. Drifa loved to bring the outdoors inside with her numerous arrangements, which Tyra admitted made the keep look more cozy, but which the men hated for the same reason. Once, she'd even brought fifty rose bushes inside, to everyone's consternation, because they were looking frail and in need of special attention.

Her father had grumbled last year that soon she would be putting flowers in the privy. To which Drifa had shot back, "Let me marry and you won't have to worry about all my flowers marring the horrid rooms of your horrid keep." And then she'd run off, weeping. Her father, dunderhead that he was betimes, had looked at Tyra and her other three sisters and said, "What? What did I do?"

But now Drifa reacted angrily, to Tyra's surprise. "Well, why not? It appears I am never going to be a bride, and the way Rashid describes the . . . um, pampered position, it sounds like a very good life for a woman. Besides, flowers bloom in the Eastlands all year round."

I am going to wring Rashid's neck.

Vana was tsk-ing at the mess Tyra had made when she'd sloshed water about in the tub. She was on her hands and knees wiping the puddles off the stone floor with a thrice-folded square of linen cloth that she always carried on her person for spot cleaning. "Actually, I've been thinking about it, too . . . joining a harem, that is," Vana remarked. Even with her white-blond braids tucked under a scarf, and her slim figure barely hidden by her big, open-sided apron, Vana, too, had the physical attributes of a man's play companion.

I'm going to wring Rashid's neck.

"And what will Rafn have to say about your skipping off to some harem, Vana?" Tyra figured that question would give Vana pause to reconsider.

Vana blushed but lifted her chin with stubbornness— a trait all of Thorvald's daughters shared. "Rafn has no say in the matter. We are not wed, and may never be at this rate. If I want to join a harem, I will."

"Me, too," said Ingrith as she stirred a fragrant cauldron of fish stew with dumplings floating on the top, then checked the eel barrel to make sure there were enough of the slimy creatures for her special eel pie. "If you all are going to join a harem, I'm not staying here in this . . . this . . . prison. I want to cook for one man who will appreciate my efforts, not three hundred men who would just as soon have boiled possum, as long as ale abounds to wash it down."

I'm going to wring Rashid's neck.

"Me, too," said Breanne, who was peeling apples for one of Ingrith's far-famed tarts, "but only if the harem is in the Eastlands. I would love to study their building methods there."

"How silly of you, Breanne!" Drifa said with a soft laugh. "My mother told me much about her homeland, and I do not think houris would be permitted such freedom . . . to roam the cities gaping at buildings and such."

"They can, too," Breanne countered. "Rashid told me a *good* harem concubine can do anything she pleases."

I am going to wring Rashid's neck.

"Well, none of you are going to join a harem. So forget that. Father would never permit it. And, Drifa, stop putting those flower petals in my bathwater. I'm going to smell like a posy."

"That is the purpose, Tyra. To remove the stink of horse and ship and battle from you and make you smell more like a woman," Drifa said. Under her breath, she muttered, "Good practice for being in a harem, too. They smell like flowers there, I would wager. Desert flowers."

That last comment about houri practice didn't even merit a response from Tyra, who was the least likely to become any man's desert flower.

"As to Father not permitting it," Drifa said, "that is the best part. Rashid said the harem is the perfect solution to our problem. Since none of us can marry till you do, Tyra, and since it appears you will never wed, then how can Father object if we settle for being the next best thing? Concubines."

I am going to wring Rashid's neck.

"I think you have all gone barmy. Harems! Not in this lifetime!"

"Perhaps one of us could try it, and if it works out, the rest can follow," the ever practical Vana offered.

Borrowing a phrase of Adam's that she herself had used before, Tyra said, "No harem. Not now. Not ever."

Silence permeated the room then as her sisters harumphed their discontent and murmured such comments as "Tyrant!" or "She never wants us to have fun," or "Who named *her* master?" Tyra ignored the muttering and began washing her long hair with the aid of one of the kitchen thralls.

When she came up from rinsing the soap from the heavy strands, it was to hear that her sisters had given up on one objectionable subject only to move on to another equally objectionable one.

"What is *he* like?" Ingrith asked.

"Who?" Tyra answered, as if she didn't well know whom her sister referred to. Adam was the subject of everyone's conversation at Stoneheim. She stood and wrapped one linen towel around her head turban style and began to towel off her body with another.

"The healer, of course," Ingrith said.

"Arrogant," she replied flatly.

"Really?" Ingrith was leaning over the shoulder of the heavyset cook, Signe, who was kneading the flat, unleavened manchet bread dough for baking. The cook's assistant, Arva, also got her attention. Ingrith watched closely as Arva ground grain—rye, barley, and even peas—on the large round stone known as a quern. Little by little, Arva poured grain through a hole in the top, then turned the top stone around and around with the handle, thus squashing the grain between the two stones and eventually turning it into flour. It was a long, tedious process, especially in a keep this size, where at least one hundred loaves were consumed per day. Meanwhile, Ingrith continued to talk. "Seems to me I heard Rashid say something like 'Confidence is a great aphrodisiac.' "

I am really, really going to wring Rashid's neck . . . and his tongue, as well.

Vana stopped her flower arranging and tilted her head, as if pondering some great question. "So, you say Adam is arrogant? Hmmm. Arrogance is not such a bad thing . . . especially in a handsome man."

"He is not all that handsome," Tyra lied.

"Are you demented, Tyra?" Breanne exclaimed. She

had finished peeling apples and set her knife down. "The man is godly handsome, and you well know it."

Tyra felt her face heat with embarrassment. In truth, she'd had the same thoughts about him being godly handsome.

"Did you notice the way he moves?" Vana asked Drifa. "So smooth and . . . well, sensual, rather like a large cat."

Her other sisters agreed with a communal, "Yea."

Moves? He moves sensually? Holy Thor! Now I will be watching the way he moves.

"And his hands," Breanne added. "I like a man with competent hands. Long-fingered. One could just imagine what those hands could do when . . ." Her voice drifted off as she bit her bottom lip and got a dreamy look in her eyes, imagining the gods only knew what.

Drifa, Ingrith, and Vana all sighed. Their eyes glazed over, too.

That's all I need. To picture the rogue's fine-fingered hands doing sinful things to me. For the love of Frigg, I wager that image is now firmly planted in my feeble brain.

"Gilly, that new maid from Erin, was in the sweathouse where he went to bathe a short time ago," Ingrith confided in a whispered voice that bespoke some secret about to be divulged. "She said he has a very big—"

"That's it! Enough! No more about the healer!" Tyra interjected before Ingrith could finish whatever observation she was about to make about the brute's anatomy.

I am not thinking about what is big on his body. I am not thinking about what is big on his body. I am not thinking . . .

"She's blushing! Tyra is blushing!" Vana said with a hoot of glee.

I am not blushing. Not, not, not!

"You know what that means," Vana said.

Tyra's other sisters began to talk all at once, like a flock of cackling chicks.

"Oh, for the love of Loki! Could it possibly be?" Breanne said. She was staring at Tyra in the oddest way.

"What? What?" Tyra asked.

"Ooh, ooh, my prayers to Freyja have been answered," Vana added. She was staring oddly at Tyra, too.

"What? What?"

Drifa glanced at Breanne and Vana, then at Tyra, and exclaimed, "Thank the gods!"

"What? What?"

Ingrith stopped pouring plum custard into a large pottery bowl. She was nodding her head with some sudden understanding. "Perchance I will cook meals in my own home afore I am gray-haired after all."

"What? What?"

"It appears as if I won't have to join a harem after all." Vana put her flowers aside and came to hug Tyra. "I am so happy for you."

"What in bloody hell are you all talking about?" Tyra said when she was finally able to escape Vana's embrace. It was always embarrassing to be hugged by Vana, whose head barely reached her chin, so tiny was she . . . compared to her, leastways.

The sisters all looked at each other, one to the other, slowly, beaming as if they'd just been handed the moon.

Ingrith was the one who finally spoke for the group. "'Tis obvious, really, sister dear. You like the healer. You *really* like the healer."

Tyra drew her brows together and cocked her head in confusion. "Speak plainly."

Drifa patted Tyra on the forearm and explained, "Let us just say that, to our mind, it appears as if you would not object overmuch to playing Eve to his Adam."

Oh, my gods and goddesses!

"Rashid says she would make a good harem houri."

"Perchance she will be Adam's first. Houri, I mean."

"Nay, nay, nay! She will be his wife."

"Then we can all marry."

"Ingrith, you will take care of the wedding feast," Breanne said brightly. "Vana can make the wedding finery. Drifa, the flowers . . . and the music, too. Your voice and lute playing are the best of all of us. And I can construct a wedding canopy."

Over and over, Tyra tried to interject her objections into their discussion. Finally she took on her best military stance, legs widespread, hands on hips, and shouted, *"Silence!"*

When the kitchen became so quiet they could hear the crackle of the fire and the steady sniffle of one of the maids cowering in the corner, she spoke, calmly but with a firmness that would not be denied. "There will be no wedding betwixt me and the healer . . . or any other man. But this I promise you. If our father lives, I will find a way for me to go my own way, and for each of you to wed. Do you accept my word?"

Each of them nodded in turn. Soon, everyone was off and about her business, and Tyra walked toward the bedchamber to complete her toilette.

It was final, then. She would never wed. Everyone understood that now. Although she'd never been quite so adamant with her sisters before, it was something she'd known for a long time.

Why then did the prospect suddenly make her feel so sad?

His cold heart began to melt . . .

Adam was resting on the linen-covered straw mattress of an alcove bed in the small guest bedchamber he'd been assigned when he sensed someone tiptoeing into his room, uninvited and unannounced.

He'd lain down on the bed after returning from a bath in the sweathouse, never intending to sleep before the evening meal. But the mattress was so comfortable and he must have been more tired than he'd realized, for he'd soon dozed off.

His eyes opened to mere slits, then shot wide open. He sat up and swung his legs over the side of the bed to the rush-covered floor. For the love of the Lord! He should have pretended to be still sleeping. How was he going to handle this latest disaster?

Standing before him was Alrek, his skin pink-scrubbed and his pale hair washed and clubbed back at the nape with a leather thong. Worn but clean garments covered his skinny form.

Standing behind him was a boy of about eight. He kept peeking around Alrek's arms, gazing at Adam as if he were some fascinating creature. God knows what Alrek had been saying about him. Calling him the Miraclemaker, he would wager.

A toddler of no more than two was clinging to Alrek's neck, her chubby legs wrapped around his hips. Her blond hair had been clumsily braided and secured into a crown atop her head. She was adorable.

Another girl stood at Alrek's other side.

"I wanted you to meet me fam'ly," Alrek explained quickly, sensing Adam's rising vexation. The boy was pestsome beyond belief.

"This is me brother, Tunni." Alrek indicated with a jerk of his head the youthling standing shyly behind him. "He's eight . . . the man of the fam'ly when I'm off a-Viking."

Oh, bloody hell!

"And this heavy bundle is Besji." He shifted his hold on the toddler's bottom cradled in the crook of his right arm. She must indeed be heavy for the boy to carry about.

He should probably offer to help.

But he wouldn't.

"Besji is two. Thank the Lord she can hold her piss these days till she gets to the garderobe. What a job it was fer me and Tunni to be changing her linens every five minutes, or so it seemed. Babes do piss a lot, you know."

Yea, I know. I took care of Adela at that young age.

Which brought him to the absolute worst part of this whole scenario: the little girl, about four years old, who held tightly on to Alrek's other hand.

"And this is Kristin."

Her blond hair hung loose to the shoulders of her garment . . . an ankle-length shift covered with an open-sided, full-length apron. The thumb of her free hand was planted firmly in her rosebud mouth.

Adela, he thought, and could have wept at the bitter-sweet resemblance.

"Why are you here?" he snapped.

Alrek flinched, but, stubborn snot that he was, he raised his chin and said, "We're jest here to welcome you to Stoneheim. We're jest bein' friendly like."

That is just wonderful. A dwarf-sized welcoming troop. "Oh. Well, thank you very much. If that is all—"

"Methinks you need some helpers," Alrek added in a rush before Adam could protest or say something mean-spirited, which he most assuredly would have done.

"Perchance Tunni could run errands for you. Kristin is good at makin' up beds and such. Takes her a while, but she gets the job done by and by. And me . . . well, I was thinking I could go down to the stables and take care of yer horse."

Alrek was out of breath by the time he finished his long-winded plea . . . and that was what it was. A plea.

"Or I could polish yer sword."

Adam was horrified at the prospect of the disaster-prone child handling a sharp object or standing near a nervous stallion. "Uh, your offer is generous, but Destiny, my horse, is being cared for by one of the Stoneheim grooms. And I just honed the blade of my sword a sennight ago. 'Tis best not to overhandle a sword."

"I never knew that. Do not overhandle a sword. I will have to remember that. See, Tunni, I told you how smart the man was."

If the rascal thought he was going to soften him with flattery, he was sorely deluded. Adam was about to tell the lot of them to go away and stop bothering him, but the little girl—Kristin—the one who could be Adela all those years ago, except her hair was blond and Adela's had been black, and her eyes were honey brown while Adela's had been blue . . . well, she was losing her shyness. Inch by inch she moved closer to Adam, who would have inched away from her if his bed wasn't built into the wall.

When she was practically nose to nose with him, she put a tiny hand on his forearm and said in her squeaky, little-girl voice, "I like you."

Adam could not take much more of this agony. He put his face in his hands, trying his best not to lash out at the children, who had no way of knowing how much their very presence affected him.

The little girl hugged him then. Nuzzling her nose into the crook of his neck, wrapping her sticklike arms around his shoulders, patting him on the back as if to

comfort him, she whispered the most incredible thing:
"Be happy."

The selfsame words Adela had whispered to him just
before she died.

She was tempted but not by the food . . .

Tyra was miserable.

Her father was deathly ill and might very well pass to
the Other World on the morrow if the healer's operation
failed. Even now, the Valkyries could be preparing an
escort to Asgard for him.

Her sisters were nigh driving her mad with their constant nagging about marriage, marriage, marriage. And
as always when in their company, she felt so . . . infe-
rior.

Alrek and his brood had latched on to Adam and
Rashid like barnacles on a ship's bottom and were tripping over themselves trying to do Adam favors he neither
wanted or deserved. Like right now, they were presumably off at the well house laundering Adam's hose . . . a
job he had no doubt given them just to get them out
from underfoot.

She was no worse than Alrek, though. She, who had
disdained men for many a year, had developed this embarrassing fascination with the man. When he was out
of sight, she kept looking for him. When he was within
sight, she tried her best to avoid looking at him. And
when he was close to her—*oh, when he was close to her,
by all the gods and goddesses!*—her face heated, her
heart raced, her breasts swelled, and she felt the most
uncomfortable ache in her lower belly. She hated it!

She let her gaze roam the great hall that was so familiar to her. Raised platforms surrounded each of the
five large open hearths. On these platforms were long
trestle tables, brought in just before each of the two daily

meals, and ornately carved settles, or benches, at the lower end of the hall.

She sat at the high table on the dais of the great hall now, awaiting the evening meal . . . sure to be a feast of sorts, as all meals were at Stoneheim under Ingrith's supervision. Sure enough, a trumpet blared just then, announcing the start of the evening meal—another of Ingrith's bright ideas for enhancing their dinner, which the Viking men snickered about behind her back but put up with nonetheless. No one wanted to offend sweet Ingrith. The housecarls and kitchen thralls began filing into the hall, carrying platters and platters of food for the three hundred or more Viking men and their ladies who had gathered there, sitting at the long trestle tables, sipping their mead and beer.

By thunder! It was only a welcome-home dinner . . . and a subdued one at that because of their king's illness. Still, there were more than eight types of fish, including baked sea trout stuffed with onions and mushrooms, an enormous whole cod that had been roasted over hot coals, creamed and salt herring, pickled eels, salmon in dill sauce, a cod and leek soup, several dozen baked brown trout, and *hákarl*, or cured shark. Most Norsemen would be satisfied with plain fish, dried or raw, smeared with butter.

Aside from the fish, there were an entire reindeer pit-roasted in hot coals; pork and leek stew slow-simmered with carrots, onions, celery, and barley; a stringy goat pottage; a large goose stuffed with hard-boiled eggs; and that ever popular *hrútspungur*, or ram's testicles pickled in whey and pressed into a cake. Bowls of butter accompanied huge platters of flatbread, along with pots of horseradish and mustard. An array of hard and soft cheeses included the Norse favorite skyr, a creamy curd cheese often flavored with fruit.

And vegetables! Blessed Freyja! There were cabbages, field beans, peas, carrots, and turnips. For the sweet palate, the traditional haverbread or oatcakes, plus stewed prunes, cinnamon apples, hazelnut tarts, and fresh berries with cream.

It was a veritable feast fit for a king, but the everyday fare at Stoneheim. If Ingrith didn't wed soon, she was going to turn them all into milksops. Or fat Vikings.

With a long sigh, Tyra put her face in her hands and wondered how she was going to survive this night . . . and the next day. And food was the least of her troubles, she realized as Adam came up and sat down beside her.

He smelled of clean soap and warm male. He smelled good enough to eat.

CHAPTER SIX

❧

He was pure knightly temptation . . .

"Why are you so sad?" Adam asked.

Without being invited, he had sat down in the chair next to her, which must have become empty when Rafn went to the garderobe. Not that being invited ever seemed necessary for this rogue.

"I'm not sad, really. Just somber, thinking about everything to be done on the morrow. Worrying about my father."

He nodded his understanding. Looking about the massive hall, he must be noticing that despite the hum of conversation and laughter, the same air of sobriety had settled in like an impending storm cloud. Tension lay in the background of all that her people said and did. They were all waiting for the next day and the outcome of the medical procedure on their king.

"So, what do you think of Stoneheim?" she asked

He arched his brows and grinned. "Not what I expected."

She arched her brows back at him.

He thought for a bit while a serving maid poured him a wooden goblet of mead. He took a deep draught before leaning back in his chair and answering her. "After force-feeding all of us that disgusting *gammelost* aboard ship, I thought there would be more of the same here."

"I left Stoneheim in a hurry. There was no time to gather tasty provisions from Ingrith's larder," Tyra told him before she realized how defensive she sounded. "You thought we ate stinksome cheese all the time at home?"

He nodded . . . and grinned some more.

She punched him in the arm, hard, and he flinched. Well, not hard enough for him to flinch. He was teasing her again.

"Actually, I thought you in particular dined on sour crabapples and prickly pears and tough-as-hide boar meat. They go better with your disposition than"—he glanced down at some of the platters being placed before them—"sweet cream and late strawberries." He stretched out a hand and dipped his fingers into the cream, plucking out a plump berry. "Here," he said, offering it to her with his fingers.

"Nay . . . I do not want . . . oh, you lout . . ." She opened her mouth for his offering because cream was dripping from his fingers onto the table, making a mess. Unfortunately, he did not immediately remove his fingers from her mouth and made her lick off the cream before he drew back.

As she munched on the sweet berry, he dipped his fingers in a bowl of water and wiped them on a linen cloth. The whole time, he watched her chew. "My God!" he said finally. "You have the most amazing mouth."

Tyra wasn't exactly sure what he meant by that, but she sensed it was a compliment. Bloody hell, she *knew* it was a compliment. How could it be anything else when he was staring at her so hotly?

"My mouth is too big, and you well know it," she snapped.

He shook his head slowly from side to side. "It's just the right size."

"For eating?"

He laughed. "Not for eating."

"My sisters . . ." she said, grasping for some subject of conversation to make him stop staring at her. "What think you of my sisters? They're beautiful, aren't they?"

At first a slight smile tugged at his lips, as if he recognized her evasive tactics. Then he looked about the hall, searching out each of her sisters. First Ingrith, a Norsewoman through and through. Tall, slim, and ever so efficient, with her blond hair hanging in long braids down over her crisp blue, open-sided apron, worn over a sky-blue gunna. She glanced up from where she was instructing a kitchen carl on proper methods of ladling beer into mugs from a big wooden barrel, noticed Adam's scrutiny, and smiled at him.

Tyra's heart sank at Ingrith's interest in the man, and his apparent return of interest. And she cringed at her own attire, compared to Ingrith's. She wore a brown belted tunic and brown leather *braies*. They were clean and of fine fabric, but not at all feminine. This was how she wished to be attired . . . as an example to her men. Leastways, that was what she told herself.

While her mind wandered, Adam's gaze had moved to Vana, who came into view then, bustling about the tables, wiping up the spill from one Viking's ale horn, shooing a dog out the door—none were permitted indoors during meals—or chastising another Viking for some loathsome act . . . probably wiping his greasy fingers on one of the cloths that adorned the upper tables. Vana would have been considered merely pestsome because of her prissiness, but her cool Icelandic good looks made up for any nuisance caused by her cleanliness passion.

Rafn snagged Vana as she bustled by, backing her up against a far wall. Rafn was a fierce fighter in battle,

Tyra's right hand in a fight to the death, but he was pudding in Vana's hands and always had been. Right now he had one arm braced on the wall behind her and was twirling a loose strand of her white-blond hair in the forefinger of his free hand. Vana was laughing at something he said. If by some miracle Tyra ever married, Vana and Rafn would be married in the next instant, so much in love were they.

Then there was Breanne, who had just entered the hall. When engaged in her carpentry and building work, Breanne often wore men's attire, but at other times, like now, she adorned herself as the pure woman she was. Right now her curly red hair was pulled back off her face with a gold circlet, and she wore a gown of amber silk in the Frankish style, without the usual Viking apron. Breanne was gorgeous, and any man in the room would be glad to have her.

Drifa came up to them at the high table, swinging her hips in a saucy way. Drifa's black hair had gained silver highlights in the flickering light of soapstone candles and wall torches. Drifa had always been people-shy, and she raised her eyes demurely as one of the soldiers, clearly impressed with her beauty, asked her a question. Her eyes, a light shade of jade, matched the green apron and shift she wore. When she got to their place at the high table, Drifa made a great fuss about arranging a bowl of flowers on their table, and she saw Adam's eyes twinkle with merriment at her transparency. All the men adored Drifa with her exotic blend of Eastern and Norse blood. She was a tiny creature, but womanly and sweet-natured . . . all the things Tyra was not. Adam would probably adore her, too.

She looked to him to see if that was so, but his eyes had already wandered to a young Norsewoman far below who had begun to strum a lute. While Tyra's burly Viking comrades much preferred a louder, more vulgar form of entertainment, Adam seemed impressed. In fact, he tilted his head to the side, and a whimsical expression crossed his face.

Finally, when his attention came back to her, she couldn't help asking, "You like the pretty lady's music?"

He shrugged. "My sister Adela used to play the lute. It just reminded me of a time . . ." He shrugged again. "It just reminded me," he said with a sigh.

"And so, what do you think of my sisters?"

His gaze swept over her then, bemused. Taking in her manly attire, no doubt. And her bigness.

She raised her chin. She would not bow under any man's condemnation. She was who she was. So there!

Grasping one of her braids in his hand, he tugged her closer. "Your sisters are beautiful . . . each and every one of them in her own way."

She blinked, hoping her disappointment did not show. What was wrong with her? Of course he considered her sisters beautiful. Everyone did. Why had she even asked? Why had she invited the comparison?

He tugged more on her braid till she was forced to lean forward from her chair, till she was so close she could smell the soft soap on his skin and the mead on his breath.

"If you are asking, however, which one I would choose to share my bed furs for a night . . . if I could renegotiate our pact . . ."

She wanted to protest and tell him that that wasn't what she'd meant at all, but it was. It *was*, may the gods have pity on her pathetic soul.

He brushed his lips against hers . . . a whisper of a

kiss, but so powerful she nigh shook from the after-
effects. Like fire it was. Sweet fire.

And then he finished his statement.

". . . I would still choose you."

It was only a kiss . . .

Adam's bedchamber door swung open two hours
later without anyone having knocked. At first he thought
it might be Alrek and his brood back again, wanting to
do him another unwanted, disaster-ending favor, like the
recent hose laundering in which his hose had become
food for several hunting dogs. But, nay, it was Tyra this
time.

He looked up from his book, which he was reading
by candle light . . . a copy of Hippocrates's journal outlining head wounds and how they might be treated by
trepanation.

"You kissed me," Tyra charged. She was wearing
some kind of sleepwear . . . a voluminous chemise of
white linen, which probably belonged to one of her sisters because the sleeves were too short and the hem fell
about mid-calf. Her pale blond hair was loose and wild
about her enraged face.

She was beautiful.

Nay, not beautiful.

Different?

Sensual?

Spectacular?

He couldn't quite come up with the proper word to
describe her. She was not pretty, by any definition, but
she was definitely attractive . . . to him, leastways.

In answer to her kissing charge, though, he merely
said, "Yea, I did."

"Don't do it again."

"Why?"

"Because . . . because that's not what I agreed to."

He tapped a forefinger against his lips, which were pressed together to avoid smiling. "Methinks kissing would be good practice for nude snuggling in the bed furs. Don't you?"

"Oh . . . oh . . . oh!" she sputtered.

He was willing to wager that she rarely, if ever, sputtered in front of her fighting men. That must mean he was different in her mind. That could be a good thing. Like her being different was a good thing to him.

"Wouldst like to try again? Practice-kissing, I mean," he offered in his most conciliatory tone, as if he were offering to do her a big favor, when in fact he would be the one most favored by such an act. The woman, despite all her manly attributes, did have the most irresistible, kissome lips. "In truth, that barely counted as a kiss. 'Twas a mere brush of skin against skin. A true kiss betwixt a man and woman should last much longer."

"How much longer?" He could tell she immediately regretted her hastily blurted question.

He waved a hand airily. "Oh, five minutes or so. And tongues should be involved, of course."

Her jaw dropped open, and her eyes went huge, before she gasped out, "Five minutes? Tongues? Are you mocking me?"

"Nay," he replied. Then, "Well, mayhap a little."

"Lackwit," she snapped and stormed out of the bedchamber.

Adam went back to his journal, but he was smiling now.

If kisses could talk, there would be some story! . . .

Moments later, Rashid announced cheerily, "He kissed you."

Tyra was leaning her forehead against the corridor

wall outside Adam's bedchamber, trying to slow her heartbeat and make sense of the knave's effect on her. Thus far, she could find no sense in it . . . just nonsense. 'Twas naught more than teasing, of course. But she'd been teased before, and her heart did not go *boom, boom, boom, boom* like a battle drum.

And now the Arab wanted to discuss the ignominious subject.

"Yea, the teasing toad kissed me. But 'twas just a jest on his part. Do not make a big thing of this, Rashid."

"Big thing? Big thing? How can I not make a big thing of it when my master has remained chaste for two years? And now he has kissed a fair maiden."

"I am not a fair maiden." She thought a moment. "Did he kiss some other woman, too? A fair maiden?" Disappointment rippled through her at the idea. Was it one of her sisters? Or a serving maid? Perchance one of her soldiers' ladies?

"Nay, just you." Rashid was smiling from ear to ear.

Elation such as she'd never experienced before replaced the disappointment.

"Next step will be a harem . . . you wait and see," he said. "Praise be to Allah! I will be home afore springtime, I wager. And we have you to thank, my lady Viking."

"A harem? Are you saying that this kiss was a ploy to get me to join some gaggle of quacking sex-women?"

"Well, I cannot speak for my master, but, yea, kisses can be tools of seduction. And women can be seduced into joining harems. That is not to say that Master Adam—"

Tyra stomped off before he could finish.

'Twas all much ado about a kiss.

Starting now, she was going to stop thinking about

the kiss. For some reason, though, she couldn't stop touching her lips.

Why is everybody always picking on him? . . .

"You kissed her," Rashid charged Adam and grinned as if praising a wee child.

"Bloody hell! Why is everyone making such ado about a single kiss?" Adam set aside his book and glared at his assistant.

"You've heard that old Arab proverb about kisses, haven't you?"

"Nay, I have not," Adam admitted, knowing he was going to hear the proverb whether he wanted to or not.

"A wise man once said, 'First comes a kiss. Next come the harem veils.' "

"You bloody fraud! You made that up. There is no proverb that says any such thing."

Rashid ducked his head. "Well, there should be."

Adam shook his head at Rashid and his never-ending attempts to put together a harem for him. "Help me gather together the instruments for tomorrow's operation."

Rashid nodded. A short time later, while they examined the tools laid out on linen cloth, he tried once again. "I think she is melting."

"Who?" Adam asked . . . as if he didn't know who.

"The warrior princess. I mentioned a kiss being the first step in the seduction process leading to a harem, and—"

"You told her *that?*"

"Yea."

"Now she will think I kissed her with ill purpose . . . to gain some end."

"Didn't you?"

"Nay, I did not. It was a spur-of-the-moment decision. And 'twas no big thing, Rashid. Do not make it so."

"Hmmm."

"What does that *hmmm* mean?"

"Just that she had the same response. Told me in no uncertain words not to make much of nothing. But methinks she protested too much. Methinks it was a big ado to her. In fact, methinks—"

"Dost know what I think, Rashid? Methinks you think too bloody damn much. Stop interfering in my life." Adam closed his precious journal and was about to put it away in its leather case; it was obvious he would have no more opportunity to study it this evening. He couldn't stop himself from asking the next question, though. "So, what was Tyra's reaction to your telling her that kisses lead to harems?"

"She stomped away."

"Aaahh," he said, and would have liked to do the same.

But there was a knock at the door. A series of knocks, actually. Four of them.

Adam looked at Rashid, and Rashid looked at him.

"Enter," he called out.

And in came Tyra's four sisters, all wearing voluminous night shifts, like the one Tyra had had on. He had thought all women slept naked, as their menfolk did.

"You kissed her," they all charged as one, smiling their congratulations at him.

He pushed a path through the women and did what he should have done before. He stomped down the corridor.

Aaarrgh! he wailed inside. *When did my life become such a nightmare? When did I revert to such youthling impulses? When did I let a woman turn my brain to mush?*

He promised himself not to repeat the mistake.
Unless there were tongues involved.
Or bed furs.
Aaarrgh!

The physician began to heal himself . . .

Adam was preparing to operate on the unconscious king.

They had slipped some of the strong, amber-colored, Scottish brew, *uisge-beatha*, between Thorvald's lips to help dull the pain and make his sleep deeper, as well as a small amount of poppy juice, though henbane or mandrake might have served as well if they had been available. It would not do for him to awaken in the midst of this procedure.

"Did you boil my tools?" he asked Rashid, who was arranging the implements on a cloth-covered table near the bed. There were several knives with short, sharp blades, a special miniature saw of his own design that fit in the palm of the hand, an extra-large needle, strong thread, and, of course, the hand-driven metal drill.

"Yea, I did." His assistant knew how important it was to his master that everything that touched the patient's body be pure. It was a lesson Adam had learned well from his stepmother, Rain, who claimed to know of medical practices far into the future. He could hardly credit that, but he accepted that cleanliness was important.

"And I had the room stripped of all objects, including the mattress, and everything was scrubbed with lye soap, even the walls," Tyra said. "Plus I had the rushes swept out." Although Vana disdained rushes in the great hall, she did allow them in the bedchambers to insulate the coldness of the floors.

He nodded, but said nothing. He had not wanted Tyra to be present, but she had insisted that she be there to represent the family. "You forget, Saxon. I am a soldier. I have seen blood afore," she'd reminded him.

How could he forget? He still saw images of her in his head, wielding a broadsword against the sea pirates. "It's different when it's a loved one," he had countered.

Also in the bedchamber were Father Efrid, the monk healer, who wanted to learn more about trepanation of the skull, and Rafn, whose muscle might be needed to hold down the king.

"Is everyone ready?" Adam asked.

"Wouldst object if I said a small prayer first?" Father Efrid inquired.

Adam nodded his head. "I am willing to accept help from any quarter."

"Blessed Lord, be with this man today as he performs his healing skills. Guide his hands, and if it be Thy will, bring Thorvald of Stoneheim out of his deep sleep and back into Thy living goodness. Amen."

"Amen," they all said, even Tyra, who was presumably not of the Christian religion.

"May Muhammad be sitting on my master's left shoulder," Rashid added, "and Allah on his right. Praise be to Allah!"

Rafn coughed and put in his prayer as well, to everyone's surprise, "Odin, god of wisdom, look down upon your servant, Adam of Britain. Give him your strength and make his hands adept. No straw-death for our king. Instead, save Thorvald's journey into Asgard for another day . . . in the midst of battle."

Adam couldn't help chuckling then, despite the dire circumstance he found himself in. "It looks as if we have ourselves covered from all celestial bases."

Everyone laughed nervously.

It was two hours after that, though, before anyone laughed, or smiled, or really breathed. Adam's hands had not trembled . . . not even once . . . in the course of the operation. He had feared they might after two years away from medicine and after his failure to save his sister.

And Tyra! My God, what a wonder she was! He had not expected her to flinch at the sight of blood . . . though it was her father and not some nameless enemy . . . but he had to admit to being impressed at her coolheadedness and efficiency under stress. She had seemed to anticipate his moves, even before Rashid, who had assisted him for many a year. If the woman were not so dead set on spilling blood, she would make a wonderful healer's assistant.

He smiled to himself, and not just at the image of Tyra the Warrior becoming Tyra the Healer . . . or any man's assistant. Whether Thorvald lived or died, the trepanation had been the most horrible, exhilarating experience of Adam's life. Those final moments when his drill had broken through the bone structure had been filled with suspense for them all. As one, they exhaled with a loud whoosh. Afterward, Adam applied bruised betony to the wound so it would unite and heal, then wrapped a long, clean strip of linen about the king's temple and all around his head.

Adam, for one, felt as if he'd been touched by the hand of God.

Whether Thorvald lived or died, and despite Adam's two-year absence from medicine and his vow never to practice again, he knew one thing without a doubt.

I am a physician.

He teased so good . . .

Tyra found Adam on one of the ramparts of the castle.

He sat with his back against the outer wall and his face pressed against his arms, which were folded over his raised knees. She had no idea whether he slept, or wept, or both. Nor did she know whether he would welcome her intrusion. Probably not.

Even so, she sank down to the rampart floor beside him and put a hand on the nape of his neck. He wore one of the loose Arab robes today, like the one she'd first seen him in back in his Saxon home.

"Thank you," she said, and she meant it most sincerely.

He didn't raise his head, but he did turn it so that he could look at her. "For what? We may not know for days if your father will recover."

"It matters not," she said, and moved her hand from his nape to his shoulder, which she squeezed briefly as a further sign of her appreciation. "Oh, I do not mean that my father's life has no importance. 'Tis just that I know you did not want to practice your healing skills, and definitely not in such a serious case."

"And not in another country, where I was brought against my will," he added. There was mirth in his voice now. She knew he was teasing her . . . again.

"That, too," she agreed. "Despite all your objections, though, you did a fine, fine job. I am impressed."

"Impressed, hmmm? I like the sound of that." He sat up, which she regretted. She no longer had an excuse to lay her hand on him. And she did so like the feel of his clean hair under her fingertips and the hard muscles of his back under her palm.

"Do not be letting your ego get more overblown than it already is. Any bigger and your head might explode," she teased back. She was not experienced with teasing games . . . certainly not teasing games with men. "I merely thanked you for completing the task competently. Just say, 'You are welcome, my lady,' like a humble healer."

"Humble healer?" he snorted, apparently not liking that description of himself. Tyra's heart went out to the man. He looked exhausted, despite his teasing, and why not? He'd spent two hours working on her father, and another two hours watching over him afterward. No doubt he would return to his vigil after this respite. "I did it because of our pact, Tyra. Do not be attributing fine motives to me. You made me a promise, and I intend to collect on it sometime soon."

Her face warmed despite her resolution to stop this blushing business that had started when she met this rogue. "I do not for one minute believe that you performed your surgery on my father because of me. You did it because you saw a man in need of your help. You did it because you are a doctor."

He shrugged. "Perchance it was all of those things, *including* you and the prize I intend to collect. So, exactly how thankful are you?"

Uh-oh! "What do you mean?" She was fairly certain she knew exactly what he meant. It would be something involving bed furs.

"Will you be slipping into my bed furs this night?"

"Nay!" she said far too quickly. "That was not our agreement."

He narrowed his eyes at her. "Do you intend to renege on our deal now? Your word is your bond, or so I presumed. Has that changed?"

"My word is everything. *If* you heal my father . . . that was what I agreed to. Then, and only then."

"I suppose you are correct. I just thought you might want to show some small token of your . . . thankfulness. In advance."

"Small token?" she asked skeptically. "Like a gift? A gold coin? An etched silver arm ring? A jewel-encrusted goblet?"

"Not quite what I had in mind." The twinkle in his eye was most beguiling.

Tyra had no idea how to handle this man. A rogue, pure and simple, that's what he was. First he pricked her pride by questioning her honor. In the next instant, he twinkled his sinful eyes at her. How was a woman to know when he was serious? "What, then?" she inquired in a surprisingly cool voice.

"Oooh, let me think." He tapped his lips with a forefinger, thoughtfully. "A kiss would be nice."

"A kiss?" she practically squealed. "When I am willing to give you some priceless object, you would settle for a mere kiss?"

"It would not be mere, I assure you. And, frankly, I have more treasures than I can use. You may find this hard to believe, but I have been a knight as well as a healer these past fifteen years. Many a battle and many a prize have there been."

"Now, there's a conflict of interests," she commented with a laugh. "Did you thrust a sword in your enemy, then later sew up his wounds?"

"That very thing did happen on occasion. Eventually, I declined to serve as a soldier anymore, unless absolutely needed to defend the position of one king or another. And they did not mind. 'Twould seem my services as a healer were needed more than my sword arm. Either way, the rewards were great. I do not need your material tokens."

It was she who put a finger to her chin and tapped thoughtfully now. There was more to this man than she'd originally thought.

He stared at her hotly, waiting for an answer. "Well?" he prodded finally when she refused to respond to his request for a kiss. A kiss that would be more than a mere kiss. She was afraid to imagine exactly what that might entail, but for a certainty it was bound to prove dangerous to her equilibrium.

When she still declined to answer, he moved on to another subject. "In all honesty, I must thank you, as well."

"Me? For what?"

"You are correct in saying that I am a physician. I am also a man . . . as I intend to show you someday. I was a brother . . . at one time. I am a stepson. And I am a friend. But most of all, I am a physician. Somehow . . . God only knows how . . . I forgot that for a while. Some say that God is the Supreme Healer. Mayhap He arranged events so that I would separate myself from society and medicine for those two years . . . something I needed to do so that *my* wounds would mend. Mayhap it was also God who arranged for me to be kidnapped by a warrior-wench who brought me to this lost land."

That was the most backhanded compliment she'd ever been given. But she was well pleased, more so than if he'd given her false praise about her beauty, as men were inclined to do when in the company of women. His comment relieved her guilt somewhat, too. But, really, he used the most tangled logic she'd ever encountered. "Methinks you give your God too much credit."

"Methinks I have not given Him enough, and that has been my problem."

Religion? From this rascal? He is ever confusing me. Does he do it a purpose? Probably. "You are a good doctor, aren't you?"

"Yea, I am," he answered without humility.

She expected no less from him.

"And you, my fair Viking. Are you a good soldier?" he asked, taking her hand and twining their fingers together. She tried to pull away, shamed by the size of her hands and the less-than-feminine calluses on her palms, but he would not allow that. Instead, he freed only his thumb and began to caress her wrist, back and forth. What a glorious, glorious sensation centered there where her pulse began to beat wildly! You would have thought he was doing something intimate, or scandalous, but all he was doing was caressing her wrist with a thumb, whilst he watched her, waiting for an answer.

An answer? Blessed Thor! I forget the question. Oh, he asked if I was a good soldier. "Yea, I am a good soldier . . . the best a woman could be . . . or most men for that matter."

"I could give you an ointment for that itch."

What that offer had to do with being a good soldier, she had no idea. "What itch?" She cocked her head in question.

"The one right there," he said, waggling his eyebrows as he stared at the crotch of her *braies.*

She blushed furiously.

"The one you scratch on occasion . . . especially when you notice one of your men doing the same."

She tried to pull her hand away, again to no avail. The man saw too much by half. She did try to take on some masculine traits. The way she walked, for one thing, when she remembered not to roll her hips. Her garments, for another thing. Crude gestures, for still another. It was silly, she supposed, especially if people like this brute noticed that they were not natural movements.

"Now, now, do not be embarrassed. I think it's rather adorable, actually . . . in a silly sort of way."

"Adorable? You think my scratching my private parts is adorable? I need to rethink my actions. I really do. Adorable is not the image I am trying to convey."

He threw his head back and laughed. What a wonderful sound his laughter was! Warm and spontaneous and very, very sensual.

When he was done laughing at her, he pulled a mock-somber face and asked her the most unexpected thing: "Well, isn't there some important question you have been yearning to ask me?"

She couldn't imagine what he was referring to.

He stood and pulled her to her feet with him. An amazing feat in itself. She did not realize he had the strength.

"Don't you want to ask me what I am wearing under my robe?"

When his mischievous comment finally penetrated the daze she was in, she blushed again, because, of course, she *had* wondered idly about that very subject. But a woman, and her pride, could stand only so much teasing. She pulled hard, and he released her hand. As she stomped down the rampart path, she heard the oaf laughing.

But she did not stop stomping, and he did not stop laughing . . . until he called out, "Nothing."

And then he reminded her, "You owe me, sweet lady-warrior. Do not forget the kiss."

As if I could!

CHAPTER SEVEN

⟨⊗⟩

And so the new phase of his life began . . .
  "Pssssssttt!"

Adam was about to step down the steep wooden stairs leading from the ramparts when he heard the hissing sound. Was it Tyra, having second thoughts about the kiss? Had she decided to give it to him now, rather than later? He smiled to himself, liking the idea of all this privacy for a kiss that he guaranteed would melt her bones.

His smile immediately faded when he saw that it was Rashid, not Tyra, who stood waiting around the bend.

"What are you doing, skulking about?" he snapped.

"Master!" Rashid exclaimed, clearly offended by his charge. "I have come to warn you—"

"Warn me? Of what? Has the king worsened?"

"Nay, nay, nay!" Rashid denied. "'Tis another, uh, event I come to . . . hmmm, uh . . . warn you of."

"Well?" he said testily. 'Twas hard to go from thoughts of hot kisses, to a possible medical disaster, to whatever it was Rashid was hmmming and uhing about.

"Look over here," Rashid said, leading him to a rampart wall that overlooked one of the courtyards below.

Rashid looked and saw a large group of people lined up outside the great hall doors. They were simple folk— cotters, soldiers, their families. He frowned his confusion at Rashid, who was grinning brightly at him. That bright grin caused Adam's frown to deepen.

"What do those people have to do with your *warning* me?"

"'Tis a miracle, my lord."

Oh, God! We are back to the lord nonsense. And I am sick to the soul of the miracle nonsense, too. "Speak plainly, man."

"News has spread already of your great medical talents, Master Adam. These people suffer various ailments that they want you to treat."

Adam bowed his head. He had made much progress today, but he was not ready for this.

"Do not be afeared. I will tell them that you are overtired today from your work with the king, whom you must still watch closely. But may I be so bold as to suggest that in the morn you might begin seeing the sick?"

Adam raised his head, his nostrils flaring with anger. Rashid was pushing him.

"Just a few," Rashid was quick to insert.

Sometimes Adam had to remind himself that Rashid, overbearing and annoying as he could be, was his friend. Rashid had his best interests at heart.

"A few," he agreed.

And so, the next stage of his life began.

There are kisses and then there are KISSES! . . .

Adam trapped Tyra that evening.

She had been avoiding him all day, the threat of a kiss hovering in her mind. In fact, she had not even gone to the great hall for the nightly meal, no doubt an extraspecial production on Ingrith's part to mark their father's operation, even though they did not yet know what the outcome would be. He had not died; to the Viking mind, that was cause to celebrate.

Adam had spent much of the day in her father's chamber, watching over him. Still, she had managed to avoid meeting up with him, there or elsewhere. Till now.

She'd been ambling from the scullery through the kitchen gardens to the outer back steps leading to the second floor and her bedchamber. On the way, she'd grabbed a hunk of flatbread and a stuffed pigeon. Then she'd stopped at the well for a ladle of water. She'd been sitting on the wide well bench, eating her tasty fare, interspersed with sips of the frigid water.

That was when the rogue had sprung his trap, coming up on her unexpectedly.

He dusted off the bench with a hand, then sat down beside her. An understandable action, considering the fine Saxon apparel he wore tonight. A tunic of wool in a shade of midnight blue . . . which matched his eyes, she could not fail to note. The tunic, embroidered at the edges with silver thread, was belted at the waist over black *braies* that hugged his form. His half-boots were of butter-soft calfskin.

She felt like a cow herself next to the resplendent creature that he was.

"Were you waiting here for me?"

"I was not."

"You did not join us for dinner."

"I was not hungry," she said, then immediately realized her mistake, for she had a pigeon in one hand and a hunk of bread lying in her lap.

He laughed.

"It wasn't because of you." Another mistake.

He laughed some more.

"You have grease on your lips," he remarked in a tone that was oddly husky.

She licked her lips.

He exhaled with a whoosh.

"What does that mean?"

"What?"

"The whoosh?"

"It means that you affect me greatly, my lady warrior."

"Oh," she said, but what she thought was, *Ooooh!*

He reached out with a thumb. "You missed a spot." He used his thumb to wipe a wide swath under her bottom lip, then put the thumb to his mouth and sucked. The whole time, he watched her, and she watched him.

For the love of a Valkyrie! Tyra had never seen a man do such an erotic thing in all her life. She felt the effects of the gesture right down to the tips of her tingling fingers and curling toes, and some unmentionable places in between.

"Do not play with me, Saxon."

"I like playing with you, Viking."

"Stop now, or—"

"Or what?"

She had no idea what . . . because the impertinent, arrogant born-to-be-a-libertine was lowering his mouth toward hers. And she was frozen in place. Mayhap it was because she had a pigeon in one hand and a ladle in the other, but more likely it was because her lips had somehow parted of their own volition. She wanted his kiss. She wanted it badly.

"Tyra," he whispered against her mouth just before his lips claimed hers. The man was proving to be a master at a number of things. Medicine, for a certainty. And now, kissing. She did not allow herself to ponder what other areas of expertise he might have.

He pulled back slightly to look at her. His eyes devoured her, searching for what, she did not know.

"Well, that was . . . nice," she choked out.

"Nice?" he sputtered.

"So, now you have your thank-you kiss-token."

"Hardly," he said, even as he bracketed her face with his hands and drew her down to the wide bench with him.

The water ladle dropped to the ground with a thud and the pigeon flew in another direction . . . she hoped not into the well.

He shaped her mouth, he nipped her, he laved her with his tongue, then sucked at her. His lips were hard, demanding something of her. Finally he gritted out against her mouth, "Open."

She did.

"Wider."

She did.

Then, by all the gods and goddesses, he showed her what a man could do with his tongue in a woman's mouth. The wetness . . . she should have been revolted; instead, she sighed inwardly at the delicious taste of him. The aggression . . . she should have shoved him off the bench; instead, she allowed him to take charge. The sinfulness of the thrusting action . . . she should have felt guilty; instead, she reveled in her first experience with a man's lust for her.

Somehow, in the midst of this brain-muddling kiss, he moved himself atop her.

"Why do you whimper, sweetling?" he whispered against her ear.

Sweetling? He called me sweetling. She could not keep herself from smiling against his neck. "I thought it was you that whimpered," she whispered back.

He was leaving a trail of kisses along her jawline when she spoke. He laughed against her mouth and admitted, "Mayhap it was." Then he resumed kissing her, and his hands . . . his wicked hands . . . moved everywhere on her. Everywhere.

Tyra loved the way he kissed. She loved the way he touched her, ravenously, as if he could not get enough of her. She loved the way he made her feel . . . feminine and desirable.

"Dost know what the best thing is about these insufferable *braies* you wear?" he asked her.

"What?" she asked, though she recognized the teasing mirth in his voice.

"This," he answered, putting his hands under each of her buttocks, then twisting his ankles about her ankles and spreading both their legs wide. The result: his manhood was nestled firmly against her womanhood.

He gasped.

She gasped.

"Oh . . . my . . . God!" he said.

"Oh . . . my . . . God!" she said, too. Sometimes only a good Christian expletive would do.

Now when he resumed kissing her, she had the double pleasure of feeling him move against her *there*. Tyra thought she had died and gone to Valhalla, so intense was the pleasure.

The one time when she experimented and dipped the tip of her tongue into his mouth, he jerked against her. What a wonderful gift! To know that she . . . Tyra the Big . . . Tyra the Man-Woman . . . could have that kind of effect on a man like Adam . . . well, 'twas nothing less than a gift from the gods.

"Why are they groanin' so much?" a little boy's voice asked.

"Are they makin' a baby?" a little girl's voice asked.

"Nay. You have to be naked to make babies," a voice that could only be Alrek responded. "Leastways, I think that is the way it works."

Tyra and Adam did indeed groan then. They turned as one, with him still lying flat atop her on the well bench.

It was Alrek, all right, with the baby Besji in his arms, sleeping apparently, her little head cradled against his shoulder. On either side of him were Tunni and Kristin.

Adam pressed his forehead against Tyra's and seemed to be counting to ten. When he was done, he sat up gingerly. And she did the same.

"What do you want?" Adam demanded testily. Tyra could sympathize with his frustration.

"Rashid sent us to find you," Alrek said in a shaky voice.

"He did? Are you sure?"

Tyra understood Adam's confusion. Rashid knew what a nuisance these children were to his master.

"Tell me exactly what were Rashid's words."

"Well, he was in your bedchamber. Conductin' inter . . . inter . . . interviews, I think he called 'em."

"Interviews?" she and Adam both said at the same time.

"Yea, and what a mess it was, too! Had a dozen women lined up outside in the corridor, he did."

"Interviews for what?" Adam asked through gritted teeth, though he and Tyra both knew the answer.

"Yer harem. We wuz helpin' him with the interviews. Openin' and closin' the door, holdin' back the pushy ones. When we kept askin' him questions, that's when he said, 'Why do you not go hunt for Master Adam?' What does buxom mean, anyhow? And belly dancin'? I have heard of dancin' round the Friggsday bonfire, but belly dancin' . . . I jist can't picture it."

Adam stood abruptly and began to stalk away. "I am going to kill the man, I truly am."

The children were staring after him, worried, no doubt, that they had said the wrong thing. Tyra, on the

other hand, had her palm pressed over her mouth, stifling a laugh.

Just before he reached the outside staircase, Adam
halted and turned. Pointing a finger at her, he asserted,
"You and I have unfinished business."

Tyra didn't even bother to disagree.

In truth, she couldn't wait.

Harems, anyone? . . .

Adam had to shove his way through two dozen mill-
ing women—the number appeared to be growing by the
minute—to get to his bedchamber.

*I am going to kill him. Forget about my newfound
dedication to healing. I am going to kill him.*

As he opened the door a crack, he heard Vana the
White—*Tyra's very own sister, for the love of God!*—
asking, "Does it matter if a new harem houri is a . . . a . . .
virgin?" The last word came out on a mortified whisper.

I am going to kill him.

"Nay, it matters not." Rashid was waving a hand airily. The other hand held a parchment on which he'd presumably been taking notes on the harem candidates.
"There is an ancient Arab proverb regarding this very
thing. 'Virginity is like a blister. Once pricked, 'tis gone
forever.' " Then he smiled widely, enjoying his own wisdom, no doubt.

"Rashid!" Adam practically bellowed, opening the
door wider.

Rashid jumped, and so did the young woman.

"Out!" he ordered Vana, then slammed the door after
her.

"Do you have a death wish?" he asked his assistant,
who had the nerve to stare back at him with wide-eyed
innocence, not the least bit repentant.

"Nay, but I do have a wish to be happy. Is that too much to ask? That a man may be happy in this lifetime? Allah says—"

"Do not dare quote me a proverb now. I am in no mood. Did I not tell you, over and over, that I do not want a harem?"

"Who said the harem is for you?" Rashid placed a hand flat against his heart as if Adam's charge had wounded him greatly.

Hah! Rashid wasn't fooling him. "And who might this harem be for? The sultan of Baghdad? A desert caliph?"

"Nay, nay, nay! Just for me."

"Oh, really? And where were you planning on setting up this harem? My weaving shed in Northumbria?"

Rashid raised his chin stubbornly. "You cannot tell me what to do with my free time. And if I want a harem, and have the funds to support it . . . which I do . . . then that is precisely what I will do."

Rashid stormed out then. Adam wasn't sure if the hasty exit was because he was offended, or if he just wanted to escape his wrath.

I have insulted my best friend.

I have gained a triple shadow of pestsome children.

I might very well have to run for my life if the king should die.

I've become involved, despite my best intentions, with a female Viking soldier.

How did my life become such a tangled mess? he wondered and put his face in his hands.

What else could happen?

The comedy of life just got funnier . . .

"Your Uncle Tykir is here," Rashid called out gaily a mere one hour later, as if they had never exchanged harsh words.

But then Rashid's message sank into Adam's brain. *Tykir? Here?* Oh, good Lord, what would he make of this mess? *He will laugh at me . . . that is what he will do.*

Adam was in the king's bedchamber, checking on his condition. Thorvald had not come out of the deep sleep yet . . . if he ever would. But his breathing was normal, and his body temperature had not elevated. Fever was always a concern.

Closing the door softly, Adam left Father Efrid behind to watch over Thorvald, with instructions to call him immediately if there was a change.

As he walked down the upper corridor, Rashid told him, "They brought the new babe with them. 'Twould seem they miscalculated the birthing date, and it came six sennights ago. It is a boy . . . a fourth son for them, I believe. Allah must be well pleased with the father to bless him so."

Rashid was rambling, as he often did, but Adam suspected he did so now to cover the awkwardness of their parting a short time ago. He put a hand on Rashid's forearm to halt their progress for a moment. "I apologize for my harsh words."

Rashid nodded and patted his hand in acceptance. "No apologies are necessary between friends. Just know this, Master Adam, we come from different cultures. Do not be so quick to judge my ways."

They continued toward the great hall, where Rashid went off to find Rafn. Meanwhile, Adam was greeted immediately by his Uncle Tykir, who lifted him off his feet and hugged him warmly. He and Tykir were of the same height, but Tykir had several stones on him in weight, being a fierce Viking warrior who guarded his home at Dragonstead with an iron hand. Dragonstead was less than a day's journey by horse and a half day by longboat. They were neighbors by Northern standards.

"How is everything going, boy?" Tykir asked as he drew back. Tykir had seen more than forty winters, but age sat well on him. There were only a few gray hairs in his light brown hair. Already Tykir was leading Adam toward a trestle table where a housecarl was pouring mead for them. "We heard that you were here, and I was worried. Alinor suggested that we come. She was worried, too."

"I operated on King Thorvald this morn. Thus far he seems to be holding on," he told his uncle.

Tykir nodded, took a deep draught of mead, then plopped down onto the bench and motioned for Adam to join him. Then he did what Adam had been expecting all along. He grinned.

Adam pretended not to notice and sipped thoughtfully at his ale.

Just then Alinor came up and hugged him from behind. "How fare you, Adam dear?"

He turned in his seat to get a better look at his aunt-by-marriage. He had not seen either of them for several years. Her hair was still rusty-red and her face was covered with freckles. Tykir thought she was nigh gorgeous. Even now, after a full ten years of marriage, it was clear that the man was besotted with his wife, so sappy was the expression on his face when he gazed on her.

"Ah, and this is the new addition to the Tykirsson family, I take it," he said, peering beneath the swaddling blanket at the newborn babe.

"Yea," she said with great pride. "Our fourth son. Selik Tykirsson. Is he not beautiful? He looks just like his father."

Adam had to take a deep breath before he could swallow over the lump in his throat. They had named their babe after his adoptive father, Selik . . . who had been sort of a stepbrother by marriage to Tykir.

Adam had to smile. "Of course, Selik is beautiful. All babies are. But I do not know about his being beautiful if he takes after his father." Adam regarded the infant, not knowing whom he would favor as he grew to manhood.

Tykir punched him in the arm, then relieved his wife of her blissful burden, cradling the still sleeping child in the crook of his big arm. Adam noticed that Tykir and Alinor's firstborn, Thork, was making friends with Alrek, who was of a similar age. Although he was only nine years old, Thork already had a reputation for being wildly mischievous. Adam wondered what domestic disasters would come of Alrek's association with him. *The Wild and the Clumsy!* Tykir and Alinor's second son, seven-year-old Starri, and their third son, four-year-old Guthrom, were already chattering away with Alrek's brother and sisters.

Alinor went to take a sip of her husband's mead, then frowned at Tykir when she realized the goblet was empty.

Ignoring his wife's frown, he commented to Adam, "Well, you landed in the middle of it this time, didn't you?"

"No thanks to you," Adam answered with a snort of disgust.

"Me?" Tykir inquired, widening his eyes with an innocence he'd never had a day in his life.

"*You.* 'Twas you that was responsible for the warrior wench kidnapping me and bringing me to this godforsaken land."

"She kidnapped you?" Alinor asked.

"Yea, she did. Whacked me over the head with a sword and tossed me over her shoulder."

Alinor and Tykir tossed their heads back and laughed uproariously. As he'd known they would.

"Tyra actually did that? Carried you off on her shoulder? Like a sack of barley?" Alinor wiped the tears of merriment from her eyes, but her face was still split with a huge grin.

"You know her?"

"Of course I know her. I have lived in this country for nigh on ten years. She was at my wedding with her father and sisters. You did not meet her there?"

He shook his head, wondering how he could have missed such a . . . a . . . wonder.

They all turned as one then to stare across the room to where Tyra stood talking with her sisters. It was easy to pick her out. She was taller by a head than any of the others. And she was the only one wearing *braies*. Adam sensed Tyra's insecurities, especially in comparison to her sisters and their renowned beauty, but frankly, Adam thought she looked ten times better than any one of them, even in her male attire, even when she did manly things like scratching. Was he looking at her through prejudiced eyes, just as Tykir did when he gazed adoringly at his freckled wife? Now, that was an alarming thought!

"She looks different somehow," Alinor mused, tilting her head one way, then another as she studied Tyra.

"Yea, she does," Tykir agreed, a grin twitching his lips.

Aaarrgh! It is starting already, the jesting at my expense.

"Methinks it is her tousled hair and her—*oh, my God!*—her lips." Alinor exchanged a look with her husband.

"You are right, wife. As usual. If I did not know better, I would think the lady soldier had been kissed good and well. In fact, her lips look rather, well, kiss-swollen."

Tykir and Alinor turned their attention to Adam.

"Just like yours," Alinor hooted with glee.

Once again, Alinor and Tykir tossed their heads back and laughed uproariously.

"Kiss-swollen lips, did you say?" It was Rashid who came up to join them. He looked pointedly at Tyra, then directly at Adam's mouth, and nodded his head with satisfaction. " 'Tis well past time, too. Two years of chastity is more than enough for any one man, I tell you. Allah says—"

"Two years?" Mirth was replaced in Alinor's voice by shock and something else . . . probably concern.

"Chastity? You?" Tykir was staring at Adam, his mouth agape with incredulity. He, too, looked a bit concerned.

"Methinks this calls for a saga," Adam heard a booming voice announce behind him.

"Oh, nay, oh please, God, not this," Adam prayed even before he turned around and saw the giant Viking with the one eye-patch. "Dear Lord, please, please, please, spare me."

'Twas Bolthor, the world's worst skald.

"This is the saga of Adam the Lesser," Bolthor began.

Alinor and Tykir smiled their encouragement. Adam just groaned.

But then Adam said, "What is this 'Lesser' business? You always say, 'This is the saga of Tykir the Great,' or 'This is the saga of Rurik the Greater.' Why is it I get no 'Great' after my name?"

"Well, Tykir was much chagrined when he found out that I named Rurik the Greater, and—"

"I was not," Tykir protested.

"Yea, you were," Alinor disagreed.

". . . and he ordered me henceforth to name no one greater than he."

"Are you really that vain?" Adam asked Tykir.

"He's lying," a red-faced Tykir lied.

"Yea, he is that vain," Alinor said.

"As I was saying, this is the saga of Adam the Lesser."

"Once was a Saxon healer,
All the maids his beauty did stir.
Some said he was overly cocky,
But, till then, his life had ne'er been rocky.
Along came a Viking princess,
Warrior by trade and dress.
Wanted the man,
Clobbered the man,
Carried off the man,
Heeded no ban,
Off she ran,
Took him to her clan,
Because the lady had a plan.
Now, some say she needed his talent,
That a miracle in him the gods sent.
That very well may be true,
But on this idea you should chew:
Exactly which talent of the knave
Did the fair maid crave?
And, further, this advice I confide:
Best that Eve should watch her backside
When Adam is untied . . .
Or better yet, at her bedside."

Tykir and Alinor declared it the best poem Bolthor had ever created.

"It even rhymed this time," Alinor cooed.

"And it was long, too," Tykir added, as if that were an asset for a good saga.

Rashid was practically in a swoon and swore that he and the skald would make celestial music by combining

Bolthor's poetic talents with his own mental stash of proverbs.

Tyra had walked up just as Bolthor began to speak. She was looking rather red, so Adam assumed she had overheard the saga. And, yes, her lips *were* kiss-swollen.

Adam closed his eyes and wished he were back in Northumbria where being a hermit was sounding better by the minute.

CHAPTER EIGHT

✣

A good day's work and then . . . oops! . . .

The next morning, King Thorvald awakened for a short time and was able to swallow a bit of thin gruel. Adam started his day in a really good mood.

To mark the occasion, he pinched Tyra's right buttock on the way out of the bedchamber, which caused her to squeal, just like a woman, which she probably hated. Then he winked at her, just to remind her of their bargain, which might very well go in his favor if her father continued to improve. The wink caused her to blush, just like a woman, which she probably also hated.

He was whistling when he entered the great hall. Rashid motioned him over to a table where housecarls were sitting down to break their fast before beginning the day's work.

"There are already people lining up for your services," Rashid told him.

He nodded. "I will see a few of them this morn, but not too many. I am still not sure how I feel about returning to medicine. Do you understand?"

"I do," Rashid said. "Slowly at first. One patient at a time. One day at a time."

He nodded.

Rashid managed to get a small solar off the great hall assigned to them. It had a long table in it and several chairs, which served their purposes just fine. By noon, Adam had seen several dozen patients before he announced firmly, "No more today!"

None of the ailments had been critical. A festering ax wound. A recurrent boil on the neck. A poison weed rash on the hands. A debilitating case of morning sickness. A fractured arm that needed splinting.

And Adam found great immediate satisfaction in being able to quiet an old man's cough by prescribing horehound boiled in water and sweetened with honey. Or soothe a screaming baby's irritated bottom with his special ointment. Or stitch a knife gash. Or advise Arnora, a twenty-five-year-old mother of eight, how to avoid any more pregnancies, thanks to some information from his stepmother, Rain, who claimed to know of methods used by women far in the future.

He told Rashid they would have to gather many more puffballs after a warm rain next summer, to replenish their stock. The edible fungus was wonderful to help bloody wounds clot because of the millions of tiny spores it contained. Lichen was also good for stanching wounds, but they had plenty of that.

Quite a few people who came to him that morning suffered from severe louse bites . . . always a problem when bathing and cleanliness were ignored. He advised them to apply a salve of cammoc, crowfoot, radish, and wormwood pounded into a dust, then kneaded with oil. Fleas posed a similar problem. To prevent infestations, he told a group of women to take gorse seeds, wet them down, then sprinkle them about their longhouses to kill the fleas. This was something Ingrith already practiced about her castle, which was so clean no flea or louse would dare intrude.

There were many ailments of the eye since Norse homes were so smoky. Adam suggested that the eyes be anointed with the juice from a roasted buck liver, and that afterwards the liver be eaten. Apparently, there was some ingredient in the meat that was beneficial to the eyes.

He prescribed pennyroyal for Torgeir's flatulence and suggested he cut ale out of his diet for a while. Torgeir said he would rather have wind in his bowels.

On a more serious note, one man, a sheepherder named Kolbein, came to him because of pains in his chest. Adam told him that he could not cure his heart disease, but he suggested he keep dogbane or milkweed about. A mild dose of the dried root mixed with water could act as a stimulant when heart failure threatened. And he cautioned the man to avoid heavy exertion or stress.

Rashid had been at his side the entire time, with his medical tools and herbs and ointments at the ready. He was an invaluable assistant, and Adam told him so now.

"Does that mean you are no longer angry with me over the harem?"

"That depends. If you are even remotely thinking of establishing a harem for me, then, yea, I am still angry. If you are doing it for yourself, then, nay, I do not care. Except to say, may Allah be watching over your demented soul."

They both laughed together as they walked arm in arm toward an outer door. It was a beautiful sunny day for October, and they intended to take advantage of the uncommon warmth to take a walk about the grounds. Tykir and Alinor joined them along the way.

"Would you look at this place?" Adam said. "I have never seen so many flowers and decorative bushes in all my life. I just never expected anything like this."

"You should see it in the springtime," Alinor remarked. "Flowers blooming everywhere. All the colors of the rainbow. Why, it is downright pretty here then."

"Precisely," Rafn commented with a grunt of disgust. He was carrying an armload of spears toward the exercise fields in the distance. "Have you ever heard of a Viking fortress being pretty? 'Tis humiliating. We are a laughingstock to many of our fellow Norsemen."

Alinor went off to consult with Drifa about some of her plants, and the rest of them followed Rafn.

"Why are those men running around in a circle?" Adam asked. There were groups of men throughout the field, working on various exercises: spear throwing, swordplay, archery, knife throwing. But around the periphery of the oval field, several dozen men were merely running at a slow trot.

"I know the answer to that one," Rashid announced before Tykir had a chance to answer. "'Twould seem that Ingrith's rich foods do not sit well on the Viking stomach. Tyra claims some of her men are getting fat. She apparently noticed a pot belly on Bolli today. He had six currant custards yestereve. Tyra was very upset and said if they want to eat like hogs, they are going to have to run like horses."

Adam and Tykir exchanged quick glances of amusement.

"Well, she does have a point," Tykir said. "I must admit to having seen very few obese Vikings in my time. And those that were, most often were not fighting men."

"Leave it to Tyra, though, to come up with this solution," Adam said with dry humor. "Mayhap she will set a new custom."

The three of them laughed, shaking their heads at the spectacle of burly, muscle-bound Norsemen huffing and puffing as they completed another round of the field, sweat pouring off their faces and beards like . . . well, hogs.

That was when Adam noticed Tyra in the thick of the action. She was engaged in swordplay with a man half a head taller than she and carrying slightly more body bulk. The Viking broadsword was not intended for thrusting and parrying; it was too heavy for that. Instead, opponents wielded it in a hacking fashion, the intent being to slice the skin deeply or actually lop off a body part if there was enough force behind the swing.

Tyra was performing admirably. Oh, she staggered at times. Even fell on her arse one time, but so did her fighting partner another time. Sweat poured off her face in rivulets, causing her hair, which hung in a single braid down her back, to cling wetly to her scalp with tendrils about her face. She appeared exhausted from the hard physical labor, but that did not stop her.

"What a soldier!" Tykir remarked, staring at Tyra.

"What a woman!" Adam added without thinking.

Tykir just grinned at him.

It was a reasonable observation, to Adam's mind. Today she wore a sleeveless, knee-length leather tunic, with a wide belt at the waist. Her legs were bare except for cross-gartered half-boots, as were her arms except for etched silver upper-arm rings. All that bare skin exposed on arms and legs, which, incidentally, were exceedingly long and well shaped, spelled *woman* to Adam, not soldier. But he decided not to explain to Tykir, who was watching him too closely and grinning.

Just then, Alrek ran by, chased by Tykir's son Thork. Their squeals of laughter were a joyous childish sound. It had to be the first time in years that Alrek had behaved like the youthling he was.

I wonder where the rest of Alrek's brood is.

His answer came far too soon.

Tunni and Kristin came rushing toward him, pushing a wooden wheelbarrow. Inside the wheelbarrow was a screeching Besji.

"Can you help us?" Tunni was addressing him, unfortunately, not Tykir or Rashid.

"How?"

"Change Besji's nappy," Kristin pleaded. "She made a smelly."

"Can't you find some woman in the keep to help you?"

Kristin shook her head vehemently from side to side, even as her thumb was planted firmly in her tiny mouth. Speaking around the thumb, she told him, "Alrek sez to come to you if we be in trouble."

Tunni was nodding his head just as vehemently as Kristin had shaken hers. "And a stinksome nappy counts as big trouble, don'tcha think?"

"Absolutely," Tykir answered. "It is right up there with other big troubles . . . like being kidnapped by a woman."

"Trouble rides a fast camel," Rashid agreed, "but betimes it rides on the back of a small child."

"Where's Alrek?" Adam shouted as loud as his lungs would allow. His unexpected bellow caused several running Vikings to stumble and Tyra to drop her sword.

"Holy Thor!" Tykir exclaimed, staring at something behind Adam.

"For the love of Allah, the boy attracts disaster like rotten meat attracts maggots," Rashid remarked.

Adam peered around to see what his two companions were gaping at and saw a dazed Alrek lying on the ground. It appeared that he'd been knocked over by a fast-trotting Norseman. And Tyra! When she'd dropped her sword in surprise, her opponent had apparently sliced her forearm accidentally.

For the first time in Adam's life, the sight of blood almost caused him to lose consciousness . . . because it was Tyra's blood.

Let me check out your tush, baby . . .

"Leave off, Saxon," Tyra complained for at least the twelfth time. "It is just a tiny gash, I tell you."

"Hah! Your *tiny gash* will take ten stitches, and I intend to sew such a fine line that you will scarce be able to see the scar in your fair skin. Dost think I would let Bjorn, your blacksmith-berserker, tend to you again? Not bloody likely!"

They were in the small solar that had been assigned for his medical work. Adam had been forced to drag Tyra there for treatment, against her will.

"You have no right!"

"I have every right. You are the woman who will be sharing my bed furs—"

"Mayhap," she corrected.

"Probably," he countered. "And I did not bargain for a scarred-up naked body in my bed."

"You are insufferable."

"Yea, I am. 'Tis one of my better qualities, don't you think?"

"Aaarrgh!"

"I assume that means yes."

"Stitch the bloody wound and get it over with. Alrek is probably out there shooting arrows again, or attempting to sharpen your sword. Better yet, I heard him asking the beekeeper if he could help collect honeycombs today. Do you know how to treat bee stings?"

Now, that *was* reason to make haste.

"I like your attire today," he commented as he washed the gash carefully with soap and water.

"Save your soppy words for someone who cares."

"Lord, I love a sharp-tongued woman. Makes one wonder what else she can do with it."

He poured a small amount of that Scottish brew *uisge-beatha* on the cut to further the cleaning and to dull the sensations in the skin before he inserted his needle.

"For the love of Valhalla! Why are you wasting good brew? Do you intend to lick it up . . . like the dog you are?"

"There is a thought," he said with a laugh. "Would you like me to?"

"Nay!"

She sat in one chair at the table and he at the other. He forced her to lay her arm flat as he began sewing . . . tiny, tiny stitches that really would be almost invisible. In order to distract her from what he was doing, he asked, "So what does a woman warrior wear under a tunic such as this?"

He thought she might say "Nothing" as he had about his Arab robes, but, nay, the woman was always a surprise to him.

"A codpiece."

He had to laugh at her quick wit. "Can I see it?"

"When the sun shines in Niflheim."

"Would that be comparable to 'When hell freezes over'?"

"Precisely.

When he was done stitching her wound, he acted quickly. Grabbing her by the waist, he tossed her onto the table face down and flipped up her tunic. She was screaming like a banshee and trying to rise, but he had one hand firmly on her neck and the rest of his body weight pressed over her bottom. Leaning back, he noted that she was not wearing a codpiece, but she did have on some kind of loin cloth. He ripped it off so that he could examine her arrow wound.

"What are you doing?"

"Checking to see what kind of butchery Bjorn performed on your buttock. See, you should have let me do the work. The wound is healing nicely, but you will have a scar there for life. Not to worry, though. It rather resembles a star. Attractive, really. Methinks I should rub some healing ointment on it, though."

She made a gurgling sound of dismay, then yelled, "Do not dare put your fingers on my arse."

He laughed and let go of her, jumping back at the same time, knowing she would punch him in the face, or kick him in some unmentionable spot, if she got a chance.

Quickly she stood and adjusted her clothing, the whole time glaring at him. "I could kill you for that."

"I was just doing my job. You must not think of me as a man when I am acting in my capacity as healer."

"Hah! I do not know of any healer who gets aroused when looking at a woman's arms, or legs, or backside."

"How do you know I was . . . am . . . aroused?"

"Your eye color lightens, your nose flares, and your lips part."

What could a man say to that? All he could think of was, "Oh."

Tyra clomped over to the door and swung it open so hard it crashed against the wall. Just before she left, though, Adam decided he would get the last word in.

"One thing, Tyra," he called out to her back. "You have a very nice arse."

His life couldn't get any worse. Could it? . . .

That morning, Alrek had decided to iron Adam's best tunic. Now there was a hole over the heart.

Kristin had made up his bed, but the linens were so twisted that when he tried to arise, he fell to the floor. Now he had a goose egg on his forehead.

Tunni brought a pitcher of water all the way from the scullery and spilled most of it along the way. The chambermaid was chasing him right now.

Besji almost fell down the hole in the garderobe. Adam caught her just in time.

"Can't you put these children to work?" he begged Breanne, who was working alongside some cotters that afternoon. "After all, what trouble could they get in while helping you apply wattle and daub to those huts?"

At the end of the day, Breanne showed up in the great hall where he was about to share an ale with Tykir and Rafn. She was madder than a bull in mating season. Without ceremony, she dumped the children in his lap. "You try cleaning them up. And take note of this, Saxon, that was the last favor you ask of me."

And she stormed off. Thorvald's daughters were wonderful at storming off, he was beginning to notice.

He and Rafn and Tykir looked at the children more closely. They were covered from head to toe with mud and straw . . . even little Besji. At least there weren't any injuries that he could see. He had taken to counting small blessings these days.

Tykir was, of course, laughing uproariously . . . even when he caught sight of a white, devilish grin under the thick layer of daub on one of the stragglers and noticed his own son, Thork. Adam doubted that Alinor would be so amused.

To cap off the moment, Bolthor walked up, took in the whole scene with his one good eye, and announced, "Adam, you give me the best ideas for new sagas. I think I will title this one 'How Adam the Rooster Gained a Brood.'"

* * *

The sly king had plans . . .

Thorvald awakened in the evening, feeling weak as a newborn babe. But alive! Praise be to the gods!

"Drink," he said, pointing to his mouth.

Rafn, the only one in the bedchamber, jumped with shock. "You are alive! You are alive!"

Thorvald would have laughed if he were not weak as dragon piss. Instead, he squeaked out, "Of course I am alive, you lackwit. Now give me a drink."

Rafn raised the king's head slightly from the pillow, then lifted a goblet of water to his parched lips. *Water! What kind of drink is that for a Viking lord?* But he had not the strength to argue, and in truth the water tasted wonderfully delicious.

He dropped back down to the pillow and choked out, "What happened?"

Rafn told him, "You were hit in the head with a mace ball by that Danish rat, Ivan the Ugly. Your brain apparently swelled up, and you have been unconscious for weeks."

He still didn't understand. He raised a trembling hand to his throbbing head, where linen cloths seemed to be covering some wound.

"Adam the Healer was brought here from the Saxon lands. Yestermorn he drilled a hole in your skull to relieve the swelling. 'Twould seem that it worked."

Drilled a hole in my head? Amazing! But then something else Rafn had said jarred him. "Brought him here? Who brought him?"

"Tyra. Whacked him over the head with a broadsword, she did, and carried him off over her shoulder." Rafn was grinning as he spoke.

Thorvald grinned, too . . . or tried to. *That's my Tyra. Just like her father.*

"I suppose the healer is hell-bent on killing her now," he mused.

"Actually, I think Adam rather likes her."

"He does?" Thorvald's brain might have been injured, and he might not be thinking as clearly as he should, but he was too crafty not to recognize an opportunity when it stared him in the face. "How does she feel about him?"

Rafn shrugged. "I think she likes him, too. Oh, they exchange word-jabs at every turn. But when she is not looking, he stares at her like a hungry wolf, and when he is not looking, she stares at him like a hungry wolf, too."

Thorvald couldn't have been happier. He had given Tyra, his firstborn and most beloved, a free hand in choosing if and when she would marry . . . to the detriment of her sisters. Was the long wait finally over?

"What of his bloodlines?"

"You remember Selik and Rain . . . from Jorvik? Adam is their adopted son. Tykir of Dragonstead—who is here now, by the by—and Eirik of Ravenshire are his stepuncles, or foster uncles or some such thing."

"Good enough!" Thorvald nodded his head, although his eyes were already beginning to close with weariness. "Although I had always wanted her to find a fierce warrior to take over for me when I am gone."

"My lord!" Rafn said with affront.

"Oh, do not be getting your *braies* all in a knot, Rafn. I know you and Vana will wed the moment Tyra is settled. And I know full well that you want the kingship more than any other. It may very well come to that."

Rafn's stiffened shoulders relaxed. "There is a problem, though."

"When is there not?" Thorvald said through a yawn. He was fighting to stay awake.

"Tyra has decided on a new campaign. She renounces all ties of kinship, and then she will join the Varangian

Guard, thus leaving herself husbandless and her sisters free to marry."

"The girl always was bullheaded." *Like her father.* He wasn't sure if he thought that or Rafn said it. It mattered not.

"She appears to be determined."

No more determined than I. Cut myself off from my first child? I think not! "You must do several things for me, Rafn."

His trusty captain leaned closer to hear his whispered words.

"Do not tell anyone that I awakened, or that we talked."

Rafn appeared confused, but he nodded.

"And bring me a boar steak, along with a horn of mead . . . all under cover, of course."

"My lord?" Rafn was definitely confused.

"I have a plan," was all Thorvald would say, for he was soon unconscious again.

But the king wasn't the only one making plans . . .

"What we need here is a plan."

Drifa was speaking to three of her sisters, as well as the Lady Alinor, as they helped her sort large bunches of cut flowers and herbs, which would be dried and used in various ways over the winter. Some would be used in potpourris, others crushed into salves, some of the more fragrant ones mixed with rushes to spread about the bedchamber floors. They were in an upper solar of the wood, castle . . . one of three solars in all, thanks to Breanne's obsession with building.

"What kind of a plan?" Vana wanted to know. "We were talking about Tyra. What has that to do with . . . oh, I see."

"A wedding plan. For Tyra," Drifa announced. "We

already know that she likes him, and he likes her, though neither would admit to such. The question is how can we make Tyra more desirable to the man? Irresistible, really."

"Oh, I love it. I love, love, love it!" Alinor said, clapping her hands together with excitement ... which caused her infant to blink his eyes, squirm around in his cradle, then nestle back to sleep in the soft furs.

"Hmmmm," Breanne said and pulled out a piece of parchment, a quill, and a pot of ink. "Let's make a list."

"She dresses like a man," Ingrith complained.

"Well, then, that should be number one," Drifa suggested. "Write that down, Breanne. Womanly attire."

For an hour and more they chattered on, suggesting, rejecting, and lauding the various ideas they came up with. In the end, this was their list:

WEDDING PLAN FOR TYRA
1) Womanly Attire
2) Develop Feminine Attributes—walk with a
hip sway, purse lips, flirt, take baths, no more
scratching the groin.
3) Be Agreeable—agree with everything he
says, listen raptly when he talks, let him do the
talking, smile a lot.
4) Damsel in Distress
5) Absence Makes Heart Grow Fonder
6) Learn Sex Tricks
7) If all else fails—jealousy

Lady Alinor disagreed vehemently with Number Three. "You'll turn Tyra into a witless maid, and what attraction is there in that?"

Breanne asked Ingrith, "So, if men are threatened by strong women, exactly how long must women act shy and subservient? Surely not for the rest of their lives."

Ingrith snickered. "Nay, just till they are wedlocked."

Ingrith's statement apparently won Breanne over. Alinor was overruled by a 4-to-1 vote.

They all giggled over Number Six, and wondered where they would learn sex tricks to pass on to Tyra. But they all agreed it was essential.

"Actually, I know a few," Alinor admitted with a blush . . . a blush that caused her freckles to stand out like rust splotches on her now pinkish-ivory skin.

"You do?" The sisters were clearly impressed.

"Feathers are involved in one of them . . . and a silky harem outfit in another, complete with bells . . . but we can talk about that later."

The sisters' shoulders drooped with disappointment. Clearly, talking about sex was a timeless subject of interest to women.

"I think we should take one step at a time. Tyra will be suspicious if we try to make her do too much all at once," Breanne suggested.

"Yea, and we might not accomplish every part of the plan. That might be too lofty a goal . . . or is it a lusty goal?" Vana said with a grin. "So, yea, one step at a time."

"When shall we start?" Drifa asked, rubbing her hands together gleefully.

"No sense waiting," Ingrith offered.

They all nodded enthusiastically.

"Then we are agreed. Step One first. Womanly attire."

A man plan . . . oh, boy! . . .

"I think you need a plan to seduce the warrior wench," Tykir opined to Adam, following his eighth goblet of mead.

Adam started to choke and let loose a spray of his drink onto the table where he was sitting with Tykir,

Rafn, Rashid, and Bolthor. It was late at night, and most of the inhabitants of Stoneheim were long abed.

"Best you clean up that spill as soon as possible," Rafn advised, "or Vana will be here with her wiping rag and broom, which she will whack over your head." It was clear that Rafn was besotted with the fair Vana.

That was all Adam needed, another bump on his head. "What makes you think I need your help in that regard?" he asked Tykir, speaking of the seduction of Tyra.

"You have been chaste for two years," Rashid reminded him. "Is that not reason enough?"

"I swear, you Arab dunderhead, if you mention that subject in company again, I will do something to you which will require abstinence on *your* part for two years . . . or mayhap forever."

Rashid winced, but not for long. "I know a perfect proverb that fits your situation. 'The best thing about male chastity is that it doesn't last long.'"

"This is the saga of Adam the Lesser, also known as Adam the Chaste," began Bolthor.

Everyone laughed, except Adam, who groaned.

"Man was not made to be chaste,
Everyone knows it would be a great waste.
If the gods wanted a man to abstain,
Why give him a staff without a brain?
It hardens at a mere whiff
Of a wench with a bare midriff.
And rises to a new high
When viewing a creamy thigh.
So when he gets a kiss,
It is in sheer bliss.
And when the sword finds its sheath,
What a heavenly relief!

So, who is the more intelligent being?
The man who wallows in virtuous self-pity?
Or the man who sheds his odious chastity?"

"The reason I think you need our *expert* advice is because you are making no progress with the Lady Tyra," Tykir resumed, as if Bolthor had not just spouted one of his horrendous poems. Adam suspected that Tykir had been the brunt of so many of Bolthor's sagas, they no longer fazed him.

Rafn raised a forefinger to get their attention. "Do not forget the kiss. Right here in the great hall, he kissed the lady. On the lips."

"Are you *drukkinn*?" Tykir asked Rafn.

"Probably," Rafn answered. "Are you?"

"Probably."

"That was not really a kiss," Adam protested. "'Twas just a fleeting little brush of the lips. It does not count as a real kiss, to my mind."

"Aaah, but you are forgetting the *other* kiss," Rashid put in.

"The other kiss?" Tykir, Rafn, and Bolthor asked.

"Yea, Alrek told me all about it. 'Twould seem that they indulged in more intense kissing on the well bench, and they were in a horizontal position, if you get my meaning."

Adam wished they would all stop talking over him as if he were not there.

"But kissing, nephew? Is that as far as you've progressed? Tsk-tsk! You seem to have lost your knack, my boy."

"Actually, I wrote a saga once about a Viking man who had lost his knack. I misremember which Norseman it was about. Oh, now I recall," Bolthor mused, then looked directly at Tykir.

Now it was Tykir's turn to squirm in his seat.

"What makes you all think that I want to seduce Tyra?" Adam said. "I am not in the market for a wife."

"Who said anything about a wedding?" Tykir scoffed. "'Tis a bedding, not a wedding we refer to. And, good Norseman that I am, well, I am always willing to share my secrets."

"Rashid, grab your parchment and a quill. Let us make a list," Rafn suggested.

SEDUCTION PLAN FOR ADAM
  1) Hot Looks
  2) Compliments
  3) Jealousy
  4) Touch Her Often in Passing
  5) Erotic Conversation
  6) Kiss Her Boneless
  7) Get Her Alone
  8) Gifts
  9) Tell Her Sex Tales
 10) Be Chivalrous
 11) Viking S-Spot

"Can I write a saga about this?" Bolthor wanted to know.

"Nay!" everyone exclaimed as one.

"Alinor would kill me," Tykir said with a shiver, then smiled brightly. "Tyra doesn't stand a chance."

Adam suspected that it was himself who didn't stand a chance.

CHAPTER NINE

❧

*U*h-oh! *Why is everyone being so nice? . . .*

Tyra's sisters were acting mighty suspicious.

They had prepared a bath for her . . . in her own bed-chamber, no less. The four of them had lugged the big brass tub all the way up the stairs, and then made three return trips each, carrying water.

"It's the least we can do for you when you worked so hard in the exercise fields today," Ingrith said.

And Drifa kept sprinkling those blasted rose petals in the water, "just to make you a tiny bit fragrant." Tyra didn't have the heart to tell her that she had no desire to smell like a rose. *There is naught wrong with the scent of plain, clean skin, if you ask me, which nobody is doing.*

Vana was soaping up Tyra's hair right now . . . always a tedious task because the tresses were so long. "I've been thinking about cutting it all off," Tyra mused aloud.

"Nay!" all four of her sisters cried, and Lady Alinor as well, who had just walked into the bedchamber carrying a message for Ingrith that she was needed in the kitchens. Apparently, there was some problem with a curdled custard. Plus, Alrek had announced his intention to go gather eggs from the chicken coop. Ingrith rushed off, making her apologies—as if Tyra needed her to continue her bath.

"So, what do you think of my nephew Adam?" Alinor asked of a sudden. It was hard to picture Alinor as Adam's aunt, when she was only a few years older than he.

Her three remaining sisters cast chastising scowls at the lady, as if she'd asked an inappropriate question. Well, it was inappropriate, but then, Alinor was an outspoken woman. And, really, Tyra didn't mind the question.

"He's a toad."

Alinor clapped her hands together as if Tyra had given the correct answer. "That's exactly what I used to call Tykir, afore he became my husband. Well, actually, I still call him a toad on occasion. Toadliness is a male trait, you know. Right up there with excessive lustiness."

Everyone smiled.

"I heard that you kidnapped Adam," Alinor continued.

"Yea, I did, but 'twas necessary because—"

Alinor waved a hand to indicate the cause mattered not. "Didst know that Tykir kidnapped me at one time?"

"He did?" all of them said.

Alinor nodded. "Yea, he did, the sweet toad." She jiggled her eyebrows at them for emphasis.

They all smiled some more.

What an unusual lady she was. Tyra would like to get to know her better, but of course that would be impossible when she was in faraway Byzantium, serving with the Varangian Guard.

"I'd best be off, too, to help Ingrith," Vana said.

"Me, too," said Breanne. "Just let me pour in another bucket of hot water. Relax, why don't you, sister? Dinner won't be served for another hour."

"Um-hmm." Tyra was already closing her eyes sleepily as she sank down into the tub.

"My baby needs to be nursed soon," Alinor added.

To Tyra's sisters she advised, "Let us pick up these wet linens and dirty clothes. Take them to the laundry yard. The buckets, too."

Soon there was blissful silence. That did not happen often in Tyra's life. Always she was surrounded by noise and people, whether they be her soldiers or sailors, servants or family members. She had not realized how much pleasure was to be had in mere quiet.

The plot thickens . . .

A short time later, the quiet of Tyra's bedchamber was broken by a shrill scream of outrage. Hers.

"How could they? How could they?" She paced about her small room, stark naked, searching for her garments . . . her *male* garments. But the only item of apparel left there was a gown of crimson silk. Nor was this a Viking-style gown of modest chemise and over-apron. Nay, this was a form-fitting gown in the Frankish style with low neckline and cross-lacing that would make the gown fit snugly from under her breasts to her hips.

Desperately she searched for something else to cover herself. But her sisters and Alinor had not left even a bed linen. She had no choice. She would have to don the scandalous gown . . . one of her sister Breanne's, she would guess, since she was taller than the rest.

Blessed Freyja! She would kill them all.

Woman in a Red Dress, but no Buddy Holly in sight . . .

Tyra was missing from the great hall.

Adam hated the fact that he noticed her presence or absence. Truth to tell, he liked looking at her. He liked teasing her. He especially liked kissing her.

Was she avoiding him again?

Probably.

Alinor had told him a short time ago that Tyra con-

sidered him a toad, and she was smiling as she made
that announcement, as if he should be pleased . . . as if
it were a compliment.

Women! 'Twas hard to figure them out.

An odd silence came over the hall then. He looked up
and peered through the smokiness toward the other end
where a staircase led to the upper level. The most magnificent woman he'd ever seen was storming through the
aisle between the long tables, heading toward the dais
where he sat with Tykir, Alinor, Rafn, Bolthor, and the
sisters. She was tall, very tall, with flowing blond hair.
And she wore a long-sleeved, low-necked gown of crimson red which molded her body from truly splendid
breasts, to narrow waist, to womanly hips.

It was Tyra.

Who knew? Who knew?

Adam put a hand to his heart to still the mad pumping there. He felt hot all over, and proud . . . so very
proud . . . of his lady.

*My lady? Aaarrgh! She is not my lady. I have no
right to be proud of her. How can she be my lady if I am
her toad? My brain is splintering apart here. Do not look
at her. How can I not look at her? Oh, God, she looks
so damn good.*

"Where are my sisters?" were the first words out of
her mouth, and they were directed at him.

"Huh?" he answered, unable to move his gaze from
that vast expanse of alluring skin just above the swell of
her breasts. Shaking his head to clear it, he looked from
side to side and noticed that Alinor and the sisters had
somehow disappeared.

Ah, now he understood. They were responsible for
this remarkable transformation in Tyra.

"Sit down," he demanded, forcing her into the seat
next to him. "You are creating a scene."

"'Twill be nothing compared to the scene I create once I put my hands on four sisters and a certain lady."

"You should be thanking them," he said, placing a goblet of mead in her hands. She needed a good swig, not that he would tell her that.

"And why is that?" she asked icily.

"You are beautiful. They played some trick on you so that you would realize just how beautiful you are."

"That is pure hog swill. I am not beautiful, and fine feminine garments will not make it so. But that is neither here nor there. I am too big for such feminine finery. People are probably laughing at me behind their hands. How can I lead my men in battle dressed like this?" She waved her hand with disgust down the front of her body. Then she downed the contents of her goblet in one long swallow, belched loudly, and waved to a housecarl for a refill.

Adam barely stifled a grin. "As long as you keep belching and scratching, medoubts you will ever have to worry about appearing too feminine to your soldiers. And, besides, can you not don different apparel for different jobs . . . as Breanne does?"

"So, you notice the way Breanne dresses?" The question was asked idly, but he could tell it mattered to her . . . especially when she downed another goblet of mead and motioned for yet another.

Was that hurt in her eyes? He hoped so. He liked the idea of Tyra being jealous of him.

"I notice all women. I like women, but—"

"If you like women, why have you remained chaste for two years?"

Did everyone have to discuss his sex life? Did everyone have to pick and probe at his emotions? He might as well tell her, or she would never let up. With a deep sigh, he revealed, "Because I was in mourning . . . for my sister, Adela, who died two years past. I loved her more than anyone else on this earth, but I could not save her. I did not remain chaste apurpose. There was no vow or aught like that. I just was not interested." He shrugged, unable to add more to those bare facts.

Tyra seemed to understand. She placed a hand on his forearm and squeezed in commiseration. It was not her pity he wanted, but he *was* comforted by her silent understanding of his grief.

Enough gloom! "But what I started to say before you interrupted me, wench, is that I like women, and I notice the pretty ones, like your sisters, but you are so much more. When you are in a room, you are like a bright, vibrant flower, and they fade in comparison."

"Hmph! Me, a flower? I do not believe that for one moment. But it is nice of you to say so," she conceded with a sniff. No doubt it was the three goblets of mead she'd imbibed that prompted the concession.

"Come!" he said, standing suddenly and drawing her to her feet. "I want to show you something."

She pulled back. "They are about to serve the meal."

"We will be right back," he assured her. "And I promise you will be pleased, sweetling."

The man could make a stone purr . . .

They were out in the stables.

The stables, for the love of Loki! The man praised her for her feminine fripperies, then took her out to a stable, of all things.

Adam was holding a wall torch in one hand and pulling her along with his left hand, through the alley created by the stalls of horses on either side. Although it was cold outside, it was warm in here with all the body heat created by the animals.

"Look there," he said, putting the torch in a wall

bracket and opening the gate to the last stall, which was empty. Well, not quite empty. There was a mother cat and its litter of kittens . . . several weeks old, Tyra would guess.

She knelt down on the straw and petted one of them. It arched its back and rubbed against her stroking fingers. "Pretty kitty, pretty kitty," she cooed.

"I told you you would like my surprise," Adam said, also kneeling in the straw and picking up another kitten. This one was not so docile and fought against being taken in hand.

The mother cat hissed at them, then settled in to staring at them with her all-seeing eyes, apparently reassured that they meant no harm to her babies.

"I do like your surprise, but I don't understand why you would want to show them to me."

"This little dearling . . . that is why I brought you here." He held out his arm so she could get a better view of the scrappy kitten that fit right into the palm of his hand but was flailing its little paws, trying to scratch. Aside from its nature, it was different from the rest. Its fur was silver gray with white feet and nose, while the other cats were midnight black. And this cat's fur stood up on end as it meowed its displeasure.

"Just like you," he explained.

"I beg your pardon."

"All the kittens are adorable, in their own way, but this one is a fighter, and always will be. It stands out from the litter. Because it looks different, others will probably treat it differently, which in turn will cause it to become more feisty and independent."

Tyra laughed. "That is the most outlandish thing I have ever heard. I hope you do not consider it a compliment."

"Sounds good to me," he said, placing the kitten back with its mother and pulling her to her feet. "I think we should name her Warrior, for her namesake."

"Hmph! How do you even know it is a girl?"

"Ty-ra! For shame! I am a doctor. I know these things," he said, waggling his eyebrows at her.

She laughed. "So, you are likening me and my sisters to cats?"

He nodded, but she could tell his mind was somewhere else . . . probably in the vicinity of her exposed bosom.

She should have pulled her hand from his, but she didn't. She should have shoved when he leaned back against the wall and took her with him, but she didn't. She should have run for her life when she saw his eyes turn smoky blue with arousal, but she didn't.

"Come to my bed furs tonight," he urged, at the same time wrapping his arms around her waist and tugging so that she lost her balance and leaned against him.

"Nay," she said.

"You smell good," he whispered against the curve of her shoulder.

The feel of his lips against her bare skin was so delicious that it took her a moment to respond. "Roses."

"Uhmmm," he said, whatever that meant.

"Are you going to kiss me?" she asked, surprised at the breathlessness of her voice.

"Undoubtedly," he said. "Will you yield to me?"

She thought a moment. "I would rather be the one in charge of this kissing. Will you yield to me?"

He didn't even think for a moment. "Yea."

"You do not mind yielding to a woman?"

She could tell that he was fighting a grin. "Tyra, I would love to yield to *you*. Not any woman. *You*."

So many emotions swirled through Tyra then.

Fear . . . she knew she was treading in dangerous waters.

Excitement . . . she'd never initiated a kiss with a man before, and, ever the competitor, she did love a challenge. *Will I be good? Oh, I hope so.*

Arousal . . . she didn't understand the sensations that assailed her in Adam's presence, but she wanted to. Her womanliness seemed attuned to his manliness so that all her senses were heightened when he was in the vicinity.

Smells were more fragrant, like the particular scent of his skin, or his breath, which was surprisingly pleasant.

Food tasted better . . . his kisses certainly tasted delicious.

Her hearing was so acute these days that the mere whisper of "Tyra" from his lips seemed to carry some sensual meaning.

And her vision—the mere sight of him coming into a room caused her heart to race. And she missed him when he was gone. The way he stared at her now—with feral intent . . . like a cat . . . a *big* cat—was exhilarating rather than threatening.

Lastly, there was touch. How could it be that the feather-light brush of his lips or the press of his fingers on her arm caused her breasts to swell and her womanplace to ache?

For days Tyra had fought all these emotions . . . signs of womanly weakness, to be sure. But now she seemed to relish her femininity and was about to step willingly into the lair of the wolf.

She leaned forward so her breasts pressed against his chest, then placed her hands behind his neck. He was only a few inches taller than she; they fitted well together. Very well.

He stared at her, saying nothing. Doing nothing. He was allowing her to lead in this game. But she saw by the tautness of his jaw and the flare of his nose that he was not unmoved, and that bolstered her nerve. Well, she had to admit, the three meads she had imbibed had probably bolstered her nerve as well.

At first she just placed her lips against his, shifting and settling till she got the position right. Then she pressed, and moved, and pressed.

"Tyra," he said against her mouth.

"What?" she asked dreamily, wanting to resume her explorations.

"You're supposed to close your eyes."

"I am? Then how will I know what is happening?"

He laughed, and she felt the delicious ripple of his mirth against her mouth. Another new sensation. She liked it.

"Feel the kiss. Do not see it. Feel it."

"Oh, I see." She was outlining the contours of his lips with the tip of her tongue while she spoke. She thought he made a gurgling sound . . . of pleasure, she was hoping. But then another thought came to her unbidden. "How did you know my eyes were not closed? Were yours open? That does not seem fair."

He laughed again, causing more of those wonderful ripples against her mouth, especially when he nipped her bottom lip with his teeth. "I was just checking."

And so she closed her eyes, and he closed his (she checked), and the kiss was so much better, just as he had said.

His prior kisses were still imbedded in her mind, and she called on those memories. She moved her mouth against his. She licked his lips. She bit him lightly. She plunged her tongue inside his mouth and almost swooned at the intensity of her pleasure. He must be nigh swooning too if his groans were any indication. At some point, she could not say when, Adam joined in the kissing. Not taking charge exactly. But giving and taking. Fair play. She liked that. In fact, she was beginning to like too much about the man.

So dazed was she by this incredible exercise of kissing that she scarce noticed when he loosened the ribbon lacing of her gown, which wrapped around her body from abdomen to hips. When she felt the air on her bare breasts, it was already too late.

How could any woman resist the hungry look of a handsome man gazing at her body?

"Don't move," he ordered as he tugged the neckline and sleeves of her gown downward to her waist and wrists respectively. In truth, she could not have moved even if she had wanted to; she was trapped by the confines of her gown.

He touched her breasts then. Lightly. With his fingertips he traced the rounded globes, then the rose-colored areolas, then the hardened tips. "So beautiful. So beautiful," he whispered.

The pleasure was more than she could bear. Arching her neck, she instinctively pressed her breasts forward for more of his attentions. He gave them, and more than she had ever bargained for. Cupping her right breast from underneath, he lifted it, then leaned down and took the turgid nipple in his mouth and sucked deeply.

With a whimper, she sank down to the straw. He went with her, never taking his mouth from her breast. Over and over and over, he suckled at her breast with a rhythm that was delicious agony, alternating his sucking action with an occasional nip of his teeth or flick of his tongue.

Then he lifted his face and gave equal punishing attention to her left breast.

Tyra felt as if she were floating, floating, floating toward Valhalla . . . or some unknown heaven of sorts.

But in the midst of her arousal, she realized that what had started out as a kissing game on her part had turned into something altogether different. She was the one gaining all the pleasure, whereas Adam reaped no rewards.

Taking a deep breath to still her roiling arousal, she grabbed his head by handfuls of hair on each side and lifted him off her body so that she could see his face.

His eyes were glazed with passion, his mouth wet and panting. "What?" he inquired huskily. "Do you not like what I am doing to you?"

Her instinct was to deny her feelings, but she was basically honest, and she admitted, "I love what you do to me, but . . . but . . . well, it is all one-sided."

His eyes went wide with surprise, then filled with understanding. "Ah, sweetling, did you not know? A woman's passion is a man's greatest pleasure."

"Really?"

He nodded and began to sit up. "I'm glad you stopped me, though. I lost control."

She sat up, too, and began to adjust her gown. Disappointment rang through her like a funeral bell. He did not want her after all. "Losing control is a bad thing?"

He turned his gaze on her and smiled softly. "Nay, losing control is a good thing . . . in the right situation. But I do not intend to take you for the first time on the floor of a stable."

Take? Tyra did not like the sound of that. "What makes you think that you would *take* me? Mayhap *I* would take *you.*"

He tossed his hands in the air. "That works equally well for me."

They both stood then and helped each other whisk

the wrinkles out of their garments and pick off pieces of straw.

"Do you want to bring your pet back to the castle with you?" Adam asked.

"What pet?"

"The kitten."

"Adam," she said with a long sigh, "why do I have to keep reminding you? I am a soldier. I must exhibit warlike ways. Having a kitten trailing about after me would not be warlike."

He just smiled at her, not believing a word she said.

"Besides, Vana does not allow animals indoors."

He still smiled.

As they were walking back toward the great hall, Tyra ventured a thought that had been nagging at her. "'Tis odd, this attraction betwixt us, do you not think? I mean, I do not even like you, really."

He laughed and chucked her under the chin playfully. No man had ever done that to her before . . . made playful gestures. But then, no man had ever sucked her breasts till her blood caught afire either.

"Yea, 'tis odd," he agreed. "And betimes, I do not like you all that much either."

She should have been affronted, but she was not.

"Methinks tonight happened because I had too much to drink," she suggested. "That on top of the stress of my father's illness."

"Mayhap," he said, but not with much conviction. "On the other hand, methinks tonight happened because I saw you in that wanton gown. Or because I have been chaste overlong." This also was said without much conviction.

They were sound excuses: stress, a wanton gown, an ale-head, excessive chastity . . . perfectly logical explanations for illogical behavior.

Neither she nor Adam believed any one of them.

* * *

Something smelled fishy in Denmark . . . uh, Norway . . .

"You shoulda tupped 'er when you had a chance."

Alrek made that outrageous suggestion as the two of them were walking toward the king's bedchamber, having just finished their morning meal.

"Alrek!" Adam said in his most chastising tone. "What a thing to say! Especially for a boy your age!"

"I keep tellin' you, I am not a boy. I am a man . . . almos'."

"What a thing for an almost-man to say, then!"

"'Tis naught more'n everyone else was sayin' in the hall las' night when you and the Lady Tyra returned from the stables, red-faced and all in disarray. Whoo-ee! Looked like you were rollin' in the hay . . . leastways, thass what more'n one soldier said. But yer uncle Tykir, he said, 'Nay, the boy might have got some straw in his *braies*, but I can tell that he has not had his hay raked yet.' Thass when the Lady Alinor bopped him on the head with a ham bone. And Bolthor sez you definitely lost yer knack. What is a knack anyway? Do you want I should help you find it?"

Adam was getting an immense headache . . . one of those that made his head feel as if it were splitting. "Do you not have somewhere to go this morning, Alrek? Surely you have something better to do than tag along with me to a sick chamber."

"Nay, I do not. My day is free," Alrek said cheerily. "But, actually, there is a reason why I am goin' to the king's chamber. I wuz hopin' he would wake up and . . . and . . ."

It wasn't like Alrek to hesitate to speak his mind. His hesitation pricked Adam's curiosity. "What is it, Alrek?"

"'Tis time fer me to get me yearly coin from the

king. Besji and Kristin and Tunni all needs new clothes. And I would really like to buy me a sword."

A sword? What next?

"And mayhap a spear if I have enough left over."

The boy is going to kill himself. "Well, the king has not awakened yet, and even if he did, I am not sure this is a good time to bring up the subject. He will have more important issues to deal with. Can you not approach the king's steward, or the Lady Tyra?"

Alrek shook his head. "My arrangement wuz a personal one . . . with the king."

Adam reached into the pouch at his belt and handed Alrek a coin. "Here. Take this."

Alrek jumped away from him. "Nay, I will not be takin' charity from no one. I kin wait." With that, he turned on his heel and ran away.

Well, is that not just wonderful? Now I've offended a ten-year-old boy . . . rather a ten-year-old almost-man. He smiled at his own mental correction.

"What are you smiling about?" Tykir asked when he entered the king's bedchamber. "Seems to me you have naught to be happy about today . . . not after last night. Ha, ha, ha!"

"You know, Tykir, you have a big mouth. I heard what you said in the hall last night."

"Me? Me?" Tykir was laughing raucously. He danced away when Adam went to punch him in the arm.

"Shhhh!" Father Efrid said. "Have some decorum before the ailing king."

Adam and Tykir ducked their heads, while Rashid, Rafn, and Bolthor grinned at their discomfort.

"Has he awakened again?" Adam asked Rashid.

"He is in and out of consciousness, but never for very long. Leastways, not whilst I've been here," his assistant said, already laying out Adam's tools and medicants on a clean, linen-draped table.

Everyone stepped back so he could examine the patient. Someone must have been in to bathe the king, because he smelled of Drifa's pine-scented soap, and he wore clean apparel, though it was only a loose, unbelted tunic. Even his mostly gray beard had been trimmed.

"His skin color is improving," Adam remarked, more to himself than the others in the chamber. "And Ingrith told me that she managed to get a whole bowl of beef marrow broth down his throat today. If only he would regain consciousness for longer periods of time."

"He spoke to me a tiny bit yesterday," Rafn informed him. "He wanted to know what happened. Mostly, I did the talking, but he seemed to be aware of his surroundings. Is it really so unusual for a man to 'sleep' so much after such an operation?"

Rafn's long-winded speech seemed odd, though Adam couldn't quite put his finger on the reason why. Perchance it was because he'd kept his eyes averted the entire time. Adam had a sneaky suspicion about the king's continued unconsciousness, but the notion was too outlandish for even this rascally king.

Adam changed the linen dressing on the head wound, checked the King's eyes and mouth and ears, and listened to his heartbeat. All seemed normal . . . or as normal as a man with a hole in his head could be.

He stepped away from the bed and said, "I will stay with him for several hours. Mayhap he will awaken whilst I am here. I would like to see myself how he reacts."

"Uh, master, didst know that folks started lining up afore dawn for your medical services?" Rashid informed him.

"As I said, I will remain here several hours. This afternoon I will see some people," he said firmly. "Please, Rashid, not too many yet." There was a hidden message in his last statement . . . a plea for his assistant to understand that he needed to move slowly back into his medical practice . . . that he still suffered misgivings.

Rashid nodded.

No one left right away, though. He and Rashid were gathering up his supplies, setting aside those items to be destroyed and those to be boiled for another use.

"Are you planning to wed Tyra?" Rafn inquired without any warning.

"Huh?" *Now, that is a really intelligent answer.* "You overstep your bounds, Rafn."

"I know you are attracted to her . . . do not try to deny it. And, if I overstep my bounds, 'tis with good reason. I want to marry Vana. Five years I have been waiting for her. And the only thing standing in our way is Tyra."

"'Tis not my responsibility to pave the way for you two lovebirds."

"It may not be your responsibility, but if you intend to marry our lady, then I would appreciate knowing. Holy Thor, man, you would be saving Tyra's sisters and many Stoneheim warriors much heartbreak if you could take her away with you."

"That doesn't say much for Tyra, does it? She has been a fine chieftain to you all, in her father's stead, and how do you all show your thanks? By making her feel less than a woman . . . and less than a leader. Has anyone asked Tyra what she wants?"

There was a stunned silence in the room.

Finally Tykir noted, "You are defending the wench? Uh-oh. Sounds serious to me."

"I think I will write a saga about men who do not know what they want," Bolthor said.

"I think I will throw you in the moat," Adam replied.

"I think I would like to see you try," Bolthor countered.

"There is a famous proverb that goes like this: 'Sad is the man who searches the world over for brass and finds gold in his own tent.'"

"What the hell does that mean?" Adam snarled. Then, "Never mind." He turned on Rafn. "In answer to your question, I have no intention of marrying Tyra . . . or any other woman. I can understand perfectly how Tyra must feel, with everyone nagging at her all the time. I never wanted to return to medicine and here I am in the midst of a sickroom with ailing people lined up to who-knows-where. Picking, picking, picking at my bones. Now you want to start on me and marriage. Well, I have had more than enough. All of you, out of here and leave me in peace!"

Four men's jaws gaped open with shock at his outburst. But at least they got the message and left in stunned silence.

Once they were gone, Adam turned back to the bed. He could swear there was a smile on the old man's lips.

CHAPTER TEN

❦

Mischief and mayhem galore . . .

"You need to flirt," Vana told her.

"For the love of a troll! You came out to the exercise field to tell me that?"

"If you want the man, you have to take some drastic actions. Flirting, that would be my solution."

"What makes you think I want the man?" Tyra was wiping sweat off her brow with her forearm. Two hours of spear throwing and she still couldn't stop thinking about the rogue who had lured her to the stables. And that stupid kitten kept following her around. She'd had to lock it in the stable finally when it kept wandering onto the exercise fields, where it would have surely been speared.

Not that she cared about the mangy little cat. Even if it was named after her.

"Please, Tyra, give me some credit. You came back from the stables last night with your hair looking like a haystack, and Adam was no better. I do not mean to embarrass you, sister, but I swear there were whisker burns on your chest. And both of you were panting."

Oh . . . my . . . Valhalla!

Rafn was about to stroll by, a battle-ax in one hand and Alrek in the other. He carried the squirming boy by the scruff of his neck. Tyra didn't even want to know what Alrek had been doing now. Nor did she want to know where Thork, that wild son of Tykir and Alinor, was at the moment. What Alrek did not need was mischievous ideas planted in his head, and Thork was mischief himself. Mischief and Mayhem . . . that's what those two were. Bolthor ought to write a saga about them.

"Good day to you, Vana," Rafn drawled.

"Good day to you, Rafn," Vana drawled back at him.

Rafn winked at Vana.

Vana fluttered her blond eyelashes at Rafn.

Tyra was thinking seriously about tossing up the contents of her stomach.

Once Rafn was gone, Tyra told Vana, "If you think for one moment that I am going to start batting my eyelashes at a man like a mush-brained maid, then you are surely demented. Flirting! Hah! That is not in my nature."

"Tyra, Tyra, Tyra," Vana sighed. "Flirting is in every woman's nature. But it does not just have to be fluttering your eyelashes, though that always works for me. Try this sometime."

Tyra's eyes nigh bulged out at the sight of Vana pursing her lips. "What is that supposed to accomplish? You look like a puffy fish."

"Tsk-tsk! Open your mind to suggestions, Tyra. When a woman makes a moue of her mouth this way, men think of kissing."

"Are you sure they do not think of fishes . . . or that you have eaten a sour apple?"

"And you have got to stop that scratching business. Really, Tyra, what could you be thinking to engage in such a vulgar touching of your female parts?"

"Men do it."

"Aaarrgh! Are you even listening to me? I am trying to make you more womanly, not manly."

"Why?"

"Dost really need to ask that question? So you can seduce the man and get married so the rest of us can have lives of our own."

"In other words, the same old blather."

She could tell that Vana wanted to throw her hands in the air with disgust, but her sister took several deep breaths for patience. "One last thing . . . and, yea, I know I should not toss too many bits of feminine wisdom your way at once, but, Tyra, you must change your walk."

"My walk? What is wrong with my walk?"

"You swagger, dear. A woman should sway gracefully when she walks." Vana looked left and right, then picked up one of several bricks that Drifa had arranged around a newly planted cherry tree. "Watch this," Vana instructed. Then she placed the brick on her head, held her arms out from her body, and proceeded to walk a straight line, first in one direction, then back again. Vana did, indeed, appear graceful, and, blessed Thor, her hips did sway mightily.

"I could never do that," Tyra asserted.

"Yea, you could," Vana insisted, pushing the brick into Tyra's hand. "Practice."

Tyra had a hard time concentrating on spear throwing the rest of the morning when all she could see in her imagination was herself with a brick on her head. No, that wasn't all she saw. She also saw a too-handsome-to-be-true Saxon doctor with his mouth on her breast.

Could I really learn to flirt? And walk like a longship riding the waves? And purse my lips? Never! Never ever! Well, mayhap once. Nay, never, never, never!

Save me, Odin, she prayed.

But all she heard in her head was Loki laughing.

* * *

God spare him from pestsome friends . . .

Adam was headed toward the solar just before noon when he saw Tykir and Bolthor approaching him.

He'd sat with Thorvald for three solid hours, and not once had the king awakened, to Adam's dismay. So now he was off to treat some other patients.

"Adam, I want to give you a few bits of manly advice," Tykir said, walking along with him on the right. Bolthor matched his strides on the left side.

"Go away, Uncle."

"I have had many more years of experience with women than you have, and believe you me, the female animal is a difficult one to understand. You should listen to me," Tykir expounded.

"Go away, Uncle."

"Before Alinor, I had a reputation as a good lover. Even now, I am sure Alinor would vouch for me in that regard . . . if you catch her on a good day, that is."

"Except for that time you lost your knack," Bolthor reminded Tykir.

"Both of you, go away. I do not want or need your advice."

Tykir totally ignored his protests and blathered on. "We already know that you have mastered the art of kissing a maid witless, as evidenced by last night. And you already know the importance of catching a wench alone, also based on last night. You must act quickly to seduce the maid, in case her father awakens . . . in which case I see a forced marriage for compromising his daughter. Actually, whether the king lives or dies, your chances of landing in her bed furs are diminishing by the day."

Thank God they do not know about the pact I've made with Tyra. I will be in her bed furs, for sure. Well, I am fairly sure.

"We have decided that you must give Tyra more hot looks," Bolthor said.

"Who is *we*?"

Tykir waved a hand airily. "Me, Bolthor, Rafn, Rashid."

"You are all discussing my sex life amongst yourselves? Have you naught else to do with your time?"

"We care about you," Tykir said. And he probably meant it.

"I have written an advice-poem for you," Bolthor added. Already that dreamy expression covered the skald's face which indicated that another awful poem was about to burst from his lips.

Tykir was grinning at Adam's discomfort till Bolthor told him, "You could learn from this, too, Tykir."

Tykir blushed. He actually blushed.

"I call this one 'Manly Rules of Love.'

"Man is a witless creature
When it comes to women lore.
But the ancients do say
There is a way
To win your woman-prey.
Make her hot.
Kiss her a lot.
Win her with words,
Many compliments poured.
Then tease her with indifference,
Even if 'tis only pretense.
Touch her ofttimes in passing,
Soon her senses will be singing.
If all else fails . . .
Beg."

* * *

Who can explain sexual attraction? . . .

"Wait a moment, Tyra."

It was Adam who called out to her. Mortified by her behavior of the previous night, she had been avoiding him. He'd caught her now in the late afternoon as she was about to ride out with her men to survey their southern border where some scurvy Danes had been spotted eyeing a village outpost.

"What is it, Adam? I must make haste." She did not look at him as she spoke. If she did, she knew she would blush.

"Come, sit down here on this bench for a moment. I must needs speak with you about Alrek."

"Alrek?" Now, that was a surprise. She wasn't sure what she had expected Adam to say, but not this. "What has he done now?"

"Nothing. Well, he has done something . . . most recently, he rearranged all the pottery vials in my medical bag, and now Rashid must go through them all to decide which is which. But that is not why I beckoned you now."

Tyra looked at Adam, and that was a mistake. A big mistake. He was wearing a plain brown tunic today over plain brown *braies* with a plain brown leather belt, but in truth there was not an inch of this man that was plain. He was just the right height. He had just the right amount of muscle bulging at his arms and legs . . . and, well, other places she dared not even think about. And his face was a sculpture made by the gods. No man should be so fair of face.

But then she noticed something else. A small bite mark on his neck. From her? Well, who else?

"Alrek has an arrangement with your father whereby he trains to be a Viking and, in return, once a year he is given a silver coin."

"My father agreed to pay him for all his disasters?"

Adam shrugged. "The point is, the time has come for him to be paid. Your father is dead to the world, so to speak. And Alrek is in need of coin to support his family."

"We give him all he needs," she said with affront.

"Apparently not."

"Why did he not come to me?"

Adam shrugged again. "Pride."

"That is a lot of pride for a little boy."

"Pride knows no age, my lady . . . nor gender." He reached out and flicked a piece of lint off her tunic . . . which called to her mind other ways in which he had flicked her the night before. She fought it but could not curb the blush that heated her face again. Then, as if unaware that he had befuddled her senses once more, he went on, "I tried to give him a coin, but he would not accept it from me."

"What would you have me do?"

"Find a way to give him the coin without bruising his pride."

She nodded. She could do that. She wanted to do that. "You are a contradictory man, Adam."

"How so?"

"You are clearly annoyed by Alrek and his pestsome brood, and yet here you are, going out of your way on his behalf. You fight your fate mightily in regard to medicine, and yet you spent many hours today serving my people. You are a Saxon, and yet you have the spirit of a Viking."

"You are probably correct," he conceded, to her surprise, "but I can think of still other ways that I am riddled with contradictions. I mislike your mannish ways, and yet I like you. I do not want a permanent relationship with you, or any woman, and yet I sniff after you like a randy dog. I try my best to focus on your ill-mannered, masculine characteristics, but all I can see is the woman in you. Can you understand that?"

She could not.

But the woman in her did, and she exulted.

Tyra was walking away from him, and he was enjoying the event immensely.

In her tunic and tight *braies*, her hips swayed from side to side in the most enticing way. Did females have any idea how sensual their arses could be when viewed by the male from this angle? If they did, they would probably always back away from their men. He couldn't stop gaping.

"Tyra," he called out. "Why are you walking like that?"

She halted and looked back at him over his shoulder. "How?"

"Like . . . like you have a brick on your head."

"A brick?" she choked out, and turned to face him directly, though she was some distance away. He still sat on the bench. "That's ridiculous. A brick? Ha, ha, ha." Her face bloomed a lovely shade of pink, as if she were guilty of some wrongdoing.

A wrongdoing involving her walk? Nay, that could not be.

"It must be the chain mail I am wearing," she explained, still blushing profusely.

"Chain mail? Why are you wearing chain mail?" he asked, alarm ringing in his voice.

"I am off to check our borders with my men. Some Danish outlaws have been pillaging the area."

"Is it dangerous?"

"Of course it's dangerous."

"Don't go," he urged before he could bite his hasty tongue.

"Don't go? Are you demented? I must go. It is my job

as chieftain to lead my soldiers. How could you think otherwise?"

"I don't know." He just knew that he wanted her safe. He did not want to picture her lying on the ground covered with blood. He wanted her close by so that he could help her, if necessary. He wanted her . . . well, suffice it to say, he wanted her.

"What is that look you are giving me?"

"A look? What look?" He tried to recall what expression might have been on his face.

"A hot look."

He smiled then, especially when he remembered that Tykir and Bolthor and Rafn and Rashid had advised him to give Tyra just that—hot looks.

She was scowling at him, waiting for an answer.

Well, a hell of a lot of good their advice had done. Hot looks, indeed!

"Methinks I will go with you," he announced, again without thinking.

"You . . . will . . . not. Besides, what about the people who come to you for your services?"

"They can wait. Father Efrid is here . . . and Rashid."

"And my father?"

"He is getting better by the hour. *Surprisingly* better."

"You are not coming with me."

"I just want to protect you." Another hasty, blurted mistake, he realized immediately.

Now her scowling face was replaced with an angry face. "Dost question my competence, Saxon?"

"That is not what I meant." He stood and walked toward her.

"I know what this is about. You think because I showed a woman's weakness last night that suddenly I am less of a warrior. Well, think again." She was backing away from him as he approached. Putting up a hand, she said, "Don't come any closer. No more of your seduction ploys will you use on me."

"Ploys? What ploys?" Now he was offended. "Go! Go play your man-role, if you must. But do not dare get yourself killed, my lady, because . . . because . . ." He was so furious, he could not complete his sentence.

She tilted her head in question, and when he refused to finish, she turned and walked stiffly toward the groups of men and horses waiting for her. He noticed that there was not even the tiniest bit of sway to her walk now. *Damn it.*

Too late, he completed his sentence, but only to himself: ". . . because I care."

The news was not good.

When Tyra and her troops arrived at the small outpost village of Fagrfjord, the Danish outlaws had already come and gone. Apparently, news of her father's impending death had spread to their enemy camps, and the scurvy lot, led by Ejnar the Evil, had attacked, sensing an opportunity. They'd burned some timber longhouses, stolen cattle and sheep, taken a few women and children who were unable to run to the mountains, and killed a half dozen fighting men.

"Unless my father awakens soon and begins to show his face in public, this will be the first of many such strikes, and not just by Ejnar, either," Tyra told Rafn. "Every malcontent from here to Birka will be on the move, sniffing out any weakness in our flanks."

"You are correct, of course," Rafn said. "But we caught this raid early on. Now that we are forewarned, we will send reinforcements to man all of our vulnerable border lines. And, my lady, do not be fearful about your father's return to leadership. I *know* that he will recover and resume his overlordship of his land and his troops."

"Is there something you know and have not told me?" she asked, suddenly alert to the tone of his voice.

He shook his head quickly . . . too quickly . . . but Tyra had no time to ponder that now.

"Are you not concerned about Dragonstead?" Tyra asked Tykir, who had ridden along with them.

"Nay. Not really. I left two hundred soldiers back on my estate. The likes of Ejnar only attack where they sense weakness."

While Rafn and a small troop rode out in search of the culprits, she and Tykir and the other men-at-arms spent the next few hours putting out fires, setting up guards, feeding the poor cotters who had been under siege for more than a day, and tending to the wounded . . . some of whom would have to be brought back to Stoneheim for more expert ministrations.

It was late that night when they rode slowly back to Stoneheim, exhausted and somber of mood. Fagrfjord would be safe for now, but there was much to ponder regarding Stoneheim and its vast holdings. Ironically, outlaw Norsemen had no interest in the land itself, not this far north, because it was wild and much too difficult to cultivate, especially for lazy sluggards such as these malcontents. They were more interested in treasure, or animals, or people to trade into slavery, all of which Stoneheim had aplenty.

There was a full moon out tonight, and when the long line of her retinue made its way home, over the drawbridge and into the courtyard, she saw one thing clearly.

Adam.

He was waiting for her.

* * *

The wench was a constant worry . . .

It was close to midnight when Tyra's troop returned to Stoneheim.

Adam had been standing near the gate for more than three hours. He wasn't sure if he was more worried or angry.

There were wounded, he noticed, slung over saddles or lying in quickly constructed pole litters which trailed behind the horses. None of the men appeared to be Stoneheim warriors, as far as he could tell. More work for him, though, he presumed.

But where was Tyra? His heart beat frantically with panic. Was she left behind, too wounded to be moved? Or dead?

Please, God, not again!

Just then the line of troops parted and Tyra rode forward through the ranks. Tears of relief misted his eyes.

I should not care so much, he told himself. Then, *Thank you, God*.

When she started to dismount, her knees gave way—no doubt from the exhaustion of the long day—but he was there to catch her in his arms.

"Are you all right?" he whispered against her ear, still holding her upright in his arms. "Have you been hurt?"

She shook her head slowly from side to side, dazed.

"You will never do this to me again, that I swear."

"Do what?" She cocked her head with confusion.

"Leave me behind to worry, like a . . . like a . . ."

"Husband?" Tykir offered with a laugh as he rode his horse up next to them.

Adam knew he was acting foolishly, but his emotions were roiling out of control. Taking a deep breath to calm himself, he told Tyra, "We will discuss this later," and went off to join Father Efrid, who was already examining the wounded.

Almost immediately, he turned around, came back, and kissed her soundly on the lips. Then he was off again.

"Has he lost his mind?" he heard Tyra ask Tykir.

"Undoubtedly," Tykir said. "Either that, or his heart."

James Bond, he was not . . .

Even though it was not quite dawn, Alrek was humming a bawdy tune he'd heard some *drukkinn* soldiers sing one night. He was in the process of carrying a bucket of fresh drinking water into King Thorvald's bedchamber.

"Good day to you, boy," a rumbly voice said.

Alrek almost wet his *braies*, so frighted was he. Setting the bucket down on a bench, he glanced right and left, searching the room. He was the only person about, aside from the king, who was still in a deep sleep from his head wound.

Tentatively, he approached the bed.

The king's eyes shot wide open, and he winked at Alrek.

Alrek nigh jumped out of his skin.

"Yer highness!" he exclaimed. "Let me go call yer daughters and the physician. Thanks be to Odin, ye are back from the dead."

The king raised a halting hand. "Nay, I want no one to know that I am awake. Come here, boy, and help me."

When Alrek was next to the bed, the king threw the linens back, exposing a trencher made of manchet bread. On it sat two roast chicken legs, several hunks of hard cheese, and some slices of pickled reindeer tongue. Held between his knees was a huge wooden goblet of ale. "Are you as hungry as I am, Alrek?"

Alrek nodded. He was always hungry.

So at the king's bidding, Alrek locked the bedchamber door, then crawled up onto the bed with his king, and they both broke their fast together.

While they ate, the king remarked, "I owe you a coin about now, do I not, boy?"

He shook his head. "Yer daughter Tyra paid me. She denied it, but methinks Adam the Healer reminded her to pay me in yer stead. He is a good fellow, Adam is. Me hero, actually."

The king nodded, even as he chomped away on the ample, tasty fare. "That Ingrith of mine is a mighty fine cook. It will be a sad day when she weds and leaves Stoneheim . . . not that that will be happening anytime soon, the way Tyra dawdles in the marriage market. But that is going to change, if I have my way." The king was speaking more to himself than Alrek, who was too stunned by his circumstances to speak anyhow.

"So, Alrek, tell me everything that has been going on in my castle."

And Alrek did, leaving nothing out. The king was especially engrossed by the events surrounding Tyra and Adam, but he was also more than interested in the outlaws who'd attacked his holdings the night before. Alrek thought he heard the king mumble, "Rafn did not tell of this yet. Where is the man? Has he become a slugabed now?"

Alrek wasn't sure he'd heard right, so he withheld comment.

"I need your help, Alrek."

Alrek sat up straighter.

"Can I trust you?"

"With me life." Oh, this was the best day of Alrek's life. To think his king was going to trust him with some special assignment. "Shall I tell the smithy to make me a sword? Even the lowest knight needs his own sword to slit his enemy's gullet, or cut out his heart, or lop off his head. I do so want to lop off a head or two."

"Uh, I do not think a sword will be necessary just yet," the king said. A weak smile slashed his still ashen face. Mayhap the king was not as well yet as Adam had thought. "The task I would set for you requires a sharp mind, not a sharp blade."

Alrek tried to look intelligent and alert, but he feared he just looked bug-eyed.

"Firstly, you must tell no one—*no one*—that I have awakened."

He nodded his understanding.

"You must be my eyes and ears about the castle. Report everything to me, no matter how insignificant it might seem. Can you do that?"

"Yea, I can that. Am I to be yer spy, then?"

"Exactly."

Alrek stepped off the bed and rose to his full height, which wasn't all that much. *A spy! I am to be a spy. Praise the Gods! 'Tis just as Adam predicted back on the longship. Mayhap he made this miracle come true fer me. I should thank him, but nay, I cannot thank him properly because it is a secret. Still . . . me, a spy!* Alrek wiped the smile of pure joy from his face and tried to appear somber and responsible. "I will not let ye down, Yer Highness. Even if they torture me with burning splinters. Even if they chop off me ear. Even if they shave me head. Even if—"

"I don't think it will come to that," Thorvald said with lips that twitched oddly, as if he were suppressing a smile.

"Now, Alrek, summon Rafn for me. Do not tell him I called for him, especially if others are about. Just say that you must go to the garderobe or some such thing, and that you hate to leave your king alone."

Alrek kept nodding at each of the king's orders.

"And remember, this is *our* secret."

A hole in the head and a harem, too . . .

"It will be *our* secret," Tykir assured the king.

Rafn had summoned him to the king's bedchamber after spending some time there himself, asking if he would keep the sleeping king company whilst he prepared for the early morning patrol.

It appeared that the Stoneheim ruler had come out of his sleep state but wanted no one to know about it yet except Tykir, Thorvald always had been a wily man . . . and smart. Tykir was not about to question his motives.

"I want you to report back to me what you see around my keep," the king said. "It is important that I know not just what is happening with my men-at-arms and the Stoneheim cotters, but with my daughters, as well."

"Why not just ask them?"

"For shame, Tykir! Methought you knew better than that. Women never answer a question when it is put to them directly."

"I suppose."

"Now, what think you of a match betwixt my daughter Tyra and your nephew Adam?"

"'Tis not for me to say, Thorvald. It's what they want. I will say this: the sap of lust is running high in both of them."

The king clapped his hands gleefully. "Perfect! Perfect! All according to plan."

"What plan?" Tykir asked, wondering if the king had heard of the plan he and Rashid and Rafn and Bolthor had devised for Adam, but nay, that was impossible.

The king never answered him. Instead he ordered, "Send that rascal Rashid to me. Do not tell him I am awake. Just say it is his turn to sit a spell with the king."

"Why would you want the Arab here?"

"I have heard strange murmurings of a harem. A harem, indeed! There will be no harems at Stoneheim . . . unless they belong to me."

Seriously, a Viking harem? . . .

"So, tell me about your master, Rashid. What is he like?"

Rashid was honored to be taken into the king's confidence, especially since he was the only one the king had confided in.

"My master, Adam, is a good man. Honorable. But these last two years have been hard on him since he lost his sister. Before that, he was adventuresome, full of life and wit. Now, he is somber and reclusive. But methinks he is changing back to his old self, day by day."

"Thanks to my daughter?"

Rashid was surprised that the king knew so much about the developing relationship between Tyra and Adam—and it *was* developing, no matter how either of them protested. A person would have to be blind as well as deaf not to see that something was going on between those two.

"They fight the attraction mightily," he told the king, "but you know what they say, 'Lust is love's handmaiden.' "

"Huh?" Then he waved a hand as if it mattered not. "You will report back to me? You will be my eyes and ears? And you will keep my condition a secret?"

To all of these, Rashid nodded and replied, "I swear on the feet of Allah!"

But what he thought was, Tyra and Adam were in

way over their heads, and not just because lust was in the air, but because the king was putting his finger to the wind.

"Now, my Arab friend, tell me how one goes about setting up a harem."

CHAPTER ELEVEN

*B*etimes the dolt melted her with kindness . . .
    Tyra awakened just after dawn the next morning, prepared to ride off again with her horse *hersirs* to patrol the borders. She would go in one direction, and Rafn with an equal number of men on horseback would go in another. Two of the twenty longships in the harbor would also be dispatched to inspect the coastal and river shorelines. They were taking no chances of being caught unawares again.

The first thing she saw when she stepped outside her bedchamber was Adam leaning against the corridor wall, waiting for her. The second thing she saw was Warrior hissing and biting at Adam's boot. While the kitten had developed an attachment for her, she seemed to have developed an aversion to Adam. Vana would have a hissing fit if she saw the cat in the keep.

"You are *not* coming with me," she asserted before he could even speak. Still angry with him for his words and actions of the previous night, she began to walk away toward the steps that led to the great hall.

He fell into step beside her, then took her by the arm and drew her to a halt. Warrior trailed behind them. "Not so fast, my bloodthirsty lady. Do not attempt to read my mind, for it is deep and hard to fathom."

She stood still and faced him, waiting for him to elaborate.

"You are wearing metal, aren't you?"

"Of course, I am wearing a chain mail *shert* under my tunic. Do you object to that, too?"

He shook his head sadly. "Nay. If you must ride like an Amazon warrior into danger, 'tis best that you are protected." He hesitated, then reached behind him and handed her a silver-embossed shield with a crest of writhing wolves. "Here. Take this with you . . . for luck. It is mine."

It was a fine piece of armory, but that was not why she was so stunned. It appeared she had jumped to the wrong conclusion. "You did not come this morn to chastise me again for my warlike ways, did you?"

He shook his head.

"You did not come to insist that you accompany me, either, did you?"

He shook his head again, then smiled, but the smile did not quite meet his eyes. "Actually, I probably would have . . . chastised and insisted . . . except that Dagma the dairymaid has chosen today to bring forth her first child, and it is a difficult delivery."

Dagma was only fourteen years old, and her pregnancy was the result of a rape the previous winter by a passing tradesman. The man had been executed Viking-style, but that did not help Dagma and her predicament.

Just then Tyra noticed the dark circles under Adam's eyes. "You have been up all night with Dagma, haven't you?"

He nodded.

'Twould seem she had misjudged Adam in many regards. "Will she be all right?"

" 'Tis hard to say. The girl has a child's slim hips, and

the babe is overlarge. Moreover, she has been laboring for a full fifteen hours already, to no avail." He shrugged. "God willing, she will survive."

Tyra could tell that Adam cared more than he was saying. "I'm sorry you are set in the midst of this. I know you did not want to resume your medical practice, and here you are, not just treating my father, but everyone else as well. You do not have to help Dagma. Let the midwife care for her . . . or Father Efrid."

"I must."

She frowned her confusion.

"I promised Dagma I would stay with her to the end."

"And your promises are solid as rock."

"Even rocks can be broken, and I have not always lived up to my promises in the past, my lady. Do not set me on a pedestal where I do not belong."

Tyra recalled then what Rashid had told her about Adam and his dead sister, Adela. Her heart went out to Adam, but she knew his pride was great, and he would not appreciate any overt sign of her pity.

"Should you not be with Dagma now?"

He nodded. "The babe will not come for several hours yet, though the birthing canal has finally started to open."

"So be it. I wish you well, physician."

"And I wish you well, soldier."

They nodded at each other.

Their conversation was presumably ended, but they both stood staring at one another.

Finally he said, "We are so different. You let blood, I stanch blood."

"There is no future together for the likes of us," she agreed, reading his inner meaning. But then she asked, "Have you never killed anyone, Adam?"

He stared at her for a long moment. "I have."

"More than once?"

He laughed grimly. "Yea, Tyra, more than once, and I did not like it any more the second and third and fourth time than the first."

"I do not enjoy it either, you know, but it is a fact of my life."

"I do not judge you, Tyra. I really don't. It's just that I have chosen a different path."

She nodded her understanding. "And so you will never take a life again."

"I did not say that."

She arched her brows in question.

"If I needed to defend myself, I would fight to the death. If the lives of Tykir and Alinor, Eirik and Eadyth, or their families were in jeopardy, I would not hesitate to take up the sword." He reached out a hand to her chin and raised it so that she would meet his gaze. "I would kill in a trice to save you."

Tyra was touched by his regard, but the fact remained that they were opposites. She sighed at the hopelessness of the attraction that thrummed between them.

"Will you take my shield Brave Wolf as a token?" Adam asked, looking down at the shield that she still held in her right hand. "It belonged to my grandfather, Dar. He claimed it carried much battle luck."

"I will be honored to carry it, Adam." The words came out hoarse over the lump in her throat.

He leaned forward, kissed her lightly, and whispered against her mouth, "Be safe."

Then he was gone.

But not from Tyra's mind . . . or heart.

It was a smelly, stinksome business . . .

Ingrith sniffed the air that morning, noticed the frost

on the herbs in her kitchen garden and a few snow flurries in the sky. Clear signs that winter was almost here.

Satisfied, she gave a hearty shout of "Butchering day!" in the great hall where everyone was breaking fast.

She was not the least deterred by the equally hearty communal groan, nor by the few youthlings who attempted futilely to escape.

Tyra and Rafn and a hundred soldiers were off on patrol. Adam and Rashid were engaged in doctoring duties. But everyone else was forced to heed Ingrith's call to arms.

It was only early October, but already there was frost on the ground at night. Soon the days would grow shorter. In fact, this far north, there were long periods of time when daylight appeared only one or two hours a day. And so frigid cold was it that a person could not venture outdoors unless they were covered with numerous layers of furs.

It was a harsh land, but one which suited the Vikings well.

Throughout that day, everyone at Stoneheim, regardless of age, except for the guardsmen on duty, was enlisted to help with the fall butchering of the pigs . . . one hundred fat acorn-fed hogs. Eventually, the animals would hang by their tied hind legs from long poles suspended across tripods, which had been constructed by Breanne. The poles extended the length of one of the far fields. Huge cauldrons of boiling water were ready to scald the skin for scraping, then to make the various dishes that would be savored on winter nights far distant.

A gruesome, smelly process it was, but one of many that were necessary for their survival during the winter months. Hay was already stored for winter silage. Massive amounts of wood had been cut to fuel the many hearths. Fruit and vegetables had been preserved. Hundreds of fish had been dried or salted. There were many other jobs to be done before snow and ice cut them off from the rest of the world, but the hog butchering could not wait.

By the end of the long day, every part of the hogs was put to good use, even the tongues and brains. The skins would be dried for leather. Hams, shoulders, and sides were cut and salted away in the smokehouse. The ears, head, and feet were boiled for many hours, then chopped and put back into the liquid to gel and be sliced into a delicacy called souse . . . an acquired taste, some said. Intestines and the stomach were cleaned and used to make sausages. Rendered lard that settled on the top of the boiling liquids was scraped off to be saved for cooking or making soap.

The air was decidedly cold that day, but the people were hot, sweat dripping off their faces and arms. By the end of the afternoon, everyone was satisfied with a job well done, but they were dirty and greasy, men, women and children alike.

Because of the large number of people who required a bath, the bathing house and sweat rooms were set aside first for the women's use, then the men's.

It was there that Ingrith finally rested her weary bones next to Breanne, Vana, and Drifa, along with Lady Alinor. Naked, the women sat up to their necks in the bubbling, steamy water of the natural spring that came up from the ground into the stone pools. Later, after they'd soaped themselves off, they would move to the clear, cool water of the pool in the next room. There was also a separate steam house for those who were interested.

"And so, one job completed. What shall we do about the next one?" Ingrith asked with a long sigh of contentment.

"Please, Ingrith. If you suggest another butchering job, like cattle, I think I may vomit," Breanne said.

Ingrith laughed. "Nay, this is a task of another nature altogether. *Tyra.*"

"Aaaahhhh!" the other ladies said.

"I recommend we skip ahead to the last step of our plan. Jealousy. Adam has got to do something to make Tyra jealous," Vana suggested. "But we cannot go to him for help. He is as bad as she is."

"I know, I know," Drifa said. "I can do it!"

"You?" the other ladies asked skeptically.

"Me! Really, it will be perfect. I will go to Adam to discuss my flowers and plants. I will ask for his advice on ways to use my herbs for medicinal purposes. Actually, I have wanted to do so for some time anyway. And then I can mention in passing to Tyra that since she is not interested in any lasting relationship with the man, then I am setting my cap for him. What think you?"

"It could work." Alinor tapped her chin thoughtfully. "I must go find my babe, and I must find Thork and have him eat soap for the new word he has been teaching all the children of Stoneheim today, but let me add this thought. Women have swarmed around Adam all his life. Tyra can see he is an attractive man. To be jealous, she must believe that Adam returns the attraction. So Drifa's suggestion may work. Adam loves to talk about his herbs and he will appear interested." At the sound of a squalling babe in the adjoining room, Alinor rose from the waters, her breasts heavy with milk, and grabbed for a robe.

"I could keep offering him tasty bits of food," Ingrith offered. "You know, show him preferential treatment."

"And I could ask for his advice in building a hospitium here at Stoneheim," Breanne said. "I know he would talk in earnest with me about that. Tyra would not have to know the subject of our conversation."

Everyone nodded.

Vana asked, "What can I do?"

"Nothing," the others agreed. "Tyra would never believe you have eyes for Adam when Rafn is anywhere about."

"Well, then, do you think we should engage any other women to help in our cause?" Vana asked, not at all perturbed by their assessment of her value in the jealousy scheme.

The four of them thought for a long moment.

"'Tis best that we keep this amongst ourselves," Ingrith said, and all concurred, especially when she added, "'Tis our secret."

Like minds and all that . . .

"I'm thinking that perhaps it is time to go home to Dragonstead," Tykir told Bolthor as they rode back to Stoneheim. The patrols had finished early and should be back enjoying a horn of ale by late afternoon. "I am getting too old for this nonsense. Riding hither and yon, freezing my nose and toes and possibly other more important body parts. Pretending to be having a grand time when I would much rather put my feet up before the fire and bounce my little one on my knees."

"You are not yet a graybeard, my friend. Nor am I . . . though you do have five years on me, now that I think on it."

Tykir reached over and punched Bolthor on the upper arm, even as they rode side by side. The skald winced as if he'd been hurt, which was impossible with all the furs he wore. In truth, Tykir would never do anything to harm the man. Despite Tykir's complaining about always having the inept poet at his side, Bolthor had been a good and true friend through the years.

Unaware of Tykir's rambling thoughts, Bolthor continued the discussion of Tykir's discontent. "Methinks you are just frustrated with your nephew. You are not a man accustomed to defeat, and thus far Adam has not jumped into the wench's bed furs, as you had hoped."

"Mayhap you are right. Am I an interfering busybody just because I want to see the boy happy?"

"He is no longer a boy, Tykir. He can make his own decisions."

"Hah! Two years of chastity! What kind of decision is that? Grief must have turned the boy barmy. And that Arab is no help. Trying to set up a harem for him! Adam needs a bedmate, not a litter."

"Do my ears play me false?" Rafn said, trotting his horse up so that they rode three abreast. "You are going to leave Stoneheim, with all these matters unresolved? I thought we had a plan, did we not . . . a seduction plan for Adam?" He had been riding behind Tykir and Bolthor on the wide fjordside path leading to Stoneheim, along with several dozen other soldiers. And he'd obviously been eavesdropping on their conversation. "If you people leave now, I am condemned to remaining unmarried. Vana and I will never wed. I will no doubt have to live the chaste life as Adam does, except in my case it will be forever."

Tykir had to smile at Rafn's doleful tone. "What would you have us do, Rafn?"

"We cannot just give up. What is the next step in the plan, Bolthor?"

"Hmmm. Let me think," Bolthor said. "First was hot looks, and Adam gave her those aplenty when she showed up in that crimson dress. Second was compliments. I daresay he tossed a few compliments her way, too, if his tongue was not tied into a twist. Third, methinks, was jealousy."

"That's it!" Rafn exclaimed. "We will make Adam jealous by having various men pay special attention to his lady."

"Which various men?" Tykir wanted to know. "I hardly think anyone would believe *you* are interested in Tyra when your tongue hangs out every time Vana enters a room."

"I resent your insinuation," Rafn said, but he was grinning as he spoke.

"And Bolthor is not a believable suitor, either." Tykir appeared to be thinking out loud.

"And why not?" Bolthor sat up straight in the saddle and puffed his massive chest out.

"Well, perchance I spoke too fast. You could pay her special attention, Bolthor, but we must have more than one man to make Adam jealous."

"Leave it to me," Rafn advised. "I will line up several of my soldiers. They will be glad to do me the favor, and if Tyra wears garb like that wicked-to-the-bone crimson gown again, I will not even have to pay them. They will court her on their own."

"So it is agreed, then. Step three of the plan. We can't lose this time."

What Tykir thought inside, though, was, *Dumb, dumb, dumb. We are dumber than dirt, as Alinor would say. Bloody hell, I hope she never hears of this.*

Who knew flirting was so much trouble? . . .

I must be losing my mind, Tyra thought.

Why else would she have donned the scandalous red gown again tonight? Why else would she have taken special care with her hair, letting it hang loose down her back except for thin braids on either side. Why else would she have used Ingrith's scented soap causing her to reek of roses? Why else would she have searched and searched through her chests till she found a pair of soft slippers to fit her big feet? Why else would she have chewed on mint leaves to freshen her breath?

On the way down to the hall where the evening meal would soon be served, Tyra stopped in her father's bed-chamber.

"Any change?" she whispered to Father Efrid, who was counting his rosary.

He shook his head. "He awakened not at all today, and we were unable to force any gruel down his throat, either. One time, I could swear, he spit it out. 'Tis almost as if his stomach is full . . . which is impossible, of course."

"What does Adam say?"

"He does not say it outright, but the message is there nonetheless. The longer it takes your father to awaken, the less chance there is for recovery. In truth, I think the healer fears brain damage."

"Br-brain damage?" she stammered. "You mean Father might be like Igor, the village idiot?"

The monk nodded, a gloomy expression on his face.

Tyra could have sworn she heard a snorting sound from the bed, but when she and Father Efrid glanced that way, the king was dead asleep.

She sat down on the edge of the mattress and took her father's hand in hers. Ignoring the priest's presence, she began to speak to Thorvald, hoping he would be able to hear her.

"I have made a decision, Father. I will be leaving Stoneheim soon . . . certainly before the fjords freeze over. I hope you will awaken before then so that we can say our farewells in person. But even if you do not, Rafn can take over as chieftain in my . . . your stead. It is time, Father. Past time."

She could have sworn her father's hand jerked in hers. Mayhap he did hear her. She hoped so.

By the time she reached the great hall, she had wiped the melancholy tears from her eyes. Dinner was already being served, and what a lot of pork it was, too.

No sooner did she enter the hall than Gunter Storrsson walked up to her. Gunter was one of the best swordsmen at Stoneheim and a favorite amongst the ladies because of his blond good looks. Tonight he had glass beads woven in the war braids that hung on either side of his fair face. Maids would be fighting amongst themselves to share his bed furs later.

"Wouldst care to join me for a cup of ale?" Gunter inquired, taking her by the elbow as if to lead her to his table.

"Huh?" Gunter Storrsson had never shown the least interest in her in all the years she had known him, which was practically since birth.

"You are looking especially lovely this eve," he said smoothly, seating her next to him on a bench.

"What a crock of *skyr!* Is this a jest, Gunter?"

"'Tis true, my lady. You are a vision of loveliness. Far more lovely than the brightest flower in Drifa's gardens." The whole time he spoke, his eyes were nigh plastered to her chest.

"Stop staring at my breasts," she admonished. 'Twas best to be blunt with a too-bold man. Set him straight from the start.

Gunter started to choke on his ale.

"You, too, Egil," she said to the soldier across the table. She took a sip of the strong ale and continued, "Blessed Freyja! You men act as if you've never seen a pair of teats afore, and I know good and well that you have. All of you lackwits have been drooling over Inga the chambermaid for years and all because her breasts are the size of cow udders. Never mind that her brain is the size of a pimple."

Egil started to choke, too.

Just then her gaze wandered to the high dais where Drifa was sitting in a chair next to Adam. They had their heads together, discussing some matter intently. Every so often, he would laugh, or she would giggle. And the whole time, Drifa had a hand laid on his forearm.

Can it be? Is Drifa flirting with my man?

Aaarrgh! Adam is not my man. I have no man. Certainly not Adam.

And the healer . . . has he now developed an affection for my sister? Has he no morals at all?

A wave of overpowering emotion swept through Tyra. Although she had never felt it before, she recognized it instantly. Jealousy. She wanted to leap over the tables and get to the dais, where her greatest desire was to pummel Adam, the rogue, and to toss Drifa, the flirt, out into one of her flower beds.

Despite her jealousy, Tyra had to admit that Adam and Drifa looked good together. Two beautiful, dark-haired people. He, godly handsome. She, with her exotic appeal.

"If they have dancing tonight, willst thou partner me?"

Tyra turned to Gunter, who'd apparently been talking to her the whole time she had been staring daggers at Adam and her sister. "Why would you want to dance with me?"

"You are a very attractive woman, Tyra. Surely you are aware of that." He had the nerve then to place his palm on her thigh and squeeze.

"You never thought so before." She firmly removed his hand from her thigh.

He shrugged and gave her his most winsome smile . . .

the selfsame one she'd seen him giving to Drifa during last summer's Frigg Festival. *Drifa*, she thought. *Mayhap two people can play at this game. But dare I flirt with a man? Do I even know how to flirt with a man? Well, how hard could it be?*

"You have a very nice smile, Gunter." She leaned in close as she spoke, and batted her eyelashes at him as she'd seen her sisters do. She felt absolutely ridiculous doing so, but the most amazing thing happened. Gunter placed a hand over hers on the table.

"Dost think so?" he asked in a husky voice.

Well, for the love of Valhalla! Is he going husky over me? And what a barmy smile!

"Yea, your smile is bright and . . . and . . . big." *Big? Now that is a really half-brained compliment . . . even for me.*

Egil snickered.

Gunter simpered. "There are other parts of me that are big, too," he answered, waggling his eyebrows suggestively at her.

Does he mean what I think he means? Hah! I know exactly how big IT is. I've seen it on more than one occasion while the men bathed in river streams on our journeys. How does one respond to such an outrageous statement?

"Well, aren't you lucky!"

"Nay, 'tis my women who are lucky." He waggled his eyebrows at her some more.

The oaf made the mistake of placing his hand on her thigh again and squeezing.

To reciprocate, she placed her hand on the giant worm lying at rest between his legs and squeezed, really hard.

Gunter's eyes crossed as he tried to speak but could not.

Really, this flirting business is a lot of botherment.

Why can't people just say what they think? "Do you want to bed with me?" she asked bluntly.

His face went all red and flustered. Apparently *his women* were not so forthright in their dealings with him. Or perchance he was all red and flustered because of the "caress" she'd given his cock. "Well, yea, I guess I do."

"Nay."

"Nay?"

"You heard me. I said nay. Nay, nay, nay! You are behaving very strangely tonight, Gunter. Methinks you ought to see the healer for a tonic."

Just then she looked up to the dais where the healer had risen from his seat and was glaring at her and Gunter, as if he'd like to leap over the tables and pummel Gunter and toss her . . . somewhere.

The most outrageous idea came unbidden to her then. Could Adam be jealous of her?

She studied him more carefully, especially when he rose from his seat and began making his way doggedly in her direction. Thinking quickly, she tugged the bodice of her gown lower, leaned slightly forward across the table, and asked Egil, "And how are your male parts?"

Not a bad start for a first lesson in flirtation, Tyra thought, giving herself a mental pat on the back.

And the gurgling sounds Gunter and Egil were making . . . well, she chose to translate those as compliments . . . even if only to her bosom.

"What in bloody hell do you think you are doing?" Adam asked when he reached their table. His eyes were plastered on her bosom, too. *Really, I am living in a world of lustsome louts.*

"Flirting," she answered honestly. "How about you?"

CHAPTER TWELVE

❧

Oh, the games lovers play! . . .

"Go right ahead, Tyra. Quaff down another horn of ale. But do not come to me later for an ale-head remedy."

She made the most ridiculous yet enchanting face at him, which involved deep inhaling and exhaling and puffing out her cheeks . . . and drank some more.

"And whilst you are at it, take another deep breath like that, and you will be giving me and the rest of the world a full-blown view of your bare breasts."

For some reason, Adam had taken a proprietary interest in Tyra's breasts. He knew he was being unreasonable, but he did not like other men gazing upon what he considered his. In truth, jealousy was the least confusing of the emotions assailing Adam at the moment. Inner conflicts battered him at every turn.

He was repulsed by the idea of a woman who spilled blood for her life's work. But he was attracted beyond all reason to Tyra, despite her being a warrior . . . or mayhap even because she was a warrior. Who could explain his splintering mind?

He wanted no lasting relationship with any woman. That would mean staying in one place, having children, responsibilities, a firm idea of where his future lay. Whereas he could scarce take care of himself these days, let alone a bothersome female and even more bothersome children, like Alrek and his siblings.

He wasn't sure he wanted to engage in the healing arts anymore, and yet here he was, seeing patients left and right. The decision seemed to have been taken out of his hands.

And that was the whole problem. He had lost control of his life. An untenable situation! A man should steer his own destiny . . . not a dying king, an interfering uncle, an outrageous warrior princess, an Arab insistent on giving him a harem, or a brood of bothersome bratlings.

"You certainly are in a grumbly mood," Tyra responded to his tirade.

By now he'd forgotten what he'd said to make her think he was in a bad mood. Or was he just frowning overmuch?

"I thought you liked this gown."

Oh, *that* bad mood. "I adore your gown. I especially adore what is nigh hanging out of it. Must you show it to one and all?"

She narrowed her eyes at him. Then she did what he should have expected . . . the exact opposite of what he'd suggested. She put both hands on the fabric at her waist and tugged downward.

"Bloody . . . damn . . . hell!"

Now the neckline of her crimson, wanton gown barely—just barely—covered the nipples and areolas of her breasts. He could not bring himself to glance out at the hall, but it was his guess that wagers were being placed all over the place: Would she or wouldn't she? Pop out of the gown, that is.

"So, have you taken Drifa out to the stables yet to practice your wicked wiles?"

"What?" he practically squawked. *Where did that question come from? I did not even know I had wicked wiles in my repertoire. Well, mayhap I did know, but I hardly expected others to notice.*

"You heard me, Saxon. I saw the two of you with your heads together, exchanging simpering smiles."

Simpering? I do not simper when I smile. I definitely do not simper. Except mayhap when I look at you. Oh, I hope I do not simper when I look at you. He set a very serious expression on his face and looked at Tyra.

"What were you and Drifa talking about? Kisses? Bed furs? Her beauty?"

"Herbs." He grinned at her, finally understanding Tyra's seemingly irrelevant questions. The warrior princess was jealous of his conversation with Drifa.

"Herbs?"

"Yea, she wants me to read my herb journals to her so that she can try transplanting some wild plants into her gardens for medicinal purposes. We arranged to meet tomorrow morn for just that purpose. You could join us, but I expect you will be off doing warlike things. Lopping off heads and such." He flashed another grin her way, just to irritate her. A grin, not a simper.

"Adam, would you care to try a new delicacy I have invented . . . pig's gizzards in dill sauce?" Ingrith had just come up and was holding out a small tray toward him, which held a hollow manchet loaf containing the concoction.

Tyra took the small knife from the shield at her waist and was about to spear one for herself when Ingrith smacked her hand. "They are not for you, sister. They are for Adam to try." She smiled coyly at him. "I made some honey and walnut cakes for you, too, which are still cooling. They are a favorite of yours, are they not?"

"Huh?" he and Tyra said at the same time.

If he didn't know better, he would think Ingrith was flirting with him.

"Why are you flirting with him?" Tyra asked.

No one could accuse Tyra of beating around the bush.

"Well, why not? You do not seem particularly interested. I assumed he was fair game. And Drifa said he is ever so nice."

Fair game? Me? Nice? He wasn't so sure about being considered nice, but he rather liked the concept of being fair game. So he puffed out his chest and smiled warmly at Ingrith. He made sure it was a smile, not a simper.

Tyra used one of her big feet to stomp on his toes and murmured something about, "Lecherous, loathsome lout."

"Ouch!" he said, pulling his booted foot up to rest on his knee and rubbing it with great exaggeration.

Just then Breanne walked up and sat down in the empty chair on his other side.

"Adam, I need your advice."

Tyra made a most unflattering, masculine-sounding snort on his other side. She'd better not scratch her groin. He could not bear to picture her in the gown, which was temptation itself, performing lewd manly gestures.

He cocked his head, indicating Breanne should elaborate.

"I have been thinking about building a hospitium here at Stoneheim. What think you of the idea?"

"Do you have someone to man it for you?"

She batted her eyelashes at him.

Good Lord, another of Tyra's sisters flirting with me! What is going on here? "If Father Efrid and the midwife are willing to work in it, then I think it is a wonderful idea. I will not be here much longer, though." He wanted to make it absolutely clear to one and all that his stay at Stoneheim had not been his idea to begin with, and it would end as soon as King Thorvald recovered . . . or died.

"Planning on going somewhere, Saxon?" Tyra asked, slurring her words.

"Exactly how many horns of ale have you drunk?"

"Not enough, apparently. I can still see your leering face."

Leering? First she says I simper, now I leer. The ale must be affecting her perceptions. 'Tis past time for me to take the offensive here. "Nay, I am not going anywhere soon . . . leastways, not till a certain pact is fulfilled." He watched with great satisfaction as her face bloomed with color.

Then he turned his back on Tyra and began to discuss the potential hospitium project with Breanne in earnest. They ate and talked at the same time . . . about the size of the building, examining tables, chests, windows, its location . . . over dozens of dishes, each more elaborate or tasty than the previous ones. Ingrith truly was an artisan in the kitchen. Breanne was an artisan in her own way, and brilliant of mind. Not to mention being beautiful, both of them . . . Ingrith with her Norse blondness and Breanne with her redheaded Irish good looks.

It was some time before Adam turned back to Tyra, only to realize that the meal was over and the entertainment about to begin . . . and that Tyra had collected her own set of admirers. She was flirting, like her sisters, except not with him. *Dammit!*

A Viking soldier by the name of Gunter, reputed to be the best swordsman in all Norway, was tugging on one of her war braids, teasing her about some saucy remark she'd made earlier. The maids all swooned when Gunter walked by, but he was too pretty by half for a man, if you asked Adam . . . which nobody did of course.

Egil Iversson, another noted warrior, was asking her if she'd like to take a stroll with him about the ramparts. Egil's *braies* were so tight you could see his prodigious maleparts. He was wearing an enlarged codpiece, no doubt. Beware of men in tight *braies*, that was Adam's philosophy, which he would pass on to his daughters someday, if he ever had any daughters. Or mayhap he would pass it on to Tyra . . . once he was within ducking distance. Adam decided to follow Tyra's suit and downed a horn of ale in one long swallow. He felt it all the way to his toes.

"Really, Tyra, you should come for a stroll with me," Egil was saying. "There is something interesting I would like to show you."

I'll bet there is. What kind of stroll does the filthy fornicator have in mind? 'Tis dark outside. And cold. I hope he freezes off his . . . codpiece.

"Nay, Tyra cannot go strolling with you. She promised to dance with me later." 'Twas Gunter the Peacock speaking now.

"I did?" Tyra appeared a bit disoriented, whether from the ale or the male attentions he could not tell.

Both men's eyes kept straying to Tyra's exposed bosom.

Adam tightened his fingers on the wooden arms of his chair to prevent himself from drawing his sword, which he'd unfortunately left back in his bedchamber . . . or perhaps fortunately.

"What kind of saucy remark did you make, Tyra?" he asked casually.

"She asked if I wanted to couple with her," Gunter revealed in a gloating fashion.

"Also, she made an astute observation about the size of a woman's breasts compared to the size of her brain," Egil added.

Both men were still staring at her chest.

I have heard enough!

Apparently, not enough, for Bolthor came up just then and gave Tyra an adoring look from his one good eye. The giant skald looking adoring was a sight to behold . . . rather like a one-eyed randy bear.

"I have a gift for you, my lady."

"For me?" Even Tyra appeared startled by Bolthor's interest.

The poet nodded his head vigorously. "A praise-poem, written just for you. Wouldst like to hear it?"

Nay, nay, nay!

"Well, of course, Bolthor." He would have liked to shake Tyra thoroughly, but her breasts would undoubtedly pop out.

"This saga is called 'Lady in the Red Gown.'"

Uh-oh!

*"There once was a lady fair
Whose love no man could snare.
All her beauty she did hide
Under male garb of leather dried.
A sword she did carry,
In battle she did tarry.
Methinks the lady knew not her worth
Till the day a crimson gown came forth.
Then the lady did bloom,
Like the finest peacock plume.
Now the lady gets her pick
Of all the men lovesick.
But she best not too quickly stir
Or she will have a spillover,*

And more suitors than she would prefer.
Praise be to Tyra, Warrior Princess
And her crimson dress."

"That was truly awful," Tyra murmured under her breath. But to Bolthor she said, "That was wonderful."

"Would you like another?" He was gazing at her like a moonstruck calf.

"Perhaps later," she said graciously. "Right now, methinks Ingrith is in need of a good saga. She is in the scullery, I believe, overtired from preparing this fine meal. Dost think you could cheer her up?"

Bolthor's one eye lit up as if he'd just been handed a great treasure. "I know just the one. 'Praise Be to Pork.'"

Well, Bolthor's saga-saying had accomplished one thing, to Adam's mind. Gunter and Egil were nowhere to be seen . . . for now, leastways. Adam had feared having to challenge them to a duel, or some such gruesome feat of challenge.

"You certainly handled Bolthor well," Adam congratulated Tyra, trying for a pleasant tone.

"Go away," she replied.

That rules out pleasantries. Apparently, she was still upset with him, and he couldn't even remember why. Oh, now he recalled. She thought he was flirting with her sisters.

"Tyra, dearling, I have no interest in your sisters."

"Do I look as if I care? And do not call me dearling."

"Yea, you do . . . dearling."

"Well, I don't. And stop, stop, stop with the endearments. It makes me feel as if I am just one of your women."

"Women! For pity's sake, Tyra, you already know, thanks to Rashid's flapping tongue, that I have been chaste for two years. So, no women!"

"You can still *have* women without tupping them," she persisted.

"I would like to bloody well know how," he muttered. Best to change the subject. "It would be nice if you would reciprocate now, and say that you have no real interest in Gunter or Egil . . . or Bolthor."

"I do have an interest in them. A huge interest."

His shoulders sagged. "Why must you always be at cross-wills with me, wench? Can't you be biddable just this once?"

"In fact, I have decided to share my bed furs with them."

"All at one time?" he asked, barely stifling a laugh at her ludicrous lies.

Her eyes went wide. Obviously, she had no idea what she might do with three men in her bed furs at one time.

So, of course, he told her.

Her jaw dropped.

"Can we start over? Why don't you say something saucy to me like you did to Gunter and Egil? 'Tis unfair for you to say saucy things to other men and not me."

She said something so vulgar and outrageous that he was speechless for a moment. It took saucy to a new level. He was spared having to react because of the shuffle of chairs and tables. Thank God! An entertainment had been planned for that evening. An open space was being created in front of the dais by moving the trestle tables and benches to the outer edges of the hall.

A number of people moved up to the dais—all the sisters, Rafn, Bolthor, Tykir, Alinor, and their oldest son, Thork. It was a better vantage point for watching, but there were not enough chairs. Tykir lifted Alinor onto his lap, resulting in a little shriek from her before she nestled sweetly into his embrace, and he motioned for Thork to sit at their feet, thus emptying a chair. Thork was being punished for his wild shenanigans that day. Rafn sank into the empty chair and pulled Vana onto his lap. Vana just sighed, not even bothering to protest.

Do I dare? Adam wondered, casting a sideways glance at Tyra.

Bloody hell, do I dare not? he countered to himself, even as he stood, picked up Tyra by the waist, then sat back down with her straddling his lap, her back to his chest. Breanne immediately took the vacated seat, with Drifa and Ingrith sitting on either arm. The three of them smiled their thanks at him.

"You brute!" Tyra tried to squirm away, to no avail. He had both arms wrapped firmly around her waist, and the table blocked her from the front.

"Keep squirming, wench. It gives me a good view of your nipples," he said into her ear.

She immediately stilled and looked downward . . . then groaned. "Did everyone else see, too?" she asked in a mortified whisper.

"Nay, just me. And very nice nipples they are, too."

She tried to pry his hands off her waist, but he held tight, like a vise.

"I ought to cut off your fingers with my dagger."

"If you did that, I would be unable to finger-pleasure you."

That certainly caught her attention. He could practically hear her brain pondering what he'd just said. "What . . . what is finger-pleasuring?" she finally choked out.

He had no idea, that word being a sudden inspiration of his. Well, actually, he could imagine what it might be. But words would do it no justice. That kind of erotic wisdom deserved a demonstration. So, while he still held on tightly to her with his left hand, he deftly slipped his right hand under the hem of her gown onto the bare skin of her leg.

"Oh." That was her only response. He was fairly certain she liked it if her soft sigh of delight was any indication . . . and the fact that she didn't chop off his fingers.

Because of the table, the dim light, and the fact that all eyes were on Agnis, the young maid singing and playing the lute, no one noticed what Adam was about.

His hand was only on her calf, but she went stiff as a pike.

Deliberately he spread his knees, which caused her knees to spread as well. He had her exactly where he wanted her . . . on his lap, and exposed.

"You cannot," she said as his hand moved in a slow caress from her calf to her knee, then up, up, up to her thigh.

"I can," he countered, and moved his hand from her outer thigh to her inner thigh. With just his fingertips, he lightly caressed her inner thighs in slow circles, from knees almost to her woman's fleece. Up one thigh, down the other, up one thigh, down the other.

Not only was she stiff as a pike now, but she was holding her breath.

"When I caress you here, do your breasts begin to ache?"

She nodded, to his surprise. He had not expected such honesty.

"Do you feel a throbbing here . . . as I do?" He put the heel of his hand against that lowest portion of her belly, just above the pubic bone.

She released her pent-up breath and tried to hold his hand there, through the cloth of her gown, which still covered her discreetly. But he was already back to finger-brushing her thighs.

"Adam, I heard about the babe you lost today," Alinor said in the short break between entertainments. The lutist was done, and now Rashid was preparing to tell one of his long Arab tales . . . something about a young man and a magic tapestry. "I am so sorry you were unable to save the wee one."

Not now, Alinor. Oh, please, God, not now. He hoped his silent nod, accepting her sympathies, would be enough.

But already Tyra was turning in his lap, looking at him over her shoulder. "I forgot to ask you about Dagma. Oh, nay, don't tell me . . ."

"Dagma will be fine," he was quick to assure her. "She lost much blood, and is very weak after a full day and a half of labor, but the babe died in the womb."

"Oh, Adam," Tyra and Alinor said at the same time.

"It could not be helped; the cord was wrapped around the infant's neck. It must have been dead for days now."

"Oh, Adam," they repeated.

"Sometimes things, even bad things, happen for a reason," Alinor said then. "She is very young. She can have other children, can't she?"

"Probably."

"I should go see her," Tyra suggested.

"Not now!" He immediately realized how shrill his voice sounded. More calmly, he informed her, "I gave her some healing herbs that will make her sleep deeply through the night."

I cannot believe I am sitting here with my hand up my lady's gown, about to part her most intimate folds, with an arousal that could scorch the hair off a hog, and I am discussing medical affairs. Can this conversation not wait till the morrow? If Drifa overhears and starts asking me which herbs I used, I think I might just weep.

"Adam, you look as if you are about to weep," Tykir commented. Adam saw the twinkle in Tykir's eyes. He was looking from him to Tyra and back to him, his head cocked in question. He might not know exactly what was going on, but his suspicions had been aroused.

"This is the story of Ala Din and his amazing adventures with a magic tapestry."

Never in all his life had Adam thought he would be relieved to hear Rashid begin one of his never-ending stories. It would probably involve harems in one way or another. The hall went silent as everyone leaned forward and listened intently, not wanting to miss a word of the tale. Vikings ever did love a good story. Adam did, too, but not now. For God's sake, not now!

Alinor turned forward.

And Adam said a silent prayer of thanks.

"Thank you for staying with Dagma," Tyra whispered over her shoulder at him, then turned to stare at Rashid, who sat on a high stool, surrounded by candles and torches, which gave an eerie cast to his Eastern features. Then, for the first time since he'd pulled her onto his lap, she relaxed and let her head loll back onto his shoulder.

Well, hell, if I'd known a little sympathy or a little thankfulness would gain me this result, I could have told her about the old crone with the pus-oozing eyes I helped today. Or the little boy's broken leg I set. Or the burn I soothed with ointment on Alrek's palm from picking up hot kindling.

Tyra squirmed on his lap to get more comfortable, and Adam saw stars before him, so intense was the pleasure-pain in his groin. Good thing she could not feel him pressing against her buttocks! He did not want to shock her.

"You may resume now," Tyra said.

"Huh? Are you speaking to me?" he asked. *She must be addressing me, because Alinor is not even looking in our direction, and there has been no break in Rashid's talking. The only thing she could be referring to is . . . oh, my God!*

"Of course I'm speaking to you, lackwit," she said with as much cordiality as a captain addressing a thick-headed soldier. "You may continue the finger-pleasuring game now."

Game? She views this as a game? So much for her being shocked!

"Have I shocked you?" she asked, apparently having second thoughts.

Nay, no second thoughts permitted. "Yea, you shocked me," he said, "in the nicest possible way."

"Shhhh!" Ingrith, Breanne, and Drifa all hissed at the same time. They were engrossed in Rashid's tale and wanted no chatter to distract their hearing.

And so, while Rashid told his tales of magic in an Eastern land, Adam began to weave his own form of magic.

He teased the hairs of her woman's nest with fluttering fingers, then palmed her, rotating the heel of his hand against her. She arched her back and whimpered softly. He would have liked to touch her breasts, but that would be too open a demonstration in front of an audience. Instead, he whispered into her ear, "Open more," and when she did, he dipped his fingers into the honey of her arousal and spread it up and down over her slick folds till he came to that bud which was the essence of a woman's pleasure. When he touched her there, she jerked and moaned aloud.

"Is something wrong?" Alinor inquired.

He was strumming Tyra *there* now, and at first she was unable to speak.

"Nay, just a little indigestion," Tyra said.

Tykir snorted his disbelief.

"You should chew on mint leaves," Drifa offered. "That is the best thing for cramps in the abdomen."

"I told you the pig's liver in dill sauce was not for you," Ingrith said huffily. She must have come back to the hall to escape Bolthor's sagas in the scullery.

"Shhh!" someone down below protested.

Meanwhile, Adam was doing his best to contribute to her "indigestion." Strumming, and strumming, and strumming, till the bud became bigger and harder, and the folds furled open like the petals of a flower, and the dew was hot and thick.

He was feeling rather hot and thick himself.

Sensing that she was about to reach her peak, he eased a long middle finger up inside of her, and was rewarded by the rhythmic spasm of her inner muscles welcoming him to her world. Her hands grasped his forearms in an iron grip, trying to fight the overwhelming ripples that passed through her. He would have bruises tomorrow, for a certainty . . . bruises that he would relish as a reminder of her sweet surrender. In the end, just before she crashed through that barrier that separates a woman from ecstasy, her knees gripped his and she put a fist to her mouth, trying to stifle her cries, but he heard, "Oh . . . oh . . . oh . . . for the love of Freyja! . . . oh!"

Then she sank into a relaxed heap of satiety.

Adam got great satisfaction out of Tyra's pleasure . . . not as much as if he'd climaxed himself, but close. Her open sensuality was a delight. He never knew what to expect next from her . . . as was proven in the following seconds.

When her soft panting died down and she was able to speak, Tyra turned slightly to face him and asked, "When can I finger-pleasure you?"

CHAPTER THIRTEEN

I'll tell you my fantasies if you tell me yours . . .

"So, exactly how many kinds of pleasuring are there?" Tyra was asking Adam a short time later.

He groaned and put his forehead on the table. "What kind of monster have I created?" he murmured, but he was smiling as he spoke; Tyra was fairly certain he did not consider her a monster at all. In fact, the hot looks he kept giving her would indicate just the opposite.

Rashid had finished his tale, none of which Tyra could remember, and several village boys did some acrobatics, none of which Tyra could remember, and most everyone had left the dais to engage in other pursuits, including dancing, which was taking place at the other end of the hall to the accompaniment of several fiddle players. But Tyra could not think of that. The only thing on her mind was the incredible experience Adam had just introduced her to.

"I mean, you have shown me mouth-pleasuring and tongue-pleasuring and now finger-pleasuring . . . none of which I would have expected. So exactly how many types of pleasuring are there?"

"Tyra, must you analyze everything?" Adam asked, raising his head to look at her. Almost immediately, he added, "If you do not raise that bodice, I very well might jump into *your* lap."

She hitched her neckline upward. "Yea, I do analyze everything. How else can I understand things?"

"This is not a battle where each and every strategy and method of fighting must be studied. The best kind of lovemaking is spontaneous."

She tapped a forefinger against her lips. "Nay, I think you are wrong. Not that I have engaged in actual lovemaking, precisely. This did not count as lovemaking, did it?"

"Not precisely," he said, mimicking her playfully.

"But methinks there must be delights in all kinds of lovemaking . . . planned or unplanned."

Adam shook his head hopelessly at her. "No doubt you are right."

"So what other kinds are there?"

"Kinds of what?"

"Aaarrgh! Pleasuring, you lackwit. Do you deliberately misread me?"

He grinned. Then he put up his hands in surrender when she made a growling sound. "There is mouth-pleasuring and tongue-pleasuring and finger-pleasuring, as you have said. Then there is eye-pleasuring, and talk-pleasuring, and swive-pleasuring. But best of all is a combination of these."

She frowned in confusion. "Give me an example of talk-pleasuring."

He laughed. "Why don't you come to my bed furs and I can demonstrate all of these things?"

"Not now," she said. "Not yet."

"Well, then, if I were going to talk-pleasure you, I might tell you some of the things I intend to do to you once I get you naked and alone. I might tell you of my desire to thrust and thrust and thrust myself into your tight sheath till you scream with pleasure. Or I might tell you of my fantasy of licking my way up one side of you and down the other, then licking where you are hottest and wettest with want of me."

"Oh, you wicked, wicked man. That is such a lie! People do not do *that*."

He threw his hands in the air as if to say, *You asked*.

"Well, what of eye-pleasuring?" she asked, figuring that was safer territory to explore.

"I would see you adorned in the sheer veils of a desert houri with bells that tinkled with every sway of your hips and bracelets on your ankles. Or I could arrange you on the bed furs and ask you to watch as I undress slowly for you. Very slowly."

"I like that latter one," she said. In truth, she liked it all.

He smiled, as if he knew.

"Would you like to know something particularly scandalous?"

"I do not know," she said, but almost immediately changed her mind and said, "Yea, I do."

He laughed. "I would like you to wear a special adornment I saw one time in Baghdad. It is a thin gold chain that hangs low on the waist, but there is another chain attached to it that runs from the center in back, through the buttocks crease up through the woman-cleft, over the belly, to attach at the waist. This adornment is to be worn under clothing during the day . . . when riding a horse, or walking to the garderobe, or eating a meal, or . . . whatever. Always it is a reminder of the man who placed it there."

Tyra was at last speechless. He had been right. It was a scandalous fantasy.

He reached over and took her hand in his. "I am half teasing you, Tyra. Not that all these things can't be done, or that we won't do them, if you want."

"I do," she put in quickly.

He laughed. "Keep surprising me like that and you will land in the bed furs afore you can blink. Just know this: If Bolthor or Tykir or Alinor tell you I was wild at one time, they would be telling the truth. I used to be a connoisseur of all things dangerous or sexual or adventuresome. But now I have come to believe that the best sexplay comes from the simple acts of two people involved, not in practiced arts."

A wanton thought came to her unbidden. "I just thought of another kind of pleasuring. I overheard Lady Alinor mention it to the cook."

"Well?" he prodded when she just smiled secretly at him. He raised a goblet of ale to his lips, waiting.

"Feather-pleasuring," she announced gleefully.

For several long moments, he choked on his ale . . . till she slapped him on the back, so hard he began choking all over again.

"I went too far, didn't I? Men like to lead, whether it be in battle or loveplay. I was too aggressive."

When his choking fit was over, he let his gaze travel over her, intimately, and he told her, "Too aggressive? There is no such thing in loveplay."

"Then you are not upset with me?"

"My warrior princess, I think I have died and gone to Viking heaven."

Tyra exulted that she could affect a man so . . . nay, that she could affect *this man* so. She felt as if she'd crossed some important line in her life, and not only because of the incredible pleasure she'd just experienced at Adam's wicked fingers. She fought through the fuzziness in her brain to understand just what it was.

Pact or no pact, I am going to make love with this man.

He still held her hand and stared at her, as if understanding her inner turmoil. Perhaps it was an important step for him, too.

As the effects of the ale began to wear off, she hitched her bodice up till she was decent. She prayed that sanity would return . . . not so that she could change her mind . . . just long enough for her to understand the implications of this momentous decision.

"Tyra?" Adam inquired.

"If I do this thing . . ."

"If . . . ?"

She smiled at the distress in his voice. "After the taste of loveplay you have given me, I would be a fool not to want to sample the full meal. But I am not an impetuous person. I need to think things out. To study—"

"Oh, nay, nay, nay! The worst thing you can do when in a lustsome mood is to think. Thinking is a sure lust killer."

She smiled at him. "Are you saying I am lustsome?"

"Hah! If you or I were any more lustsome, we would be drooling."

"What I'm trying to say is you have convinced me to make love with you, but there still must be some rules."

"Rules?" He groaned.

"Just because I choose to couple with you does not mean I consent to marriage."

Adam turned three shades of purple before he said, very carefully, "I do not recall bringing up marriage. Not even once. And, really, Tyra, men are the ones who are supposed to fear that dreaded word, not women."

"I am not like other women. You already know that."

"So, aside from scratching your crotch and spitting, you have other masculine traits . . . such as aversion to marriage?"

She could tell he was trying to make light of what

she considered a very serious subject. "You already know that I am being pushed from all directions to wed. Well, you will be subject to the same pressures if anyone suspects our naked bodies have touched."

"Naked bodies?" He grinned at her.

"Do not try to change the subject."

"All right, so we must be secretive. And we must avoid pressure to wed. Agreed. Any other rules?"

She nodded. "I intend to leave Stoneheim soon . . . definitely within the next month. I cannot wait till the fjords freeze over. Then it will be too late."

"To Byzantium?"

"Yea, it is the best thing for me. My mind is made up, regardless of my father's fate. Rafn is ready to step into his shoes if the worst should happen."

"I cannot say that I approve. It seems a hard life for a woman." He raised his hands in surrender when he saw she was about to protest his characterization of females as being softer than males. "But if that is what you want, that is your decision."

"Will you be leaving Stoneheim, or will you stay the winter?"

"Hah! I'm not staying here if you aren't. Actually, no offense intended, but even if you are, I have no intention of wintering in this land of ice."

"Perhaps you could travel partway with me . . . you and Rashid. He speaks often of a yearning to return to the warmer clime of his homeland."

Adam shook his head. "Nay. Rashid might go with you, but I am for England. The only home I have is there."

"One last thing," she said, and took a deep breath for nerve. "If there should be a babe, you give up all rights."

He dropped her hand and stared at her incredulously. "Nay!"

At first she was not sure she'd heard him right. "Nay?"

He stood and glared down at her. "You heard me. Nay! My lady, you offend me deeply. How could you think that I would abandon my child?"

She tilted her head and studied him as he clenched and unclenched his fists with anger.

"My sister Adela and I never knew our father. We were adopted by Selik and Rain, who opened an orphanstead in Jorvik. I saw over and over what the lack of a father does to a child. That will never happen to mine. Never!"

"But, Adam, you are not making sense. You have said you do not want to wed."

"I don't." He gave her a direct look, which carried some hidden meaning.

When understanding seeped into her brain, she stood, too. "You would take my child from me?"

"I would. An unwed mother who fights for a living? Please, Tyra, even you must see how unsuitable that would be."

"You think I would be an unfit mother?" All her life, Tyra had been subjected to criticism. She was too big. Too rough. Too unattractive. But this was the harshest blow to her pride she'd ever been dealt. It struck at the very heart of her.

"That is not what I said." He tried to take her hand, but she shoved him away, so hard he almost tripped against the chair and only righted himself at the last minute. "Tyra, there are ways to avoid having children."

"There are?" Now, that was a surprise. Why did men and women, especially those with more offspring than they could feed, not practice these "ways."

He nodded. "They are not foolproof, of course."

"Aahhh!" she said. "So, in the end, making love is still a game of chance for the woman. In the end, your seed could take hold in my womb?"

He hesitated, then nodded.

"And you would take that fruit from me?"

"If you are serving in the bloody Varangian Guard, yea, I would." He was as angry as she was now.

She shook her head sadly at him. "Leave my presence now, Saxon, afore I run you through with my dagger." And she meant it, too.

He stared at her for a long moment, anger and sadness warring on his face. Then he turned and walked away.

Tyra should have been happy to know that she had just escaped what might have been the biggest mistake of her life. Why, then, were tears streaming down her face?

Strange bedfellows . . .

Adam tossed and turned for many hours. 'Twas not the way he had expected to spend his night.

He lay restless in his comfortable alcove bed while Rashid snored away on the other side of the central hearth where a low fire burned. If Rashid had his way, the fire would be roaring. As it was, Rashid was buried under three bed furs . . . two of his and one of Adam's.

How could so many things go wrong with his life? How could so many things go wrong between him and Tyra? How could he have come to care so much in such a short time?

He was not entirely to blame, either. Really, if Tyra thought things through, she would have to admit that there was no place for a babe in a soldiering life.

And why were they even discussing a babe betwixt them anyhow? It would probably never happen. Especially since it appeared he would never have the opportunity to do the deed that might produce a babe. Why look for trouble when there was plenty to be found at hand?

The most contradictory thing of all was the way Adam's heart felt, as if a fist were clenching it. He couldn't stop picturing the babe he and Tyra might produce. The child would be tall, of course, and blue-eyed. It could have black hair or blond. Either way, any person formed of the two of them was sure to be comely.

I do not care. I do not care. I do not care. 'Tis best that it ended afore it began.

But what if . . . ?

Once Adam finally started to drift off to sleep, he felt someone slide under the bed furs beside him. At first he thought it might be Tyra . . . come to ask his forgiveness. Hah! It was Kristin, the little imp, staring at him through big blue eyes, with her thumb planted inside her rosebud lips.

"Why are you here, Kristin?" he growled, or attempted to growl. 'Twas hard to be gruff when he was adjusting the wee mite to fit into the cradle of his arms—*just like Adela*—and brushing loose strands of hair off her face.

"I had a bad dream," Kristin revealed. A big fat tear ran down her little face.

"Shhh, 'twas just a dream."

"Alrek went away agin. And you went, too. I wuz all alone, and I wuz scared. In my dream." That was a mouthful of words for Kristin. Actually, what she described was not some horrible nightmare; it was reality. Alrek *would* go off a-Viking again. And Adam most definitely would be leaving before long.

No sooner did the words leave her mouth than Kristin fell asleep. 'Twas the way of children to go from chatter to slumber in the blink of an eye.

When he awakened groggily at dawn, it was to find not just Kristin in the cradle of his arms, but Besji asleep at the foot of the bed, and Tunni on the floor at his side.

Alrek was standing at the hearth, trying to stoke what was already a blazing bonfire.

As he stumbled out of bed to prevent Alrek from setting himself afire, trying not to awaken the other children in the process, he made himself a promise.

Today is the day I take back control of my life. Today is the day I make arrangements to leave Stoneheim.

The blabber mouth blabbed . . .

"Did you bring extra horseradish sauce for the venison steak?" The king licked his lips hungrily as he addressed Alrek, who was carrying a huge, cloth-covered tray into his bedchamber.

"Yea, I did, but I had to hide out in the corridor ever so long afore Father Efrid left yer room to go say matins." Alrek couldn't see why the king didn't just get up out of bed and eat in the hall like everyone else. But who was he to question the secrecy that his master required? After he set the tray on the mattress, Alrek went back to lock the door.

"Did you have any trouble getting the food?" the king asked even as he dug into the morning repast and waved for Alrek to join him.

"A little," Alrek said, biting into a delicious honey oatcake. In truth, he was eating better than he ever had, since the king had taken him into his confidence. "Ingrith wanted to know where I thought I was going with all these pilfered goods, and I told her it wuz fer Master Adam."

"Good thinking, boy. Did it satisfy her?"

Alrek shrugged. "Seemed to. She added the honey cakes for him, special like."

"By thunder! I hope she's not setting her cap for him, too."

"I don't think so. To tell you true, all the ladies seem to be conspiring in some way . . . Ingrith, Breanne, Vana, Drifa, not to mention the Lady Alinor. Methinks they have some plot goin' to match up the Master Adam with the Lady Tyra."

"Hah! Just like a brood of mush-brained females! Plots and secret doings. As if that would do them any good!"

Alrek started to point out that plots and secret doings seemed to be what the king was engaged in, too, but he bit his tongue just in time. He was following Master Adam's advice . . . to think afore he flapped his tongue. The healer had given him that bit of wisdom when Alrek had told him that he'd seen Rafn poking his . . . uh, poker . . . into Vana's woman-fire one night.

"So, tell me all the news," the king said, having eaten his fill and pushed the tray aside. "And leave nothing out." He reached for the stoppered pottery jug of ale and proceeded to take a long swallow.

"Well, I can tell you one thing. 'Tis a new word I heard Master Adam sayin' to yer daughter Tyra. Mayhap it has some significance. Mayhap not." He frowned. "Or was it my lady speakin' ter Master Adam? I misremember now."

The king waved a hand as if it mattered not. "Get on with it, boy. What word is it that has you flummoxed?"

"Finger-pleasurin'."

The king started to laugh and choke at the same time. As he laughed and choked and laughed and choked, Alrek feared he might be single-handedly responsible for killing the king. Bolthor might even write a saga about it: "The King Who Laughed Himself to Death."

Alrek was thinking it was past time for him to go a-Viking.

* * *

Time to rise from the dead . . .

"Finger-pleasuring?" Tykir exclaimed. "What the hell is that?"

"I have no idea," King Thorvald said. "I thought you would know . . . being a woman-lucky man, as you are famed to be."

"Thorvald! I have been wed for ten years now. Any woman-luck I have would be with Alinor."

The king shrugged. "And a shame that is, too . . . that you would disdain the *more danico*."

" 'Tis more like I value my life . . . and my manparts. Alinor would kill me if I took multiple wives . . . or make sure I am incapable of doing anything more than twiddling my . . . uh, thumb." He poured the king and then himself another goblet of ale. "So, why do you want to know what finger-pleasuring is?"

"I heard that Adam might be doing that to my daughter Tyra. Or mayhap she is doing it to him? Or mayhap they are just considering it."

Tykir narrowed his eyes at the king. "How did you hear this? I thought I was the only one who knew of your recovery."

"You are. You are. But a person hears much when people think he is dead to the world. They speak as if they are alone. You would be surprised at the news I garner just lying here."

Tykir wasn't entirely satisfied with the king's explanation, but he let it ride for now. "What do you want, Thorvald?"

"I have got to get the girl married, and it appears that fingering is as far as they have gotten. A Viking man would not settle for fingering, I will tell you that. The Saxon blood in him must make him weak-sapped."

"Adam is not weak-sapped," Tykir contended. "Furthermore, the way I hear it, those two are not even speaking today, let alone fingering each other. The way I hear it, Adam threatened to take her baby away."

"What baby? Tyra has a baby, and no one bothered to tell me? Have I no loyal subjects who would tell me this?"

"Nay, Tyra does not have a baby . . . yet. But if she has a baby . . . with Adam . . . he will take it away."

"He will not! I will lop off his head if he dares try. By the by, is it a boy child or a girl child? May the gods be merciful, 'tis past time for a boy child to be born in my line."

"There is not going to be a child. They are not even speaking . . . did you not hear me say that?"

"Can't anyone do anything right?" Thorvald threw his hands in the air. "It looks like I will have to do it myself."

"Go ahead. Awaken from the dead, you old schemer, you. Scare your entire clan by walking into your hall during dinner tonight. Or pretend to be a ghost. I do not care. But get out of that damn bed. This chamber is starting to reek . . . of ale and horseradish. I'm thinking of going home to Dragonstead, where everyone is sane . . . well, everyone except Rapp of the Big Wind."

"Go if you must," the king said grumpily, "but you might want to stay a bit longer. Perchance I will soon have something special to show you."

Tykir stopped at the door and turned back to the king, who was propped up in the bed, his hands folded behind his neck and his long legs crossed at the ankles. He had a crafty expression on his face.

"And what might that be?"

"My harem."

CHAPTER FOURTEEN

&

She wanted to give him children, but not hers . . .

S It was a bright sunny day at Stoneheim . . . the kind of uncommonly fair day known as Odin's Summer. A day when the sun shone brightly, deceiving one into thinking there might be more clement weather ahead, when in reality there could be snow and a freeze afore morning. In truth, one of the shipwrights who suffered a soreness of the joints told Tyra that a storm was on the horizon, because his knees were aching in premonition.

Tyra was taking advantage of the lull in weather by examining one of her longships, *Wild Serpent*, which was raised up on sawhorses. She had sent workmen soon after dawn to begin preparing it for a journey. Breanne was helping her, reluctantly, by setting her carpenters to sanding down the rough edges on the rails. Vana was checking the sails for any tears; she was not so reluctant. Oh, Vana would be sad to see Tyra go, but she would be more glad to finally wed Rafn.

"Are you going somewhere, Tyra?"

She glanced up to see Adam standing before her. He was wearing one of those Arab robes, which might have appeared silly on one of her Viking soldiers, but on him looked as if he'd been born to the Eastern culture.

"I thought you were seeing patients."

"Are you going somewhere, Tyra?" he repeated.

"You know I am. Go away, Adam. I have work to do if I am to leave by Friggsday."

"Friggsday? You are leaving on Friday? That's only three days from now."

"That is right. Now go away."

"Are you not even going to wait to see how your father fares?"

She shook her head and continued to run her hand over the hull, looking for cracks or leak holes. "Viking women may gain a divorce from their husbands by merely stating their desire afore witnesses. The same is true of a daughter or son separating from parents. Once I perform the ritual, I will be off."

"To Byzantium?"

She nodded, then raised her chin haughtily. "Lesser woman though I may be in your opinion, I at least choose my own life path. And I embrace it wholeheartedly. You, on the other hand, keep running from your fate. I pity you, Saxon."

Now it was Adam who raised his chin haughtily.

"There is one more thing that must be settled. Alrek wants to come with me, to travel to far lands. I would not deprive him of that adventure, except for one thing."

He arched his brows at her.

"Only the gods can fathom why, but Alrek wants you to take Tunni and Kristin and Besji with you . . . to give them a home."

"Nay!" he nearly shouted, turned abruptly, and practically ran away.

Some men are sharp, even with a hole in the head . . .

"I want all of you here to bear witness for me."

Tyra stood at the side of her father's bed as she made

the pronouncement to Adam, Father Efrid, Rafn, Rashid, Tykir, Alinor, Bolthor, and her four sisters . . . all of whom she'd called to meet her here for the formal ritual. Today was the day she would renounce her bloodlines. Today was the day she would become a homeless wanderer. Today was the day she would finally take control of her life.

The royal bedchamber was large, with a central hearth and a massive bedstead against one wall. The room was hot, due to the blazing fire, and smoky, though there was the usual smoke hole in the roof. It reeked oddly of venison and horseradish.

"Do not act in haste," Adam cautioned her.

She cast him a fierce glower and gritted out, "Mind your own business, Saxon cur." Then she began, "In the way of the Ancients whose laws we obey, I, Tyra Thorvaldsson, do hereby—"

"To leave your homeland forever . . . oh, Tyra, are you sure about this?" Alinor interrupted anxiously.

"Tyra knows what she is about. 'Tis the only way," Rafn said, taking the hand of Vana, whose hair was looking particularly white today in the gloomy bedchamber. He and Vana moved up next to Tyra, as if to show whose side they were on. But, really, there were no sides here. She was doing, finally, what must be done to ensure her sisters' futures.

Everyone's eyes were growing misty . . . whether from emotion or the increased smokiness in the room, it was hard to tell. Alrek must have brought up green wood for the fire today.

"With all due respect, m'lady warrior, the country rooster does not crow in town." It was Rashid offering his opinion now.

"Huh?" Tyra said. Was he classifying her as a country

bumpkin, unable to live in a city like Byzantium? How many insults should one woman be subjected to before she started lopping off heads . . . or tongues?

"Shut up, Rashid," Adam said.

"Shut up, Adam," Tyra said.

"Would everyone shut up! You're making the hole in my head hurt."

Tyra looked right and left to see who had spoken. The other occupants of the room were doing the same. Then all eyes moved to the unmoving figure in the bed.

"Father, was that you?" Tyra asked, taking one of his hands in hers . . . a hand which remained lifeless.

Adam pushed her aside with a rude swing of his hips, almost knocking her over. She was about to protest, vehemently, but she restrained herself when she saw that Adam was reacting as a healer. He was listening to her father's heart rate and lifting his eyelids. Under his breath, he murmured to Rashid, who had joined him and was helping to remove the head wrapping to examine the wound, "I have been suspicious for days now. Is it possible the king is not really unconscious?"

Rashid shrugged and took the soiled wrappings from him, handing him some clean ones.

"Looks deader'n a door hinge to me," Bolthor mused.

"Mayhap he is dead and 'twas his ghost speaking," Ingrith whispered in a voice of awe.

"I was saving some of my best dried flowers for his funeral," Drifa confessed.

"You could always stick a bouquet in the hole in his head," Rafn quipped.

"Rafn!" Vana chided and pinched him in the ribs.

Rafn just grinned at her.

"I was thinking that if father lives, he could put a jewel in the hole," Breanne said with a bite of sarcasm.

"You know how much he likes to adorn his hair with beads and ornaments. He is ever so vain about his hair."

Suddenly Alinor punched Tykir in the arm. "You lout! You did that, didn't you?"

"Did what?" Tykir was rubbing his upper arm with great drama.

"Projected your voice to make it appear as if the king had spoken. Like you did that time with the sheep at Dragonstead. For shame! Making jest on such a serious occasion." She punched him again.

All of Tyra's sisters were listening raptly to the interchange between Tykir and Alinor. No doubt they saw them as an example of longtime lovebirds.

"For shame, Alinor! That you would make such false charges against me . . . your beloved husband. And you know why I pretended to be a ram speaking to you at Dragonstead. Dost recall the message?" He waggled his eyebrows at her.

Alinor giggled in response. "Willst thou never grow up, Tykir?"

"I hope not . . . and you should, too. Forever young, that is us." He waggled his eyebrows some more. "I at least have some decorum. You never heard me mention *finger-pleasuring*."

Every person in the bedchamber let loose an interested exclamation of "Finger-pleasuring?" except Tykir, who was beaming brightly, and Adam and Tyra, who were turning red with embarrassment, and the king, who continued to lie motionless.

"How could you, Adam? How could you? Did you have to tell everyone?" Tyra addressed Adam in a mortified whisper.

"Me? I said naught."

Tyra, even without a hole in her head, was developing

the world's biggest headache. For a certainty, it felt as if
her brain was leaking out.

"What exactly is finger-pleasuring?" Vana wanted to
know.

Rafn whispered something in her ear.

Vana squealed with incredulity before she clamped a
hand over her mouth. Tyra could tell she was smiling
behind the hand.

Tyra groaned.

Adam groaned. Then he immediately seemed to pull
himself together as he straightened and went over to a
chest where he proceeded to wash his hands from the
water in a pottery bowl and dry them on a linen cloth.
When he was done, he declared, "It would be best for
my patient if all of you would leave his sick chamber."

"How is he?" Tyra asked quickly.

He gave her a long look, as if to say it was about time
she gave concern to her father.

"He is fine," he said, addressing everyone in the
room. "Methinks he will awaken soon." In an undertone, Tyra thought he added, "If he hasn't already."

"That is wonderful news," Tyra said. "It will gladden
my heart to leave the Norse lands knowing my father
will recover."

"Can you not wait another day?" Adam's question
was asked with little inflection in his voice. To Tyra,
that meant he did not care one way or another.

She shook her head. " 'Tis time for the ritual." Everyone stepped back to give her room. She stood at her father's side and began once again. "I, Tyra, daughter of
Thorvald Ivarsson, do hereby renounce—"

"Nay!" a booming voice pronounced.

It was the king. With a snarl of disgust, he sat bolt
upright in his bed. "Have you all gone barmy?" he
snarled, and tried to disentangle himself from the furs

that had covered him. "Must I do everything myself . . . even coming back from the dead?" He leaned wearily against the pillowed headboard.

"Father!" Tyra and all her sisters exclaimed and converged on his bed to give him hugs and kisses.

"Leave off! Leave off!" he protested. "You will smother me."

"Step back," Adam ordered. "Let me examine the king."

As he leaned over the old man, she heard her father ask, "And who be you? Ye have the look of a bloody Saxon about you?"

"I am Adam the Healer. And, yea, a Saxon. The very one your daughter Tyra kidnapped to come save you."

"That you did. That you did," the king acknowledged. "And my thanks you have in abundance."

"Father, now that you are on the road to recovery . . . do not take this personally . . . you have been a good father . . . most times, least ways . . . but I want to renounce our blood ties, and—"

He muttered something like, "When snow falls in Valhalla!"

Tyra sighed. "You owe me this favor in return for bringing the physician."

Her father raised his hand in a halting fashion. "Not now Tyra. You will not bedevil me with this nonsense the moment I escape the raven's fate."

"It is not fair, I tell you. You cannot keep putting me off. You cannot put my sisters off." It was unlike Tyra to argue with her father, especially in these circumstances. But she needed to act, and soon.

"I will handle it, daughter. Trust me, dearling. Just this once. One more day will make no difference, will it? I promise this situation will be resolved, and soon." Her father's voice was weakening, and she recognized that she was not helping matters by forcing an answer now.

"One more day. That is all," she agreed.

Her father nodded, though he muttered under his breath, "Obstinate, unbiddable girl!

"I would ask you all to take leave of me so that I may rest," he said then. But first he turned again to Adam. "Ask any boon of me and it is yours."

Adam thought for a long moment, then said, "Transport home. I ask for one longship to take me home . . . now . . . afore winter . . ."

The king nodded. "It is done. And a fair request it is, too."

Tyra's heart sank. Unreasonably. Whether she left first for Byzantium, or he left first for Britain, the result would be the same. Separation . . . and soon.

". . . and I insist that the captain of that longship—" there was a long pause—"be your daughter Tyra."

A stunned silence filled the room before Tyra gasped and said, "Nay! You cannot ask that, you . . . you . . ."

"Loathsome lout?" Alinor offered with a grin.

"Yea, you loathsome lout!" Tyra said to Adam, who remained grim-faced, waiting for the king's answer.

"Good strategy," Tykir congratulated Adam, clapping him on the shoulder.

"Methinks this calls for a saga," Bolthor announced. "How about, 'How the Lady Warrior Got Caught in Her Own Snare'?"

"I give you this word of caution, my lady warrior," Rashid said. "She who rides the tiger should be careful how she dismounts."

"That is the most nonsensical proverb you have spouted thus far," Tyra told Rashid.

"It means that you have been tempting me as if I were a castle cat, when in fact I am a tiger," Adam explained to her. He added a tigerish growl and a wink to make his point.

The growl and the wink touched Tyra in the most sensual way . . . well, actually, in the most sensual place.

"You are clearly some sort of disgusting male creature," Tyra informed Adam, clicking her tongue with disgust.

"Faults are thick where love is thin," Rashid opined.

"Shut your teeth, Rashid," Adam said cheerily.

"I still want to know what finger-pleasuring is," Breanne said.

"Me, too. Me, too," chimed in Ingrith and Drifa.

"Enough!" the king roared.

When there was silence in the room, he addressed Adam. "Your request is granted. She who kidnapped you shall return you to your home."

Tyra put her face in her hands and moaned. As she heard everyone leaving the bedchamber and calling out their good wishes to her father, she wondered how her life had reached such a chaotic state, and how it could get any worse.

She soon found out.

When she opened her eyes, she realized that her father had fallen back asleep . . . a relaxed slumber, by the sound of his even breathing . . . and she saw that Adam remained in the bedchamber.

Meeting her eyes directly, he said simply, "Tonight."

Tyra required no further explanation. Adam had healed her father. Now she must fulfill the pact she'd made with him.

One night. His bed furs. Naked.

She answered him with the same simplicity, "Tonight."

But what she thought was, *May the gods help me. Tonight.*

* * *

He would make his own miracles . . .

"Come with me," Adam told Alrek.

"Me?" Alrek almost swallowed his teeth on hearing Adam address him directly. He'd been moping about the courtyard, shuffling his boots in the dirt. He'd heard about Adam's imminent departure for Britain, and it was finally sinking in that he and his siblings would not be going with him.

Now that he had finished treating patients for the day and had checked on Dagma and then the king, Adam had strapped on a belted sheath to hold his sword. Then he'd gone searching for Alrek.

Adam took Alrek by the upper arm and led him out of the main courtyard toward the blacksmith building. "I have something to show you."

Usually, that kind of statement would have brought forth elation in the youthling, so desperate was he for attention, but he just nodded forlornly now.

They stepped into the exceedingly hot building where Bjorn was working on a sword over a blazing fire. A young thrall kept the flames high by working a bellows from the side.

The sword Bjorn was working on was not a large one, but it was finely worked. Using the damascening method, he twisted together iron and steel rods of different textures and shades and then forged them into a single blade. Intermixed with the twisting and pounding was frequent heating and quenching to harden the metal. The result was a beautiful flame pattern ingrained in the surface of the blade.

When he was done, Bjorn handed the sword to Adam and muttered under his breath, "I still think ye are demented. He will kill himself . . . that he will."

Walking out of the smithy, Adam handed the sword to Alrek and said, "This is for you."

"Me?" Alrek's eyes went huge with wonderment. Alrek took the short sword by the hilt and almost tripped forward, not being prepared for its weight.

Adam winced at Alrek's first near-accident with the weapon. He could just hear people telling him, "I told you so. I told you so."

"Why?"

"It's a gift."

"No one ever gave me nuthin', 'ceptin' the king, and that was a job."

"Well, I am giving you something, but there is a price attached."

Alrek was staring at his new sword adoringly. "Whatever you say."

"You know that I am going away soon, and I am not . . . *cannot* take you with me."

The boy immediately stiffened at that reminder. "I do not see why—"

Adam put up a halting hand. "You should be able to live as a boy, but God . . . the gods . . . have dealt you a different fate. That means you must continue to be the head of your family. Being the head of the family also means protecting those under your shield. That is why I'm giving you the sword. That is why I will practice with you as much as possible till it is time for me to leave. Having your very own weapon means being responsible, Alrek. You must learn to be more careful. A sword can be your friend or your foe. Make it your friend. Do you understand?"

Alrek nodded, but Adam wasn't sure how much the youthling understood. Well, he would once Adam was done instructing him. Some people believed that they were helping children by keeping all dangerous objects out of their path, but he was of the opinion that people— even little people—must learn to deal with the dangers that surrounded them.

'Twas as Rashid always said, "Do not stand in a place of danger and pray for miracles." Well, Alrek kept looking to him for a miracle. Adam chose instead to provide Alrek with his own means to a miracle. But, bloody hell, he hoped the boy didn't kill himself first.

By the time dusk rolled over the Norse mountains, Adam and Alrek were both feeling proud of the youthling's accomplishments. He was not yet a skilled swordsman, but he had made progress. And the two of them had only a dozen or so nicks on their arms to show for the effort. Alrek promised to practice with him early the next morning and again in the late afternoon. Adam would speak to Rafn about tutoring the boy after he left.

It was the best he could do.

As they trudged back toward the keep and the sweat house where they planned to heat up their aching muscles, Alrek turned to him and said, "A man's sword should have a name, should it not?"

"Absolutely."

"I know what mine will be."

"Now, Alrek, remember what I said about so many of your problems being the result of acting before thinking. Stop, think, act. That is to be your motto."

"I do not need to think about this. The name of my sword shall be . . ."

Adam just knew he was not going to like this.

". . . Miracle-Maker."

Always keep a woman guessing . . .

From a distance, Tyra had been watching Adam and Alrek practicing swordplay at the far end of the exercise field. For three hours, Adam had worked patiently with the accident-prone youthling. He would have cuts up one arm and down the other to show for his efforts.

At first, when she'd heard that the healer had commissioned a small sword to be made for the boy, she'd been furious. Storming out of the smithy, she'd stomped over to the exercise fields and had been about to chastise the healer for interfering in the affairs of Stoneheim. Arming and training a Viking boy was her business, not his.

But Rafn had put a hand on her arm to hold her back. "Adam is doing the right thing. We cannot continue to overprotect Alrek. The boy must learn himself."

"Even if he hurts himself?"

Rafn had nodded. "Even if he hurts himself."

So Tyra had watched and marveled at the tolerant manner in which Adam instructed his pupil . . . over and over, teaching the same lesson. The Viking short sword was not made for the thrust-and-parry action of the longer, lighter Saxon sword. And so Adam and Alrek practiced the hacking, slicing motions with their swords against a tall tree stump.

Most surprising of all was the expertise Adam displayed as he hefted his sword and wielded it in smooth, fluid motions. The healer had told her that he had been a soldier betimes over the years, but she must not have believed him.

"He is a handsome devil, is he not?" Tykir asked as he came up to stand beside her.

"That he is," she admitted. Despite the coolness of the air, Adam and Alrek had stripped off their tunics and were exercising bare-chested. Adam's dark hair and Alrek's blond hair were both tied back into queues at their napes with leather ties. Alrek would no doubt be a handsome man when he was grown . . . if he lived that long. Adam was already as handsome as a god.

"Who is he?" Tyra asked. The man was clearly full of contradictions. He could be a soldier, or a healer. He could be as crude as the most ignorant cotter, or sensitive to the needs of others. He claimed to want no family, and yet he threatened to take her child if it were ever born of his seed.

"Do not judge Adam too harshly," Tykir said. "I'm not sure he knows, himself. He has lived a harsh life, and a privileged life. In the end, he is a survivor. But at a cost."

"Have you known him long?"

"Since he was seven years old, and his sister Adela was four. A more foul-mouthed, enterprising, wild rascal you never met in all your life! My stepsister Rain and her husband Selik adopted the two orphans. Only the gods know what horrors the two experienced before that, living on the streets of Coppergate in Jorvik. I do know that the wildness never really left him. He tries to hide it under a veneer of civility, but on occasion it emerges. And always there is this invisible shield he has erected around himself. He lets people in only so far, even family and friends. There are wounds inside him that have never been healed . . . and not just the death of his sister."

"You sound like an advocate for the man."

"I'm being long-winded, am I not? Alinor would say 'tis time to freeze my flapping tongue. But, really, my lady, Adam needs no advocate. If he wants something, he gets it himself."

That is what I am afraid of.

"Still, you seem protective of him."

"We all are. Me, Alinor, Eirik, Eadyth, Bolthor. His prolonged grief these past two years has alarmed us all."

"That's why you came to Stoneheim, then? Worry over Adam, not my father."

He nodded.

She should not be asking these questions of Tykir. He would think she had a personal interest in the rogue. After tonight, he would be out of her life completely. Well, not tonight, she immediately amended. First she had to deliver him to his home in Northumbria. Then she would be off to Miklagard, the "Great City." It was a rich, powerful, sophisticated city of gold and marble. She could scarce wait. Once there, she would have no cause to think of Adam again.

But first she had to get through tonight.

CHAPTER FIFTEEN

❧

Timid she was not . . .

Adam was in his bedchamber with Rashid, helping to pack their belongings for the return trip to Northumbria.

They probably wouldn't be leaving till two days hence, but all of the medical supplies that Rashid had packed in haste were now in disarray. Decisions had to be made about which ones to leave behind with Father Efrid and the midwife, and which were so rare he must needs keep them for himself.

"I still cannot believe that the king has recovered so rapidly. 'Tis a miracle. Praise be to Allah!"

"Rashid, please do not use the word miracle in my presence. It has come to leave a nasty taste in my mouth. And, frankly, methinks the king's recovery is not as rapid as he would have us think."

"Really?"

"For days he has displayed the symptoms of a recovering man, not one who was unconscious."

"Why would he pretend to be sicker than he was?"

Adam shrugged. "He is a crafty fellow . . . always has been, I understand from Tykir. His motives are beyond my understanding. And, really, I do not care. We will be going home. That is the most important thing. I cannot wait till we are gone from this hellhole of the North."

"From one hellhole of the North to another hellhole of the North," Rashid murmured, still chagrined over Adam's refusal to return to the Eastlands and the world of harems. Rashid squinted his eyes at Adam with confusion. "Why did you insist that Tyra be the one to accompany us? Why not cut your ties with Thorvald completely?"

"Revenge. Pure and simple. She kidnapped me. In essence, I am kidnapping her by forcing her to make the return trip."

"Be careful, my friend. Revenge has a way of coming back to bite a man in the arse."

Adam laughed. "Is that another of your ancient proverbs?"

"Nay," Rashid replied with a grin. "That is a bit of Rashid humor. Speaking of humor, master, could you believe all the jests that were being made at dinner about the king's condition? And Thorvald was the worst of them all."

"Vikings do have a great sense of humor. They especially like to laugh at themselves. But even I thought the hole-in-the-head jokes went too far. Especially the one about the king making a good candle holder . . . now that he has a hole in his head."

"Or, 'How did the *drukkinn* Norseman misplace his horn of ale?' "

Adam laughed and finished for him, "It was sitting in the special horn-holder in his head."

"I give you fair warning, master. I heard the king telling one of his soldiers that ever since the operation, his manpart seems to have regained new virility. Harder and bigger it is now, he claims."

"Oh, my God!" Adam exclaimed. "You know what that means, don't you? If word of this spreads, I will have Vikings by the dozens asking me to drill holes in their heads. Just so they can have better sexplay."

They both burst out laughing.

Just then the door flew open and Tyra stood there like an avenging angel . . . hands on hips and legs spread in the battle stance he loved. Unlike them, she was not laughing. She must have come recently from a bath, for the hair in her long braids was still damp. She wore only a short-sleeved, knee-length hide tunic with a thick leather belt. On her legs were cross-gartered half-boots. The only adornments that indicated her rank were the etched silver armlets on her upper arms.

Her hair and apparel were neat and perfectly in order, but the only word he could think of to describe her was *wild*. Yea, Tyra was wild tonight, and he didn't know why, but her being wild ignited a spark of wildness inside him, too.

The Stoneheim princess pointed an imperial finger at Rashid, whose mouth was agape with the same wonder that filled Adam, and ordered, "You! Out!"

Rashid didn't hesitate. Without even a questioning glance in Adam's direction, he left the room, shutting the door soundly after him.

Tyra turned and locked the door.

That click of the lock rang in Adam's ears like the gong of a bell. It had some significant meaning, but for the life of him, he couldn't fathom what . . . not when his mind was consumed with the warrior woman standing before him.

Their eyes held in a smoldering gaze that neither would break, not even when she sank down onto a bench near the door and began to unlace her right boot. She toed it off and kicked it high in the air to land at his feet. With a gloating smirk of victory at her superior aim, she did the same with her other boot. Then she stood and proceeded to unbuckle her belt.

"Tyra, what are you about?"

"You hurled the gauntlet. Now I am taking up the challenge."

"What gauntlet? What challenge? Do you refer to our pact?"

"Our pact is a moot point. I gave my word. It will be done." She waved the hand holding her now loosened belt high in the air. "Nay, this is about your insisting that I transport you back to England, against my will. This is about your saying I am less than a woman."

She was reaching for the leather lacing at the neckline of her tunic.

Adam could scarce concentrate on her words when it appeared she was about to disrobe, without any fanfare. If it were up to him, there would be a blaze of trumpets aforehand . . . or at least a chance for him to take a gulping breath.

"Are you trying to shock me?" he asked.

"Are you shocked?"

To the bone, wench. To the bone. "Not a bit."

She laughed, unconvinced.

"Tyra, slow down a moment. Let us talk first."

"The time for talk is long past." She tossed the leather lacing directly in his face. Luckily, he caught it or he might have been blinded. The last thing he wanted at this moment of revelation was to lose his sight.

But then her previous statement sank into his muddled brain. "I *never* said you were less than a woman."

"Not in those exact words. But you implied it. I am here to prove you wrong, you lackbrain son of a Saxon bastard."

Those last words of hers gave Adam a tiny inkling of

just how angry she was under her seeming calm. "Do you hope to intimidate me by being the aggressor, Tyra? Well, think again, warrior wench, because I like aggressive women. I am not . . ." His words trailed off as she pulled her tunic up over her head and dropped it to the floor.

She was stark, gloriously naked.

He made a point of clicking his jaw shut, just in case he did something dimwitted, like drool.

The woman was magnificent when clothed . . . doubly magnificent when unclothed. She was big, of course, but perfectly proportioned, with sinfully full and high breasts. The rose tips were also big, to suit her size, and maybe her arousal. *I can only hope!* Her waist and hips were trim, her legs exceedingly long. And the nest of curls between her thighs, of the same blond color as the hair on her head, begged for a man's touch. *I can only hope!* Most impressive were the muscles that delineated her arms and abdomen and thighs and calves . . . probably her buttocks, too. The muscles should have made her appear masculine, but instead they added beauty to her woman's body. They made a man imagine how those muscles could be used to draw him into her woman-place, to ride him, to force him to give her pleasure. *I can only hope.* She was like a statue he'd seen once in the Roman lands . . . but better.

As an afterthought, she seemed to recall that her hair was still in braids. She released the ties of first one braid, then the other. Raising her arms, she finger-combed the braiding out of her hair with long, sweeping movements of her arms, which caused her already upraised breasts to rise and fall with her motions.

He felt each of those strokes over every inch of his sensitized skin and most especially on his fully engorged manpart. At first she just stood, staring at him through those clear blue eyes, arms at her sides, watching him watch her. But then she seemed uncomfortable with that posture and resumed her earlier battle stance, hands on hips and legs spread in a vee.

If only the woman knew what that pose did to him!

Her sexual turnabout backfired wonderfully . . .

Tyra knew how her belligerent pose affected the man. Even when she was clothed, his eyes glazed over and his mouth parted with arousal when she stood thus. Now she was as naked as a newborn babe, and Adam was as lustsome as any man could be, if that bulge in his breeches was any indication. Too bad she was shaking like a leaf inside . . . trembling so hard she was unable to appreciate the effectiveness of her deliberate game of turnabout. Tyra was not embarrassed to expose her body, but she *was* embarrassed by all her imperfections. She was too big, too muscular . . . too, too, too . . .

"Well?" she said finally.

"Well?" he choked back.

Good! Choking is good! This is a war we are waging here, and if there is anything I know, it is battle strategy. "Keep your enemy off guard" is the first rule a Viking soldier learns. "Methought we were supposed to *both* be naked in the bed furs. Correct me if I'm wrong, Saxon, but all I see is one nude body in this chamber."

His eyes flashed at her sarcasm. *Two can play this game* was the silent message his eyes threw her way just before he toed off his right boot, flicked it high in the air, and watched as it sailed end over end and landed directly in front of her, toe facing her toes. He smirked, saying nothing.

"Lucky shot," she remarked.

He arched his eyebrows at her challenge. The left

boot followed suit, not just landing next to the other boot, but right in front of the toes of her other foot.

"Show-off!" she muttered.

He smiled at her, and the tight knot in her stomach clenched and unclenched in response. His smile was a lethal erotic weapon.

"What is your goal here? What would you have us do when we are both naked?" he drawled out as he ever so slowly removed his belt, then quickly lifted his tunic up and over his head.

Tyra inhaled sharply at the sight of his bare chest.

He smiled knowingly.

Tread carefully, Tyra. He is the expert in this game. Do not give him any more advantage than he already has. And whatever you do, stop panting. "I thought you already knew," she said. "'Tis as we agreed afore. One night in the bed furs, naked. That is all."

He made a grunting sound of disbelief as he shimmied out of his tight *braies*. She thought he muttered something like, "Dream on, wench." Once he stepped out of his *braies*, he was left wearing long hose and a loincloth type of undergarment, which was exceedingly tight at the moment.

Do not look. Do not look. Do not look. She looked.

He looked, too, then shrugged. "What can I say in my defense? *It* has a mind of its own . . . especially within striking distance of a beautiful, naked goddess."

She was the one making a grunting sound of disbelief now. But her breasts believed . . . their nipples growing tight with interest.

And Adam, the rogue, noticed, too. "Jesus, Mary, and Joseph!" was his only response. Then, as his hose followed the route of his *braies*, he murmured, "This may be the longest night of my life."

"I hope so."

"Please, Tyra, do not say things you do not mean," he pleaded as he began to unravel the cloth that covered his maleness. "And do not look at me so, or I will surely embarrass myself like an untried youthling."

Tyra couldn't stop herself. She had to look at him. He was like a statue she'd seen once of a Greek god . . . only better. She was not unfamiliar with the male genitals, living in close proximity with men on a daily basis. But she'd never witnessed a fully erect man whose arousal was due to her, and only her. She was struck by the beauty of the way the human body was designed. Male and female. Attraction, desire, connection, satisfaction. 'Twas the way it had been at the beginning of time. 'Twas the way it would be ages hence. And now, finally she was part of the process.

"Do you like what you see, Tyra?"

"I do," she said. "And you?"

He laughed and waved a hand toward his groin. "How can you ask?"

"There is one thing I should tell you about our pact." She was starting to feel rather exposed, standing naked before him for such a long period, especially when he continually surveyed her with such intensity. She fought against the instinct to cross her arms over her chest.

"You cannot back out now. You cannot." Shaking his head vigorously, he waved a hand, indicating he would like her to turn around.

Not bloody likely. "Oh, it is not that I want to renege on our agreement . . . just add to it."

Adam did not answer at first. Since she had declined to spin for his pleasure, he had walked a little forward and to the right so he could see her from a side angle. The brute was staring at her buttocks, and she could swear his manpart twitched.

"Just how big can that thing get?" she blurted out.

"Immense, it would seem, when you keep staring at it." His voice was husky. Had she finally shocked him?

"I am sorry," she said.

"Do not be," he said. "I like it. *It* likes it."

"You are teasing me," she guessed. "Women are not usually so blunt, are they?"

"Nay, they are not. It is a refreshing change."

"Well, how would this be for bluntness? I want you. You want me. Let's do it."

His eyes went wide. His face reddened. A sputtering sound came from his mouth. He reached for a nearby tabletop to support his presumably shaky knees. And his manpart looked as if it might explode.

The temptation was too great . . .

Adam was out of control.

He inhaled and exhaled several times to calm himself. It didn't work.

"Tyra, what is going on with you? We discussed this two days ago. Remember that conversation that prompted you to stop talking to me?"

"I thought about it . . . a great deal, and I came to this conclusion. I knew I was going to have to sleep in the same bed furs with you . . . naked . . . because that was what I agreed to."

"Of course. The honor-bound soldier would never do anything so feminine as change her mind. Thank God!"

She glowered at him and continued, "But I also knew that I had fallen under your erotic spell."

"I have no magic powers. If I did, I would have wielded them long ago. Like back in Northumbria when you first kidnapped me."

"No man has ever wanted me the way that you appear to."

I do. I do. "Your Norsemen must be blind."

"This is my view of the situation. I can always find a man to couple with me . . ."

A wave of intense jealousy overcame him.

". . . but I may never have the opportunity again to mate with a man who makes me feel so . . . so . . . desirable."

He started to reach for her, then stopped himself. There were still obstacles to overcome.

"Plus, the women of Stoneheim are all abuzz over the advice you gave to Arnora."

"Arnora?" He frowned. "Oh, the young woman with eight children."

She nodded. "You told her of a method to prevent conception. You said a woman is *safe* three days afore her monthly flux and eight days after."

"*Safe* is not the correct word." He shook his head vehemently. "The cycle technique is not infallible. My stepmother Rain was a famous physician in her land . . . in fact, she was a bit barmy at times . . . claimed to have come from a future time when women practiced many forms of birth control . . . men, too. The one thing she emphasized was that it was not perfect."

Tyra waved a hand airily. "My monthly flux is due two days hence. Therefore, I am in that safe zone."

"Tyra, Tyra, Tyra. Are you listening to me? What happens if it does not work? What happens if you become pregnant?"

"This is the way I figure it. We make love tonight, and only tonight . . . during a time of presumed safety. We should be on board ship, on the return trip to Northumbria, when my monthly time comes. If the flux fails to occur, you will know, and we will deal with it then."

"You do not agree to give up rights to a child you carry?"

"I do not." She sighed and seemed to decide on a

different tactic. "Of course, there is another solution. I could bed with Gunter and Egil tomorrow night. Then if I do increase, no one will know who the father is."

"Absolutely not."

She held his gaze, waiting. Then her face reddened and she reached down for her tunic. "It appears I made a mistake coming here. I will depart."

"Nay!" he practically shouted. "Do not go."

She halted, and tilted her head in question.

He walked around the table and took her hand, leading her to the alcove bed. "One night?"

"One night only," she agreed.

"The deed will be done, then. We will make love," he said, lowering her to the mattress and following her down. "And damn the consequences."

Where did he get all these ideas? . . .

"I want it all," she said.

Too aroused to wait, Adam was adjusting himself atop her, about to spread her thighs and thrust inside. He paused but a second before replying, "Of course you shall have it all," and took her hand in his to wrap it around the prodigious width of his full-blown arousal.

"Not *that*," she said with a giggle against his neck.

Tyra had had no idea that she could giggle! And who knew that a giggle could have the effect of cold water on a man's hot staff?

He sat back on his haunches, straddling her legs. "What *all* are you referring to?"

"All the different ways of pleasuring that you told me about. The sight-pleasuring . . ."

"I think you and I have had more than enough of sight-pleasuring for one night. If I look at you any more, my eyes might pop out."

She smiled. "I like when you look at me. Your scrutiny is like a caress. See? Even now, when you gaze upon my breasts, the fine hairs stand out all over my body."

"For the love of God, Tyra! Are you trying to torture me?"

"Am I torturing you?"

"Yea. Sweet torture."

"Aaah," she said, pleased with herself. Then she continued her explanation, "I want the other types of pleasuring, too. Kiss-pleasuring. Tongue-pleasuring. Finger-pleasuring. Talk-pleasuring. All of it. I have much to cram into one night."

He pondered what she'd said; then a wicked grin split his face. "Whatever you want, wench."

Lifting himself off her, he stood and went over to the hearth where he stoked the fire higher—to give him more light, she presumed. Then he set a half dozen already-lit candles about the bed, also for light, she presumed. Finally he grabbed a large harem-style pillow from Rashid's pallet and brought it to her. Arranging her on the bed so that she half reclined against the pillow, he then dragged a chair to the side of the bed, where he sat down with his feet crossed at the ankles and propped on the edge of the bed frame.

Thus casually sitting, he began telling her a story. "There was a desert sultan renowned for his sexual prowess, and his ability to satisfy all the houris in his harem."

"Is this a true story?"

"Absolutely true," he said, but there was a decided twinkle in his eyes.

"Abn Fadin—that was his name—told me once that a man's greatest pleasure came from seeing his woman's pleasure. And the way that a woman gained the most pleasure was when she knew her own body."

Abn Adam is more like it, she thought. "I know my

own body. What kind of soldier would I be if I did not know my body's strengths and weaknesses?"

"Not that kind of knowing, sweetling."

Oooh, I like it when he calls me by that endearment.

"Push your hair behind your ears. Now close your eyes and examine each of your ears by tracing the whorls with a forefinger. Lightly, lightly. Push the finger in, too. Do you feel how sensitive they are? Now imagine how the same thing would feel if done by a man's teeth and tongue. It will be wet there, and he must blow you dry."

The oddest thing happened then. She was touching her ears, but she felt the sensation down lower in her body. Much lower. "Does everyone know about this phenomenon?"

"Only me and Abn Fadin." She could tell he was lying by the mirth in his voice. "Now keep your eyes closed. Examine your lips now. Trace them with your finger. Lick them. Stick out your tongue as far as it will go, then slide it back in, out again, in again. Set a rhythm. Holy hell!"

"Why did you curse? Am I doing it wrong?"

"Nay, my warrior witch. You are doing it just right. That is the problem . . . not a problem, actually . . . just *my* problem."

She opened her eyes to see exactly what his problem was and noticed it immediately . . . standing at attention in his lap, once again. Her giggle had turned him limp earlier. He was not limp now.

"Stop smirking, Tyra, and close your eyes. In punishment for that disrespect, we will move directly to your breasts. Lift them from underneath. Feel their weight."

"Oh, I don't know about that."

"Do it."

She cupped her breasts from underneath and lifted.

She licked her suddenly dry lips as she did so and sighed.

"We may not have to worry about my spilling my seed inside your womb at this rate," Adam said.

She was fairly certain that meant he liked what she was doing.

"Now lift, and rub. And lift, and rub. Learn their size and texture. Would you like it if I were doing that for you?"

"Most certainly. Would you like to try?"

"Not yet."

"Touch your nipples. Play with them. Pull at them. Flick them up and down and side to side."

She did as he asked and almost swooned at the intensity of pleasure she felt there and between her thighs, where she suspected a wetness had begun to form. "I would definitely like you to be doing this, not me. I feel wanton . . . perverse . . . doing it myself. Well, actually, I feel wanton when you do it, too, but not perverse."

He laughed. "Now lower . . . move your hands lower . . . little by little. Lay them over your stomach. Skim over your woman hair. Now your thighs. Part them."

"I . . . I can't."

"Yea, you can. Do it for me. Do it for yourself."

She spread her legs slightly and continued to skim her fingers over the hair there. Who knew there could be such pleasure in touching one's self? Adam had been correct from the start. She did not know her own body.

"Wider," he coaxed. "Come now, Tyra, you can do better than that. Wider. Now bend your knees and put your feet flat on the mattress."

She practically yelped at that suggestion. There was no way in the world that she would be able to expose herself in that manner. It would be too mortifying. It would be a surrender. It would be . . . incredible. So, of course, she did it.

She gritted her teeth, arched her neck, and groaned aloud as ripple after ripple of flutters hit her right in that most vulnerable center of her. When she caught her breath, she asked, "Is the talk-pleasuring over yet?"

"Oh, Tyra, we have scarce begun. Examine yourself there now, dearling. Discover which folds are most sensitive. Find the bud that is the essence of all your sex. There."

She whimpered. "I am wet."

"I know, and you have no idea how much that pleases me."

Her lower body jerked when she hit upon the tiny bud.

"Don't stop. Circle it. Make it grow. Does it ache?"

She nodded. Every part of her body had tensed up. Her heart was pumping madly. She felt as if she were rising and rising and rising toward . . . something.

Opening her eyes, which seemed heavy and lethargic, she said, "I cannot do it anymore. I cannot. Something is wrong with me."

"Shhh. Trust me." He crawled up onto the bed, pulled the pillow from behind her head and placed it under her hips. Then he proceeded to do the most sinful, wanton, scandalous, unimaginable things to her woman folds . . . *with his tongue.*

She screeched.

She tried to push him away.

She tried to pull him closer.

Her hips started to jerk in a rhythmic undulation.

His mouth found that bud of sensation and suckled softly.

She screamed. She actually screamed as wave after wave of pleasure hit her there. It would not stop. He would not stop. She arched her hips up high. Her inner muscles clenched and unclenched, and she knew exactly what they wanted. Him. Inside her. Now.

"Please, please, please, please, please, please, please . . ." Her litany was a plea for satisfaction only he could give her.

She probably took the lead in dancing, too . . .

Adam knew what Tyra yearned for, but if he entered her now, the bedsport would be over afore it began.

But he should have known that his warrior princess was like no other woman. If his mind had been more clear, he might have been prepared.

Sensing his hesitation, she lifted her hips slightly, grabbed at the pillow under her, and tossed it to the floor. Then, before he could blink, she grabbed his head by the ears and pulled him up and over her. Within seconds, he found himself lying atop her, her strong legs wrapped around his hips, and his manpart pointed directly at her female portal.

"Wait, Tyra. Slow down. I must needs—"

"Slow down? Are you demented? I am like a boulder sliding down a slippery slope. I could no more slow down than—"

Before he knew what she was about, his own personal boulder slammed her hips against his, an instinctive movement as old as time, and he was inside her tight, spasming sheath to the hilt. It was hard to say whether he was more stunned or thrilled.

"You fill me," she said in a voice of utter awe.

Well, yes, he did fill her. Oh, God, he filled her so well. "Are you all right? Are you in pain?" After all, she had been a virgin. And in truth, he was in a bit of pain himself.

"I am fine."

Apparently, all the years of exercise and horseback riding had taken their toll on her maidenhead. He had heard of such afore. Even so, their coupling was proceeding at lightning speed. It was all too much, too soon. And after all, it had been two long years since he'd tupped a woman, he told himself defensively, sensing what was about to come. He pulled out slowly, then thrust . . . once, twice, three times, and roared his ecstasy. Wonderful as it was, the performance was all over for him in seconds.

"What happened?" she asked in a panic. "Your staff has gone limp inside me. I want it hard. Make it hard."

Should I laugh or cry? "I told you to wait."

"It is not over yet, is it? Do not dare to stop now."

He leaned down and gave her a quick kiss on the lips. "Give me time to regroup, Tyra."

"Time?" she shrieked, thumping on his chest with her fists. "There is no time. I need you now." Apparently, the quick kiss was not going to suffice.

He should have known. He should have been prepared for what Tyra did next. After all, this was Tyra . . . warrior woman . . . a person accustomed to going after what she wanted. An out-of-control boulder, by her own description.

With a twist of her hips, she flipped him over on his back and sat on him, his embarrassingly limp member still held inside her slick walls.

"Well?" she prodded.

"Well what?" he gurgled. The sight of a wild Amazon goddess straddling him, naked as Eve in the Garden of Eden, was enough to make any man gurgle. Adam— *that would be him*—would love to accommodate Eve— *that would be her*—but, unfortunately, the "snake" was uninterested . . . at the moment.

"Regroup," she ordered.

"Tyra, a man cannot get erect on command," he explained to her patiently. "He must be aroused . . . again." This was the most outrageous situation Adam had ever found himself in, and there had been plenty in his illfamed past.

"Tell me how to arouse you, then," she said with all the logic of an illogical female. In other circumstances, he would probably be enticed by such a suggestion from a female, but not now. Meanwhile, she squirmed on his lap to make herself more comfortable.

The "snake" perked up at her squirming, and Adam saw stars. "That would be one way," he choked out before inhaling and exhaling several times. "Hey, hey, hey, Tyra," he called out to her, placing his hands on her hips to still her motions. "Just relax."

"Relax," she repeated after him. Then she, too, inhaled and exhaled several times. "Now what?"

He grinned at her enthusiasm. "I do not want you to say anything, or do anything. Let me lead."

She nodded her head slowly, but then she raised one hand, as if asking his permission to speak.

Now what?

"There is just one thing. I'm weeping all over you."

At first he didn't understand. When he did, he started to laugh, which caused his "snake" to jiggle, which caused Tyra's eyes to widen. Finally he said, "The 'weeping' is from both of us, and it's natural . . . to be expected."

"Oh. All right. Proceed then."

"No more talking," he reminded her.

"No more talking," she agreed, running the back of her hand across her lips to demonstrate just how shut her mouth was.

For several long moments, he just gazed at her. Still straddling his body, trapping his half limp member inside her, she gazed back at him, waiting. God, she was magnificent.

"Lift your hair and place your hands behind your neck," he instructed.

She did so without question, and Adam decided then and there that there had never been a more beauteous or desirable female in all the kingdoms of the world. With just his fingertips, he traced her upraised inner arms from elbows to armpits, then the muscled planes of her sides and waist and hips.

The position of her arms caused her breasts to be outthrust. Leaning up off the bed, he took one nipple and areola into his mouth, just licking it at first with the tip of his tongue.

She made a soulful whimpering sound . . . the kind that makes a man thank God he is . . . well, a man. He hoped to elicit more of those sounds from her.

Pleased with the progress of what he hoped would be a slow assault, Adam began to suckle her. Slowly. Deeply. Rhythmically. Each time he drew on her, her inner muscles contracted around his staff, and soon he was hard enough to serve as the mast pole of a longship . . . certainly erect enough to give her all the pleasure she could want. But it was too soon for that. This time, he wanted to prolong her arousal, to double . . . nay, triple . . . her rapture when she finally peaked.

Tyra in the throes of ecstasy would be a sight to behold.

He hoped he survived.

CHAPTER SIXTEEN

What lackwit said sex was a burden for women? . . .
Tyra was so excited she could scarce contain herself. How she would survive this wondrous night, she had no idea, but she could not wait to find out.

She sat as still as any woman could in her position. And wasn't that an amazing feat . . . that two people . . . a man and a woman . . . could fit together so well? She was not sure what she had expected, but not this . . . fullness, accompanied by the most delicious tension. Why didn't women tell other women how wonderful it was? Why keep it a secret? Or could it be that she was the only woman who experienced such bliss . . . or that only this man could bring it on?

"Why are you smiling, witchling?" he asked, chucking her playfully under the chin with his knuckles.

"It is a secret," she replied, hoping the smile on her face was one of mystery now, and not a silly grin.

"Ah, then, I will have to torture your secrets from you." Even as he spoke, he put his hands on her buttocks and rolled them over so she was on her back once again. Luckily, his manpart had remained within her, but then, mayhap it could not escape once it reached this size. She would have to ask . . . later.

Adam began an assault on her then that could only be described as sweet agony. He kissed her and kissed her and kissed her till she did not know where he ended and she began, whether his tongue was in her mouth or hers was in his.

He wet the inner whorls of her ears, then blew them dry with such erotic appeal that she felt as if there were a thread connecting her ears to that special place between her legs. She wanted so very badly for him to move *there*, but she was following orders, for a change, and she liked it.

He allowed her to return his kisses and caresses, but nothing more. She liked that, too.

He worshiped her breasts. She would be sore on the morrow, but that soreness would be a reminder of how much she had enjoyed his attentions.

He whispered wicked, wicked things about her body and the things they would do. Some of them were surely physically impossible, though she would be willing to try.

They were both panting loudly by the time he sat back on his haunches and pulled out of her slightly. Wrapping his heels under her thighs, he spread her wider, then ordered, "Watch this, dearling. I want you to see yourself."

She propped herself on her elbows and gazed downward where she could see her woman-folds and the portion of his manpart that was not inside her. He did the most tantalizing thing then. He wet his middle finger in the moisture they had made there and began to strum the exposed pleasure bud that rose up, distended.

At the first touch of his finger, she let out an agonized, wail, then began to keen, "Stop, stop, stop, stop, stop. It is too much." In truth, it was not enough.

"Shhhh. Let it happen, sweetling," Adam said, his voice hardly recognizable for its hoarseness.

Flutters began inside her that quickly turned to clasps

of his male organ, then a continuous series of full-blown spasms. She thought she might have screamed at the peak, so mindless was she.

"Now it is my turn," he said. "God willing, I will last longer this time than a boy with his first maid."

His turn. She had thought it was over. She certainly felt complete. But no, he had raised himself up on straightened arms and now began to thrust in and out of her . . . long strokes that went on forever, dragging on her inner walls, sucking her back into the vortex of passion with a jolt of even more intense pleasure.

She could not think. She bucked her hips. She writhed from side to side. She wailed her building arousal, much, much more powerful than the previous ones.

"Do something," she screamed. "Do it, do it, do it!" She had no idea what she was urging him to do to put her out of her agony. All she knew was that the infuriating man just continued those long, slow strokes that were driving her mad . . . although she noticed that his teeth were gritted now, and veins stood out on his arched neck and forehead.

She reached out behind him and squeezed his buttocks.

He rewarded her with a groan. Only then did he begin shorter, harder strokes that drove her across the bed. She was meeting him, thrust for thrust, her legs spread as wide as they would go with her feet flat on the mattress. Her insides were grasping him so hard, it was a wonder he was not in pain. Finally it was too much. He roared out his male triumph as his hot seed spurted into her womb, and her pleasure spiraled and spiraled and spiraled till her insides shattered into a million small ripples of woman-joy.

Adam lay atop her for a long time, breathing as heavily as a warhorse. She sounded no better.

When he finally raised his head to look at her through glazed blue eyes, he kissed her swollen lips and whispered, "That was wonderful, my sweet warrior lady."

Her heart sang at his softly murmured sentiment. She asked a simple question then—one which any sensible-minded woman would have asked, in her opinion, but which prompted long peals of laughter from the rogue. "Oh, Tyra, you are priceless," he sputtered as she shoved him off her and onto the floor.

And all she'd said was, "Can we do it again?"

Some sports need no intermission . . .

Tyra was straightening out the bed linens, and Adam was making crude but complimentary remarks about her buttocks and what he referred to as her "butt-scar" as she bent over the mattress, when there was a soft knock on the door.

She looked at Adam, who shrugged.

"Tyra, are you all right? I heard you scream." It was Drifa, and her voice was definitely worried.

Adam made a muffled snorting sound and muttered something about her having screamed more than once.

"I'm fine. I . . . I saw a mouse." She glanced pointedly down at the object lying at rest between Adam's thighs. He was leaning casually against the wall, waiting for her to finish fixing the bed.

"A mouse! You have never been afraid of mice." It was Ingrith speaking now.

"I was startled, that is all. Besides, this was a particularly hairy mouse."

Adam made great show of examining his male part for hair. Then he silently mouthed at her the words, "You . . . will . . . pay."

"Let us in," Breanne insisted, rattling the door latch, unsuccessfully. Holy Thor! Was the whole tribe here?

"Mayhap the Saxon has kidnapped you and he is holding a knife to your body, forcing you to mislead us."

Tyra made a little squeal, but not in response to what Breanne had said. She was reacting to the Saxon coming up behind her while she was still bent over the bed. And it was not a knife he held to her body. 'Twas something altogether different, though it was hard.

"I heard a squeal," Vana said. Yea, it was the entire tribe, come to cheer her on . . . or something.

"Must be the mouse." Tyra could scarce breathe, let alone speak, for the ingenious man had lifted her up onto the mattress so that she was on all fours, and he had come up behind her. Into her ear he whispered, "Have you ever seen a stallion mount a mare?"

While her very own "stallion" fondled her breasts and mounted her from behind, and her eyes rolled back in her head, she managed a forceful, "Go away!" to her sisters. She couldn't be absolutely sure that they had left. They might have their ears pressed against the door. To be on the safe side, she made sure that she uttered no neighing noises.

They had no sooner completed their "ride" and were lying limp on the bed with satiety . . . she on her stomach, Adam on top of her . . . when there was another knock on the door, more forceful this time.

"Adam, open the door. I was in the hall under this room, and the ceiling is shaking. Has your Amazon lady been beating you?" It was Tykir.

"Amazon lady?" Tyra exclaimed and attempted to pummel his shoulders from behind. "Did you refer to me as an Amazon?"

"Only in the nicest possible way."

"Tyra's sisters are worried about her. Let us see that she is well." Bloody hell! It appeared that Alinor was there, too. What next?

A child's voice added. "The king sent me with a message fer Master Adam. 'My eldest daughter has a hu-u-uge dowry.'" It was Alrek now.

"Adam does not care about money. He is an honorable man, with more than enough coin of his own," Alinor asserted.

"God bless the woman," Adam declared. "Sometimes she is not her usual pain-in-the-arse busybody self."

"I think he is looking for love," Alinor continued.

"On the other hand . . ." Adam said.

"Love?" all four of her sisters said in a swooning voice. They must have returned.

"That is ridiculous woman-nonsense." Tykir was talking to his wife now. "Men do not think of love when the lust is running high. Hey, why did you hit me?"

"I hit you because you are behaving like a troll, you troll."

"Really, Adam, just open the door so I will know you two have not killed each other," Tykir implored. "Then I can be off to my bed where I will prove to my winsome wife just how much of a troll I can be."

With a sigh of disgust, Adam lifted himself gingerly off of Tyra. "It seems they will not leave till one of us makes an appearance." He wrapped a bed fur around his middle and stomped to the door. Opening it a mere crack, he said, "See, I am fine. Now go away." He tried to slam the door shut, but Tykir stuck a foot in.

"Why is your hair standing up like you combed it with a hay rake? And is that a bite mark surrounding your nipple?" Tykir asked with the innocence of a seasoned rascal.

Adam looked down. Then he looked over at Tyra and winked.

She hated it when he winked at her. It set off all kinds

of strange ripples through her body . . . a body that needed no more ripples tonight, thank you very much.

"Holy Valhalla! Our lady is stark naked, and she looks as if she wuz flattened by a warhorse." It was Alrek, who had scooted down to his knees and was peering around Tykir's legs and into the bedchamber.

Tyra scurried to cover herself.

"That is it! I am closing the door now." Adam was tired of being the brunt of everyone's speculations.

"Wait! Just one minute. I have something to say," Alinor shouted. She shoved her husband and Alrek aside, then advised Adam in a surprisingly warm, almost motherly way, "Treat her well."

Adam closed and locked the door, then dropped the bed fur. Tyra wasn't sure if he was talking to Alinor or her when he said, "That is precisely what I intend to do. Very well indeed."

Tyra hoped so. This was to be her one night of love. It would have to last her a lifetime.

Ah, yes, the famous Viking S-Spot . . .

After midnight, when most of the keep was abed, he and Tyra slipped outside to the sweat house, where they soaked their aching muscles in the hot springs.

It had been his plan to soap her body from crown to toes with the soft soap that was kept there . . . to minister to her like the princess she was. But Tyra surprised him once again. Taking charge, as she was wont to do, she lathered him up, rinsed him off, then laid him down on the stone slab outside the pool and kissed him up one side and down the other. But that was not all. Oh, God, that was not all. The enchanting woman, ever the apt pupil whether it be the art of battle or the art of love, brought her mouth down on him till he begged for mercy.

He thought he might be in love.

But many a man thought he was in love when his cock was tickling a lady's throat. So he did not speak the sentiment aloud. He planned to ponder the question later, though, when his eyeballs were no longer rolling in his head.

They went back to his bedchamber, arm in arm, where he massaged her still sore muscles with one of his special ointments . . . in this case, sandalwood scented. She kept saying she had not known there were muscles *there* or *there*, but he kept assuring her that there were still more muscles he would show her that she'd never imagined. In fact, some time later, he showed her the famous Viking S-Spot, the secret of which had been passed on to him by his stepfather Selik, as well as his uncles Tykir and Eirik. Tyra claimed to be extremely impressed. That must have been why she fainted at the end. It was Adam's opinion that a man who could make a woman faint in the bedsport had performed admirably. He intended to tell Tyra so when she awakened.

Adam was enthralled with Tyra. Her lack of inhibitions . . . her enthusiasm for everything he suggested . . . her ability to laugh while making love . . . all these made her an incredible bed companion. But it was more than this . . . much, much more, he suspected. And that prospect both frightened and elated him.

He fell asleep with a smile on his face.

In the still of the night . . .

Tyra awakened just before dawn.

The one night she'd committed to Adam was over. She could not be unhappy about what she'd given him. He had given her so much more in return.

But it was over now, and she must go on from here. A

new life . . . a new path awaited her. But she would never forget Adam, or this long night of loving. It was a gift from the gods.

She slipped out of the bed, careful not to awaken Adam, who slept soundly on his stomach, his face resting on his folded arms. Once she was hastily clothed, she gazed down at him, gloriously naked.

Adam thought he would have another sennight or so in her presence as she transported him back to his home in Britain, but he was wrong. Tyra had made a decision the previous evening. The agreement to captain the longship back had been made under pressure. It was an unreasonable request her father had made, and she felt no dishonor in disobeying him.

She was going now to Father Efrid's bedchamber, where she would renounce all her rights as a daughter of Stoneheim. She would never dare do so in front of her father. He would just laugh at her, or deny her request, or lock her in her bedchamber till she did his will. After the ritual denouncement before Father Efrid and two witnesses, Gunter and Egil, she intended to tie the priest up so that he would not warn her father of her actions. A fully manned longship awaited her in the harbor. She would be gone before first light.

There was one twinge of guilt she felt. Placing a palm over her stomach, she wondered if she might even now be carrying Adam's child. Probably not. But if she was, for once in her life she was going to entertain a female prerogative and change her mind. She had told him they would discuss the situation if it occurred. Well, they would not discuss the fate of any child she might carry. However, she would inform him, some way, if there was a birth . . . after the fact.

So now it was over. She would have liked to give

Adam a good-bye kiss, but he might stir if she did. Instead, she opened the door softly, looked back at him one last time, and mouthed the words she would never get to say aloud.

"I love you."

It was past dawn when Adam awakened and stretched languidly. There was nothing in the world for a man like the feeling of complete satiation after a night of good bedsport.

He reached for Tyra to give her a good-morning kiss, but found her side of the bed empty. He was not overly alarmed. His warrior wench was, no doubt, out spear throwing with her soldiers, or engaging in some other ridiculously energetic exercise. You would think he'd given her enough exercise the night before, but not his Tyra!

God! When did I start to refer to her as mine? But she is, by damn. If any other man dares to touch her, I will kill him on the spot.

He smiled at his inner vehemence. There were so many questions to be resolved with Tyra, but he had a sennight or more to come to some understanding with her while she transported him back to Britain. He was not sure if he loved her, and he did not know if marriage was a possibility, but now that he'd had her, he never intended to let her go. That decision gave an odd buoyancy to his spirits. It was as if his mind had been in a daze for a very long time. How refreshing to finally know what he wanted!

There was a knock on the door just as he slid his legs over the side of the bed and attempted to stand. He was chuckling at the weakness in his knees as he pulled on a pair of *braies* and opened the door.

He was not surprised to see Tykir standing there once again.

He *was* surprised at his uncle's announcement, though.

"Tyra is gone."

Misery does not need company . . .

By that evening, Adam was drunker than he'd ever been in all his life. The ale-head that would follow on the morrow would surely bring excruciating pain and stomach upheavals, but he could not care now. All he knew was that he was suffering from fierce anger alongside fierce hurt, interspersed with a bit of humiliation. Dousing himself with ale was the only thing that helped, and even that only numbed him.

Perhaps he would drill a hole in his own head and let his brain seep out. It hardly seemed as if it would make a difference in terms of his intellect.

How could she? How could she? he kept asking himself. What had transpired between the two of them the night before had been amazing. Now he was wondering if he'd been the only one who thought so. No—he refused to believe that she had been pretending. Tyra had been just as affected as he had. *Then why did she go?*

As if it weren't bad enough that she'd abandoned him so ignominiously . . . and, yes, it felt like abandonment . . . he'd found out this afternoon that Gunter and Egil had accompanied her on her longship to Byzantium. He swore that if either of those Viking peacocks dared to touch Tyra, he would kill them both. But then, he realized, Tyra could do whatever the hell she wanted. Hadn't she proven that by renouncing her family ties while her father slept, and defying his own wishes regarding any child that would come of their coupling by taking the decision out of his hands, by removing her person?

Adam put his face in his hands. He was torturing

himself with all these questions. He had to stop. A long-ship awaited in the harbor that would take him back to Britain on the morrow, if he wanted. That was what he should do. Put Tyra and this whole disaster of a forced visit to Stoneheim out of his mind.

"Adam, dost think you should be drinking so much?" Tykir asked, coming up and putting a hand on his shoulder.

"Yea, I do."

"Well, then, mayhap I will join you," Tykir conceded all too quickly. In Adam's opinion, Tykir would be better off discovering his son Thork's whereabouts. Adam had noticed him a short time ago tiptoeing out of the hall in a most suspicious fashion, with a half dozen youthlings tiptoeing after him.

Alinor, sitting on Tykir's other side, swatted her husband with a slab of manchet bread. She was able to do so with her free hand even though she held her sleeping babe in the cradle of her other arm. "Dumb dolt! You are supposed to be helping Adam, not joining in his misery."

"What? Drinking is a misery now?" Tykir said, grabbing his wife about the waist and pulling her onto his lap with a big kiss on the mouth. He was careful not to disturb his sleeping son in the process. "Drinking can be a man's best friend when his woman-luck has run out."

"Drink makes the wise man a fool," Rashid opined. If Rashid did much more opining, Adam was going to sew up his mouth with some physician's thread.

"You are so right, Rashid. Well, husband, who gave you that bit of lackwitted wisdom? *'Drinking can be a man's best friend.'* Rurik?" Alinor scoffed. Rurik was a close comrade of theirs who thought he knew everything about everything, especially women. "You are supposed to be giving Adam sound advice, not drivel."

"Never give advice in a crowd," Rashid said.

All of them looked at Rashid as if he'd lost his mind, but no one asked what he meant. No one cared. Really, Rashid was getting to be as pestsome as Bolthor.

Speaking of Bolthor, just then the skald stood. "I feel a saga coming on," he announced.

Adam felt his stomach churn. "It had better not be another one about me," he mumbled.

"This is a saga of Thorvald the King."

Adam exhaled with relief, and the king, who was not speaking to Adam because of his failure to hold on to his daughter, puffed out his chest with pride. Thorvald had not yet learned that a Bolthor saga was nothing to be proud of.

> *"Thorvald was a mighty king,*
> *In battle his sword did sing.*
> *Alas, a mighty head wound did he gain*
> *Which caused him much sleep pain.*
> *His daughter, the princess soldier,*
> *Brought her father a far-famed healer,*
> *Who drilled a hole in the king's head,*
> *Thus bringing the man back to life.*
> *The only trouble is now the king has a hole*
> *Which many a randy Viking, high in the mead,*
> *Might try to swive,*
> *Thinking it is a hole . . .*
> *Of an entirely different kind."*

Thorvald seemed stunned at first. That was most people's reaction to hearing one of Bolthor's sagas for the first time. Then he threw his head back and released great peals of laughter, which gave all the other Vikings in the hall permission to join in.

Adam had to give Norsemen credit for one thing . . . they did have an ability to make mock of themselves.

"I give you fair warning, Tykir . . . you had best not be thinking about leaving Bolthor behind with me when you return to Dragonstead," Adam told Tykir even as he took another long swig of ale.

"I am deeply offended that you would think such," Tykir said, placing a hand over his presumably wounded heart.

"That is precisely what you told me you were going to do," Alinor pointed out. "Your exact words were: 'Adam needs a poet to brighten his life.'"

"For the love of Allah, do I not brighten your life enough?" Rashid asked. He also put a hand over a presumably wounded heart.

"Best you examine your tongue and where it might lead you," Tykir chastised his wife. Meanwhile, he patted his restless baby on the head, clearly a doting father despite all his arrogant man-talk.

"You liked my tongue well enough yestereve," she answered saucily.

"Al-i-nor!" Tykir exclaimed with pretended shock, accompanied by a huge grin. "A biddable wife would never speak in such a wanton way."

"I thought you liked my wanton way."

"I do. I do."

"Would you two mind taking this conversation elsewhere?" Adam suggested. "I am busy turning my brain into gruel."

"Which brings us back to the original subject," Alinor said. "Advice to Adam."

"I do not want any advice," Adam protested.

But no one was listening to him.

Tyra's sisters had just come up and had apparently overheard part of the conversation.

"Forget about advice," Breanne remarked. "It will probably go just as badly as our seduction plan for Tyra."

"Well, the feminine attire seemed to work," Drifa said.

"Yea, I may have to get one of those red gowns for myself," Ingrith added.

"And jealousy . . . don't forget jealousy. It worked when Gunter and Egil expressed an interest in Tyra," Vana said. "Adam was nigh livid at the sight of other men interested in her."

"We never could get her to walk in a feminine way, though. She does have a tendency to swagger," Alinor put in. "And as for acting like a damsel in distress, forget that. Even I have trouble swallowing such silliness in a woman."

"Whoa, whoa, whoa!" Adam said, raising his heavy head and trying to make sense of what they were blathering about. "Are you saying that Tyra had a plan for seducing me?"

"Nay, you dimwit. *We* had a plan for getting Tyra to seduce you," Alinor explained.

"We? What *we?*" Adam was getting more confused by the moment.

"Me, Vana, Breanne, Drifa, and Ingrith," Alinor replied.

"Alinor! For shame, that you would stoop to such devious means to entrap a man!"

"Well, it was not really so different from *our* plan," Rafn said, coming up to join the group. "Except that our plan was for Adam to seduce Tyra."

Adam narrowed his eyes at Rafn, who should be in heaven now that Tyra was gone. He and Vana would be

...rry now . . . in fact, he'd overheard Ingrith
of a wedding feast to be held in a sennight.
"Exp.. yourself, Viking," Adam ordered, though the
words came out a bit slurred and not as threatening as
he intended.

"Our plan . . . mine, Tykir's, Rashid's, and
Bolthor's . . . was no doubt more enlightened. It involved hot looks, compliments, constant touching, kissing, and jealousy."

"Do not forget the erotic conversation," Rashid
added.

"And the telling of wicked tales," Bolthor added.

"I was the one who suggested the Viking S-Spot,"
Tykir said proudly.

"What's an S-Spot?" Ingrith, Drifa, and Breanne
wanted to know.

"Never mind!" Vana inserted, then immediately
turned bright red at her telling slip.

"My God, you have got to be the biggest bunch of
bungleheads I have ever met," Alinor said to all the men,
and the sisters nodded their agreement, though some of
them were still mumbling questions about the S-Spot.
"As if women could be won over with hot looks!"

The men looked sheepish, except for Adam, who was
growing angrier by the minute. "Are . . . are . . . are you
saying," he sputtered out, "that all of you . . . men and
women alike . . . have been discussing me and Tyra in
such intimate detail? That you have been plotting behind our backs to get us together?"

An awkward exchange of glances followed, but the
silence was telling. Adam groaned, firmly convinced
that his life could not get any worse. He was wrong.

Bolthor stood and announced, "This is the saga of
Adam the Lesser, called 'Advice to a Dumb Dolt.'"

"Sometimes a man has woman-luck.
Sometimes a man does not.
But methinks the gods have a master plan
For each and every one of us.
One man, one woman destined to meet,
Their fate sealed in the heavens.
But men have a tendency betimes
To think with their cocks
Instead of their hearts.
That's when the dumb dolts of the world
Need the advice of all their friends.
Thus sayeth Bolthor the Skald."

You could say she was a Viking Anne Landers . . .

Alinor found Adam the next morning coming from the garderobe, where he had been hurling the contents of his stomach for the past hour. His head felt as if it had been cleaved with a broadax. And he swore there was hair growing on his tongue.

"Not now, Alinor," he warned. "I cannot take any lectures this morning."

She reeled back a bit, no doubt from the stench of his breath, not his words.

But then she handed him a goblet and said in a surprisingly kind voice, "Drink this. It will make you feel better."

He took the goblet from her and sniffed. He recognized some of the herbs that would indeed help alleviate the head pounding and stomach nausea. He downed the drink in one long swallow, then exhaled with a loud belch.

"Come," she said and led him over to a stone bench. The air was cool and they were both wearing fur-lined cloaks.

He sat beside her, as miserable as he had been before he'd started his drinking bout. "Where's the babe?"

"Asleep. With his father." She smiled. "Tykir imbibed a bit too much, too."

"What a mess I have made of my life!"

"Yea, you have," she said bluntly. "But that is a good start . . . admitting your mistake."

"You're going to give me advice, aren't you?" He groaned softly at the prospect.

"Did you tell her how you feel?"

He shook his head, and felt as if there were rocks rolling about inside his skull. "I do not know how I feel."

"Yea, you do, dearling. You just haven't admitted it to yourself yet. As far as I know, the only thing of substance you told her was that you would take her babe away from her . . . if it should be born."

He looked at Alinor, then shrugged sheepishly. "That was rather overbearing of me, wasn't it?"

Alinor nodded. "As Rashid has been saying, 'Even the strongest team of oxen cannot take back ill-chosen words once spoken.' In any case, did you ever consider what place she might have in your life, or you in hers?"

"Well, I did have one thought. When I operated on her father, she was a magnificent assistant. She did not blanch at all the blood, or hesitate to handle tools. In truth, she anticipated what I would need before I asked."

"So you are saying that you two might have made a good healing team?"

"Mayhap."

"And what did she say when you suggested this to her?" Alinor stared at him for several long moments. Then she grunted with disgust. "Let me guess. You never shared that idea with her."

Both of them sat in silence then, staring off toward

the harbor where a longship was being prepared for travel.

"Let us cut to the marrow here, you thickheaded fool," Alinor finally said. "What . . . do . . . you . . . want?"

He did not even hesitate to answer. "Tyra."

"Well, then," Alinor said, throwing her hands up in the air, "you have your answer."

He smiled for the first time in a day and a half and yelled for Rashid, who was walking toward him from the courtyard.

"Yea, master? You called," Rashid replied dolefully.

"It appears we are going back to the Eastlands, after all."

"To Arabia?" Rashid asked hopefully.

"Nay, to Byzantium."

CHAPTER SEVENTEEN

✧

A Viking road trip, or a circus on a longship? . . .
Adam was living his worst nightmare.

It started the following morning, one full day since he'd ended his drunken binge and decided he wanted Tyra enough to go after her . . . even to the ends of the earth.

"'Twould seem the longship on which you planned to travel is going to prove unsuitable," Rafn commented dryly as they stood on the wharf just past dawn, waiting for the crew to assemble.

"Huh?" Adam responded.

"The royal bedstead and those six stallions would never fit on the longship you planned to use. Oh, I see a *knarr* is being brought forth. Yea, one of those deeper, larger trading vessels will serve your purposes better."

"Huh?" Adam said again, then turned to follow the direction of Rafn's gaze. "Oh . . . my . . . God!"

A large, ornately carved bedstead was being carried by four burly Vikings down the incline from the Stoneheim castle to the harbor. Following in its wake were many servants carrying a thick straw mattress and many chests, even a thronelike chair. Still others led six nervous stallions.

There came also King Thorvald, relying on a long staff for a cane. He was dressed to the gills in regal attire—a red tunic embroidered with gold thread in a writhing dragon pattern, over black *braies* and high leather boots. A deadly broadsword with a spectacular silver hilt was strapped to his side. Over all was a massive ankle-length cloak of rich black sable pelts. He looked like a Norse god . . . a Norse god about to take a long journey.

Rafn was grinning at Adam's shock. Now that Rafn's future was sealed—his wedding to Vana being a foregone conclusion—he did a large amount of grinning. But Adam did not appreciate the grinning now, at his expense.

"I have directed my men to prepare a *knarr*," the king told Adam, panting slightly from his exertions. Truly, the man should be resting in his sickbed, not traipsing about, dragging his household furniture with him.

"Wh-what?" Adam stammered, then quickly asserted, "Nay, nay, nay, you are not coming with me."

Thorvald arched his imperial eyebrows, even as he waved the servants to begin loading his bed and his stallions onto the large vessel. A canopy with leather sideflap curtains had already been erected in the center of the boat, presumably for the bed and other royal trappings.

"Be reasonable," Adam urged the king. "You have undergone a serious medical procedure. You are supposed to be recuperating. You have a hole in your head, for God's sake!"

"And your point would be?" The king was already looking weary as he leaned on his staff and watched the provisioning of the *knarr*.

"My point is that you need to be in your sickbed."

"I have brought my sickbed with me. Besides, is it not best that I stay close by my personal physician?"

"I am not your personal physician. Father Efrid is."

The king swished a hand through the air dismissively. "A man cannot have two physicians?"

Adam made a low growling sound of frustration. "Why can't you trust me to find Tyra and bring her back? After all, it is not as if she is in any real . . ." His words trailed off as a thought came unbidden to him. Hesitantly, he asked, "She is not in any real danger, is she?"

"Of course she is in danger. The Byzantine court, like any court, is a cess pit of intrigues. A knife in the back can be more deadly than a battle wound."

"Oh, this is just wonderful! I really need more things to worry about." He glowered at the king, who did not even have the grace to look guilty. "What makes you think you would be better able than I to rescue her from such a situation? I have served in various Eastern courts. And just because I am a healer does not mean I cannot fight when the need arises. I can handle a weapon if need be."

"Mayhap you can, mayhap you cannot. But with your charm and my clout, we will be doubly sure of rescuing her."

Rescue. The king is being overprotective. Tyra is a warrior. She is perfectly capable of escaping danger. But what if . . . ? Adam's shoulders sank with surrender.

Then the next crisis came barreling down the hill toward him with a shrill, wailing cry, "Naaaaaayyyyy!"

It was Kristin. No sooner did his mind register who it was than the little girl hurled herself through the air at him. He had no choice but to open his arms and catch her. Immediately, she latched her arms around his neck and held on tight, sobbing loudly.

" 'Twould seem young girls develop attachments to you. First Tyra, now this one. You must have charm oozing from you," the king remarked.

"It is not just young girls," Rafn pointed out. "Young

people in general think he is the best thing since honey custard was invented . . . by Ingrith, no doubt." He motioned his head toward the newest arrivals.

It was Alrek, huffing and puffing as he tried to simultaneously run and carry the baby, Besji, his sheathed sword slapping at his leg with each stride. His whole side would be bruised by nightfall. Close behind Alrek was the little boy, Tunni. Besji and Tunni, frightened by all the commotion, were crying, their sobs creating a counterpoint to the continuing wails of Kristin, who was spouting a river of tears down Adam's neck.

Adam had no idea what to do.

"I am going with you," Alrek declared.

"You are not," Adam said. And he meant it.

"Me, too," Kristin blubbered, echoed by, "Me, too. Me, too," from Tunni and Besji. He hadn't even been aware that Besji could talk, though he supposed at two years she should be able to.

Aaarrgh! What am I to do?

"I am sorry to disappoint you, my lord, but I cannot obey your orders this time," Alrek said. "You told me I must think before I act . . . start behaving as a man. Well, that is what I am doing. I have thought, and now I am acting. I am going with you to Byz . . . Byz . . . that place where Lady Tyra went."

"How many times do I have to tell you that I am not a lord? And, really, Alrek, this is impossible. You cannot bring all these children with you."

"Actually, we have a perfect solution," Vana announced brightly. She and the other sisters seemed to appear out of nowhere. "While you are off to Byzantium, taking Alrek with you, we can take the other children back to your home in Britain. Tyra told me what a dirty mess it was. We will prettify it for you . . . make it a home for you to bring Tyra back to."

Prettify? She says that as if it is an attribute to be desired. "We? What *we?*"

"Us. Tyra's sisters," Vana answered. "Well, except for Breanne, who wants to go to the 'Great City' to study the buildings there." All four of Tyra's sisters were staring at him expectantly, as if they'd just offered him a gift for which he should thank them profusely.

"You are not going to Byzantium with us," King Thorvald told Breanne. "'Tis too dangerous."

There it was, that danger business again.

Breanne burst into tears and shouted at her father . . . something he was clearly unaccustomed to, if his wide eyes were any indication. "'Tis not fair. Tyra gets to do everything. I am going, I tell you. I am going." Now she was stamping her foot petulantly.

Adam put a hand to his throbbing forehead . . . not an easy task with Kristin still clinging to him as if her very life depended on it. Were these people actually suggesting that they all invade his home? The children. The sisters. Probably an army of servants. By the rood! The possibilities were horrifying. At the least, his peace and privacy would be a thing of the past.

He had to pry Kristin's fingers from his neck in order to disengage himself from her embrace. With much relief, he set her on the ground next to Alrek. Her thumb shot immediately into her mouth as she gazed up at him, reproachfully. He inhaled and exhaled to calm himself. He could not bear to look at the little girl, so he didn't.

"Now, Vana," he said, trying for a reasonable tone, hoping he didn't sound as panicked as he felt. "'Tis true that I have dirt aplenty in my keep, but it would be asking too much of you to straighten out my household back in Britain. After all, you have much to do here at Stoneheim, preparing for your wedding to Rafn."

"That is the best part," she said with much cheeriness. "Rafn will be especially busy protecting Stoneheim while Father is gone, and we must wait till Father's return for the wedding anyhow."

"Furthermore," Thorvald declared wheezily, "'tis best to keep the prospective bride away from the randy groom afore the wedding, lest I come home to a big-bellied daughter."

"Faaa-tther!" Vana exclaimed, her white face turning bright red.

Rafn, in true man-fashion, just nodded his head.

"Everyone, be quiet!" Adam practically shouted. "Let me make myself perfectly clear. I do not want my castle cleaned. I do not want flowers planted in my moat. I do not want my cook to learn how to prepare myriad menus. This may surprise you all, but I like my home the way it is, rusty drawbridge and all."

"You have a rusty drawbridge?" Breanne asked with sudden interest. Clearly, she was now pulled in two directions. Should she go to Byzantium and study new building methods? Or should she go to Britain and take on a re-building project? "Oh, all right, I will not go to Byzantium this time. But next time I am definitely going."

"Aaarrgh!" he said with as much brilliance as he could muster.

"That is all well and good," Rashid remarked, coming up from God only knew where. He'd probably been hiding. "But what about the children?"

You Judas, you! Adam thought. Out loud he said, "They are not my responsibility." He did not look at the children as he spoke. He could not. But he was the one who felt like a traitor . . . which was ridiculous.

Rashid shrugged. "If you say so, master."

Adam bristled. "What is that supposed to mean?"

Rashid shrugged again. "With all due respect, my

lord, there is a famous proverb that says, 'Love and commitment are two sides of the same coin.' "

Adam's jaw dropped open. "Who said anything about love?" He slanted a quick look at the children, and all four of them looked as if he'd just stabbed them, even Besji, who couldn't possibly have understood what he'd said.

It was an absurd situation, and he was sick of having these people foisted on himself. With a snarl, he turned on his heel and began to stomp up the hill to gather the last of his belongings. He had no intention of returning to Stoneheim . . . leastways not in the next decade or so.

Halfway up the hill, he stopped dead in his tracks. At heart, Adam was an honest man. He abhorred lying, even to himself. *What if Selik and Rain had decided they were not responsible for Adela and me?* That question hammered inside his head, almost as if his two foster parents were asking the question. *The kindness must be passed on. As you were treated, so must you treat others. As you were saved, so must you save others. And, yea, you have the power to provide miracles.*

He muttered a sincere "Bloody hell," then turned around and announced to the gaping crowd, "All right. But only for a short visit."

At first there was a stunned silence. Then Ingrith asked, waving a hand to indicate herself and her sisters, "All of us?"

"Yea. God help me, but you are all welcome, for a *short* visit. But make no substantial changes."

Vana was already wringing her hands with anticipation, and he thought he heard Ingrith ask Rafn, "Dost think they have wild reindeer in Britain? I'm thinking a reindeer feast would be good for the homecoming festivities. If not that, how about boiled wolf?" *What homecoming? What festivities? And wolf? I am most definitely not eating wolf.* Drifa was rushing off to get a shovel, no doubt to dig up some bushes for transplanting. And Breanne was still pondering the temptations of a rusty drawbridge.

"And the children?" Rashid asked. There was a crafty smirk on his face that Adam did not like . . . not one bit.

"Yea, for a visit. Then they will return to Stoneheim." Inside, Adam knew—*he just knew*—that he was committing to much more than that.

Adam had not finished speaking before Kristin was running up the hill, her gown gathered to her knees, her skinny legs pumping wildly. This time, when she hurled herself into his arms, she was smiling, not weeping. As she patted his face reassuringly, she confided in her little-girl voice, "You doan hafta luv us . . ."

Adam braced himself for what would come next.

". . . but I luv you."

Adam knew he was lost then. Good and truly lost.

Or was he found?

New beginnings aren't all they're cracked up to be . . .

Elsewhere . . .

The trip to Byzantium—referred to as Miklagard by the Vikings—was a grueling one, and thank the gods for that. Tyra needed hard physical labor and concentration to keep her mind off her misery.

The work should have taken up all her time and thoughts. Unfortunately, it did not. Weather-luck had been with them, the climate getting increasingly warmer each day, but that was the only good thing about the trip thus far. She could not even share in the enthusiasm of her men-at-arms, who were looking forward to the adventure of a new country and service in the imperial army's prestigious Varangian Guard.

She had known from the start that forgetting Adam

and their night of lovemaking would be impossible. But she had underestimated just how miserable she would be. She was losing weight, sleep, and the joy of living.

She missed Stoneheim.

She missed her sisters and her father.

Above all else, she missed Adam.

To make matters worse, she was not pregnant. Her monthly flux had been late, and deep inside, a foolish part of Tyra had wished for Adam's seed to have taken root in her womb. But it was not to be, she'd found out yestereve.

In order to avoid the more difficult voyage around Jutland, the land of the Danes, Tyra had directed her small contingent of sailors to cross the stormy Baltic Sea. Then they would follow the trade route down the Volkov to Old Ladoga, the Norse Aldeigjuborn, where a trading post stood, offering a brief respite from the journey. If their ship had gone by way of the Dneipr, as many Norsemen did, they would have had to face cataracts, sandbanks, and dangerous shoals. As it was, they'd had to employ portage on more than one occasion.

Gunter and Egil came up to stand at the rail with her as her boat approached the Golden Horn harbor of the "Great City," Constantinople, capital of the Byzantine Empire, which occupied the eastern half of the old Roman Empire. It was a spectacular view, even for those like herself who had visited here in the past. There were three sets of walls enclosing the city, one inside the other, accented periodically by one hundred massive towers, each sixty feet high. The ancient walls were almost six hundred years old. Surrounding the outer walls were moats, and along the sea wall were iron chains that blocked the harbor from invaders. There was much to protect, too, since the city had several hundred thousand inhabitants and vast wealth.

"Are you having second thoughts?" Gunter asked, looping an arm around her shoulders. She looked pointedly at the hand, its fingers pointing toward her breast, and Gunter laughed. "Now, now, m'lady. I am just being friendly."

"Like our first night out, when you tried to crawl into my bed furs?"

Gunter pretended to wince. "You cannot blame a man for trying. What kind of Viking would I be if I did not offer my services to a pretty maid?"

"Oh, please, Gunter!" It was she who laughed now. "All these years we have traveled together, and not once before did you offer your services. Why now?"

He shrugged. "You have changed."

"How so?" *Does the fact that I am no longer a virgin show?*

"You are softer somehow."

That is just wonderful! A soft soldier! A voluptuous Varangian! A weak woman! It appeared she would have to work more on her masculinization. More groin scratching, and swaggering, and spitting. She already knew how to curse like a sailor.

"As to your question," she said, changing the subject, "nay, I have no second thoughts. This is the right thing for me."

"Me, too," Egil remarked, coming up on her other side.

"Do not even think of touching my arse," she warned. If Egil put his hand on her buttocks one more time, as seemed to have become a reflex with him, she swore she was going to pull out her dagger and slice him across the knuckles.

He put a palm to his chest, as if wounded by her words. "My lady, your words do me wrong. I am betrothed to be married."

"Oh, really! That did not stop you from making indecent proposals to me."

"What indecent proposals?" an interested Gunter wanted to know.

"The same ones you have been making," she told Gunter.

"Oh," Gunter said, clearly disappointed that there was not some new form of indecent proposal he had not yet heard of. *Men!* "But I am not affianced, Tyra. So I am free to provide for your pleasure. Unlike Egil here. By the by, Egil, who are you trying to impress with those tight *braies?*"

"What has my being affianced to do with having sex with another woman? My Inga does not expect me to remain chaste whilst I go off earning treasure for her bride price. And as to my tight *braies*, at least I have something substantial to fill them."

Gunter stiffened and dropped his arm from her shoulder. Next they would be calling for the *holmganga*, a duel that was fought within a ten-foot square according to strict ritual rules.

"Would the two of you just stop? We are about to dock." With that in mind, she called out to Ivan, the rudder master, "Pull up to the Gate of Phanar. That is closest to the Palace of Blachernae, where the emperor and empress should be in residence."

Ivan nodded, and soon they were docked.

"Go to Romanus and send my regards. Request an immediate audience for me," she ordered Gunter and Egil. "I met him five years past when his father, Constantine, was still alive. He was only seventeen or so at the time, but he should remember me. If not, give him this as a gift." She handed Gunter a velvet-lined box containing a large piece of rare amber on a heavy gold chain. Although she was not much given to ornamentation, she had been wearing it at the time over her tunic, and he had admired it.

Tyra stepped over the plank then. She had been aboard ship too long now and much preferred to await the emperor's summons on land. When she stepped ashore, carrying with her the shield that Adam had given her, she sighed deeply.

With those first steps onto a new land, tears welled in her eyes. A new episode of her life was about to begin.

ONE SENNIGHT AFTER DEPARTURE FROM STONEHEIM

Samsonite? Did someone say Samsonite? . . .

"When I made the decision that I wanted Tyra . . . that I should go after her . . . I never realized that she carried so much baggage with her," Adam grumbled aloud. He was standing at the prow of the ship, which was riding the large waves of a stormy Baltic Sea.

In truth, Adam was growing excessively tired of longships and stomach-churning waves and wet boots and watery horizons. Once he got back to his home in Northumbria, he swore he would not travel again for a good long time, and definitely not over water.

"What baggage would that be?" Tykir asked.

How his uncle had come to be on this journey was another story altogether. But here he was, and Alrek, too. Not to mention Bolthor, who was off somewhere composing an Ode to the Ocean, or Saga of a Shark, or some such thing. You would think that Tykir—a man with a newborn child—would feel the need to stay close to home, but, nay, Tykir had sent Alinor back to Dragonstead under heavy guard. For some reason, he believed that Adam needed him more than his wife and children did. Alinor had agreed to let him go, but adamantly refused to allow their son Thork to accompany his father. Tykir appeared alternately prideful and dismayed by his incorrigible son, who

was surely a miniature version of himself as a youthling.

"The baggage I refer to is a troublesome family,"
Adam explained. "I did not realize that caring for
someone"—he still had trouble saying the love-word—
"meant involvement with all these other appendages."

Tykir laughed. "Appendages, huh? That is a good
way of describing family members. But, really, Adam,
you should not be surprised. It is the same for everyone.
For example, when I fell in love with Alinor, I also had
to deal with her barmy twin brothers, Egbert and He-
bert. When she fell in love with me, my family became
hers, and that included not just Rain and Selik, Eirik
and Eadyth, and all their children, but you and Adela,
too. Plus our friends Bolthor and Rurik and all the rest."

Adam winced at the mention of Adela. "But don't
you ever just crave privacy?"

"All the time. Well, not all the time. When things get
too loud or bothersome at Dragonstead, I go off on an
amber dig to the Samland Peninsula, or to Hedeby for
trading. But you know what is really odd? No sooner do
I leave the fjord harbor at Dragonstead than I am missing my wife and family . . . even all the chaos that ac-
companies them." Tykir shrugged.

"She will change my life, won't she?" Adam asked.

Tykir chuckled at his nephew's woeful tone and informed him with much glee, "Oh, Adam, she already
has."

ABOUT THAT TIME, IN BYZANTIUM

The golden city didn't shine for her . . .

"You wish to join the Varangian Guard?" Romanus
asked Tyra incredulously. Thank the gods, she and her
men understood the Byzantine tongue, being far-traveled

people. Romanus sat upon a great silver throne under a golden canopy in the palace reception room, several marble steps up from where Tyra stood with Gunter and Egil.

Romanus's keen eyes surveyed her, from her long blond hair, plaited on each side into war braids, over her soft leather tunic and *braies*, down to her overlarge feet encased in half-boots. He gave particular attention to the broadsword sheathed at her side, and the battle-ax slung over her shoulder with a special strap.

"I do . . . along with three dozen fine fighting men who have accompanied me," she answered, not at all intimidated by Romanus, who was several years younger than herself.

Romanus rubbed his chin thoughtfully, his eyes twinkling with delight. She could see that she and her entire retinue amused him. It was true that she and her men were attired differently from these Byzantines. Her men wore hip-length tunics with thick belts over *braies* and leather boots. Some of them even wore wolf skins. No matter how fine their fabrics or the jewels they might wear, they were primitive in appearance compared to these more sophisticated Byzantines, who wore loose silk or linen ankle-length gowns of a T-shape, highly ornamented with embroidery. Their necks and arms and various fingers held jewels worth a king's treasure.

At twenty-three, Romanus was an impressive man, and not just because of his garments of royal purple encrusted with pearls and rubies. The young man had inherited his father's fine physique and charming manners, not to mention his mother's beauty. And vanity—he had that in abundance, it was clear. Already he wore her amber pendant around his neck, hanging over his golden breastplate.

He was nothing compared to Adam, though. No one was.

"But a woman in the Imperial Army, Romanus? It is unheard of." The woman speaking at Romanus's side was Theophano, a breathtakingly beautiful woman with sleek dark hair reaching down to her knees and wide ebony eyes. The sapphire torque around her neck could purchase five longships. Theophano was clearly in love with her husband, and he with her. They could not seem to stop touching one another . . . a hand on the wrist here, a pat on the head there. Theophano had already given him three children and was pregnant with a fourth. No wonder, with all that touching!

"But perhaps that is the best part, Theo," Romanus said as if thinking aloud. "No other king or emperor could boast of the same. Mayhap if the Princess Tyra works out, I could establish a separate female guard. Truly, my dear, I will be the envy of every monarch in the world."

Theophano was not convinced. "Like a freak dwarf, or a double-headed cow?" she sneered.

Tyra bristled with outrage, but held her tongue when Gunter and Egil squeezed her forearms from either side in warning.

Even more alarming, Theophano kept looking from Tyra to Romanus, as if she suspected that her husband had a personal interest in Tyra . . . which was ridiculous, of course, especially when he had a woman of Theophano's outstanding beauty.

Unfortunately, that suspicion proved true when Theophano whispered to her husband, loud enough for Tyra to overhear, "She is so *big*, dearling, and not at all pretty."

Romanus, the dumb dolt, answered, "Dost think so, dearling? On the contrary, I think she is stunning. Tall, yes, and perhaps not pretty, but very attractive."

Holy Thor! That should put an end to her hopes of joining the Varangian Guard. A jealous wife would never allow her husband to employ an attractive woman. Not that Tyra considered herself attractive. It must be something Adam had done to her that made her appear different to men. She and Gunter and Egil exchanged meaningful glances, and shrugged. Perhaps they could continue on to the Rus lands and find mercenary work there. Or they could backtrack to Trelleborg and become Jomsvikings, but Tyra misdoubted the knights would allow a woman to join their ranks. Or her men could stay and become Varangians while she went off on her own.

Romanus clapped his hands together as if making a decision. "It is done. You and your soldiers are welcome to join my army, Tyra." He motioned for a man standing off to the side to come forward. "Let me introduce you to my general, Nicephorus Phocas. Nicky, you can find a place for several accomplished fighting men . . . and a woman, ha ha ha . . . can you not?"

Tyra was in awe. Who had not heard of General Nicephorus Phocas? Nicephorus was famous for his spectacular triumphs in recent years in Crete.

Whereas Romanus was young and handsome, Nicephorus, at fifty or so years, was short and squat with broad shoulders and a barrel chest. His complexion was swarthy from years of serving under the Syrian sun. His eyes, piercing and sad, were small and dark, under heavy brows.

He stared for a long time at Tyra before speaking. "We are constantly involved in battle to drive the infidels back to the desert. That is my brother Leo's area of command," he told her. "Do you have any problem fighting Arabs?"

For some reason, an image of Rashid flashed into her mind. But she gave the answer that was expected of her. "The enemy of my friend is my enemy, too."

He nodded his acceptance of her words, then waved a hand in the emperor's direction. "It is as you wish, Your Majesty." Then he walked away.

Romanus walked down the steps toward her, smiling widely. "Welcome to Byzantium," he said warmly, kissing her lightly on one cheek, then the other.

Over his shoulder, Tyra saw Theophano glaring at her with venom. It appeared that her welcome to Byzantium was not a universal one.

"Be careful," Gunter advised her in an undertone. "Be very careful, my lady."

Egil concurred by adding from her other side, "You have entered a real vipers' nest here. And the queen asp has her eye on you."

Their words of caution were reinforced when the empress stepped down from the royal dais and went off to the side, where she and General Phocas put their heads together, looking up from time to time toward her.

An uncomfortable ripple of foreboding swept over Tyra's body. Battles she could fight—'twas what she'd been trained to do. But court intrigues were another matter.

Gunter and Egil were here with her, and several dozen of her *hersirs*, but still Tyra came to an alarming conclusion.

I am all alone.

Tyra's fears were reinforced that night as she prepared for bed in one of the small castle chambers that had been assigned to her. Gunter and Egil and all her soldiers had been given quarters in the army guardhouse. She was virtually isolated from her men.

Azize, a Turkish slave assigned to her, whispered a

warning as she smoothed out the bed linens. "Be careful of the empress, my lady. Her beauty is a facade to hide much evil. Nothing and no one stand in the way of her ambition."

Tyra was surprised that a servant would speak so bluntly, but she was not about to question the maid's good intentions. "Perhaps your view is biased because of your situation," Tyra suggested kindly as she began to take off her clothing. From her language, it was clear that Azize was not of common birth. No doubt she was a prize of one battle or another and resented the empress's royal position, which she might very well have held in another country.

Azize shook her head vehemently. "The empress tolerates no rivals . . . real or perceived. When Romanus became emperor, she had his mother and five sisters relegated to a distant part of the castle, like prisoners. Then, after his mother died, Theophano forced all five girls into nunneries, against their will. The Patriarch Polyeuctus himself was called in to shear their hair in public. Ahhh, the wailing and lamentations were so sorrowful! All five of them were then sent to different convents so they would never see each other again in this lifetime. They are now slaves as much as I."

Tyra decided then and there to heed Azize's warning. The sooner she was out of this palace, the better. She slept with her sword that night. Adam's shield on the floor by her low pallet served as an odd comfort to Tyra as she began her new life in a foreign country.

CHAPTER EIGHTEEN

❧

Humor is ageless . . .

"What has a hole on the top and is full of mead?" one Stoneheim soldier asked another Stoneheim soldier.

"A barrel of mead?" a third soldier interjected innocently, though he had to know the answer.

"Nay, the *drukkinn* king of Stoneheim."

"Ha, ha, ha!" the men sitting around the alehouse table laughed.

"Didst hear that the king tupped Bertha last night?" another soldier called out. Bertha, the alehouse whore, straightened up. "The only problem is, he tupped the wrong hole."

"Ha, ha, ha!" More communal laughter.

"The king tupped himself," the soldier explained to one man who hadn't understood the jest.

These men must be demented to find humor in these endless hole-in-the-head jokes, Adam thought, but after a forced two-sennight stay in the trading town while the king recovered from a high fever, he and his friends were bordering on demented, too.

"You'd better be careful that Thorvald doesn't overhear these jokes," Adam warned. "He may not appreciate your laughing at him."

"Nay, you are wrong there," Bolthor spoke up. "Thorvald seems to enjoy the hole-in-the-head jests best of all. In fact, I have composed a saga about this very thing, 'Viking Men with Humor.'"

Bolthor was already starting to perform before Adam had a chance to groan. Rashid, the traitor, was applauding.

> *"Viking men are fiercesome fighters,*
> *Skilled with sword and axe.*
> *But off the battlefield, some say,*
> *Their greatest talent is*
> *The ability to laugh at themselves.*
> *No man or god is ever so great*
> *That never does he trip.*
> *If man cannot laugh at himself,*
> *He might as well be dead."*

There was stone silence in the ale room. Bolthor was a giant of a man . . . too big for them to taunt with laughter or ridicule.

Finally Adam said, "Very good, Bolthor," though he gritted his teeth in saying so. Then he added, "I noticed that you had no rhyming words in that one."

"How sharp-witted of you to notice, Adam! I like to mix my sagas . . . some rhyming, some not."

"Excellent idea!" Tykir said.

Adam's head swiveled toward Tykir so sharply he would probably have a crick in his neck tonight. "Excellent idea?" he mouthed silently.

Tykir just grinned.

"Someone ought to tell Bolthor the truth someday," Adam grumbled.

"He who tells the truth should have one foot in the stirrup," Rashid advised him.

"Sagas and proverbs! I think I have landed in hell and no one bothered to inform me."

"It is good to know the truth, but it is better to speak of fig trees," Rashid continued.

"Aaarrgh!"

"Methinks I will go over and talk to Bertha," Rashid said.

"If you dare to offer her a spot in my harem, I swear I will tell the world you are a eunuch." Adam shoved his trencher and wooden goblet aside and placed his forehead on the table before him. Then he banged his head several times. *Welcome to the world of the demented!* "I have to get out of this place. I am dying of boredom. Soon I will be composing sagas and proverbs myself."

"Now, Adam, we will be gone from here in a day or so. Even you have said that the king is much improved," Tykir said.

Adam should be thankful. It had been questionable at one point whether the king would survive the fever that overcame him soon after leaving Stoneheim. "But two whole sennights we have lost here. The king planted the idea in my head that Tyra might be in danger in Byzantium, then succumbed to the fever. All this time, even as I tended to Thorvald, I have been worrying that we will be too late."

Tykir nodded his understanding, then leaned back on his bench against the wall, a dreamy expression on his face. "There was a time, afore Alinor and I were wed, when we were separated for a short time. You may not be aware of this fact, but my lady can be a very stubborn person."

Adam made a snorting sound and said, "And you are not?"

"Not as thickheaded as she. But do not tell her I said so," he quickly added. "In any case, during those several sennights when we were apart, I worried about her welfare. She had two evil twin brothers, you know? But mostly, she occupied every moment of my every day because I was coming to accept the fact that I loved her, and I had never told her. I was all twisted up inside."

Mayhap Tykir had the right of it. Betimes Adam felt as if he'd been turned inside out. He wasn't sure what he thought anymore. Sometimes he even forgot to eat. "I'll tell you one thing, Gunter's pretty face is going to be not so pretty when I am done with him, and Egil's overtight *braies* will fit him much better. Furthermore, Tyra had better not be scratching her groin again. After seeing her in that red gown," *and seeing her naked*, "I cannot bear the thought of her trying to act the man."

"That is the least of your troubles, boy. I can see clearly that you are in the same spot I was in then. You have not yet come to terms with your feelings."

"Oh, God! Spare me from Vikings who speak of feelings. Next Bolthor will be . . ."

Uh-oh! I spoke too soon. Already he saw that the verse mood was coming onto the skald's face, *again*.

"This is the saga of Adam the Lesser, also known as the saga of 'Three Dreaded Words.'"

"Three words there are that all men fear
More than sword, or ax, or spear.
Why is it such a dreadful thing
For a man to admit his heart can sing
At the mere swish of a fair maid's hip
Or the mere upward turn of her lip?

Some say there are stages to life:
Birth, death, first swive, first babe, first wife.
But I say there is another step man must
    go through,
One which brings terror to his heart so true.
'Tis the first time he says, 'I love you.' "

STILL IN BORING BYZANTIUM

Boredom breeds hasty decisions . . .

Another sennight had gone by, and Tyra was in the exercise arena, practicing battle skills with other members of the Varangian Guard. She was bored, and more than a little chagrined by her service in the Guard thus far.

Romanus was indeed treating her like a freak. Her uniform was the same as other members of his Guard, except more feminine in subtle ways. Tucks and folds he had apparently ordered resulted in her attire clearly showing that she was a woman with breasts and rounded hips and long legs. And he paraded her before every emissary who visited his court from other countries. It was hard to miss their smirks and rude stares or blatant invitations to couple with them, like a court whore. Worst of all, the empress's hatred toward her was becoming more and more evident.

Inside the palace enclosure there were supposedly fifty thousand retainers. Up till now, Romanus had kept Tyra as part of his private imperial bodyguard, though some Varangians served on active duty, too. During any reception or public event, the emperor had three lines of soldiers arranged in a semicircle behind him. The first arc included those fighting men who had recently distinguished themselves in the ruler's service. The second group was less important, but still meritorious of royal recognition. The third group, where Tyra had been assigned, included the "Barbarians," or "Varangians." All of them stood at attention, eyes lowered the entire time, in full uniform, armor, and weaponry.

In the evenings, she would be invited to dine with the royal family and their guests. In the large dining chamber, which held a huge table made of gold and was surrounded by thirty-six couches, meals were served on plates of gold. But even the smaller dining chambers with only a dozen couches held splendors unimaginable to the average person. Between courses, they would be entertained by jesters, mimes, dwarves, acrobats, musicians, poets . . . and her.

Ingrith would be really, really impressed with the staggering number of exotic dishes served each day. Vana would bemoan the amount of work to be done in polishing all the marble. Drifa would swoon at the profusion of heavy-scented flowers. And, Breanne . . . holy Thor! The ideas for building and renovating she could come up with here boggled the mind. She would no doubt be inspired to put marble pillars and indoor fountains in their father's great hall at Stoneheim.

Tyra never would have guessed that she could miss her bothersome sisters so much. And her father . . . the egotistical fool! He could teach this monarch much about reigning with dignity, even if his Norse castle was lacking the Byzantine's splendor. She hoped her father's health was continuing to improve, but she trusted that Adam would not leave Stoneheim till he was assured of that fact.

Personally, she thought these Byzantines took themselves far too seriously. *They need a good hole-in-the-head joke, if you ask me.* Tyra had to smile to herself when that thought occurred. She must be going barmy if she missed Viking humor.

Occasionally, she and her soldiers had free days.

Then some of them would go to the Hippodrome for entertainment, usually horse races or the circus. All of the men found women on whom they could ease themselves at night, she supposed. She never asked.

It was at Tyra's insistence that Romanus finally allowed her to join her fellow soldiers in the practice fields. And even there, they treated her like a curiosity. Many of the Byzantine soldiers wanted a chance to fight her one on one, no doubt to boast later of what great men they were to have triumphed over the Amazon soldier in combat. Some of them had been surprised when she trounced them soundly. In other cases, she'd been trounced herself. But mostly, she'd performed admirably, and slowly she was gaining their respect. She was unaccustomed to having to earn respect, and it grated on her.

Just then a soldier she recognized as an aide to General Phocas came up to her. "The general would like to speak with you at once," he said without preamble.

She was bent over at the waist, hands on her thighs, trying to regain her breath after her latest bout of swordplay. She straightened and swiped a forearm across her forehead to wipe off the perspiration. "Now? Immediately?" she asked, trying to catch her breath.

He nodded.

"Should I not go off to bathe and change my dirty garments?"

"Now!" he repeated. "Follow me." And off the rude fellow went.

She glanced over at Gunter and Egil, both of whom shrugged, and she went off to meet with the general in his quarters.

Within moments, she learned what was so urgent to the gnomelike commander. She did not let his almost ugly appearance mislead her. She knew he was an excellent soldier and leader. Good looks mattered not in battle, as she well knew.

"My sources tell me you are anxious to get into active battle," he said straight off.

Well, anxious to be out of Byzantium itself . . . anxious to no longer be a spectacle . . . anxious to be given a useful job. "I would welcome an assignment," she said carefully.

"My brother, Leo Phocas, is general of the Army of the East. Always we are plagued by our greatest enemy there, Saïf ed-Daula. 'Tis time to end the life of that pestsome gnat and to take the Syrian lands into the Byzantine Empire. Will you join him in his fight there?"

Lately, Tyra had been uncomfortable with aggressive warfare. She had no qualms whatsoever about defensive fighting to protect a homeland, or an ideal. But battle motivated by greed was different.

Inwardly, she struggled with all these issues, especially since she had come in contact with Adam the Healer and his criticisms of her warlike attributes. But for now her most important priority had to be getting out of the imperial city. Yea, 'twas best to accept the general's offer. Later she would have time to resolve her inner conflicts.

"I accept your assignment, provided all my men may accompany me," she finally said.

"Why must your men be with you? Can you not stand alone?" A shifty look came over the general's face, the same look Tyra had seen on too many occasions lately when he was in whispered consultations with the empress.

"Yea, I can stand alone, but we Stoneheim warriors came here as one unit, and that is how we intend to stay. Take one, take all," she insisted.

Nicephorus frowned at her, and a tic worked rhythmically to the side of his mouth, causing his lips to jerk up in a rather grotesque fashion. In the end, the general said, "So be it. You will leave on the morrow."

Tyra left the general's quarters and went off to give the news to her men. A heavy cloud settled over her mood, however. With this latest action, she would be taking herself another step farther away from Stoneheim . . . another step farther away from Adam, wherever he was.

What will my future hold now?

THE EASTERN BYZANTINE FRONTIER

Felled by a jealous queen . . .

"I never thought I would miss the cold of the Northlands, but I do." Tyra was sitting under the overhang of a tent, fanning her sweltering face with a palm leaf.

"I agree," Gunter said. "Thor's balls! Two sennights in the Syrian deserts and I would like nothing more than an icy Stoneheim wind, accompanied by a good dose of snow."

The two of them were watching a patrol of soldiers, including Egil and some of their comrades, come back from night duty. It would be their turn to go out soon. Wherever that slyboots Saïf ed-Daula was, he hadn't made an appearance yet . . . leastways not for any direct confrontations. Instead, there were constant hit-and-hide assaults that were driving them all barmy.

A shortage of men was always a problem for the Byzantine armies, especially this Eastern division. As a result, soldiers were given land in return for service. The men were permitted to live on and work their own properties, but they had to present themselves fully armed and mounted whenever summoned to the frontier army. To say they were not dedicated soldiers was an understatement. Mercenaries and soldiers like the Varangian Guard were rewarded with huge salaries and the right to take booty after battles. Tyra thought they had the better deal.

Soon she was saddled up and about to ride out on what turned out not to be the usual guard duty. Instead, General Phocas assembled a large troop, almost two hundred soldiers, and announced they were going farther than they had in the past. This would be an overnight foray to a distant village, where Saïf had presumably been raiding the last few days.

The odd thing was that, at the last moment, the general ordered Gunter, Fegil, and Tyra's Stoneheim warriors to stay behind while she went alone. They protested vehemently, but the general claimed he needed the accomplished talents of the Northmen to hold down the garrison post. So, at least this time, they gave in.

By that evening, Tyra understood why she and she alone had been singled out from the Stoneheim contingent to go on this foray. As they approached a desert oasis some distance from the village where they were headed, Tyra's horse suddenly went lame. When she dismounted and examined the mare's foreleg, she saw immediately that it had been gashed. Before she had a chance to stand and confront whoever had done this dastardly deed, Tyra was struck from behind. She lay in the sand staring up at a hazy image of General Phocas bending over her, smiling grimly.

"Kill the horse," the general ordered, even as her heavy eyelids were closing. The pain at the back of her head was unbearable. Was this how Adam had felt when she'd whacked him with the flat side of her broadsword?

"Should we leave her here, unattended?" one of the Byzantine soldiers was asking the general.

"Aye. Leave her. She will be *rescued* shortly. It will be as the empress desires."

There was much chuckling and soft laughter then as the men mounted their horses and prepared to ride off.

Then Tyra's world went black.

When Tyra awakened later that day, she was in strange surroundings. Bit by bit, she took in her situation. She was lying on a marble slab. There were cool breezes from water falling into a courtyard fountain. She noticed the pungent scent of desert flowers, the sound of giggles and soft feminine chatter.

Tyra's head throbbed painfully. Still, she glanced to the right, then to the left. There were scantily clad, beautiful women everywhere, of all ages and colors.

She recognized two facts then:

She was totally naked.

She was in some sultan's harem.

Tyra gasped and felt her heart begin to race with panic. A hysterical reaction to an unbelievable situation. Rashid had suggested one time that she would make a good harem concubine, and she'd laughed. It would seem that the decision had been taken out of her hands.

For a certainty, she wasn't laughing now.

BYZANTIUM . . . AT LAST!

Betimes just prayer is the best plan . . .

Six sennights of travel, and they were finally arriving in Byzantium. Adam felt as if dozens of butterflies were fluttering their wings in his belly, so anxious was he at the prospect of seeing Tyra again.

What should I say?

How will she look?

How do I look? Rashid says the blue tunic matches my eyes, but mayhap I should try the red-fox-lined cloak

*instead. Better yet, I should probably wear armor . . .
appear more soldierly.*

Bloody hell, what difference does it make how I dress?

*On the other hand, some women are swayed by fine
trappings.*

Not Tyra. Never Tyra.

Well then, how best to handle her?

Fool! Handling is the worst thing I can do.

I must be firm with her.

*Nay, I cannot be firm. She will consider that over-
bearing. Gentle is better. Yea, gentle . . . but firm.*

"Why are you talking to yourself?" Tykir asked,
looping a companionable arm over Adam's shoulder.

"Fear."

Tykir nodded his head, as if that was perfectly understandable. "Do you have a plan?"

"Nay, and do not think of suggesting another of your
lackbrain plans, like the one all of you concocted back
at Stoneheim."

Tykir blinked his eyes rapidly, pretending affront.
"You did not like our *Seduction Plan for Adam?* There
were many good points in that plan."

Adam was not about to get involved in that silly
discussion again. "Shouldn't the emissaries be back by
now? 'Tis almost noon, and they have been gone for
two hours."

King Thorvald, resting on his ship bed, had sent some
emissaries to seek permission from Emperor Romanus
for their contingent to enter the royal sector of the city.
His health was much improved, but he tired easily. Today he wanted to appear at his best.

Tykir shrugged. "We still have plenty of time. The
imperial gates do not close till three. Once inside, we
have the rest of the day to find Tyra."

"I have decided to stay behind here on the ship with some of the soldiers and Alrek," Rashid said. He was on Tykir's other side. "The Byzantines do not have much love for us Arabs, and I prefer not to take a chance."

"Mayhap that is a good idea," Adam agreed. "With luck, we will be leaving this harbor on the morrow. You are right about Alrek, as well. Good Lord, the boy is proving a real handful."

At the moment, Alrek was running from one end of the ship to the other, trying to get the best view of the "Great City." Adam could not blame him. It was a spectacular sight, even for those like himself who had been here before. He had come to study a unique hospitium, and Tykir had made innumerable visits during his amber-trading days.

Byzantium occupied a triangular promontory at the northern end of the Sea of Marmara. What had Alrek wide-eyed, though, was the Pharos, a famous lighthouse that guided mariners but also sent signals to distant parts of the empire by means of a relay system. In addition, Alrek was agape at the many palaces that could be seen from the harbor; some of their gilded domes were prominent from a far distance.

Adam would have liked to show Alrek the royal zoo or aviary, but there would be no time for that. Tyra was his main priority.

"Are you ready?" Thorvald asked. "I see my men, along with the emperor's guard, approaching."

Adam nodded. The butterflies in his stomach now felt like hummingbirds.

"I hope you have a plan, boy," the king added.

"Wh-what? I thought *you* had a plan," he stammered out. When King Thorvald had insisted on making this journey, Adam had assumed he knew what protocol to follow.

"See, Adam, I told you that you needed a plan," Tykir said.

Adam closed his eyes and said a prayer . . . the first time he'd prayed in two long years. *Please, God, hear me this time.*

Someone was going to pay for plucking her . . .

Harems were not all they were touted to be.

Of course, the only persons Tyra had ever heard touting harems were men. And Rashid, who was of course a man. That had to be taken into account.

It had only been three days since Tyra had joined the harem of Amin ed-Daula, some desert sultan who was a cousin or half-brother or something of Saïf ed-Daula, but already she was bored to the point of numbness, and angry to the point of . . . numbness. She had yet to meet her "master," who was presumably off fighting Byzantines, or capturing more slave girls for his harem, or hiding from her. He only had two hundred females in his harem so far. About one hundred eighty of them hadn't seen the old guy, who was more than fifty, for five years or more. She'd sure like to see him. She'd like to give him a piece of her mind . . . or a piece of her sword if she could recover the weapon.

To be fair, she was certain that the leaders of this tribe . . . rather, harem . . . would like to get rid of her, too. In fact, she had taken to sleeping with her eyes half open, just in case she pushed someone too far. "Troublesome, loud, big, barbarian" were words often used to describe her.

Her first day in the harem, they'd left her pretty much alone.

The second day, she'd taken a bath, willingly, in a marble tub big enough to hold twelve people. Then it took eight eunuchs of considerable size to hold her down while every single hair on her body was plucked off. She was now hairless *everywhere* except for her head. Somebody was going to pay for that atrocity.

Today, she was attending harem school. The lesson of the day . . . bloody hell, the lesson of every day, she would guess . . . was the best way to please the master. The instructors were the head eunuch, Selim, and an aging houri Salome. She thought it ironic that a man with no manparts should be teaching women how to please those who had such parts . . . along with a lady whose female parts had long ago dried up.

There were three dozen women lying about on low divans sucking up this sexual knowledge like thirsty camels drinking water. Tyra's contribution was to snort her disbelief or make rude comments at various inter- vals, especially when they recommended such things as rouging the nipples, which they referred to poetically as flower buds. "Not unless the male is going to rouge his *lily*, too."

"M'lady," warned Kareem, a surly-looking eunuch who stood near her. He was about three feet tall and three feet wide. With an evil grin, he caressed the small whip he held in his hands. "Wise females know when to curb their tongues."

She stuck her tongue out at him, which probably wasn't a smart choice, if his low growl was any indication.

"Always keep one's eyes downcast with meekness," was another morsel of wisdom the two instructors tossed out.

"Hah! Only if you want to fall flat on your face." Almost immediately, she said, "Ouch!" Kareem had switched her across the back.

"Then there is piercing one's belly button with a gold ring," Selim was saying. He ordered a young woman in the front row to stand and demonstrate. She had a gold ring, all right, smack in the center of her belly.

Tyra winced and thought, *Ouch!* "That is attractive? Really, ladies, are you believing this hog swill?"

This time, Kareem took great pleasure in putting his full force behind the swish of the whip across her back. Mayhap she would rest her tongue for a bit, after all. She adjusted her position on the divan and heard the tinkle of tiny bells. All the women were scantily clad, mostly in diaphanous pants and vests with lots of little bells. "What are we? Cows? Do we need bells to find our way home?" she muttered. Actually, Tyra would be mortified if anyone other than two hundred women were to see her in this attire. She looked like a six-foot scarf, in her opinion. Of course, she'd forgotten that she was not going to speak anymore, but Kareem had not. Three hits she got this time.

She was going to make Kareem eat that whip when she got out of this place. If she ever got out of this place. Nay, nay, nay, she could not think that way. Someone was sure to come for her. Gunter. Or Egil. Or her soldiers. They'd better come.

But wait. The program was finally getting interesting. Selim and Salome were handing out smooth marble rods to all the ladies. They were about the width of her forefinger and twice as long. She frowned, trying to figure out the purpose of such an object.

"Today you are going to be taught how to strengthen a *new* muscle in your bodies . . . one which will enhance the pleasure of the master during bedplay. And your pleasure as well," Selim added as an enticement.

Muscles? That was a subject with which Tyra was well acquainted, but she did not think there was any muscle that could be considered new to her.

She was wrong. As one of the houris demonstrated the purpose of the marble wand, Tyra's eyes widened.

"There is an inner muscle that you must learn to control." Selim instructed, "Clench, unclench, clench, unclench, clench, unclench . . ."

As he repeated the order over and over, Tyra began to understand the principle. And all she could think was, *For the love of a Frost Giant! What would Adam think of this trick?*

But then she immediately chastised herself. *I am never going to see Adam again.*

Am I?

The intrusion of Adam into her thoughts erased all interest in the demonstration. At some point she was going to have to face her feelings about him, and the mistakes she might have made. In that moment, Tyra made a vow to herself. If she ever escaped this harem . . . and she had no doubt that she would . . . she was going to return to Stoneheim and make peace with her father and sisters.

Then she was going for Adam.

Really, every good soldier knew that there were times when it was best just to cut one's losses. She was unhappy here in the Eastlands. She had been unhappy in Byzantium. And it all had to do with Adam . . . or his absence from her life. It didn't matter where she was; she could be happy if he were there.

Yea, she was going for Adam. Even if she had to kidnap him again. They had unfinished business . . . the least of which involved marble wands.

Well, mayhap not the least.

CHAPTER NINETEEN

⬥

Princess, where art thou? . . .
     King Thorvald was lying on couch number three in the Hall of Nineteen Couches, as indicative of his high standing in the court of Emperor Romanus. Adam, Tykir, and Bolthor were on couches much farther down the line, as indicative of their lower standing.

It was late on the night of their arrival, and Adam could not care less where he sat, whether his plate was gold or silver, whether he got one more dish served in grape leaves, whether his face was fanned by a dancing girl, or his fingers washed with rose water. If Adam spoke with one more Byzantine physician about herbs and healing, he was going to scream. Medicine was his profession, but Tyra was his obsession.

Six hours in the emperor's presence, and they had not yet been given permission to discuss the purpose of their mission. They had not seen or heard of any of the Stoneheim contingent.

"Protocol," King Thorvald had advised him. "We must follow protocol to accomplish our ends. Diplomacy is the key if we want to leave this land where we are far outnumbered."

He had told the king exactly what he could do with

his diplomacy, and the king had told him that mayhap he wouldn't give him his daughter after all.

It was probably a good thing he and Thorvald were separated. Angry words spoken in haste needed time and space to heal.

He took another sip of the wine in his goblet and turned to speak with Tykir, who was listening to something being said by a slave girl wearing a clinging garment. Assigned to feed Tykir grapes or fan his face in case a bead of sweat dared to pop out, she purred to him, "You are such a fascinating man."

Tykir must have heard Adam's snort of disgust, because he blushed and told the slave girl, "I am not all that fascinating."

"Alinor is going to kill you when she hears about this," Adam remarked.

"That is assuming *someone* has a death wish and chooses to tell her," Tykir said out of the side of his mouth.

On his other side, Adam heard Bolthor grumbling to his slave girl, "Just because I speak slowly does not mean that I think slowly."

The girl just giggled. She probably did not understand the Norse language, and thought he was commenting on her rouged nipples, which were visible through the fabric of her gown.

"Here is a saga for you two," Bolthor said. "A Viking View of Life."

> *"Some lands are filled with riches*
> *Which oft leads to excesses.*
> *Gold plate, silk robes, jewels galore,*
> *So much food that the belly gets sore,*
> *Horses, boats, women, slaves, and what's more,*
> *There ne'er seems to be enough of anything,*

So greed and dissipation become king.
Methinks there is much to be said
For the simple life led.
Food, shelter, fire, and wife . . .
That is all one really needs in life."

For once, Bolthor's saga made sense. Tykir nodded, and Adam told him how impressed he was. There was something revolting about the excess of this court. There should be a better balance between rich and poor. Strange idea, that. Who would have thought it would come from Bolthor? But then, perchance Adam had been guilty like many others of thinking Bolthor was slow-witted just because he spoke slowly.

Adam's slave girl, who had to be all of thirteen years old, had gone off to deliver a message for him to King Thorvald. She was returning now.

"Your king says to come forth. The emperor will speak with you now," she told him in her girlish voice. "You two, as well," she added, indicating Tykir and Bolthor.

Adam nodded and stood, noticing that Thorvald was doing the same, with the help of two servants, one of whom handed him his staff. If Adam wasn't so worried about Tyra, he would be concerned about the king, who was not as strong as he believed.

Within seconds, the four of them stood before the emperor and empress, whose divans were on a dais elevated slightly from the rest of the room. Romanus and Theophano—both extremely handsome people—did not rise for them. Instead, they remained half reclining on their low sofas.

The four of them were dressed in their best finery . . . quality cloth, exquisite embroidery, amber jewelry, silver armlets . . . but they looked like paupers compared to these two, and most others at the court.

"Welcome to Byzantium, Thorvald. I believe you were a friend to my father."

Thorvald nodded. "And to his son, as well."

After Thorvald introduced the three of them, Romanus said, "I understand you had a miraculous operation performed on you of late."

Here we go again with the miracle business, Adam thought.

"Yea, I did. A hole in the head."

Oh, God, please, no hole-in-the-head jests.

"This is the physician who cut into my scalp and saved my life," the king went on, waving a hand at Adam.

"Aaahh!" the emperor and empress both sighed, duly impressed, he supposed. Or bored.

"Would you care to tour my hospitiums on the morrow? I have five of them. Mayhap you can explain this head drilling to my healers," Romanus suggested to Adam.

"I would be honored to do so . . . at another time. There is a more urgent matter on my mind . . . *our* minds . . . first."

He could tell that the emperor was not pleased with his answer. Still, Romanus inquired, "And what would that *urgent matter* be?"

"My daughter," the king said. "I must see my daughter Tyra."

At the same time, Adam said, "My betrothed, Tyra."

"Your betrothed?" the empress asked with surprise.

Equally surprised, the emperor turned to his wife. "She did not tell us she was betrothed, did she, Theo?"

"She does not know yet," Adam admitted, feeling his face heat up with embarrassment.

Romanus and Theophano both smiled, while Thorvald, Tykir, and Bolthor chuckled on either side of him.

"Where is she?" Adam asked bluntly.

The emperor narrowed his eyes at him and replied with equal bluntness. "Serving with the Army of the East."

Theophano put a hand on her husband's sleeve, a crafty expression sweeping over her face. "Did I forget to tell you, husband? The Stoneheim soldiers are serving with the Varangian Guard under General Leo Phocas, but the warrior princess known as Tyra . . ." She shrugged, and said no more.

"What of Tyra?" Adam and Thorvald both prodded at the same time.

"Alas, she is missing," Theophano explained.

A bull-like roar emerged from Thorvald's chest, and Adam saw for the first time where the king had got his reputation as the Wolf of the North. In truth, Adam was as angry as the king over the empress's seemingly indifferent attitude about Tyra's fate.

The emperor was clearly shocked at his wife's words, but not about to challenge her in such a public forum. He gave his wife a long look which made it clear that there were explanations to be made on her part later. For now, he stood behind her by proclaiming, "There you have it, then. My wife has told you . . . Tyra is somewhere in the East . . . missing."

Adam and Thorvald exchanged worried glances then. Thorvald had warned him of the dangers of court intrigue. Now he was experiencing them firsthand. He would bet his bag of herbs that the empress knew more than she was saying.

The king's face was red with suppressed fury and his hands were clenched into tight fists, but Thorvald, to his credit, spoke in an even tone when he addressed the emperor. "Romanus, I am the king of a small section of a small country, but I am ruler there, just as you are here. And my daughter Tyra is a princess in her own right, no matter how she may portray herself. You have not shown the proper respect for a daughter of Norway. And I can tell you this for a certainty. Not only do I take umbrage at your lack of concern, but my fellow kings of Vestland and all the Norse countries would join in my outrage if they learned of this. We protect our own."

Romanus sat up on his divan, then stood abruptly. His Imperial Guard behind him drew their weapons, ready for any command. Romanus's face was as red as Thorvald's when he asked, "Do you threaten me, Viking?"

Thorvald said nothing, just held his chin high as he held the gaze of the equally arrogant emperor.

Adam stepped in then. "Let me add this, Romanus. My uncle Tykir, Jarl of Dragonstead, is a warrior of great repute in Norway, and my uncle Eirik is Lord of Ravenshire in Britain. Both of them would join me in a trice if I called on them to help recover this woman."

Romanus waved a hand airily. "You would still be far outnumbered."

Adam shrugged. "Yea, we would be. But do you really want to risk a war over a mere woman?"

Several of the Byzantine advisers of high rank rushed up to the emperor and engaged him in hasty conversation, too low to be heard from their position at the bottom of the steps. Soon Romanus announced, reluctantly, "I apologize for the treatment of Tyra, Warrior Princess, whilst in my land. I put my troops at your disposal to help recover her."

The empress looked as if she might be choking on her tongue as her husband spoke. She must take his words as an indirect slap at her.

Adam and Thorvald nodded their acceptance of Romanus's apology and his pledge of help. What else could they do?

"Well, it would seem we are off to the Eastlands," the

king pronounced in a voice that brooked no argument, not even from an upstart emperor half his age, nor from a devious empress.

Oh, Tyra, where are you?

Off to rescue a princess bride . . .

Tyra was in a harem. A harem, for the love of God!

Adam didn't know whether to laugh, or cry, or both.

"I'll tell you one thing," he told Rashid, "if that randy desert sheik has dared to lay a hand on her, I will cut it off."

"Best you drop your anger and concentrate on getting inside the harem compound," his assistant advised him. "'Tis said that only a man without balls may enter a harem."

Adam was about to snarl something sarcastic to Rashid, but really, the man had been invaluable to him with his Arab contacts. He had arranged for Adam—and Adam alone—to enter the sacred confines of the women's quarters with a contingent of physicians who would be giving the houris their annual examinations. The examinations would involve checks for continued virginity in some, resulting in a death sentence if it was missing; sexual diseases in others, which also resulted in a death sentence since it indicated adultery; and various everyday complaints, like rashes, which could also mean death, depending on how they had been contracted.

Thorvald and a troop of one hundred Norse soldiers—both Varangians and regular everyday mercenaries—would be waiting for him and Tyra a half-mile away from the palace. Assuming they were able to escape, that is. Among the men-at-arms were the guilt-ridden Gunter and Egil and the Stoneheim troop, who suffered much personal regret that they had not protected Tyra better.

General Phocas had been forced to help them in every way possible on orders from the emperor.

Adam donned his Arab robe, pulled up the hood, and tugged one side across his face so that only his eyes were visible. Under his robes, he was fully armed with sword and dagger. He mounted his horse then and was about to ride over to join the five other physicians, who were similarly attired.

"Allah be with you," Rashid called out.

"May Odin watch your back, and Thor lead your sword arm," Tykir added.

"Bring my daughter home, I pray thee," Thorvald directed, gruffly.

"Please, God," Adam concurred in prayer. And he was off.

Her knight in shining . . . robe? . . .

"If any of you lackwit doctors think you're going to stick a finger inside me to check for a maidenhead, you are sorely mistaken."

The other harem houris shrunk away from her. She was always getting in trouble, and they probably feared contamination by association. Or else they thought she was demented . . . which she very well might be.

The Arab physicians who had entered the harem a short time ago probably didn't understand a word she'd said, although she could have sworn one of them chuckled, but she announced, "Here is some news for you. I am not a virgin anyhow."

The chuckling doctor chuckled some more behind his hood.

Kareem wasn't chuckling, though. He hissed a warning from behind her and waved his little whip.

They were in the round tower of the castle. The women would be led, one at a time, into separate rooms off the central reception area where they stood now. Each of the rooms opened onto a balcony that encircled the entire tower and looked down over a beautiful fountain garden. The serene picture was deceptive. The garden was pretty, and 'twas true there were no iron-grilled windows on this balcony, but it was a prison just the same . . . like a gilded cage. Beyond the bright flowers and tall bushes were high stone walls and iron gates. It was an impregnable fortress, not a pleasure place, as far as Tyra was concerned.

When Tyra's name was called, four eunuchs had to prod her with pointed spears into the appropriate examining room. She balked, but to no avail. Well, she might not be able to fight off the eunuchs, who were bowing out of the chamber, but there sure as hell was going to be a physician with a broken finger if that appendage meandered into forbidden territory.

"Listen, I have about had it up to my gullet with this harem business," she said to the hooded doctor, "so let us not make something you do be the last straw. I am a warrior, you know, and . . ."

Her words faded away as she turned to confront the physician, who was just now lowering his hood.

"Oh . . . sweet . . . Jesus!" he murmured as he stared at her scandalous costume. Then he grinned.

She would know that grin anywhere.

"Adam?" was the first utterance out of her mouth, immediately followed by, "Stop looking at me. And don't you dare grin at my attire."

Adam grinned some more. "I could no more stop looking at you than breathe, especially in that garment. Make sure you bring it with you. But hurry, there is no time for talking now. Put this on." He shoved another Arab robe at her, similar to his.

Before she could pull the robe over her head, though,

Adam yanked her into his arms and kissed her hotly. "God, I was worried about you. Do not ever do this to me again."

She had no idea what he meant. *Do what again?* she wanted to ask. *Run away? Be a soldier? Join a harem?* She would have to save the questions for later. But she had to warn him, "Adam, it is impossible to get out of here. You should not have come. The danger is too great."

"Shhh! For once, let someone else take care of you." He shoved her away and was already out on the balcony wrapping a long rope with a three-pronged hook on the end around one of the columns. "I hope you do not fear heights," he said, motioning her forward. "We have only a few moments to accomplish this, and it is three floors down." He kept glancing from right to left to make sure no one emerged from one of the other examining rooms, then down below to the gardens to make sure no one had wandered into the area for a stroll.

She rushed forward, tying the rope belt of her robe as she ran. "Any fear of heights I have is outweighed by my fear of beheading . . . which is the penalty for escape from a harem."

"Beheading?" He laughed. "I never would have come for you if I'd known beheading was involved."

She smacked him on the arm. "What a time for teasing!"

Minutes later they had both shimmied down the rope . . . an experience she never wanted to repeat . . . and were running as stealthily as possible through a maze of corridors till they came to a hidden door that led out onto a public street. With a forefinger to his lips, cautioning silence, Adam lifted the hem of his robe and handed her a long dagger. He pulled his sword from its waist sheath for himself. This was the most dangerous part of all, she realized. Much coin must have been paid to clear their way through the oddly absent inside guards, but there were sure to be guards posted at intervals all along the castle walls . . . too many to be contacted or bribed.

"Your father and your troops are awaiting us a short distance away."

"They are?"

"Oh, Tyra, how could you think otherwise? You are a much-beloved daughter and military leader and friend."

And lover? Why that omission should bother her so much, she could not say, but it did, even in the midst of all this danger.

He took her hand in his, entwined their fingers, then raised her hand so he could kiss the knuckles.

"This is it, heartling. Here's hoping we live to see the stars tonight."

She nodded. As long as she was with him, she was not afraid . . . even of dying. "Nay, here's hoping that Bolthor will compose a saga about this successful adventure aboard a longship tonight."

He laughed at the thought of the two of them welcoming one of Bolthor's sagas. "Better yet," he said over his shoulder even as he opened the creaking door and pulled her forward, "here's hoping we will be telling this story to our children for a loooong time."

They both ran for their lives then, but Adam's last words rang through her ears like a joyous refrain.

Our children. Our children. Our children . . .

STILL IN THE BLOODY DAMN EASTERN DESERT

The best laid plans of men and fools . . .

That night, Adam approached the tent that had been set aside for Tyra. He was so nervous he could scarcely breathe.

"Thor's toenails, Adam! Your hands are shaking," Tykir pointed out to him.

"Allah be praised!" Rashid piped up. "You rescued your lady. You and you alone! You have naught to fear. She will be so thankful she will fall into your arms with thanks. And think on this, master. She has been in a harem. She no doubt *knows* things now." He waggled his eyebrows to convey what things he was referring to.

"What things?" King Thorvald wanted to know.

Adam groaned. He really, really did not need the company of the father of the woman he hoped to swive this night.

"Actually, I think you should just toss her over your shoulder, like she did you. Ride off to some secluded spot and *convince* her to be yours." The king beamed at him after expounding that wisdom.

Adam clicked his jaw shut. He was not about to ask her father what he meant by *convince*.

"I wrote a saga one time titled 'How to Convince an Unconvinceable Maid.' 'Twas very popular at Anlaf's court, as I recall." Bolthor was stroking his chin as he tried to remember the details.

"Enough!" Adam shouted. He stopped dead in his tracks, which caused everyone else to stop dead in their tracks, too. "I do not need an escort. I do not need advice. I do not need any of you here with me. Go away!"

As one, his four companions turned on their heels and stalked away, with the king muttering, "Ungrateful Saxon whelp!" and Bolthor saying something like, "He will be sorry," and Rashid intoning, "Allah cannot be everywhere; that is why he created friends." Tykir just laughed.

Adam stared at the tent before him, bracing himself.

This morning, he and Tyra had made it safely away from the desert palace to the Stoneheim troops, despite being followed by the sultan's guard. They all had ridden off without any fighting ... something that had rankled with Thorvald, who wanted desperately to lop off a head or two in retaliation for his daughter's kidnapping. Adam was certain he would find an opportunity to take revenge in the future, once he was in a position of greater strength.

Now they were back at the desert outpost of the Army of the East. Tyra and her soldiers had already informed General Phocas that they would no longer be serving in his army. The general had argued fruitlessly the whole time, denying any involvement in her being taken by the desert sultan. Since she had no proof besides the evidence of her own eyes, they'd decided to accept his word. The only other choices were: one, to confront the devious commander on the issue in a Byzantine court, which would be heavily weighted in the general's favor; or two, to lop off his head during the night—Thorvald's preference—but then they would have a thousand soldiers chasing after them.

Thorvald swore that he would take his revenge at a later date. Already he'd talked five hundred Norse soldiers into deserting the Byzantine ranks and returning with him to the Northlands, at great cost to his royal treasury. This depletion in ranks would hurt General Phocas more than any court fine.

To say that the general was livid was a vast understatement. He would have lopped off Thorvald's head himself if he could.

On the morrow, they would travel back to Byzantium and their two longships. The king intended to purchase several more to carry the additional soldiers who would return with him.

From there, the ships would be heading on separate paths. Most would proceed to Stoneheim. But at least one of them would be going to Britain and Adam's home at Hawkshire.

The question he nervously faced now was whether Tyra would be coming with him to Britain . . . or not.

Should he first tell her of his feelings and the future they might have together? Or should he make love to her first, and leave the explanations for later? He was leaning toward the latter.

And besides, he was still angry with her over her desertion immediately following their night of loving. Although they definitely needed to talk, he was thinking it might be a good idea to wait till his temper cooled.

Inhaling deeply, he opened the flap of her tent and called out in what he hoped was a husky voice filled with erotic promise, "Tyra? Sweetling?"

He stepped inside.

Then he bellowed with outrage, "Aaarrgh!"

So much for erotic promise!

Pulling at his hair with frustration, he stomped around the carpeted floor of the tent, exclaiming over and over, "I should have known. I should have, should have, should have known!"

Tyra was gone. Again.

Now she was in big trouble . . .

Adam caught up with her halfway to Byzantium.

She was by herself, brushing down her horse in the stable of a small village. She had planned to sleep here for several hours on a wool blanket placed over the straw. Taking no chances, her sword would be at the ready by her right arm and a battle-ax near her left.

That plan was cut short when she glanced up and saw Adam standing in the open doorway of the stall. He was leaning back against the door frame, his arms folded over his chest, his ankles crossed casually at the ankles.

His nonchalant pose didn't fool her, though. He practically had smoke blowing from his nostrils.

"Adam," she acknowledged, trying to sound calm, when inside her heart was thundering. She resumed her brushing, as if his appearance had been totally expected.

"Tyra, you are in big trouble. The biggest trouble of your life. So big you should be shivering in your boots and begging for my mercy."

"Adam, I can explain."

"Oh, I am sure you think so. But we will save that for later. We have a longship to catch now."

She tilted her head to the side in question. "For where?"

"Northumbria."

"Don't you think you should ask if I want to go to your home?"

"The time for asking is long past."

She did not like his domineering tone . . . not one bit. But she would save that battle for a later date. "Where are my father and the others?"

"Following close behind. They will meet up with us at Hawkshire . . . some of them, leastways. Not Tykir or the hundreds of soldiers your father hired. They will go directly to Stoneheim."

"My sisters will be overwhelmed with all the extra work caused by the new arrivals."

"Your sisters are at Hawkshire."

Her mouth dropped open at that news. "How did that come about?"

He waved a hand dismissively, obviously not wanting to discuss it now.

She sighed deeply at all the changes that had happened. "I need to go back to Stoneheim for a while . . . to think."

"You are going to Britain with me," he declared, "where you can think all you want . . . or not think. Frankly, I do not care. Your fate is in my hands now, my warrior wench. Do not doubt that for one moment."

"Of all the . . . !" Her words trailed off as Adam grabbed her by the nape of the neck with one hand and raised a large broadsword over her head with the other. Was he going to lop off her head? He looked angry enough. But, no, the tap on her head was light, but the pincer-squeeze on her neck was hard. She found her legs buckling and her vision fading away. She was about to faint. As a doctor, he must know just the right spot to pinch to get that result, she decided with utter irrelevance.

Even as she was drifting into blackness, she felt the brute lift her by the waist, toss her over his shoulder, and carry her off to his mount.

The tables had truly been turned now. She and Adam had come full circle.

But what did that mean?

CHAPTER TWENTY

⊗

ONE SENNIGHT LATER, HOME AT LAST

A wedding? Whose wedding? . . .

Tyra was locked in one of the towers at Hawkshire.

Adam had barely spoken with her since he'd whacked her over the head and carted her off. He'd kept waving her off and saying, "Later!"

The tower she was in was new, one which had been erected by Breanne in Adam's absence, much to his consternation. In fact, when their weary retinue had ridden up the dirt road to Hawkshire that morning, Adam's eyes nigh bulged out of his head. Not only had the rusted drawbridge been oiled and repaired, but there were several new outbuildings, including a large structure that Breanne proudly proclaimed to be Hawkshire Hospitium.

To give Adam credit, he hadn't exploded with angry words at her sister, but Tyra could tell he'd wanted to.

Of course, that was before he'd noticed Drifa's handiwork. It was October, well past the growing season, but somehow she had managed to wield her magic trowel. There were colorful bushes and trees that had not been there before, not to mention a newly planted herb garden off the scullery. Drifa had assured him there would be a myriad of colorful flowers sprouting in the spring all along the moat, to which he'd replied in an undertone, "Oh, joy!"

When they'd entered his keep, there were further surprises. To say his great hall was now clean would be a vast understatement. Vana had done her work well. Not a spider web in sight, or a speck of dust. Vana had an aversion to rushes, but because Adam's great hall had a dirt floor, she had laid new rushes, mixed with lavender and juniper tops. Even the ancient weaponry hanging on the walls had been polished to a new brightness. And there were vividly colored tapestries everywhere. The now spotlessly clean tower solar where he did his work had new shelves built for his precious books and special compartmentalized boxes for his herbs and ointments.

They had not needed to go into the kitchen to know that Ingrith was brandishing her spoon there, creating her own form of magic. The delicious odors that floated through his wood castle bespoke a fine meal ahead . . . no doubt having dozens of courses.

Every time he had seen one of the changes, Adam had groaned anew. Tyra had kept her groans inward, but she was highly embarrassed at the way her sisters had taken over Adam's home, as if they had a right to do so.

And then there was the way Alrek's brother and sisters had jumped on Alrek . . . and all over Adam. The three had looked as if they'd made themselves at home in his home, and had no intention of leaving. In fact, it had been as if they were welcoming Alrek home and Adam, too . . . even though it was Adam's home and not theirs. Adam had appeared confused and embarrassed by their actions. She vowed to herself that she would take care of the situation for him once she was free. It was not fair to unload the youthlings on him.

So now Tyra sat on the pallet in her tower room waiting for Adam to finally speak with her, as he had promised an hour ago before sending her up the stairs. She did not have long to wait.

"Tyra," he said wearily as he came inside, locked the door, and plopped down on a chair that faced the mattress where she sat. "We have a real problem here."

"You mean other than you kidnapping me and refusing to speak to me for more than a sennight?"

"Or other than you deserting me, not once, but twice? Yea, we do. Lord Eirik and Lady Eadyth from Ravenshire have arrived this very moment with all their brood, including John, who resides in nearby Hawk's Lair. Rain and Selik should be here by eventide."

So that was the cause of the additional commotion out in the courtyard. "Your uncle and aunt? Your foster mother and father? Why is that a problem?" *Uh-oh! He is looking extremely serious. Something is amiss.* "Why did they come?" She narrowed her eyes at him suspiciously.

"Tykir sent them missives."

Tyra put a hand to her forehead. "Explain yourself, Saxon. Why have they come?"

"The same reason your father, Bolthor, and Rashid will be coming tomorrow, along with a small contingent of Stoneheim soldiers." He took a deep breath, then informed her, "For the wedding."

She frowned. "Whose wedding?" Were Vana and Rafn to be married here, rather than on Norse soil? That would be odd, especially since Rafn was not even here.

Adam shook his head. "Ours."

"Ours?" she squeaked out. "Me and you?"

He nodded, a pitiful expression on his face.

That pitiful expression caused her neck to prickle with alarm. "Did my father force this on you? Well, I will not stand for it."

"It was not your father, precisely. I think I may have given him the idea."

"You?" Tyra squeaked again.

"Well, I went after you to Byzantium, didn't I?" he grumbled.

"And in your mind that is a marriage proposal?" By the runes! Men could be dumb dolts betimes.

"Sarcasm ill suits you, my lady. I may have told a person or two that I was going after you because I wanted you, and it all took on a life of its own, like a snowball which grows and grows into an avalanche. I must tell you, Tyra, your family has a tendency to take over. Well, mine does, too. Eadyth is down there even now planning the wedding feast with Ingrith, and I suspect that Eirik has invited half of Northumbria to the festivities. Alinor, who happens to be a noted weaver, is sending you a wedding gown, posthaste. My friend Rurik and his wife Maire may even come . . . all the way from bloody Scotland."

"Whoa! Whoa! Whoa!" Tyra said, as if speaking to a horse. She was looking into Adam's sad eyes. "You *wanted* me. What does that mean?"

"I do not know. I truly do not." He put his elbows on his knees and his chin in his palms, gazing at her directly. By the gods! He had the most beautiful eyes. Soulful, they were. "I suspect it means that I . . . that I . . ."

"What?" she prodded when he seemed unable or unwilling to go on.

". . . I love you."

She started to cry then, big loud sobs, accompanied by fat tears brimming in her eyes and running down her face.

"This was not quite the reaction I expected," he said, reaching for her.

She swatted his hands away. "What *did* you expect?"

"I expected . . . nay, I hoped . . . that you would say you loved me, too."

"Of course I do, you idiot."

"You do? Then all the other problems are nothing if we have that." He frowned as if something was bothering him. "If you love me, why did you go away . . . two times?"

"The first time is easy to explain. I knew we could have no life together . . . with your feelings about me and motherhood . . . which I presume have not changed, by the by. So, yea, we do have problems that seem nigh insurmountable. Plus, I had to leave to give my sisters a chance at marriage."

He pondered her words, then nodded. "It is a twisted logic, but I guess I understand, though why you could not tell me afore leaving, I do not know."

"You would have tried to talk me out of it."

"That is true, that is true," he agreed. "Which brings us to the second time. I rescued you, returned you to safety, and you deserted me again. I was mortified in front of all the others, and devastated by your lack of feeling for me."

"Oh, Adam it was never lack of feeling."

"Then what?"   •

She felt her face brighten with embarrassment. "I cannot tell you."

"You'd better."

"Something happened to me during the short time I was in the harem."

He immediately stiffened. "You were raped? My God, I will go back and kill the old buzzard. I thought you said you had not been touched."

She raised a hand to halt his tirade. "I was not raped. Nor was I touched in *that* way. Adam, I knew you were coming to my tent after we returned to the army camp. I knew you would expect to make love with me. And I could not do if . . . not after . . . I just could not."

"You are not making any sense, Tyra."

"They plucked all the hair off my body. So there! Now you know." She started to weep again, this time with mortification.

"Huh?"

"There are times when you can act the total lackbrain. Other than the hair on my head, those stupid eunuchs . . . it took eight in all to hold me down . . . plucked every hair off my body. Including . . ." She waved a hand to her groin area.

At first he did not understand. When he did, he grinned. "Let me see."

"Nay! And do not grin at me. There is no cause for mirth in this."

"Yea, there is, Tyra. Are you saying that you ran away because you are hairless *there*?"

She nodded. "You know how I feel about my body. I am too big. My feet are like snowshoes. I talk too loud. I scratch. Now this. Big and hairless. That is me."

"Let me see."

"I told you nay, and I meant it. I look like a plucked chicken."

"It will grow out," he said, trying for a consoling tone, but ruining it with his continuing grin. "Won't it?"

"I suppose. But not for a long time."

"How long?"

She shrugged. "Six months, mayhap."

"And you think you can keep me from your bed furs for six months?"

"I can try."

"Wedding or no wedding, I will be betwixt your

hairless thighs by nightfall. That I promise you, you silly wench."

"Nay, you will not." She lifted her chin stubbornly. "And do not dare tell anyone about this. I swear, if I hear Bolthor compose a saga about this atrocity, I will blame you. And I had absolutely better not hear any chicken jokes, or your life is in peril."

"Ch-chicken jokes?" he sputtered out.

"Yea. I can just hear it now. 'What chicken laid that egg in the courtyard?' 'Oh, never mind, 'twas just Tyra.'"

She had shocked him with her bluntness, she could tell.

"This really bothers you?"

"Did I not say so?"

He stood suddenly and kicked his chair aside. Then he began to remove his clothing. His belt, his tunic, his boots, for a start.

"What are you doing?"

"You will see."

When he was totally naked—*and what a sight that was! The man was too handsome for his own good*—he walked over to a table on which were a pitcher, bowl, and jar of soft soap. With deliberate care, he lathered the hairy region around his manparts. Then he walked back to her and handed her a sharp dagger which had been in his belt.

"Shave me," he ordered.

She dropped the dagger to the floor. "Have you lost your mind?"

"Nay, just my heart," he said with such simplicity it melted all her resolve.

Just my heart. Did the man know how much those words would mean to an affection-starved woman such as herself? There wasn't a woman alive who didn't yearn for a special man to say those words to her. And Adam *was* special. Very special.

"If it will make you feel better to have us both be hairless, it is a small price to pay."

She jumped to her feet and wrapped her arms around his wide shoulders, kissing every part of his face. "I love you. And not just because of that sweet gesture. I love you. I love you. I love you."

"Does that mean I will remain unshaven?" he asked against her ear.

"It does."

"Whew!" he said. "Two plucked chickens in one bed is a bit too much."

She smacked him for his teasing.

He tried to tickle her . . . in the area of her mortification.

She really did punch him then, and while he wrestled with her to restrain her pummeling, he lowered himself to the bed, taking her with him. Then he rolled over smoothly so she was on the bottom.

He held her face in his hands as if she were a delicate object to be cherished. He laid his lips carefully over hers so they fit perfectly; then he breathed in and out, putting his breath into her mouth, taking her breath into his.

It was a brief kiss, but more than that. It was a kiss that promised so much. Forever. It was a forever kiss.

"I have missed you so much," he said. "There was a time, not so long ago, when I cherished my aloneness. I thought that I wanted nothing more than peace and quiet. But now"—he shrugged—"now I cannot imagine living in this cold, dark keep without you and all the turmoil that surrounds you. In truth, I cannot imagine living anywhere and being happy unless you are there.

Eirik and Tykir and Rurik have all warned me that when a man meets the right woman, it will feel as if they are soulmates. I never believed them . . . till now."

Tyra felt as if her heart were swelling and swelling. The man aroused so many emotions she could scarce breathe. He knew just the right things to say while she stared at him in dumb wonder that he could care for a woman like her.

He began to undress her then, article by article. Despite her protests and struggles, he persisted, the whole time speaking softly to her. "Tyra, I do not want to hear any more about those thoughtless words I spoke regarding you and motherhood. I do not want to hear how you must be a soldier. I do not want to hear how the only way your sisters can marry is if you are disinherited. I do not want to hear how unattractive you think you are. I do not want to hear about any of the problems that you and I have." He had her totally naked now, and he was gazing at her . . . all over.

She closed her eyes in shame.

"Open your eyes, Tyra." When she did, he told her, "There is only one thing I want to hear from you."

She knew exactly what that was. "I love you, Adam."

He smiled then . . . a glorious Adam smile . . . the kind only he could give . . . the kind that made a woman think she was the most important thing in the world to him.

"You are the most important thing in the world to me, Tyra. And I love you more than I can say. I do not know why or how it happened, but I suspect you had me from the first moment you stepped into my hall, wearing armor and scratching your groin."

His words were so precious to her, she could not speak for several moments . . . even the part about scratching her groin. Little did he know that she sometimes felt itchy there now as her hair began to regrow, and might truly have a need for scratching.

"There is one thing you must know, heartling. I come with baggage, just as you do with your bothersome family."

"Baggage?"

"Yea. Baggage by the names of Alrek, Tunni, Kristin, and Besji. I need to adopt them, Tyra. For some reason, I believe that God, and mayhap Adela up in heaven, sent them to me. Just as Selik and Rain adopted me and Adela, I cannot do any less for them. Do you understand? Are you willing to take me *and* my baggage?"

"You will never have another moment's peace, I suspect."

"Undoubtedly."

"Then of course I will marry you, and I love you all the more for your charges." A sudden thought came to her, and she chuckled to herself. "In return, you will have to adopt one of mine."

He raised his eyebrows in question. "One of your sisters? Why would you want to do that?"

"Nay, not one of my sisters. My cat."

"Warrior? Oh, good Lord! My life will really be raucous then, won't it? That cat loathes me." He was smiling as he spoke, which Tyra took for a good sign.

Adam made slow, slow love to her then . . . the kind where a man professes his love with his body instead of words. He made her whimper and beg. He even kissed her *there*, though she suspected his lips were twitching with suppressed humor as he did so. When he entered her and began the long, slow strokes that would bring them both to ecstasy, he pleaded, "Never leave me again. Promise, Tyra. Tell me, no matter what, you will not leave me again."

How could she promise that?

How could she not?

"I promise," she said, though how she would fulfill such a promise, she had no idea. She had to trust Adam that they would work things out.

And then she could not think for they were riding the crest of a huge wave of pleasure. When they exploded, together, she spasmed around him with after-ripples of sweet agony.

She knew he was well pleased, too, because he moaned.

Adam had the nicest moan in the world.

When they lay sated in each other's arms for a while, with Tyra lying on her side, her face on his chest and one leg tossed over his thigh, Adam inserted a hand between them and placed it on her stomach. "I want to have children with you, Tyra. Will you stay with me and bear my child?"

Tyra's heart stopped at his question. She suspected there was more to the question than what was immediately apparent. "Do you think I could be a good mother?"

"Yea, I do," he said, kissing her lips lightly.

"What made you change your mind?"

"I don't think I ever felt different. I was fighting my own feelings for you. And you have already promised to stay with me. That is enough."

"Then, yea, I would love to have your child. Though I still do not see how we can reconcile our differences. You are a healer. I am a soldier. We are so different."

"Ah, dearling, I celebrate our differences. But actually, I have had many long sennights to ponder this, and I was wondering . . . would you consider working with me? Hell, I already have my own hospitium, thanks to your sister."

"I do not understand. Work with you *how?*"

"I noticed how well we worked together when I was

operating on your father. You do not flinch at the sight of blood. You anticipated my needs. You would make a wonderful assistant. In truth, you could become a healer yourself in time, if you so chose. God knows, there is enough work for me and you and Rashid."

"Me? A healer?" The idea was so new and preposterous she could barely take it in.

"You do not have to decide now. And besides, you can still perform your soldierly duties here at Hawkshire . . . amassing a guard, patrolling, defending. I would not stop you from doing that . . . as long as you are here, not off in some other country, fighting some strange king's wars."

She nodded. He was a remarkable man. Truly, he was.

Adam slipped out of the bed then, got down on one knee, and said, "Tyra, dearling . . . my fair Viking . . . I only intend to make a fool of myself this once. Will you marry me?"

Tyra was no fool. She said yes.

EPILOGUE

⊗

Happily ever after, Viking style . . .

Chaos reigned at the Hawkshire wedding of Tyra, Viking warrior princess, and Adam, the Saxon healer.

To Adam and Tyra's amazement, two hundred people showed up to watch them exchange vows and celebrate their union. Some said it was the event of the year in both Norse and Saxon worlds; others said it was just a slow social season.

Half of the time, Adam was asking Tyra, "Who *are* all these people?" The other half of the time, Tyra was asking Adam, "Who *are* all these people?"

Lord Eirik and Lady Eadyth of Ravenshire were there with their five children: twenty-four-year-old Larise who was the young widow of a Saxon merchant; the heart-meltingly handsome, twenty-three-year-old John of nearby Hawk's Lair with his raven-black hair and clear blue eyes, who had developed a sudden fascination with flowers and with Drifa, though next week his interest might change to cooking; shy Emma, who at twenty-two wanted to enter a convent but found Rashid's harem stories oddly intriguing; and the fifteen-year-old twins, Sarah and Sigrid, whose gray eyes danced with mischief.

Eadyth had presented them with barrels of her famous mead, which was contributing greatly to the high mood of everyone in attendance. She had already given Ingrith many cloth-wrapped combs of honey for use in the sweet dishes that had been prepared.

Adam's good friend Rurik and his wife Maire showed up, too, coming all the way from Scotland. Their gift was an abundance of that potent amber beverage the Scots called *uisge-beatha*. It also was contributing to the jollity of the crowd, along with the mead. Not contributing to the jollity was the set of bagpipes that they had given to Bolthor. Rurik and Maire came with their growing brood. There were eleven-year-old Jamie, the spitting image of his father, except for the blue tattoo down the center of Rurik's still handsome face; six-year-old Grace; and three-year-old Angus. Maire was breeding again.

Jamie had made good friends with Alrek, who was regaling him with exaggerated tales of his trip to Byzantium. Even though Alrek had never stepped off the longship on that foreign soil, Jamie was very impressed. Of course, Alrek was equally impressed that Jamie was a Highland laird-to-be.

Since his arrival at Hawkshire, Alrek had fractured his foot tripping over Ingrith's broom, skinned two knees when he fell off a horse, got bitten by a stable cat, singed his hair when he tried to light a bonfire, and almost died of mortification when Bolthor wrote a saga about his discovering his first pubic hair. People were holding their breath to see what Alrek would do next.

Harald Bluetooth, self-proclaimed all-king of Norway, and a large contingent of his followers came as well . . . no doubt for his own political purposes. Ever since the death a few years ago of Haakon the Good,

Harald had been fighting with the minor Norse kings to gain control of the entire country.

The Saxon king Edgar did not come, but he sent high-placed officials of his realm, along with the real power behind the throne, Archbishop Dunstan, who actually participated in the religious nuptial rites. Not that he had been asked. Hardly anyone argued with the dogmatic cleric, not even the king . . . except for Tyra, who was resisting his efforts to baptize her.

Most important, Rain and Selik came with their children and some of the Rainstead orphans. These were most welcome guests, though it tugged at Adam's heart to see all these reminders of his missing sister, Adela, who had worked at the orphanage. The oldest, twenty-five-year-old Theta, was running the orphanage almost single-handedly now. Adam could no longer justify cutting himself off from these reminders of his sister and promised to help more in the future.

Selik pulled him aside at one point and reminded him, "Adela's last words . . . dost remember them?"

"She said, 'Be happy,'" Adam recalled.

Selik nodded. "I believe she is with us here today, and that is what she would wish for you. Be happy."

Later, when the vows were exchanged in the makeshift chapel in the new hospitium, Tyra pledged to her new husband in the Christian rites, "As God is my witness, I promise to love and honor you all the days of my life." There was no mention of "obey."

When it was Adam's turn, he said, "I promise to love and honor you all the days of my life . . . because you are my beloved and will be forevermore."

All the women in attendance sighed at his gentle words. The men groaned, claiming Adam was setting too high a standard.

Afterward, following Viking tradition, Adam chased Tyra up the steps of the keep. Getting there first, he laid his sword across the threshold. Once they both crossed over, the marriage was completed. He whacked her across the backside then with the flat side of his sword. That, too, was a Norse tradition . . . leastways, one which had been started by Tykir at his own wedding.

Because so many people were commenting on the differences between the bridal couple, Bolthor naturally decided to recite a saga about it. "This is the saga of Adam the Lesser," he began, "also known as 'Why Opposites Attract.'

> *"Love is a strange emotion,*
> *When all is said and done.*
> *Sparks do fly,*
> *And lust runs high*
> *When bold man meets maiden shy,*
> *Or wanton wench attracts timid guy.*
> *Tall and short, fat and thin,*
> *Homely and handsome, slovenly and neat as a pin.*
> *Why do opposites attract?*
> *'Tis obvious, in fact:*
> *Sex, food, and life . . .*
> *Need spice."*

To which Rashid added, "Allah cannot be everywhere; that is why he created sexual attraction."

It was now mid-afternoon, and Adam was sitting next to Tyra on the dais. They'd eaten one fine course after another. They'd imbibed more than enough honeyed mead. They'd watched countless entertainments.

Tyra wore a gown of softest blue wool, sent to her by Alinor. It was adorned with seed pearls and a border of embroidered hawks. Her flowing blond hair was held back by a slim gold circlet. She was so very beautiful. *My fair Viking.*

Adam watched with amusement as Tyra admired, once again, the large gold ring with the hawk crest that he had placed on her finger this day. "So, do you like your bride gift, wife?"

"I love it, husband," she said, smiling softly at him.

They were both getting much pleasure out of saying the words "husband" and "wife" to each other. Each wondered if the novelty would ever wear off.

"Oh, oh!" she said suddenly. "I forgot to give you your husband gift."

As she struggled to pull something out of the cloth placket on her belt, he tugged on the war braids on either side of her face, which had been threaded with pearls to match the beading on her gown. "You are not supposed to buy me presents, heartling."

"Why? If there can be a bride gift, why not a husband gift?"

He shrugged and smiled at her. In truth, he could not stop smiling today.

"Is this a jest gift . . . like mayhap chicken feathers?" He waggled his eyebrows at her.

"Adam . . ." she warned, narrowing her eyes at him.

She looked adorable when she narrowed her eyes at him. Adam couldn't resist saying, "Bok! Bok!"

She narrowed her eyes some more. "If you bring up that subject one more time, there is not going to be a wedding night . . . if you get my meaning."

He did, and immediately wiped the grin off his face. He didn't even say what he'd been going to say . . . that the best thing about chickens was plucking them. He would save that one for a later time.

Into his hand she shoved a piece of blue velvet, tied

with a thick gold cord. "Here," she said, her face blooming a lovely shade of pink.

That blush intrigued him more than the gift.

Slowly he opened it, then stared with confusion at the marble wand that lay in his hands. It was about the size of his middle finger and twice as long.

"What is it?"

She leaned close and whispered an explanation into his ear.

"Tyra!" he exclaimed, then threw his head back with laughter. The woman continually surprised him. And he was *really* surprised now.

"If you don't like it, give it back to me," she complained and tried to grab for it.

"Hah! Not bloody likely!" he said, holding it out of her reach. Then he stood abruptly, pulled her along the dais, down the steps, across the hall, and up the stairs to his bedchamber. It was a scandalous way to act, really, in front of all their friends and family. Neither one of them seemed to care.

Tykir called out, "Where are you off to, Adam?"

Adam said, "To polish some marble."

There was a collective gasp amongst the ladies, and chuckles from the men. They thought he was referring to his staff. Little did they know!

The next day, many guests said it was the first time they had ever heard of a bride and groom leaving the wedding feast while it was still daylight . . . and not emerging again till the next day.

Bolthor promised to write a saga about it.

Tyra just smiled.

Adam beamed.

READER LETTER

Dear Reader:

I hope you liked my revised version of *My Fair Viking*. Yes, I actually did unkill beloved characters who died in the original version of this story at the request of so many of you who loved Rain and Selik. And I added the funny scene tags which I hope you enjoyed.

Look for similar changes in new reissues of my old books. I am having fun going back and updating them.

I do not take credit for all the Arab proverbs quoted in this book. Some of them are products of my creativity, but most are ancient proverbs, anonymously written, usually of Arab provenance.

To my shame, I do take credit for Bolthor's horrible poems.

And, yes, head drilling, or trepanning, did take place in the tenth century, believe it or not. Ancient remains show holes drilled into skulls to release evil spirits, to alleviate headaches, and to relieve pressure created by a bruised and swollen brain.

Thus far, there have been nine books in this loosely linked (stand alone) series: *The Reluctant Viking, The Outlaw Viking, The Tarnished Lady, The Bewitched Viking, The Blue Viking, My Fair Viking, A Tale of Two Vikings, Viking in Love*, and *The Viking Takes a Knight*. And more to come. Check out my website for more details on reissues, ebooks, and for genealogy charts on the characters in all these books.

As always, I enjoy hearing from readers. Please write to me at:

Sandra Hill
P.O. Box 604
State College, PA 16804
shill733@aol.com
www.sandrahill.net

GLOSSARY

Berserker—an ancient Norse warrior who fought in a frenzied rage during battle.

Blindfuller—drunk as a lord.

Braies—slim pants worn by men, breeches.

Codpiece—a flap or cover (even a bagged appendage) for the crotch of a man's hose or tight breeches.

Danegeld—in medieval times, especially Britain, a tribute or tax paid to Vikings; in other words, you pay or we plunder.

Drukkinn (various spellings)—drunk, in Old Norse.

Ell—a measure, usually of cloth, equaling 45 inches.

Hersir—a military commander who owed allegiance to one jark or King.

Hnefatafl—a board game played by the Vikings.

Holmganga—a form of duel fought on a ten-foot-wide cloak. Whoever steps off the garment is considered a coward. Whoever wins such a fight to death gets all of the loser's property.

Hospitium—a type of hospital usually attached to a minster and attended by monk healers.

Housecarls—troops assigned to a king's or lord's household on a longtime, sometimes permanent basis.

Jorvik—Viking word for Viking-Age York, known by the Saxons as Eoforic.

knarr—a Viking merchant ship.

Midden—a refuse dump.

Minster—a church, often connected to a monastic establishment.

Mjollnir—the name of Thor's hammer.

More danico—multiple wives.

Nithing—a person of no worth, less than nothing.

Norns of Fate—three wise old women who destined everybody's Fate.

Northumbria—one of the Anglo-Saxon kingdoms, bordered by the English kingdoms to the south and in the north and northwest by the Scots, Cumbrians, and Strathclyde Welsh.

Sennight—one week.

Skald—a poet.

Soapstone—also called steatite, a soft rock composed primarily of talc, often used for hearths, tabletops, carved ornaments, etc.

Thrall—a slave.

Trepannation (or Trepanning)—one of the oldest medical procedures in the world in which holes are drilled in the skull to relieve pressure or to cure some malady, or as part of a religious ritual, or to release evil spirits from the mentally disturbed. It was done as early as 3,000 B.C.

Uisge-beatha—Water of Life, early name for Scotch whiskey.

Valkyries—Odin's female warriors who led valiant fighting men after their death in battle to Valhalla, the hall of the slain.

Varangian Guard—the legendary elite guard made up of Viking mercenaries assigned to the Byzantine emperor.

Wergild (various spellings)—a man's worth, paid in reparation for a death or some crime.

Can't get enough of *USA Today* and
New York Times bestselling
author Sandra Hill?
Turn the page for glimpses of her amazing
books. From cowboys to Vikings, Navy
SEALs to Southern bad boys, every one
of Sandra's books has her unique blend of
passion, creativity, and unparalled wit.

Welcome to the World of Sandra Hill!

The Viking Takes a Knight

❦

*F*or John of Hawk's Lair, the unexpected appearance of a beautiful woman at his door is always welcome. Yet the arrival of this alluring Viking woman, Ingrith Sigrundottir—with her enchanting smile and inviting curves—is different . . . for she comes accompanied by a herd of unruly orphans. And Ingrith needs more than the legendary knight's hospitality; she needs protection. For among her charges is a small boy with a claim to the throne—a dangerous distinction when murderous King Edgar is out hunting for Viking blood.

A man of passion, John will keep them safe—but in exchange, he wants something very dear indeed: Ingrith's heart, to be taken with the very first meeting of their lips . . .

Viking in Love

❧

*C*aedmon of Larkspur *was the most loathsome lout*
Breanne had ever encountered. When she
arrived at his castle with her sisters, they were
greeted by an estate gone wild, while Caedmon
laid abed after a night of ale. But Breanne must
endure, as they are desperately in need of protection . . . and he is quite handsome.

After nine long months in the king's service, all
Caedmon wanted was peace, not five Viking prin-
cesses running about his keep. And the fiery red-
head who burst into his chamber was the worst of
them all. He should kick her out, but he has a far
better plan for Breanne of Stoneheim—one that
will leave her a Viking in lust.

The Reluctant Viking

&

*T*he self-motivation tape was supposed to help Ruby Jordan solve her problems, not create new ones. Instead, she was lulled into an era of hard-bodied warriors and fair maidens. But the world ten centuries in the past didn't prove to be all mead and mirth. Even as Ruby tried to update medieval times, she had to deal with a Norseman whose view of women was stuck in the Dark Ages. And what was worse, brawny Thork had her husband's face, habits, and desire to avoid Ruby. Determined not to lose the same man twice, Ruby planned a bold seduction that would conquer the reluctant Viking—and make him an eager captive of her love.

The Outlaw Viking

⟐

As tall and striking as the Valkyries of legend, Dr. Rain Jordan was proud of her Norse ancestors despite their warlike ways. But she can't believe it when she finds herself on a nightmarish battlefield, forced to save the barbarian of her dreams.

He was a wild-eyed warrior whose deadly sword could slay a dozen Saxons with a single swing, yet Selik couldn't control the saucy wench from the future. If Selik wasn't careful, the stunning siren was sure to capture his heart and make a warrior of love out of **The Outlaw Viking**.

The Tarnished Lady

❦

*B*anished from polite society, Lady Eadyth of Hawk's Lair spent her days hidden under a voluminous veil, tending her bees. But when her lands are threatened, Lady Eadyth sought a husband to offer her the protection of his name.

Notorious for loving—and leaving—the most beautiful damsels in the land, Eirik of Ravenshire was England's most virile bachelor. Yet when the mysterious lady offered him a vow of chaste matrimony in exchange for revenge against his most hated enemy, Eirik couldn't refuse. But the lusty knight's plans went awry when he succumbed to the sweet sting of the tarnished lady's love.

The Bewitched Viking

☙

Even fierce Norse warriors have bad days. 'Twas enough to drive a sane Viking mad, the things Tykir Thorksson was forced to do—capturing a red-headed virago, putting up with the flock of sheep that follows her everywhere, chasing off her bumbling brothers. But what could a man expect from the sorceress who had put a kink in the King of Norway's most precious body part? If that wasn't bad enough, Tykir was beginning to realize he wasn't at all immune to the enchantment of brash red hair and freckles. Perhaps he could reverse the spell and hold her captive, not with his mighty sword, but with a Viking man's greatest magic: a wink and smile.

The Blue Viking

❧

For Rurik the Viking, life has not been worth living since he left Maire of the Moors. Oh, it's not that he misses her fiery red tresses or kissable lips. Nay, it's the embarrassing blue zigzag tattoo she put on his face after their one wild night of loving. For a fierce warrior who prides himself on his immense height, his expertise in bedsport, and his well-toned muscles, this blue streak is the last straw. In the end, he'll bring the witch to heel, or die trying. Mayhap he'll even beg her to wed . . . so long as she can promise he'll no longer be . . . **The Blue Viking**.

The Viking's Captive

(originally titled MY FAIR VIKING)

❧

Tyra, Warrior Princess. She is too tall, too loud, too fierce to be a good catch. But her ailing father has decreed that her four younger sisters—delicate, mild-mannered, and beautiful—cannot be wed 'til Tyra consents to take a husband. And then a journey to save her father's life brings Tyra face to face with Adam the Healer. A god in human form, he's tall, muscled, perfectly proportioned. Too bad Adam refuses to fall in with her plans—so what's a lady to do but truss him up, toss him over her shoulder, and sail off into the sunset to live happily ever after.

A Tale of Two Vikings

⊗

*T*oste and Vagn Ivarsson are identical Viking twins, about to face Valhalla together, following a tragic battle, or maybe something even more tragic: being separated for the first time in their thirty and one years. Alas, even the bravest Viking must eventually leave his best buddy behind and do battle with that most fearsome of all opponents—the love of his life. And what if that love was Helga the Homely, or Lady Esme, the world's oldest novice nun?

A Tale of Two Vikings will give you twice the tears, twice the sizzle, and twice the laughter . . . and make you wish for your very own Viking.

The Last Viking

He was six feet, four inches of pure, unadulterated male. He wore nothing but a leather tunic, and he was standing in Professor Meredith Foster's living room. The medieval historian told herself he was part of a practical joke, but with his wide gold belt, ancient language, and callused hands, the brawny stranger seemed so . . . authentic. And as he helped her fulfill her grandfather's dream of re-creating a Viking ship, he awakened her to dreams of her own. Until she wondered if the hand of fate had thrust her into the loving arms of . . . **The Last Viking**.

Truly, Madly Viking

🜨

A *Viking named Joe? Jorund Ericsson is a tenth-century Viking* warrior who lands in a modern mental hospital. Maggie McBride is the lucky psychologist who gets to "treat" the gorgeous Norseman, whom she mistakenly calls Joe.

You've heard of *One Flew Over the Cuckoo's Nest*. But how about *A Viking Flew Over the Cuckoo's Nest*? The question is: Who's the cuckoo in this nest? And why is everyone laughing?

The Very Virile Viking

ॐ

Magnus Ericsson is a simple man. He loves the smell of fresh-turned dirt after springtime plowing. He loves the feel of a soft woman under him in the bed furs. He loves the heft of a good sword in his fighting arm.

But, Holy Thor, what he does not relish is the bothersome brood of children he's been saddled with. Or the mysterious happenstance that strands him in a strange new land—the kingdom of *Holly Wood*. Here is a place where the folks think he is an *act-whore* (whatever that is), and the woman of his dreams—a winemaker of all things—fails to accept that he is her soul mate . . . a man of exceptional talents, not to mention . . . **A Very Virile Viking.**

Wet & Wild

❀

What do you get when you cross a Viking with a Navy SEAL? A warrior with the fierce instincts of the past and the rigorous training of America's most elite fighting corps? A totally buff hero-in-the-making who hasn't had a woman in roughly a thousand years? A dyed-in-the-wool romantic with a hopeless crush? Whatever you get, women everywhere can't wait to meet him, and his story is guaranteed to be . . . **Wet & Wild**.

Hot & Heavy

॥

*I*n and out, that's the goal as Lt. Ian MacLean prepares for his special ops mission. He leads a team of highly trained Navy SEALs, the toughest, buffest fighting men in the world and he has nothing to lose. Madrene comes from a time a thousand years before he was born, and she has no idea she's landed in the future. After tying him up, the beautiful shrew gives him a tongue-lashing that makes a drill sergeant sound like a kindergarten teacher. Then she lets him know she has her own special way of dealing with over-confident males, and things get . . . **Hot & Heavy**.

Frankly, My Dear . . .

⚮

*L*ost in the Bayou . . . *Selene had three great passions:* men, food, and *Gone with the Wind*. But the glamorous model always found herself starving— for both nourishment and affection. Weary of the petty world of high fashion, she headed to New Orleans for one last job before she began a new life. Little did she know that her new life would include a brand-new time—about 150 years ago! Selene can't get her fill of the food—or an alarmingly handsome man. Dark and brooding, James Baptiste was the only lover she gave a damn about. And with God as her witness, she vowed never to go without the man she loved again.

Sweeter Savage Love

❦

The stroke of surprisingly gentle hands, the flash of fathomless blue eyes, the scorch of white-hot kisses . . . Once again, Dr. Harriet Ginoza was swept away into rapturous fantasy. The modern psychologist knew the object of her desire was all she should despise, yet time after time, she lost herself in visions of a dangerously handsome rogue straight out of a historical romance. Harriet never believed that her dream lover would cause her any trouble, but then a twist of fate cast her back to the Old South and she met him in the flesh. To her disappointment, Etienne Baptiste refused to fulfill any of her secret wishes. If Harriet had any hope of making her amorous dreams become passionate reality, she'd have to seduce this charmer with a sweeter savage love than she'd imagined possible . . . and savor every minute of it.

The Love Potion

☙

*F*ame *and fortune are surely only a swallow away* when Dr. Sylvie Fontaine discovers a chemical formula guaranteed to attract the opposite sex. Though her own love life is purely hypothetical, the shy chemist's professional future is assured . . . as soon as she can find a human guinea pig. But bad boy Lucien LeDeux—best known as the Swamp Lawyer—is more than she can handle even before he accidentally swallowed a love potion disguised in a jelly bean. When the dust settles, Luc and Sylvie have the answers to some burning questions—can a man die of testosterone overload? Can a straight-laced female lose every single one of her inhibitions?—and they learn that old-fashioned romance is still the best catalyst for love.

Love Me Tender

*O*nce upon a time, in a magic kingdom, there lived a handsome prince. Prince Charming, he was called by one and all. And to this land came a gentle princess. You could say she was Cinderella . . . Wall Street Cinderella. Okay, if you're going to be a stickler for accuracy, in this fairy tale the kingdom is Manhattan. But there's magic in the Big Apple, isn't there? And maybe he can be Prince Not-So-Charming at times, and "gentle" isn't the first word that comes to mind when thinking of this princess. But they're looking for happily ever after just the same—and they're going to get it.

Desperado

❦

Mistaken for a notorious bandit and his infamously scandalous mistress, L.A. lawyer Rafe Santiago and Major Helen Prescott found themselves on the wrong side of the law. In a time and place where rules had no meaning, Helen found Rafe's hard, bronzed body strangely comforting, and his piercing blue eyes left her all too willing to share his bedroll. His teasing remarks made her feel all woman, and she was ready to throw caution to the wind if she could spend every night in the arms of her very own . . . **Desperado**.

NEW YORK TIMES BESTSELLING AUTHOR

SANDRA HILL

Viking in Love

978-0-06-167249-8

Viking princess Breanne and her four sisters are forced to flee
to the castle of Caedmon of Larkspur. The Viking warrior
is a distant relative and his home is very much in need of a
feminine hand, but Breanne never expected he would try to
lure her into his bed.

The Viking Takes a Knight

978-0-06-167350-4

All Ingrith wants is refuge for herself and a group of orphans
from a vicious Saxon commander. John of Hawk's Lair longs
for peace and quiet, not a nagging wife and noisy children. But
despite their differences, an uncontrollable attraction sparks
between him and Ingrith.

The Viking's Captive

978-0-06-201908-0

A journey to save her father's life brings Tyra face to face
with Adam the healer. He's tall, muscled, and perfectly proportioned. Here's the physician who could cure her father,
and the lover who could finally seduce her to his bed furs.

At Avon Books, we know your passion for romance—once you finish one of our novels, you find yourself wanting more.

May we tempt you with . . .

- **Excerpts** from our upcoming releases.

- Entertaining **extras**, including authors' personal photo albums and book lists.

- Behind-the-scenes **scoop** on your favorite characters and series.

- **Sweepstakes** for the chance to win free books, romantic getaways, and other fun prizes.

- Writing **tips** from our authors and editors.

- **Blog** with our authors and find out why they love to write romance.

- **Exclusive content** that's not contained within the pages of our novels.

Join us at
www.avonbooks.com